MEMBERS ONLY

MEMBERS ONLY

Sameer Pandya

MARINER BOOKS / HOUGHTON MIFFLIN HARCOURT

BOSTON   NEW YORK

2020

For information about permission to reproduce selections
from this book, write to trade.permissions@hmhco.com or to
Permissions, Houghton Mifflin Harcourt Publishing Company,
3 Park Avenue, 19th Floor, New York, New York 10016.

hmhbooks.com

Library of Congress Cataloging-in-Publication Data
Names: Pandya, Sameer, author.
Title: Members only / Sameer Pandya.
Description: Boston : Houghton Mifflin Harcourt, 2020.
Identifiers: LCCN 2019033955 (print) | LCCN 2019033956 (ebook) |
ISBN 9780358098546 (hardcover) | ISBN 9780358100508 (ebook) |
ISBN 9780358379928 (trade paper)
Classification: LCC PS3616.A368 M46 2020 (print) |
LCC PS3616.A368 (ebook) | DDC 813/.6 — dc23
LC record available at https://lccn.loc.gov/2019033955
LC ebook record available at https://lccn.loc.gov/2019033956

Book design by Chrissy Kurpeski
Typeset in Warnock Pro

Printed in the United States of America
DOC 10 9 8 7 6 5 4 3 2 1

For Emilie

MEMBERS ONLY

Sunday

WE WERE JUST starting our third night of interviews, and I felt the kind of weariness that comes from having wasted time.

"Raj," I said, introducing myself to the first couple.

The man was wearing a casual half-sleeve shirt, and his wife was refreshingly unremarkable — in a loose dress, her hair in a simple ponytail. I liked them for it, but only for about ten seconds.

"Rog?" the wife asked, leaning in.

It was a question I had been asked too many times in my life.

"Raaaj," I exaggerated.

"As in Federer?"

I feigned a smile, unsure if she was joking. They moved on, introducing themselves to the rest of the membership committee.

The committee — Suzanne, the efficient and disciplined

chair; Stan, a balding sixtyish lawyer; Richard, a leather-skinned club pro; Leslie, a childhood friend of my wife; and I — had a particularly difficult task. Over the course of two evenings the previous week, we had already spoken with ten different couples about why they wanted to join the Tennis Club, simple nouns elevated to proper status. Tonight, we would talk to still more and then choose five out of the total fifteen to let in.

The club had opened several decades before, in the early seventies, when couples were riding high from breaking rules in the sixties and yet wanted to make sure their children knew how to slice a backhand properly. The original membership had been a mixture of old money and lawyers and doctors, all of whom downplayed the breadth of their bank accounts. But the past several years had brought the movie and hedge fund people, who'd bought up the old estates and come driving into town in cars that were never more than a year old. As the town's gilding glowed ever brighter, the club — or the TC, as it was known among members — had continued on, a simple place with eight courts, a swimming pool, and a rustic clubhouse with worn wicker couches. No flat-screen TVs, no towel service; there was a soda machine that still charged fifty cents for a Coke. Simplicity was the brand. And the simpler it stayed, the more people wanted to join, perhaps to rub off some of their new-money sheen. The membership committee was tasked with bringing in families that had some sense of that earlier, understated ethos, as well as some of the newer sort, who paid their monthly dues but generally preferred to use their home swimming pools and tennis courts.

My wife, Eva, had grown up coming here, her parents a little ambivalent about its clubbiness and yet appreciative of that selfsame simplicity. When we moved to town, we had joined together, though both of us were concerned by how quickly we were losing our urbanity. I, in particular, had fought the idea of the place, though quietly, somewhere inside, I knew I had been drawn to its luster. But for me, tennis courts and swimming pools were meant to be public. I had honed my tennis skills on muni courts in the East Bay, after my family had moved to California from Bombay. I was hazed into playing better by a group of Filipinos who worked the night shift at the post office, slept several hours in the morning, and then set up shop at the courts until they had to go to work again.

In high school, I secretly hated the kids on our team, who, with their multiple, freshly gripped racquets and unscuffed Nikes, went off to private clubs after practice for further instruction. They had at least one parent who came to all their matches, while my parents were always working. I could sense then the deeper differences between us, though I didn't yet have the language to articulate them, or the experience with which to understand them.

But, somehow, now, I had grown to love belonging to my own club — or at least parts of it. I loved the late afternoon matches when the soft winter California sun lit up the surrounding hills in orange phosphorescence. I loved grilling meat with our friends while the children swam and swooped in for bites of hot dog. I loved diving into the pristine pool, swimming the length in one breath, and appearing at the other end, refreshed and alive. And most of all, I loved being there with Eva and our boys when the place was empty, hitting balls on a court and then jumping into the pool, the four of us a perfectly self-contained pod.

In most every way, the club was not so different from the club my family had belonged to before we left Bombay. We'd joined a gymkhana—one of many clubs that had originally been made for British colonials, but later, by the time we were members, were populated mostly by Bombay's upper middle class—after my father had gotten a big promotion. That was where I'd swum in a pool for the first time, and after swimming I'd lounge in the comfortable, dilapidated clubhouse with a mango lassi and a vegetable frankie.

I had easily blended into the background at the gymkhana; not so much at the TC.

"Can we get you anything?" Suzanne asked, pointing to a side table spread with cheese, dried meat, and wine. The couple and their sponsors—every prospective new member needed a sponsoring couple—sat on one side of the center table, and we all sat on the other. They said no. The couples who declined a glass of wine were usually the nervous ones, the ones I tried to put at ease.

"Why don't you tell us a little about your family and your interest in tennis?"

Suzanne exuded order—her milky, unblemished skin, contrasted by her shiny dark brown hair; her expensive outfits draped over her wispy body, always impossibly pressed; her immaculate Tesla. Suzanne easily fit in with countless other women at the TC who spent their days marinating in their luck and good fortune. But she was also something more: driven, smart, restless. She'd had a full, successful career as a management consultant before she stopped to have kids. Now, our older sons were in the fourth grade together, and she was the head of the PTA. She brought a certain fat-trimming zeal to that group, as well as the TC's membership committee, several nonprofit boards, and her own home, none of which seemed to burn her substantial reserve of fuel. Eva liked her for who she had been, but not for what she had become — a sharp, skilled woman who now devoted too much of her time to the success of her children. I liked her for the impatience she was unable to hide from her face during some of the interviews. Like this one.

"Who doesn't love tennis?" the husband asked. At first it seemed like a rhetorical question, but then he continued, lowering his voice a bit and raising his eyebrows so that his eyes got bigger: "But actually, I do find myself getting a little bored after a while. Like, is this all there is? A game comprised entirely of hitting a yellow ball back and forth into a bunch of squares?" He was holding his arms out and his palms up in mock exasperation, as if he had just delivered the punch line in a comedy routine.

I bit my lip not to laugh. I appreciated his honesty, but man, he'd gotten his audience wrong. His wife seemed to lean slightly away from him. Both Suzanne and Leslie gave him a tight, polite frown.

"I know that feeling," I said, trying to pull him away from the nervous wilderness he was entering. "I'm often thinking about other things on the court, but then a ball comes whizzing by and I'm back."

The husband just sat there, not taking my help. I wondered if he would have taken the lead if Stan or Richard had offered.

Sensing that things might be going south, the sponsors interjected, talking about how wonderful the applicants were, how much their children would take to the game. And for the next ten minutes, the committee discussed family, tennis, and community, topics that had been preassigned to each of us by Suzanne. I talked about the strong communal sensibility of the club.

As the fifteen-minute mark neared, Suzanne interlaced her fingers and placed them on her lap, her tell that she was ready to wind the interview down. "Thank you so much for coming in. We're going to be meeting at the end of the week and we'll let you know."

As we were all saying our goodbyes, the wife turned to me and said, "It was lovely meeting you, Kumar."

I looked straight at her for a few long seconds before responding. Messing up my easy name earlier was one thing. But this was something else entirely, not even in the same ballpark. I could feel my back tighten. "It's Raj," I finally said, feeling a sliver of heartbreak.

The expression on her face changed. I couldn't tell if it was embarrassment or defiance or indifference. At least if she'd been embarrassed, I'd know she felt bad. I noticed, too, that Suzanne was listening to the exchange. Her face had slightly contorted, as if she'd just witnessed a car crash and knew that I had gotten rear-ended. The rest of the committee had either not heard it or, as was typical with this group when something untoward happened, didn't know how to react.

The woman had leaned closer to her husband and was now cradled in his arms. They were amiably chatting with the other committee members.

A few months before, Suzanne had asked me to be on the committee, saying that I would be "a perfect addition, a friendly face." I remember the quote because the words, and their juxtaposition, had wormed through my ears for days. What exactly was I adding? I was, indeed, quite friendly. But was my presence also a show of diversity? Did they all think I was the token who wouldn't rock the boat? I hated the idea that this was what they thought of me, and yet I'd proven them right by not barking at that woman for calling me Kumar. There were already too many TC events — Labor Day barbecues, Wednesday evening doubles socials — where I clearly stood out, but pretended not to. And that's why at first I didn't want to be on the committee. And yet I knew that if I didn't do it, the TC would likely continue on the same as ever.

Privately I had a plan: I wanted to darken the TC, which had only a handful of nonwhite members, all of whom had white spouses, as I did. It was my midlife project, after years of ignoring the fact that all of the social circles I had been part of — high school, college, graduate school, work — were overwhelmingly white. I had tried not to make too much of this fact. I had convinced myself that my presence in these circles was the start of the change I wanted to see in the world. But then that change never seemed to come. It was almost always just me and a lot of kind, well-meaning white folks. There are members here who still refer to "Orientals" and ask me about the "African mind." And in the face of it, I've mostly said nothing, because I just want to play some tennis and not give a lecture.

My family had arrived in America not long after my eighth birthday, and I had started the third grade in a threadbare public school. The first friend I made lived upstairs from us, his family recent refugees from Vietnam. Perhaps because of the basic lunches we all ate in the school cafeteria together or the small apartments we returned to at the end of the day, I got along with the white and black kids, moving easily between them. But starting around junior high, I noticed that there were classes filled with mostly white kids and classes filled with all black kids. I was placed in the "advanced," white classrooms. And by the time I arrived in high school, the divisions felt cemented. I spent the school hours with my white friends, who, at the end of the day, walked home up the hill, while all the black kids and I took buses back to our neighborhoods far away. It was only some years later that I connected the image of all those buses lined up after school with the policy of busing. The black students were brought in to diversify the school, but remained very much separate within it.

And throughout this time, there was only the smallest handful of Indians. In that environment, I'd come to see myself as the person in the middle, someone who could talk to everyone, translate across the aisle, and bring people together. Maybe it was that I hated conflict, or maybe I could genuinely empathize with different points of view, find some common ground.

When we'd first started the interviews the previous week, it was a thrill to sip local wine, sit back, and watch how the machinery operated. Couples came in, some nervous, others overly confident. Their sponsors peacocked, we dog-whistled about the importance of family and the culture of the club, and I pulled out my go-to phrase about how this was "our shared backyard." I was very aware of the fact that, for once in my life, I was in a position of judgment, and I could sense — like a dog can sense a coming earthquake — that this made a lot of the potential candidates uncomfortable. When a couple first walked in, they would chat easily with the other committee members, but with me they seemed at a loss for how to make small talk. I enjoyed it all in the way my historian friends enjoy discovering a hidden corner of an archive, a trove of formerly redacted documents returned to their original integrity that finally prove whatever they'd long been hypothesizing about a certain time, place, and event.

Now, as we were reaching the end of the selection process, not having interviewed even one Asian-American couple, I had the sinking feeling in my belly that I was on a small raft, trying to make my way up the white water instead of down. I knew most of these sponsors. I liked many of them. We tended to share similar views on organic produce and politics. And yet, no one had sponsored a couple who did not, in some much more literal way, replicate themselves. I couldn't help but feel that my efforts at darkening the TC were going to be thwarted despite my best intentions; at the end of this whole process, I'd still be one of the darkest folks around, which didn't say much. And thus, as the next couple and their sponsors filtered into the room, I continued to be struck with the weariness that comes from having wasted time.

For the next three interviews, I kept mouthing incensed lines to myself: "It's Jane, right? Oh, Amy? Sorry, they sound so similar." "No, it's Raj, not Kumar, but I do a pretty decent brownface, if that makes it easier for you." "Why is 'Raj' so hard to pronounce? I get 'Becky' right." I couldn't quite parse the source of my anger. I was mad at that woman for getting my name wrong twice, but perhaps even angrier with myself, for hoping that, given time, I could be part of this club without losing some vital part of myself and my dignity.

Another couple left and I gazed out the clubhouse window at the fading daylight. Before I could catch myself, I let out a full, uncontrolled yawn.

"Are we boring you?" Suzanne asked in a tone that seemed to cut and soothe at the same time.

Of course I was bored. And disgusted. But I didn't want to let Suzanne or anyone else in on how vulnerable I felt. "No, no. The kids haven't been sleeping well lately. Bed-wetting." A lie, but the first excuse I thought of.

Suzanne's boys seemed as if they had never peed or eaten or talked out of turn. On the court, they mimicked perfectly the strokes the pros had taught them; they seemed destined to become either the Bryan or the Menendez brothers.

I could sense a slight tremor on her face, as if my fibbed account of our familial chaos would rub off on her.

"There are ways to stop that," she said.

"I'm sure there are," I said.

I got up, walked over to the food, poured myself more wine in a plastic cup, tossed a sweaty piece of aged Gouda in my mouth, and went back to my seat.

"The Browns are our last family," Suzanne said. "And funnily enough, their sponsors are the Blacks." She let out a slight snort.

It was a stupid joke, one I wished she'd not made. But unlike the woman who'd come in earlier, I could clearly sense Suzanne's embarrassment. If I were to be charitable, perhaps she'd said it because she recognized that, in fact, there had not been any browns or blacks in these interviews. But where before I might have smiled, wanting to make her feel OK about it, wanting to be part of the joke even as I felt guilty about smiling and thereby offering my approval, now I ignored her as I sat back down. If there was one of us who was going to say something stupid and inappropriate, it was Suzanne. For all her decorum, she had a need to elicit laughter. But then again, so did I.

Eva had warned me that this tendency would get me in trouble, and it had, on more than one occasion. In Suzanne's case, of course, we would all laugh it off and move on. I didn't always have that luxury.

Once, when I was in my first year of graduate school, I was at the anthropology department potluck, waiting in the food line in front of a senior visiting scholar who'd written a remarkable book on matrilineage in an East African tribe which rethought ideas of power, hierarchy, and seemingly everything else. I admired her work so much it left me tongue-tied. As I piled my plate with too much pesto pasta, I tried hard to figure out the right thing to say so that she might remember me. I wanted to take a class she was offering the following semester that I knew would be packed. I should have just told her how much her book had shaped my thinking and taken my chances with that, but instead, this came out of my mouth: "So how was it spending so much time with all those strong women for a change?" I had meant it to be a genuine question, with a playful chaser — something that gestured at our mutual struggle, as different kinds of minorities in a field traditionally dominated by old white men. But the second the words were out of my mouth, I knew I'd missed my mark. Did she think I was suggesting that she had no strong women in her life already? That she had to travel halfway across the world to find them? Maybe she didn't like me suggesting that we were similar, considering that she was at the top of this particular academic totem pole and I was the Indian at the bottom.

She didn't answer my question. Instead, she turned to the table with the food, took a few slices of a beautifully glazed ham, and walked away. I didn't bother trying to get into her class. And a few days later, my advisor stopped me in the department hallway and suggested I needed to work on my professionalism.

It was the same advice I now wanted to pass on to Suzanne.

"Here they are," she said. Two couples walked into the clubhouse.

The Blacks, of course, were white. But the Browns were black. I looked at the handsome couple and breathed a sigh of relief. It was as if an alternate, younger version of the Obamas had just walked in.

I glanced at the rest of the committee, all of them looking at the alt-Obamas with big, friendly grins. The room was completely silent. We could hear the cicadian murmur of kids finishing up at the pool outside.

"Let me introduce you to Doctors Bill and Valerie Brown," Mark Black said.

Bill was roughly six feet tall and fit. He was wearing lean, perfectly fitting khakis, loafers, a button-down, light pink shirt, and a navy-blue wool blazer. I had recently read an article somewhere about how every man needed a perfect navy-blue blazer. Bill's certainly was that. On one of his wrists was a bracelet of Tibetan prayer beads, and on the other, a blue-faced octagonal Audemars. I placed my hand on my stomach and sucked it in a bit. I wished I went to the gym more often, got my shirts pressed more regularly.

Valerie was a tall, striking woman who stood comfortably on her own, close enough to be intimate with her husband, but not subsumed by him.

The Browns' sponsors were Mark Black, a well-regarded cardiologist in town, and his wife, Jan. Mark had the confidence that comes with being able to slice open chests. I didn't see him on the courts often, but when I did, his strokes were compact and tidy, his body always moving instinctively in the right direction. He struck me as a little uptight, always appropriately dressed for whatever occasion he was attending. I don't think I'd ever seen his toes, which was noteworthy given the fact that one of the only things we had in common was access to the same pool.

Jan was pretty and put together, her prettiness perhaps

enhanced by all the time and money she had to take care of herself. They were a family obsessed with being on the cutting edge of trends. They bought their Range Rovers — his in black, hers in white — while most people were stuck in their Audis. Jan took the family to spend a year in Spain so their kids could get used to playing on real, red clay before everyone was taking a year off and calling it a sabbatical. Once, I overheard Mark say that his shoulders were sore because he had been skeet shooting the day before. I genuinely thought he was kidding, until I realized he wasn't. Who goes skeet shooting? Perhaps everyone soon enough, if the Blacks continued to have their fingers on the upper-middle-class pulse.

The Browns went around the room, shaking hands with all of the committee members. When they came to me, they lingered for an extra few seconds, their eyes asking for help managing what was clearly an awkward situation: a roomful of white people deciding whether they wanted to let a black couple into their club. I'm here for you, I tried to say as I reached out my hand to shake theirs. "Rajesh Bhatt. Everyone calls me Raj."

"I knew a Raj in college," Bill said, smiling.

I think everyone knew a Raj in college. Except, of course, the woman from earlier in the evening.

Bill had a deep, calming voice, one you might hear on a TV commercial for a Mercedes sedan. "I think he runs Google now. Or something."

"I use Google," I said, returning his smile.

"Can we get you anything?" Suzanne asked.

"Water would be great," Bill said.

I happened to be the one closest to the table with the drinks. Suzanne glanced at me for the slightest beat of a second. I looked at her as Bill looked at me.

"You know, how about a sip of something stronger instead," Bill said, moving toward the table. "I'll get it."

I stepped over to the table with him.

"What do you like?" he asked, examining the open bottles of white and red. I sensed that he knew his way around labels.

I reached for a lone, half-full bottle of a nearly translucent pinot tucked behind the mineral waters. "This is the high-end stuff."

Bill took two clear plastic cups from a stack. I gave us both a liberal pour. Bill took a small sip and then turned to me and said, "It certainly is."

Our backs were turned to the rest of the group. Bill ate a dried apricot, I had a piece of salami, and we both took another sip. Before placing the bottle back, I poured us a little more of the wine.

"Shall we?" I asked.

Bill took his wine in one hand and a bottle of water in the other. He handed the water to his wife and took a seat next to her. I sat down on the couch facing them.

For a moment, I wondered whether Bill was originally from the Caribbean. If he was, he would have grown up with Indians, maybe had a grandfather who had arrived on the island as an indentured servant, worked through his contract, and decided to stay instead of going back to the small Indian village he barely remembered. Maybe somehow, over the years, the "Bhatt" had changed to "Brown." If that was the case, I mused, going back several generations, Bill and I could well be cousins.

Since Eva and I had joined the TC, I'd slowly learned the rules of places like this — what games to join, when to engage in conversation, when to say nothing. Never to ask what someone did for a living. I'd made plenty of tennis friends, but I hadn't met anyone with whom I felt simpatico. I wanted Bill to be that guy. He and I were different kinds of doctors, but certainly he'd have some appreciation for my doctorate, in contrast to most of the rich knuckleheads I met here, who probably thought of Indiana Jones when I said I taught cultural anthropology at the university in town. I'd not been getting many invitations to matches lately. I couldn't understand why. My game had continued to improve. I'd begun to wonder if they'd realized finally that I didn't fully fit in, that when they talked about the vacations they were going on, to Marrakesh or Fiji, I usually pretended to be adjusting the strings of my racquet. But maybe Bill and I could play.

"We've read all of these wonderful letters of support you have," Suzanne said, holding up their file. "You're so new to the area, and yet you've obviously made a lot of friends and set your roots quickly. Why don't you tell us about yourselves, your family. And your interest in tennis."

I'd read the file, which had letters from the Blacks and several other members attesting to how wonderful the Browns were. As I was reading the letters, I could sense something different about them, but I couldn't pinpoint it. Now I knew that they were a master class in colorblindness. The Browns were "friendly" and "laid-back." The phrase "they'll fit right in" had been used in three different letters.

"Where shall we start?" Valerie asked.

"Wherever you like," Suzanne said.

"Bill and I met in medical school in San Francisco, and we went to Boston to do our residencies. Bill in cardiology, me in trauma surgery. We both grew up in Los Angeles. Just a few miles apart, but we never knew each other."

I wanted to know which part of LA they'd grown up in, but I didn't ask. Inglewood always up to no good? Perhaps Baldwin Hills.

"After winters and residencies that lasted far too long, we realized we missed the sun, the oak trees, and the huge, congested freeways," Valerie continued. "And so when the opportunity opened up at the hospital, we jumped at it. We're less than two hours away from our families in LA, and the community here has been very welcoming to us. Our sons are also showing some interest in tennis, and Mark can't say enough about how much he loves this place, so it seemed like the right fit for us."

As she spoke, Valerie made careful eye contact with everyone in the room. She knew exactly how to make a roomful of strangers feel comfortable as they gawked at her, trying to piece together her beauty, all her fancy degrees, the fact that every day when she went to work, she kept death at bay.

"How old are your sons?" I asked.

"Eight and five," Valerie said.

Perfect, I thought. They'll be fast friends with my own.

"Boys are fun, but they can be complicated," I said.

"Yes," Valerie said. "Yes, they can."

I sensed from the inflection of the second "yes" that raising boys for them was going to be a particular kind of complication, similar to but ultimately different from the one Eva and I would experience. As our boys grew older, I'd talk to them about the dangers of driving while brown and how they would not always get the second chances some of their classmates would get. But Bill and Valerie would have to have this conversation on a much higher, far more sobering level.

"I'm glad your kids are interested in the game," Suzanne said. "What about you two? We have a strong, competitive interclub team you could play on."

"Bill and I had our first date on a tennis court. And I've hit the ball around with him since, but it'll be a while until I'm game-ready."

Eva and I had also had a tennis first date. I didn't want to get too far ahead of myself, but I could imagine a regular doubles match in our future.

The women's interclub matches were on Wednesday mornings, and most of the other women we'd interviewed were eager to play, especially because the TC team had won the interclub championship for the past two years running.

"I'm sure Wednesdays are busy at the hospital," Leslie interjected, distinguishing Valerie from all of the women we had interviewed who didn't work.

Leslie and Eva had grown up coming to the TC. Their parents were friends, and they'd run cross-country together in high school. Leslie had been a hippie in college, had a girl-friend her junior year, and had worked in New York and Boston for several years before returning home to get married and have a family. She and her husband Tim had sponsored us, and since we'd joined, we'd spent countless weekends together, barbecuing and drinking and talking while the kids swam and ran around. I liked her; we shared a similar ironic sensibility. Throughout the interviews, however, she'd rebuffed my attempts to dish about the inherent problems with the process — namely, that the prospective members were all so interchangeable — but Leslie liked the place a little too much to go there. Lately, I'd sensed that Eva had been pulling away from her too. I don't think they'd had a disagreement, but Eva worked and Leslie didn't, and that may have been the difference.

"Yes, Wednesdays are tough," Valerie said. "But Bill is the tennis player in the family anyway." She placed her hand on her husband's knee, handing the ball over.

"I played some in college," Bill said, a little too matter-of-factly. I sensed Bill was downplaying his level.

Stan jumped in. "Where?"

In every interview, the only time Stan spoke up was when there was a mention of a college. He'd ask about it, and without missing a beat, talk about Williams, how he'd played fullback there, *read* philosophy, went on to Harvard Law School, and settled into a life of contracts. Stan was lean and the veteran of two shoulder surgeries, brought on by several decades of playing tennis four times a week.

Before this whole interviewing process had started, I'd had

no opinion of Stan. I'd seen him around, always getting off the court with an ice pack balanced on his shoulder. But at the start, Suzanne had asked everyone on the committee about their vision for these interviews. Everyone, including me, had said this and that about considering the past to forge the future. And then there was Stan: "I've thought about it and I've realized I don't have a vision. I just want high-level tennis players. Bad tennis offends me. This is a *tennis* club."

A few days earlier, I'd seen him sitting in the hot tub reading a tattered copy of *Don Quixote*. When I asked him about it, he'd said that he was rereading all the books that he had loved as a young man to see if they still hooked him in the same way. "I'm trying to remember who I was back then." He had just finished with the Russians, and after Cervantes he was going to hit the Americans. I loved the idea that *The Great Gatsby* might help Stan see the conspicuous consumption all around us. It made me realize that, despite all the Williams business, there was much to like about him, and I appreciated that he was up-front about the fact that, in asking people about their alma maters, he was sizing them up. At least I always knew where I stood with him.

"Stanford," Bill said.

I wasn't the human *U.S. News & World Report* annual college ranking that Stan was, but I knew how to translate "played some" at Stanford. Bill was very good. Like heavily recruited in high school and nationally ranked good. John McEnroe had played some at Stanford.

"Were you there with Tiger Woods?" Richard asked, suddenly perking up. Richard wasn't a member, but traditionally one of the senior pros sat on the membership committee, perhaps to make it seem like the process was more equitable. He and I were both in our mid-forties, but working under the blazing sun had prematurely aged him.

"In fact, I was," Bill said. "I was just glad that he wasn't on the tennis team as well."

That's it, I thought. Don't ask him any more about Tiger. I was sure that at this point in his life, Bill must be tired of answering questions about Tiger just because they were vaguely alike.

"What was he like?" Stan asked. "Did you take any classes with him?"

"I didn't. I was stuck in bio and chemistry."

Bill and Valerie made the slightest eye contact.

"What did Tiger study?" I asked, wanting to turn the conversation away from whether Bill had known Tiger, toward Tiger alone. Somehow that seemed better.

"I'm not sure," Bill said. "Econ maybe. He was only there for a couple of years. Clearly, he didn't need to take any more classes. He figured out macroeconomics all on his own."

I couldn't contain my grin.

"So, did you both always want to go to medical school and become doctors?" I asked, moving us away from Tiger entirely. The main purpose of these brief interviews — some as short as ten minutes — was to let the prospective members talk so we could get some sense of them. The due diligence was performed in the letters and in whispers.

"I did," Valerie said. "My father is a doctor, so it was assumed that I'd go into the family business. I couldn't imagine doing anything else. I still can't."

"I thought about other things," Bill said. "I flirted with law school, but it didn't feel quite right."

"As usual, Bill's being a little modest," Mark interjected. Throughout the interview, he'd sat there self-satisfied, like he'd brought the fatted calf to the banquet. "He decided to forgo the Tour to go to medical school."

This bit of information dazzled the men in the room. They all seemed to lean in toward Bill at that moment. I suddenly felt sad about the state of both my game and my career. I had done just enough to get by at both. Bill, on the other hand, had excelled, and had the freedom to choose between two enviable options.

"That's not exactly how it went," Bill said. "I played in a few professional tournaments and lost in the early rounds. I couldn't deal with the uncertainty of it all. But the fact is that I haven't had much time in the past fifteen years to keep up with the game. Medical school and then residency and kids didn't leave time for doubles. But I was thinking that I'd get out there a little more now. Get rid of the rust. At least if Mark doesn't work me too hard at the hospital."

Bill's mention of work got me thinking about my own. I had papers to grade before the next morning. I'd grab a burger after this to soak up some of the wine swirling around in my head. And by the time I got home, I hoped, the kids would be asleep. I felt exhausted from all this talking and smiling.

Bill added, "It'll take me some time to catch up with you all."

I bit at my lower lip. I have a tendency to mouth words to myself before I actually say them, as a way of testing out the safety of what I'm about to say, something I'd learned from lecturing: sound out the joke before letting it loose. But this time — maybe because I was distracted, maybe because I was so desperate to show Bill that we could be on the same team, that I understood where he was coming from — as I mouthed the words, the complex mechanism that occurs between air and tongue and throat to create sound did its job, against my deepest wishes.

"Nigga, please."

For a second after I said it, I thought it might be fine. That in a room with four other committee members and two other couples, all engaged in various conversations, no one had heard me. That maybe I hadn't really said it at all.

But it became very clear that none of that was true. They all turned to me as if I'd suddenly caught on fire. And in many ways, I had.

As I sat there burning, I wondered just how bad this was going to be.

On those bus rides home in high school, I had teethed on the details and matters of black life. After some headbanging to Ozzy and Black Sabbath in middle school, listening to N.W.A for the first time felt like genuine rebellion. I certainly didn't live in Compton. But I understood Ice Cube's rage, and listening to it through cheap headphones in my bedroom gave voice to my confusion, my feeling that I was on the outside, unsure of how to get inside, of where inside would even be.

In college, I'd made a personal religion out of Ralph Ellison, the outward anger of N.W.A now replaced by a considered philosophical probing of not being seen. The first time I read the last line of *Invisible Man*, it brought me to tears. *Who knows but that, on lower frequencies, I speak for you?* You do, Ralph. Yes, you do. And maybe, on some other frequency, I speak for you, Bill? If Bill knew the invisibility that I'd felt, which I suspected he did, then I hoped that would mean he and I could see each other clearly. That he would know exactly what I meant—that I was nothing like the others on the committee, that I was reaching out to him, albeit in a stupid way.

I was staring down at my feet, and when I finally raised my head up, I noticed that Bill was running his thumb and index finger over each of the prayer beads he wore around his wrist. I couldn't bring myself to turn away from the movement of those beads, hoping somehow they would bring me peace too.

The silence lasted somewhere between a few seconds and forever. My entire back was soaked in sweat; my ears were ringing. Outside, the last of the daylight was gone.

"No, honestly," Bill said at last, flashing an absurdly handsome smile. "I'm that rusty. But let's hit some balls soon, Raj. We can team up."

It was the kindest thing anyone had done for me in a very long time. I now wanted desperately to be his friend, but I knew that the next time I saw him, he'd turn away and keep walking. I'd done something so stupid and wrong, made so much worse by the fact that I'd done it in front of this particular audience, forcing Bill and Valerie to choose between the anger that was their right and the compassion Bill had shown.

Suzanne said nothing. She just sat there horror-stricken, trying to figure out how to manage the situation and bring the interview to a close.

I don't clearly remember the minutes that followed. It felt like I was underwater, that there was conversation going on above that I couldn't piece together. But it seemed like everyone was trying hard to put the moment behind them.

"Those earrings are beautiful," Valerie said to Suzanne.

"Really?" Suzanne said, fiddling with them. "I designed them myself. They're inspired by a trip my family took to India. I so loved the place and the people. They'd look beautiful on you. I'll send you some."

I suppressed the urge to roll my eyes. She loved *all* of the one billion people in India? A lot of dumb stuff had been said that night, and that was definitely near the top of the list. But I knew that I, of course, was by far at the top.

"No, no," Valerie said, "I couldn't." She seemed taken aback by the intimacy of the offer.

"I'd like to," Suzanne said, an almost pleading tone in her voice, as if a pair of fancy earrings could ease the awkwardness of the moment.

"That'd be nice. Thank you."

"Did you play a sport in college?" Stan asked Valerie.

"I didn't," she said, turning to Stan, and added before he could ask: "UCLA. Just a fan."

There were a series of conversations going on around the

room. Leslie was busy talking to Mark and Jan about their time in Spain, telling them how much she'd loved her study abroad year in Seville. Bill was talking to Richard about the rigors of junior tennis. I was having trouble getting Bill's attention. Somehow, I needed to get him alone so that we could talk.

We were now well past the fifteen-minute mark that we allotted for each couple. Suzanne didn't place her interlaced fingers on her lap. Instead, she let the conversation die down naturally. And when it did, she said, "Thank you so much for coming. We'll be in touch very soon."

The meeting came to a close. Once again, the Browns shook hands with everyone, and when they got to me, Valerie had a kind, calm expression on her face, perhaps the one she typically reserved for when a skinhead with a bullet-ridden chest rolled into her operating room. Bill shook my hand as well, gave me a muted smile. When they left the room with the Blacks, I wanted to follow, to apologize in the privacy of the darkening evening outside.

"I'm going to see if I can catch the Browns before they leave," I said. I didn't expect any opposition. This was precisely what they all wanted to hear.

And with that, I ran out of the clubhouse, into the night and toward the cars. There were no lights in the parking lot, but at the far end I could see an SUV backing out of its spot. As it came toward me, I stepped forward, hoping it was the Browns. I wasn't sure if they knew I was out there, but as the car got closer, the headlights shined directly at me. The car slowed down. Thank god, they were going to stop. But then they maneuvered away from me, and as they passed, I could see Valerie in the passenger seat, illuminated from the light of her cell phone. Bill was saying something to her, with his eyes on the road. They drove out of the lot before I could catch their attention.

I turned back toward the clubhouse, and through the windows I could see that the rest of the committee was still there, in animated conversation.

In the dark, I felt so horribly alone, with the light from the bright stars above not quite making it down to me. It was the first cool night after a long summer, and the damp air felt refreshing on my skin. How had I become the one who, again and again, filled every last bit of silence with some stupid joke? Why was I incapable of learning a simple lesson? Shut up, Raj.

I headed to my car.

"Raj."

The sound echoed in the parking lot, the voice coming from the dark, as if a hellhound were barking my name. I heard heels tapping on the ground in quick succession. I stopped and waited. Finally, Suzanne appeared. The only light came from the clubhouse, and when she stood close to me, I couldn't see her very clearly.

When I had first met her and her husband Jack, it had been a very hot day and our kids were all swimming in the pool. We were talking in the shallow end, and after I told them what I did for a living, they spent the rest of our time together trying to persuade me that a liberal arts education was a waste of time and money.

"If they want to read books, they should go to the library. They should be learning to *do* something when they're in college. Be a doctor, an engineer."

I had reduced Suzanne to those words, convinced that she thought all human endeavors had to have utility. And yet, every time I saw her after, she did and said things that surprised me, often inquiring about and showing a genuine interest in what I was teaching that term.

The previous week, we'd been the last ones left after the membership meeting, cleaning up together. In the parking lot, as we were about to get into our cars, a little drunk off the wine and the power to say yes or no, laughing and making fun of the couples we had seen that night, she had told me about her visit to the Taj Mahal. "What a luminous place," she'd said. "I was so happy to have Jack and my boys at my side. But as I gazed at all that marble, I realized that no one would ever build something so majestic in honor of me. I know it sounds ridiculous. Of course they wouldn't. But still I was left with such a deep, profound melancholy. It was almost like my whole body was melting away."

Several seconds passed without either of us saying anything.

"Maybe it was the summer heat," I finally offered.

There were a few more seconds of silence and then she belted out this wild, beautiful laughter that echoed in the empty parking lot.

Now here we were again, though I imagined the conversation would be rather different.

"Did you catch them?" Suzanne asked in a soft voice.

"No." I'd wanted to so badly. And now I wished I'd gotten in my car immediately after the Browns had driven away. I needed to be by myself, and I certainly didn't want to talk this through with Suzanne.

"What happened back there?" Suzanne asked in a gentle yet stern tone that I suspect she used with her children after they'd thrown a temper tantrum.

My mind felt like a hive of bickering bees. I ran my fingers through my hair, as if that might help order my thinking. "I said something terrible. I didn't mean to, it just came out. Now I feel sick to my stomach." Much as I desperately wanted to, I couldn't take this back. "I get the sense that you and the rest of the committee are very concerned about it."

"Yes, we are."

I mean, who wouldn't be? But still it rankled that after years of turning the other way, they were finally taking a stand on something.

"I'm not making an excuse for myself here, but I didn't see that same concern from everyone when that woman called me Kumar. I know they're not the same. But still."

"I'm sorry about that. She's an idiot and they're going on the bottom of the list. But you know this is of an entirely different magnitude. You just called — you called an African-American man, an African-American doctor . . ." Her voice dropped off.

"I didn't," I said. "And what does it matter that he's a doc-tor?"

"Several people in there would disagree with that. Everyone heard it. We're all horrified. And no, it doesn't matter that he's a doctor, but you know exactly what I mean. It would have been equally bad if you said it to someone else."

I wasn't going to explain to her the difference in intention and the crucial replacement of the "er" with an "a" in what I had said. But then I did.

"I'm not your student," Suzanne said, snapping at me. "And I don't live under a rock. And neither do you."

I was figuring out how best to reply, but Suzanne continued on, as if reciting a script the committee had hastily put together for her.

"Do you understand that there are legal implications? He could sue the club."

"For what?"

"Hostility. Racial bias. Discrimination."

"Then I should have sued this club long ago." But I didn't want to talk about my grievances right then. "You don't understand, Suzanne. I wasn't being hostile."

"What else do you call that? I saw the way you stared at him when he came in, when he was talking about choosing medical school over pro tennis. The envy was pouring out of you."

It took me a few seconds to register what she was saying. I wanted to hang out with Bill; I wanted to be him. And so yes, I was envious. But it wasn't a hostile envy. Is that what they all thought I was feeling? "Are you kidding?" I asked, my voice louder and more forceful than before.

"Raj, I'm not going to argue with you about this, but I think you need to resign from the committee. We all do. I'll call

Mark and let him know. And you're going to have to apologize. To both the Browns and the Blacks."

"Fuck that." The words came out, once again, before I could stop or soften them. All of them wanted me to resign? I trusted Leslie with my kids. I'd had an insightful conversation with Stan the other day about Dostoyevsky.

I was certainly going to apologize to Bill. I'd stop by the hospital in the morning, or send him and Valerie an email. But I wasn't going to let Suzanne and the rest of the committee dictate how that apology went. I needed to do it on my own terms.

"Sorry. Let me start again." I ran my fingers through my hair, this time feeling like I had more control of my racing thoughts. "As I said earlier, I know I messed up. Big time. But I'm not resigning."

"We like you, Raj. We like your family. Please don't do anything to jeopardize that."

These words, more than any others that had been uttered that evening, felt as sharp as a knife, slicing the dark space between us.

"Are you threatening me?"

I couldn't see her face. And she didn't immediately respond.

"No," she finally said, in a steady, slow voice that I'd never heard from her before. "I'm just trying to make things right."

"So am I. I'll see you at that meeting on Friday." I walked to my car.

Once inside, I sat in the dark of the driver's seat and watched as Suzanne walked back to the clubhouse. My hand was unsteady as I tried to fit the key into the ignition. I turned on a light.

For years, I had been meticulous about my car, keeping it clean and organized, washing it inside and out every weekend. Now, granola bar wrappers littered the floor, shattered potato chips ground into the folds of the seats, and a layer of thick dust caked on the dashboard. I put the key in, started the car, and then noticed a headless Lego man near the gearbox. I examined it for a few seconds and, unsure of what else to do with it, put it back. I pulled out of my spot, my front left tire screeching against the body of the car where I'd gotten into a fender bender several months before. Mine was the anti-Tesla, noisily announcing itself everywhere it went.

There was no gate at the entrance of the club. As I waited to merge onto the street, I closed my eyes for a few seconds, hoping to gain some clarity, as Bill seemed to from his prayer beads. When I opened them again, I glanced in the rearview mirror. There was no one behind me. But I saw a small wooden sign attached to a stake in the ground, one that I had seen a hundred times before. Eventually, I had stopped noticing it. Now it was as if it were lit up only for me — THE TENNIS CLUB — and right below, in smaller letters, two words shining in the glow from the lamp on the ground beneath it: MEMBERS ONLY.

I put the car in reverse and drove close to the sign. When I got out, I saw the committee through the large bay window of the clubhouse. Suzanne was saying something to the rest of the group. They were all listening, but then Leslie noticed that I was outside. She turned toward me. One by one, the rest of them did as well, as if they were all on shore and I had boarded a ship set to sail. What were they all thinking? Did they think I was one of them? I looked back at the sign, still glowing, still proudly announcing its intent. I had hated that sign when we'd first joined the club, and the layers of meaning in those two simple words. And yet, I would be lying if I said I didn't enjoy being on the inside, being part of a club that others wanted to join.

I got back into my car and drove home.

Monday

WHEN I WOKE UP the next morning, it took me a few seconds to focus on the red numbers: 5:24. My eyes were parched, as if I'd slept barely an hour, though I'd been in bed by ten and fallen off instantly. I felt around on the other side of the bed with my feet, but the sheets were cool. I stayed under the covers for another half an hour, hoping I might catch just a wink more.

Still in a morning haze, with pieces of the previous night scattered in my head, I allowed myself to think, for as long as I could, that none of it had happened. I hadn't seen Eva and the boys before bed. I'd gone from the meeting to a restaurant, where I sat at the bar, drank a very quick beer, ate dinner, and sloppily graded some papers. I couldn't concentrate. I'd stayed out until I knew they'd all be asleep.

When I finally got up, I made the bed, brushed my teeth, and walked down the hall. I peeked into Neel's room and, from the bit of morning light coming through his curtains, saw an open toolbox, plastic tubing, a hammer and nails, scattered Matchbox cars, and a stack of books on the floor. A sign made of toothpicks and nails spelling out NEEL hung on his door. Across the hall, Arun had written out his name in crayon and drawn a picture of himself, and carefully taped it to his door. The floor of his room was bare; on one bookshelf, his books were organized by size, and on another, he had every Lego he had ever built, organized by genre. On his bedside table was a glass of water for when he got thirsty at night. He often called for Eva in the very early hours of the morning, and now she was spooning him, and he was spooning a large, stuffed wolf.

As names go, "Neel" and "Arun" were pretty unremarkable. But we had put a lot of thought into them. When my parents were naming me, all they considered was what the name meant. Rajesh, "ruler of kings." Raj, "king." After two daughters, the king had finally arrived. The choice was easy: they assumed that the name would only ever need to roll off Indian tongues. But then we had immigrated and I was lucky. "Raj" was easy. The question for Eva and me was how to maintain some cultural specificity for our brown boys without risking complete destruction on the playground. Thus, Neel and Arun. Both easy to pronounce, both vaguely ethnic.

Though my name meant king, as a child I'd often acted a little prince — as my sisters liked to remind me. In Bombay, on our walk to school every morning, I insisted that they each clasp one of my hands the entire way. In the rainy season, they both had to hold an umbrella over me because I hated to get wet. Once when I did, I had one of them go home and get me a dry shirt. Since then, they often bought me umbrella-themed birthday gifts — actual umbrellas, T-shirts, industrial-sized packs of cocktail umbrellas. As far as I could tell, the teasing was playful; they were both too busy, successful, and well adjusted to hold a grudge — Swati, the eldest, most of all, maybe because of how old she'd been when we arrived in America, or maybe because of her naturally sharp focus. Two years in an American high school; Berkeley undergrad; straight into marriage and a child; and then Silicon Valley, before they called it that. Now, her one daughter had graduated from Wesleyan and was working for Swati at the micro-lending startup she'd founded after cashing out at two different companies. My other sister, Rashmi, had followed in our paternal grandfather's footsteps and become a lawyer. She lived in San Francisco, had two kids, and usually worked deep into the weekends.

Between loans and legal help, I was covered in case of emergency.

We all got together a few times a year and always at Thanksgiving, at the family house in the East Bay, where our mother still lived. It was a simple tract home we'd moved into several years after we immigrated. Before that we'd lived in a dingy apartment behind a Kmart and then in a brand-new condominium that was eventually too small for a family of five. In the bare backyard of the new house, my father had dug holes and planted roses, grape vines, and peach, plum, and pear trees. After long days of work, he was happiest tending to his flora. He'd been dead a decade, but still I often thought of him, lingered on his precise movements in the garden, especially when I was working in my own backyard.

Through the kitchen window, I watched the first of the morning light streaming through the thicket of pink bougainvillea growing in the back. I'd planted them as little shrubs soon after we'd moved into this house several years earlier, and here they were, immense and unruly, needing to be cut back. I'd chosen them, along with a cherimoya tree, because they reminded me so much of India. Here, in my wife's hometown, through the alchemy of wet ocean air and dry mountain heat, the plants grew ferociously. In some ways, when we'd moved here, we'd both returned home.

I went out through the sliding door into the cool morning. The damp lawn wet my feet as I walked over to the chicken coop. Arun loved eggs to start the day, and I loved cracking them open on a sizzling pan, watching the orange yolk harden and change color. There were two waiting for me in the laying boxes, and they were warm in my hands.

In the distance, I could hear Mexican radio, and this early in the day, it sounded like a norteño morning call to prayer. We lived next door to a large organic blueberry farm, and the work of picking always started very early. We'd bought our ranch house, and the half acre of land it sat on, when the housing market had crashed, and now that the market was returning and the trees on the property were bearing consistent fruit, buying the house felt like the single best financial decision we'd ever made.

We couldn't have made it without some help. As he neared

retirement, my father had written a weekly column for a
newsletter that went out to our entire extended family: "The
Upanishad Guide to Investing." He liked the *Upanishads* and
he liked investing; he thought that the philosophical core of
this particular Hindu religious tradition — to be neither happy
in victory nor daunted in defeat — was as useful a principle
for investing as any fancy algorithms Goldman Sachs could
come up with. He took special pride in his returns and became a little obsessive about it. Not because of the money he
was making, but because — at least this is what I think — it
was his way of getting back at America for all of the promo-
tions he hadn't gotten in the years he'd been working in the
country. In India, he'd been in charge of monetary policy at a
large national bank, but here, he'd hit his ceiling quickly as the
branch manager of a local bank, spending his days and years
approving home improvement loans for garage additions and
new kitchens.

He started each of his columns with the same statement: "I
am not telling you how to invest. I'm simply telling you how I
invest. What you do with the information is up to you." He'd
then write a paragraph — with supporting numbers and charts
— justifying each new stock he picked. In addition to preach-
ing dispassion once the stocks were bought, he'd explain his
choices by applying two further principles. First, invest in companies that were at least five years old, because they were sus-
tainable yet still hungry; don't invest in companies that had
been around for more than twenty-five years, because they
were comfortable and had no desire to innovate. And second,
he picked businesses that made things or provided services

that he himself could reasonably use. For his sixty-fifth birthday, we put all the columns together in a book and printed a hundred copies to give out to the family. For a lark, one of my younger cousins put the book on Amazon. For a while nothing happened. Then a few copies sold, and then several more. An investing blog picked it up and wrote about it, dubbing my father "the Guru of High Returns." After that, we had to print more. A small business publisher paid him a decent amount of money to repackage and properly sell the book. Some of the proceeds from the book, but mainly his judicious use of the advice in it over the years, had helped pay for our down payment.

He never saw our house, but I imagine he would have liked its rural feel. To the right of us was the farm, and to the left, about two hundred yards away, were a couple of houses occupied by older neighbors. A retired art professor and his wife lived in one; inside their house, the walls were covered with the abstracts he had painted over a lifetime. In the other house was an older man named Max, whom I only saw riding on his John Deere, mowing his large backyard. The one real substantive exchange I'd had with Max was when he noticed a Bay Alarm truck in our front yard soon after we moved in. "I have an alarm system too," he'd said with a mischievous grin. "My shotgun." In the name of new neighborliness, I'd smiled back, though in truth, guns, and the Second Amendment culture that often surrounded gun ownership, made me pretty uncomfortable. I feared that the right to bear arms would loosely translate, at some point, into a right to shoot me.

In some ways, we were boutique homesteading. The daily world my children woke up to couldn't have been more different from the one-bedroom, sixth-floor apartment that I had lived in with my family in south Bombay until I was eight. The apartment had felt big to us then, with the salty air of the Arabian Sea blowing through. Every weekday morning, my sisters and I would descend into the hectic, crowded streets and walk to the Gandhian school we attended, where the principal had outlawed clapping during assemblies because he thought the motion was too violent. In my earliest memories of the city, I smell the fresh loaves of bread baking in the Iranian café near our apartment, and I walk past whole families who slept on the sidewalk, cows meandering nearby, red double-decker buses barreling past them on the street, mere feet away from their heads. I see schoolchildren like me, oil in their hair, talcum powder on their faces, trying to stay cool in the humidity that never seemed to break.

I'm not sure which set of early impressions I preferred for Neel and Arun. On the one hand, I would have liked for them to be urban children, aware that the very act of walking down the street was a complex negotiation between beauty and danger. And yet, I loved that they often woke up to the piercing sounds of a red-tailed hawk flying high above and that they flinched less and less at the sight of a gopher snake. But I did feel some parental responsibility to balance out this world they knew with the world I'd grown up in, so that when it was time for them to choose lives for themselves, they could make an informed decision.

When I got back inside with the eggs, the kettle was whistling. As I made my coffee, I wondered what advice my father would have given me about how to proceed following the previous evening's debacle. Somewhere around my freshman year in college, he had decided it was time to start communicating with me as an adult. This didn't translate to real conversation, or even the metaphoric intimacy a lot of fathers and sons find in, say, sports talk. No, my father spoke to me through photocopied clippings from the *Wall Street Journal,* which he mailed to me every month or so. Where were the originals? Perhaps in a folder called "Stuff Sent to My Son for Guidance." Those envelopes left me with so many questions. Why wasn't he writing me an actual note? Did this article mean he thought I wasn't saving my money properly? Did this one mean I was ruled by my heart? Now I desperately wish I'd saved them all, but of course I hadn't. I was young; it didn't occur to me that they were clues. My father didn't share much about himself with me; imagine what I could've pieced together from what he did.

There were some things he had revealed over the years. His favorite album was pre-radical Harry Belafonte's *Live at Carnegie Hall.* When "Jamaica Farewell," a song about sailors leaving home, came on, he would turn up the volume slightly and hum along, his mind clearly somewhere far from our living room. He'd said that he wanted to study psychology in college but it just felt too impractical. He'd once recalled to me that his favorite psychology professor had said that ninety percent of men masturbate, and the other ten percent lie about it. I had looked over at him, startled; that was as risqué and off-the-cuff as my father ever got, perhaps a sign that there had been more going on beneath his insistently calm, controlled exterior than he let on. More humor, more playfulness. I wish I could have known that side of him.

He'd loved *Guess Who's Coming to Dinner*. He thought poorly of films in general, that they were a waste of time, but when he watched that one, he seemed to be in another world, one I could neither understand nor access. I always assumed he saw himself as Sidney Poitier. But he talked most often about the Spencer Tracy character, the pissy white dude who finally comes around to his daughter's choice of a black partner. I didn't understand why until much later, when Nelson Mandela and F. W. de Klerk won the Nobel Peace Prize. I was angry that they had given it to de Klerk, who had benefited handsomely from apartheid. My father countered: the greater courage is de Klerk's, who, having seen the error of his ways, was willing to admit his wrongs to the world by releasing Mandela from jail.

Why had he been so taken with making amends, with admitting fault? Perhaps he'd done something in his life that he'd later wished he'd handled differently. Whatever the reason, I was sure that if he were here now he would tell me to apologize quietly to everyone and move on. Neither happy in victory nor daunted in defeat: the dictum that shaped his investing and the primary advice he gave his children on how to manage life's vagaries. Every day when I woke up in my sturdy house, I was thankful for that counsel. And yet this time I didn't want to move on, to smooth things over, to remain even-keeled.

Coffee in hand, I went to shower.

On my way there, I stopped in the hall between the kids'

rooms. Eva was still asleep with Arun. I walked into Neel's room, placed my coffee on his desk, and crawled into bed with him. It wouldn't be long before he outgrew his twin bed. He stirred and then turned to me, his breath sour from the night.

"Is everything OK?" he asked.

He was asking because I'd gotten into bed with him without having been called for. He was asking because when he was in that space between sleep and waking, he saw the world most clearly — he often professed deep love for us in the hazy minutes before he fell asleep at night. And he was asking because he was always tuned in to my emotional tremors.

"Everything's fine," I said. "I just wanted to see you before I left for work."

Relieved, Neel purred and leaned in close to me. I held him tight, as if the purity running through his body could somehow cool the continued burning in my chest.

I got up and went to take a shower, my coffee getting a little cold. When we'd had the bathroom redone, we'd asked the tile guy to build a small shelf for the shampoos; I preferred to use it for my mug.

The door creaked open while I was rinsing off. Eva walked in and sat gingerly on the toilet. Every American romantic comedy seemed to have this moment as a marker of a couple's intimacy. It had always made me wonder: How did this practice evolve? How many real, non-movie people actually did this? Were they just in America? Did couples in Swaziland do this? Norway? What were the cross-cultural habits of couples who peed in each other's presence? Maybe there was an essay in that for me — though the list of essays I thought about writing kept getting longer and longer, and I never seemed to sit down and draft any of them. Essays, like so many other things in life, were much better in my mind than in reality.

A few seconds later, Eva slipped into the shower and turned on the other showerhead. Her naked body, a bit of Venus on the half-shell, which, after fifteen years of marriage and two babies, still gave me a twinge.

"Don't get any ideas," she said.

The shower used to be our thing. I passed her the mug.

"How did it go last night?" she asked, taking a sip.

"Fine," I said. "We'll meet later this week to figure it out."

"Anyone interesting?"

We were that couple who talked about absolutely everything. But I wasn't quite ready to tell her about Bill Brown. I needed to process it longer on my own, to be clear about how I wanted to move forward before I heard her take on it. I trusted her opinion so much, it was easy for our thoughts to become intertwined; I wanted to have a clearer sense of where I stood myself before that happened.

"Not really."

She was rinsing the shampoo from her hair, suds streaming over her breasts.

"How were the boys last night?" I asked, stepping out of the shower and drying off.

"We had our moments, but for the most part they were fine."

I quickly pulled on my teaching uniform: 501s and a red Lacoste shirt that I always air-dried to keep it from shrinking and a pair of high-top black-and-white Vans I'd recently bought. When I was a teenager, my parents would never have bought me the shoes because they were expensive and impractical. So, of course, as soon as I'd been able to afford them, I'd bought them for myself; but now they made me a little self-conscious, as if I were too blatantly channeling my teenage self. What's worse than a middle-aged college lecturer pretending he's not? But the Vans were comfortable and reminded me that, at least when it came to shoes, I now had the freedom to buy what I wanted. I tried to leave it at that. The first day I'd worn them, I gave a particularly lively lecture and the students were engaged through the full hour. When I was done, I said, "It's gotta be the shoes." They all just stared at me blankly and shuffled out of the classroom.

I ate a piece of toast with peanut butter and started making sandwiches for the kids' lunches. On Monday mornings, I usually left early to get to my office. I did the drop-offs and pickups on Tuesdays and Thursdays, while Eva took Mondays and Wednesdays. We roshamboed for Fridays.

"You go," Eva said when she came into the kitchen, taking the butter knife from me. "I'll do it." She gave me the once-over. "Nice. Keep your door open during office hours."

"I always do."

I tried to put together the sentences that would explain and defend what had happened with the Browns. Certainly she was going to hear it from Leslie at drop-off; Leslie loved the intimacy of gossip.

"What's up?" Eva asked.

"Nothing," I said. I knew that once I told her, the conversation would go on for a while, and I wasn't ready for that. "Busy day today?"

"Nothing unusual. But whenever I say that, the earth shakes."

Eva and I had met in graduate school at Columbia, a couple of Californians bonding over long winters that neither of us could comprehend. I was getting a PhD in anthropology, and she was getting a master's in international and public affairs. I had picked Columbia because it was a highly ranked school, yes, but also because I desperately wanted to have a New York period in my life. I wanted to grow away from my family, something I had decided all young men needed to do, and going to the gloriously hectic urbanity of New York felt like returning to the urbanity of Bombay. I had also wanted to study with the distinguished Palestinian literary critic Edward Said. Years before, in college, I had seen him give a talk on the broad influence of his seminal book *Orientalism,* in which he lays out the stereotypical ways in which the East has been portrayed — as religious, feminine, exotic — within the long tradition of Western literature and history. He was brilliant; I was rapt. But I also kept my eyes on the perfectly tailored mustard corduroys he was wearing. Mustard? My god. A revelation. You could dress well and say the world was unjust and quote Foucault, all at the same time. I wanted to be that person; I wanted to share bad news about the world, and I wanted to be sharply dressed while I did it.

I did my fieldwork in India and then returned to New York to write my dissertation, before settling into my first teaching job in Queens. In the meantime, Eva had graduated and was working for various foundations in New York that collected money from billionaires and used it to fight diseases and promote democracy around the world. She swiftly climbed up. When we moved back to California, she got a job before I did, at a well-funded NGO called Rapid Responders International. Earthquake in Haiti? Rapid Responders was there within hours with food, water, and supplies, while the UN and other nations, with their various bureaucracies, were still figuring things out. Cholera outbreak in Somalia? Doctors were there treating patients before the story appeared below the fold of the *New York Times*. As the years passed, Eva coordinated bigger and bigger operations from the safety of California. She loved the job, and she was really efficient at managing large-scale, complex logistics. The hours were flexible when things were calm in the world, but she could easily be in the office for fourteen-hour days during hurricane season.

She didn't seem to mind, though the social requirements of the job did bother her. There were plenty of rich people in town ready to throw events to raise money for Rapid Responders. It was a sexy organization to support. For a while, I'd accompanied her to some of these. But I stopped going after one, at a stunning oceanfront estate, where men in tailored jackets and women wearing thousand-dollar garden dresses listened to a doctor talk about the problems of syphilis in sub-Saharan Africa. Sure, by the end of the night some money had flowed from those who didn't need it to those who desperately did. I just couldn't stomach the idea of dressing up and drinking specialty cocktails to help the poor.

But I watched from the sidelines. Eva always forwarded me emails about the various fundraisers going on around town, for her organization and for others. The affluent, I discovered, like to role-play while they give away their money. Arabian Nights, A Night in the Hamptons, The Roaring Twenties. My favorite? Bollywood Dreams — a gala at which the guests were encouraged to wear their best Indian costumes, and there were designations for the amount of money the attendees gave, from highest to lowest: Queen Victoria, Viceroy, Governor, Maharaja. The lowest category? Sahib. Donate a thousand dollars, and for a night you could wear linen and feel like a midlevel colonial functionary. The rich truly don't give a fuck.

"Let's hope things are mellow," I said, giving Eva a kiss on the cheek and heading toward the door. "Here and in the world."

"I'll pick up the kids this afternoon," Eva said, turning to their sandwiches.

I lingered at the edge of the kitchen. "I had a little disagreement with the committee last night," I said. Though I wanted to tell her, I also didn't want to relive the moment. Every time I'd replayed it in my mind, I felt a full-body cringe. "I'm sure you'll see Leslie or Suzanne at drop-off this morning. Please don't listen to them. I'll explain later."

"Oh, no," she said, with concern in her voice. "What happened?" But then she added, matter-of-factly, "What did you say?"

"Why do you assume I said something?" I hated that I had become so predictable.

Eva cocked her head slightly. She didn't need to remind me of my habit of saying things that I shouldn't. "Can you just tell me what happened?"

"It's not that big of a deal. But I have to go get some stuff done before class. I'll call you later."

Before Eva could object, Arun walked into the kitchen, wearing a pair of tight red underwear. His body was still burnt brown from the summer, his long hair lighter from days in the sun and water. Our little California-bred Mowgli.

"Going to work?" he asked.

"Yep. Wanna come and teach my classes?"

His face disappeared into Eva's belly. Sometimes I think both boys longed to be back in there.

"I'll see you tonight," I said, winking at Eva.

For a moment, as I drove away, I felt the sanctity of the early morning again, the coolness and the possibility of a day that had not yet been misspent. I might have liked the life of a monk — or at least the part where they woke up early, prayed, and then maintained uncluttered minds for the rest of the day.

I drove through our neighborhood and then got on the freeway. Much of my twenty-minute commute went along the Pacific Ocean. The first sight of water, running onto a strip of beach where we often went on the weekends to swim and tide-pool, grabbed hold of me every morning. It was so beautiful, now and at dusk when the deep orange of the setting sun blanketed the water. Every day the splendor stunned me anew, then left me feeling empty. Sadness at the heart of unrelenting beauty? There has to be a German word for that.

There were some solid five-foot waves out there, and several wet-suited bodies. I envied the seeming simplicity of surfing: arriving on the shore, putting on a thick layer of protection, pushing out against the waves, and gliding on the sea, over and over again until you hit the point of exhaustion. Every surfer I knew seemed cleansed from the water and the salt.

I'd tried it once myself, while I was courting Eva; her father had taken me out to give it a go. He'd lent me one of his wet suits.

"This should fit fine," he'd said.

I was excited to see myself in it and started putting it on, but it was so tight I could barely move my leg. Eva's father had come to take a look, and in the kindest tone said, "I think you put your leg where the arm's supposed to go."

That was that with surfing.

I'd had this feeling so many times in my life: the sense that I didn't know how to manage a situation that everyone around me seemed to inhabit so effortlessly. Even in the ocean, this frothy source of all life, I never felt truly comfortable. It was too vast, threatening, and unpredictable. Whenever we went to the beach, Eva was the one who took the boys out. She had grown up swimming in the ocean and knew the contours of the waves as they came in, how to challenge some and respect others.

Turning away from the water, I switched on the radio and quickly changed stations. I landed on the classic rock station: Springsteen and his hungry heart. I've always loved Bruce's handsome brooding, how addicted he is to attention, how he shies away from it all the same. But even as he gives voice to my inner wants and fears, I've always sensed that I'm not the kind of outsider he's singing for. And yet I listen, over and over again. Bruce and then Tom Petty, followed by Neil Young — who always manages to make me nostalgic for a life I've never had — got me to my exit.

The university where I teach also overlooks the ocean. At first, I'd been disappointed with the clean lines of the campus's form-follows-function architecture, the buildings a bunch of mismatched matchboxes. But eventually I realized their genius. The natural beauty of the ocean was so stunning, ornate buildings would have gotten in the way. Of course Oxford is spectacular and impressive; it's in the middle of dreary, rainy England.

Since it was so early, I got a parking spot right next to the six-story building that housed my office. Nearly every time I walked from my car to the building, I was thankful to work in such a beautiful place, and yet felt an ache of sorrow, leaning toward resignation, about how my career had stalled. On Mondays and Wednesdays, I arrived very early, well before the department secretary, did all my class prep, taught my three classes through the day, and did my best to avoid my colleagues. I had learned that having a very small footprint was my key to survival. But that had not always been the case. When I finished graduate school and went off to my first job, I'd felt so ascendant, confident that there would always be a correlation between hard work and success. All these years later, I'd realized that luck, good fortune, and the ability to translate hard work into usable currency can be just as, if not more, significant in professional advancement. And somewhere along the way, I'd struck out.

By the time I'd started that job, I'd lived in New York for several years. I knew that September hung in the long, humid shadow of August. And yet, on a Tuesday morning after Labor Day, in the safety of our air-conditioned Upper West Side apartment — filled with unopened gifts, even though a year had passed since our wedding — I'd showered and put on my new slacks, a button-down shirt, and a blazer, all new from Brooks Brothers.

"You'll melt," Eva had said.

"I'll be fine. I'll keep the jacket off."

"It's the wool of those pants that's worrying me."

I should have changed into khakis and a half-sleeved shirt, but for as long as I could remember, I'd had this vision of myself, stepping into the classroom for the first time, with a newly minted degree — the wrong kind of doctor, but a doctor nevertheless — wearing a properly fitted blazer instead of the oversized ones I'd borrowed from my father's closet for years. That image of a well-dressed Edward Said had stuck in my head.

"It's supposed to be cooler today," I offered.

"Well, you look sharp," Eva said, tugging at my blazer's lapel.

"Don't I?" I said. The heat hit me as soon as I left the building. By the time I'd made it to the subway station, my shirt was soaked in sweat. It was too late to take my jacket off. There were plenty of men walking on the street wearing suits and ties, all of them far fresher and more put together than me. I just couldn't understand it.

On the station platform, with sweat trickling down my legs, my wool slacks seemed to be growing fangs. But even through the endless wait for the train, as the crowd grew thicker and more agitated, I was happy to be there, with hundreds of strangers around me. So many of my friends complained about the subway, but it was one of my favorite things about living in New York. It reminded me of being a kid, going on shopping trips with my mother in Bombay. She'd stuff me onto a crowded double-decker just as the bus started moving, knowing that the adults would make room for a six-year-old, that she'd somehow find space for herself. I'd look at the Parsi women in their skirts, the Muslim men in their beards, professional men in lean suits, and the occasional Western tourist dressed in an Indian kurta with beads around his neck. My mother and I developed a deep trust in each other on those rides; no matter the crowds, we always knew we would find our way together on the other end. As I took the C train to the E, which started out sardined, the crowd gradually thinning as I made my way deeper and deeper into Queens, I felt that same wonder I had on the bus as it bounced through Bombay, strangers jostling all around.

I'd been to the college before, for my interview and then later to move into my office. But this arrival was the official one — and, I'd thought, a permanent one. I went to the department secretary, who showed me around, gave me the keys that I needed. I went into the mailroom and saw a little box with my name on it, nestled in among the rest of the faculty. I was in there alone for a minute, and then someone walked in.

"You the new guy?" an older faculty member asked, charmingly, as if I had arrived with a lunch pail and we were waiting for our shift to start at an auto plant.

He, too, was wearing slacks, a jacket, *and* a tie. I watched as he noticed my jacket, which had wrinkled a little.

"I am."

"John Williams," he said, offering his hand, warm and surprisingly large.

Of course I knew exactly who John Williams was. He'd been away when I'd come to interview on campus, so I hadn't met him then, but he was one of the reasons I'd wanted to come and teach at the college. He'd written an oft-cited book on time and memory in everyday Moroccan life.

"Raj Bhatt."

He moved past me to get his mail. "Well, Raj, if you need anything, let me know. And we should have lunch soon."

Excited about the prospect of that meal, I headed to my first class, located in a building that had remained essentially untouched since 1974. I peeked in through the glass square on the closed classroom door before I opened it. All the seats were taken. As I walked in, the fifty or so students turned their heads to me.

"Hi, all," I said. "I'm Professor Bhatt."

The chairs the students sat on were old. I was about to write my name on the chalkboard, but there was no chalk. The college had once been a distinguished place, but lately had fallen on hard financial times. It seemed that the only thing that worked in the classroom was the air conditioning. Thank the gods.

"You the new guy?" a young woman in the front row asked.

Amused by the echo of John Williams, I asked, "Were you just in the department mailroom?"

She was confused. Of course.

"Never mind," I said, smiling. "Yes, I am the new guy." I set my bag on a table and removed my notes. "I hope you're all here for Intro to Cultural Anthropology."

When I had interviewed for the job, I'd immediately been attracted to the makeup of the student body: lots of immigrants, mostly the first in their families to go to college. It seemed that half of the faculty, devoted to helping the students and aware of how much their own research and thinking had benefited from engaging with diverse classrooms, shared my enthusiasm about this. The other half were conspicuously silent when the topic came up, reflecting their disappointment that their best teaching days were behind them.

The students I had taught at Columbia knew the culture of college well — they had been training for it their whole lives. Now in front of this class, I sensed that there was something different about them. I stood there for a few long seconds, my shirt having gone from wet to dry to wet again. I was finally doing what I'd been training to do for years — to have the authority to speak and teach. I'd spent so much of my time looking ahead, assuring myself that when *this* happened and *that* went through, I would find some sense of peace. Now it felt that I had arrived at the place I'd wanted to be — an immigrant helping other immigrants navigate the new world.

I took out my notes, and as I was about to take attendance, a hand shot up in the back.

"Before you start, can I ask you something?" a young man asked.

"What's up?"

"Why anthropology? Why do we have to take this class?"

"You don't have to take this class."

"I know," he said. "But it's a class we can take to fulfill some of our requirements. I just want to know why I should take this one."

I had been asked to justify why I did what I did plenty of times, mainly by my parents' friends who couldn't understand why I hadn't just gone to business school. But this student was asking me something more profound, more inquisitive — or at least I wanted to believe he was. So I put my prepared notes aside, kept my jacket on, and for the next hour talked to the students about why I thought anthropology was important. I mentioned Malinowski, Evan-Pritchard, Lévi-Strauss: canonical men of the discipline who went out to the southern parts of the globe and came back with grand theories about how the world worked. The idea that there were deep structures that shaped societies across the globe, that we were more similar than different, had once kept me up at night. There are limits to such theories, of course. Still, though he's no longer in vogue, Lévi-Strauss has remained my secret, optimistic gospel. I had studied anthropology for all sorts of complex, high-minded, theoretical reasons, but at the core, I had done it because I loved the idea of talking to people and trying to understand them, to see how different they were. And perhaps, if

I dug far enough into their lives and histories, I could discover how similar they were too.

At the end of the period, the student who'd asked the question walked by on his way out.

"You going to take the class?" I asked.

"Maybe," he said, smiling.

I knew he'd be back.

I didn't take off the jacket until I returned to our apartment that evening.

"What happened?" Eva asked, breaking into a huge smile. "Not the right day for wool?"

I glanced down. My shirt looked like my fingertips did after I had been in a pool for two hours straight. No matter.

"I just had a perfect day."

The road to that day had not been quite as I had planned when I started college. I'd assumed I would go to law school. Until that dread eventuality, I took a lot of English and anthropology classes. I would sit in the library for hours, barreling through Walker Percy one day, Lévi-Strauss the next. But I became truly obsessed with two writers, the subject of my only published essay, "The Impossibility of Second Acts." I wrote my undergraduate thesis on the novelists Ralph Ellison and G. V. Desani, both of whom had written brilliant first novels but never published a second one, at least not in their lifetimes. Why not? I reasoned that both had formulated an entire world — and an entire worldview — in their books the first time out, so there was nothing else for them to write, even though Ellison in particular had tried and tried.

I had worked so hard on that essay. It had won the English

department prize and a college-wide undergraduate award. And my thesis advisor had helped me get it into print just as I was graduating. It had appeared in a highly reputable journal next to work by scholars who were deep into successful careers. All this didn't mean much in terms of guaranteeing me a stable career, but it did give me a window to see a life for myself beyond law school. I turned my attention fully to anthropology because I'd loved those classes the most. And by the time I was done with graduate school, and in my first job, I thought I was ready for my first act.

But it never came. The excitement of that first day never amounted to anything more than that. I had trouble turning my dissertation into a book. John Williams, who I thought would be my mentor, spent most of his time patronizing me. The phrase "Let me put it more simply" seemed to slip out of his mouth without fail during our conversations, and I was sure that as he spoke to me, he slowed down and enunciated his sentences more carefully, as if he thought I had gained fluency in English only recently. I entertained the hope that all this was in my head, until he asked to see the syllabi for my classes and recommended easier readings for the students, for their sake, but also because he thought I'd have difficulty with some of the more complicated articles.

I never complained to anyone about this, partly because I had a job and some of my friends from graduate school didn't. It seemed bad form to be upset when so many people I knew didn't even have health insurance. But also, I knew that there would be a cost to crossing John Williams. His books had given him a semblance of fame, which had translated into power, in the department and the discipline at large.

So throughout the years I was in the job, the resentments piled up between us, until eventually we had a disagreement in a department meeting. He didn't like me contradicting him in front of everybody. Afterward, in the mailroom, he got in my face. "Do you know how long I've been doing this work?" he asked. "Since before you were born." Nervous, I let out a squeal of laughter — perhaps another instance of saying the wrong thing at the wrong time — and that enraged him more. I can still smell his staleness. I then stepped away from him, and as I tried to squeeze my way out of the small mailroom, I accidentally bumped his shoulder with mine. That was it. A tap. And he flopped and fell to the ground. Since no one else was around, his seniority was all the proof he needed to say that I had attacked him.

Not long after that, the chair of the department called me in and said, without bothering with euphemisms, that the rigors of research and publishing were not for me. It was true, I hadn't been publishing. But what he was also telling me, without saying it, was that I didn't quite fit with the culture of the place. I fit in with the students, with the changes they were bringing to campus. But John and his older generation of colleagues still made the decisions, and they had no interest in fostering a new energy within the university.

Eva had wanted to return to California for a while at that point, and so I'd left the job. We headed west, and I ended up with the much lesser job I now held, taking a serious drop in rank. There were certainly aspects of it that I liked: the two-day-a-week teaching schedule; the after-lunch strolls to the ocean; the freedom to teach what I wanted; smart, engaged students.

And yet, the place was filled with lecturers like me, many of whom had fancy PhDs, but by happenstance, bad luck, lack of skill, and a shrinking supply of positions had not gotten or kept the plum tenured jobs that offered lifetime employment and the freedom to write and say whatever you wanted. We were the contingent labor that made this university — and most universities around the country — run these days. We did most of the teaching, packing more and more students into our classrooms, and wrote letter after letter of recommendation so that our students could go on to better careers than ours. But if budget cuts started, we'd be the first out the door. And thus the dull, constant ache of stress and anxiety that I felt now, that circulated through my chest every time I arrived on campus.

I opened my office door, and Dan, my lanky officemate and fellow detritus of academic life, was already there. We taught on different days and were assigned the same office, which had two metal desks and two large bookshelves. Dan had made it a point to leave his shelf completely empty, a poetic nod to the impermanence of his job. On mine, I had placed stacks and stacks of unclaimed, graded blue-book exams that students had failed to pick up after their course had ended. There must have been two thousand little books filled with scribbled pen and pencil. No one wanted to see what they did wrong anymore. Several months before, Dan had written on the back of a business card, *"Pass/No Pass," Raj Bhatt, Mixed Media, 2016,* and taped it to the shelf. Site-specific art.

Dan was tall and skinny. He always seemed uncomfortable when seated; his knees never could find their proper resting place.

"Hey, bubba," he said. He was in his boxers, an old white T-shirt, and brand-new tube socks, eating dry raisin bran out of the box and reading the *New York Times* online. He offered me the cereal. "Breakfast?"

"What the fuck are you doing?" I whispered. "What if I had been someone else?"

"Who else bothers to get here this early?"

I noticed a toiletry kit on his desk. "You didn't."

Dan shrugged his bony shoulders. "The floor isn't very comfortable. I somehow thought it would be."

"What happened?" I asked.

"I need a break."

"A break? You have a sweet, mellow daughter who likes to read books. You don't need breaks. This job is your fucking break."

"What's up with the language? A little hostile this morning."

I didn't respond.

"Don't judge me," Dan continued.

"I'm not judging you. I'm just telling you to go home."

"I can't. Julie said she isn't going to speak to me for one full week."

"She actually said that?"

"Yes. Starting yesterday. She made it very clear. She drew

a circle around the date for reengagement on the family cal-
endar."

"What did you do?"

"Why do you assume it was me?"

I just looked at him. I suppose we were all a little predictable.

He shrugged. "I'm not telling you."

"You can be in the house together but not speak," I said.
"It's easy. My parents built a marriage out of it."

"It's uncomfortable."

"But peaceful."

I could see that Dan wanted to talk more, but I turned to
my computer. I was embarrassed that it actually made me a little bit happy to know that, at the moment, his life was in more
of a shambles than mine.

While my computer powered up, I went into the department kitchen and made myself a cup of instant Starbucks coffee, a useful beverage for the long day ahead. I knew I'd need at
least two more cups to get me through my classes.

For the next hour, I busied myself with prep by going
through my PowerPoint slides, adding one here, removing one
there. I knew these lectures by heart. It wouldn't have made a
difference if I'd shown up to campus five minutes before class.
But getting here early made me feel that I was working hard.

"You expecting a call?" Dan asked.

"Why?"

"You keep checking your phone."

"Don't judge me," I said, pushing the phone away.

"Did you read this story about Jews in India?"

I ignored him.

He reached out again. "Jews in India?"

"Yes, Dan. Jews in India. Maybe you should convert and move. I'm sure Julie won't even notice you're gone."

"You think your mom wants to convert with me?"

I stuck out my middle finger as I continued to work.

When I was done with my class prep, I Googled Bill Brown and the name of our local hospital. His profile came up, which listed his bio, specialty, and education, along with his phone number and email address. I wrote down the email on a scrap of paper. What exactly would I write to him? What would I put in the subject line?

A video had also popped up in the search results: "Stanford's Brown: Long rally and then THIS." I clicked on it. It was an old video of Bill in college, very poor quality, but I could see him, in tennis whites, playing a match against a guy from USC. Bill serves and they rally, hitting the seams off the ball. Bill has an all-around game, gliding back and forth on the baseline. He almost seems bored waiting for the ball to arrive, so casual until he hits it back with full force. He has a beautiful one-handed backhand. He gets down low and explodes forward as he hits the ball. The two rally and then rally some more — the ball flies back and forth at least fifty times. I'm getting tired of watching. I'm tired for them. Then finally, Bill rushes the net, and his opponent hits the most beautiful lob, the shape of the Gateway Arch. There, I think. This is the "THIS." Bill swings around, runs toward the baseline, and with his back to his opponent, hits the ball through his legs and down the line. His opponent lunges for the ball, and misses. The camera closes in on Bill's face: the same easy smile he had when I met him the night before.

I laughed aloud at the perfection of it all. Whenever I've tried that move, I end up smacking my shin with the racquet.

Dan turned to me. "Something more interesting than Jews in India?"

"Nothing is more interesting than Jews in India," I said.

My phone buzzed. I assumed it was Eva, but it was Suzanne. I suddenly felt nervous. It was too early for her to be calling. I didn't want to pick up. But if I silenced it, she would know I was screening her. And so I let it ring.

"Pick that thing up," Dan said. "I'll do it if you won't. Who are you avoiding?"

"I'll tell you later. You'll get a kick out of it."

I waited to see if she left a voicemail. She didn't.

As I was leaving, I said, "You know they have showers in the gym."

"Gyms are for rats," Dan said.

I liked Dan. His humor was sharp, but didn't hurt. We survived the absurdity of our work together. But he also had a slackerly indifference to the world and his job that I didn't want the department to think I shared. If the budget ax fell and they could only keep one of us, I was sure it would be him. He fit the role of the disinterested scholar much better than I did.

I walked out of the office and headed to my 9 a.m. lecture. Because the campus was essentially a beautiful oceanside resort, it attracted students who felt comfortable blurring the line between beachwear and schoolwear, so I had made it my practice to keep my head down when I was outside. On the way to class, I went through the small lot where I had parked. A sporty Audi had just pulled into a spot, and I knew whose car it was.

Josh Morton was roughly my age. And that's where the similarity ended. He was the newly christened Bay Alarm Chair in Insecurity Studies, a burgeoning field studying humanity's fundamental insecurity — political, social, and emotional. And Josh was its leading light. His star had ascended thanks to complete dumb luck. He had taken a trip to Sweden with a girlfriend and come across *trygghet*, a governing principle of Swedish social life. The gist of *trygghet* is that you can't be secure and happy if your life is full of the markers of insecurity — fear, anxiety, uncertainty. Josh took that idea and ran with it.

Seemingly everyone had read and loved his book *The Poetics and Politics of Insecurity*. In it, he had interviewed people from across the American social spectrum — a prison guard in Tennessee, a twenty-four-year-old tech billionaire in San Francisco, an aging model in Beverly Hills, the black mayor of a predominantly white town, and on and on — and concluded that the country was moving into an age of insecurity, regardless of class, race, or any other difference. The book opened with this line: "If the brilliant Danish philosopher Søren Kierkegaard were alive today, how would he assess the fear and trembling occurring all around us? What would he post on Twitter? Would he have an Instagram account?" It had won nearly every academic prize possible, and become the sort of book that nonacademics liked having on their coffee tables, something that happened to about one academic book in a thousand. I'd heard a rumor that Josh had just gotten a big contract with a mainstream publisher to translate some of his ideas for a more popular audience.

I had to admire him for the sheer brilliance of using insecurity to earn him a lifetime of major security. And yet, of course, I hated the fucker. It wasn't just that he held up a mirror to me and my life; he was admiring himself in a completely different, gold-plated mirror. I tried not to think too much about it, because when I did, getting from my place of insecurity to his place of heightened security seemed as daunting as scaling Everest.

I saw Josh now, and I know he saw me, but he pretended not to. This happened on campus a lot. I was a lecturer; he had lifetime employment. He looked right through me. My insecurity was of no concern to him.

As I walked to class, my phone buzzed again. Eva often called to check in after dropping off the kids. I saw her name, but I also noticed that, as had been happening more and more of late, my phone had taken a while to register a voicemail, and Suzanne had indeed left a message. Eva's call kept buzzing. I thought about picking it up, but I didn't want to feel agitated before the lecture. Just as the phone stopped ringing, a text came in. "I know you're not teaching yet. Pick up. WTF? I just saw Leslie."

"Will call after class is done," I texted back rapidly. "Don't listen to Leslie. She understands nothing."

I could see the blinking dots, a ghostly trace of what I presumed was Eva's anger at my evasion, but I switched out of the messages and checked the list of saved voicemails. Most people left me quick, to-the-point messages. Ten seconds max, if they left one at all. In and out. I had saved a few from my last birthday, which were a little longer, topping out at thirty seconds. Suzanne's message was three minutes long — a clear violation of the social contract. What did she possibly need three minutes for that couldn't wait until we actually talked? Was she reading aloud some bylaw that justified kicking me off the committee? I stood in front of the door to the lecture hall, debating whether to listen to it before the class. I decided not to, but as I walked in, now imagining what the message said, I indeed felt agitated. I took a deep breath and tried to calm my head.

My first class of the day was a large lecture I'd been teaching for years: Introduction to Cultural Anthropology. It was the same class I'd taught when I first started teaching. But lately, the ideas that I'd been regurgitating over and over again, quarter after quarter, were getting stale. In class, I did my best to pretend they still excited me, aiming for those golden student evaluations: *passionate, enthusiastic, really cares for us.* My salary increases were dependent on a handful of adjectives.

But even as the others grew crusty, the one idea that I still remained genuinely passionate about was dirt. More precisely, Mary Douglas on dirt. I had lectured on it the previous week. When I first read her *Purity and Danger* in graduate school, I'd gravitated toward its treatment of pollution and taboo among Jews and Hindus. I finally had an explanation for my grandmother's habit of taking baths whenever she returned from being outside. In her mind, her interactions with people lower on the caste hierarchy were not at all different from the actual dirt at her feet: sources of pollution that needed to be cleansed immediately. Her kitchen was a space of strict vegetarianism. She even kept her grandchildren, who spent their days playing outside, at arm's length. Something is deemed dirty, Douglas argues, when it messes with the social order of things. "Dirt is essentially disorder." For a while, I'd written that phrase out in large letters on a piece of paper, and for all the years I spent writing my dissertation, I had it pinned at sight level by my desk. That Mary, she'd nailed it. Particularly when we first joined the TC, I often felt acutely the dirt on my shoulders. I was always worried that I wasn't wearing the right kind of tennis outfit or that my car was too old, too unwashed, that I was talking to a member about something that should have been assumed and left unsaid. After my comment to Bill, there wasn't a shower hot enough to wash the dirt away.

And it wasn't just at the TC that I felt dirty. Dan could get away with sitting in the office in his boxers. If he got caught, my colleagues would think it was a charming moment out of a Kingsley Amis novel. But if I did that, it would confirm something they already believed about my not being quite right for the department; I knew from experience. I didn't want that to happen again.

It was the third week of class. The heavy attendance of the first week was over, but with the midterm in two weeks there were plenty of students in the room. I got up to the front of the class, prepared my notes, turned on my PowerPoint presentation, and for a second surveyed the lecture hall. There were roughly 150 students scattered there, most of them with their faces illuminated by a laptop or phone. I recognized a lot of them by now, but I'd forget them soon after the term ended. Before me was a study in sociological types: the young women, some outwardly confident and others not, who got most of the best grades in class; the bros, who would come up to me at the end of the term, pat me on my shoulder, and say, "Nice job," just as their fathers had done for years with their gardeners, construction workers, lawyers, and doctors; the shy young men, who may have felt alienated in the sunny social world outside of class, but were finding their footing with the course material and gathering the courage to come chat with me; the handful of students who sat in the same seat lecture after lecture, which I knew meant that they came early every day to get their spot. I always paid close attention to the smattering of Indian-American men in my classes, who, almost without fail, would visit me in office hours, carefully ask about the trajectory of my life, and look in wonder when they realized that the narratives their parents had already written for their futures were not the only ones available. I knew that they would slum with me for a term or two before they graduated and settled into a life at Deloitte. I didn't have the heart to tell them that Deloitte was probably the safer bet.

"If you're all done shopping online, maybe I can get started," I said, with a bite in my voice left over from the tension of Suzanne's excessively long voicemail, sitting on my phone.

The lecture was on the history of Indian men who had come to America starting in the late nineteenth century and sold religion and spirituality to the masses: Vivekananda, Krishnamurti, Deepak Chopra. There were plenty of days when I taught things with false confidence, but I knew this material on Indians in the American imagination intimately. I started by talking about the arrival of yoga in the United States in the early twentieth century. "There's a long history that gets us to the moment we're in now, when you all happily pay hundreds of dollars for your yoga pants," I said, trying not to look up at the students, many of whom I suspected did, indeed, spend hundreds of dollars on yoga pants.

I turned to the various holy men who talked about India and religion, spending extra time on Gandhi, who didn't fit perfectly within this tradition, but was someone I assumed most of them knew. I showed them photos of Allen Ginsberg dropping out in Varanasi and the Beatles going through their Maharishi phase. What did all this have to do with anthropology? Nothing directly. Which is why the bone diggers in the department didn't like people like me. We gleefully ran away from the pretention that anthropology was a science. I talked about these men to underscore the larger point I was presenting in the class about the traditional methodology of anthropology: going out in the world, making claims about "natives." It was as much about the anthropologist as it was about the natives, a point I had made more forcefully lately. America's obsession with these holy men, and their yoga and Hinduism and spirituality, was about our own obsessions, our own sense of loss and emptiness. We can examine our love of yoga, in other words, to learn about the kinds of things we find important — self-care, balance, and peacefulness — qualities that are absent in other parts of our collective cultural lives.

The more I taught, the more I learned that students needed

me to be clear about the exact point I was trying to make so that they could repeat it on an exam. And so I ended the lecture with a simple slide that read: "Americans have been so obsessed with these gurus not only because they fulfill our Orientalist desires, but also because they offer an alternative to the culture and religiosity of Christianity. They offer a counterpoint to the emptiness of Christianity and Western life." I had used the slide before in other lectures, tucked away among others. I had never featured it so prominently, and for a passing moment, I questioned the wisdom of being so explicit about my point.

Most of the students were typing into their laptops. Some had their phones out, taking pictures of the slide behind me. There had been so many changes in the classroom since I was in their seats, but this one felt the most unnerving. Every time I changed slides, maybe half the class raised their phones and took a picture. I didn't like seeing myself in photographs, and now there were pictures of me, standing in front of my ideas, stored in phones all across the campus.

I was done. And exhausted. I glanced around the lecture hall.

To the left of the lectern sat a young man who had attended every lecture since the beginning of the term. He always walked in and out of class alone. The few times I had asked the class to discuss an idea with the student seated next to them, he'd sat there by himself, writing in his meticulous notebook — he was always close enough to me that I could see his pages of handwritten notes. He listened intently to what I said, wrote everything down, but never spoke to anyone. Looking at him now,

I saw that he was fiddling with his phone; when he saw me watching him, he shoved it in his pocket. I had taught enough, and engaged with enough students, to pick out the loners from the crowd. As loners go, he seemed pretty middle of the pack, but with excellent penmanship.

"Thanks for your continued attention and interest today," I said to the room. "I'll see you Wednesday."

The students filed out of the lecture hall. I packed up my things and walked up to my three teaching assistants.

"That was interesting," Carla said.

Carla was roughly my age, had teenagers at home, and was slowly finishing up her dissertation. I sometimes feared she never would. She had TAed for me so many times that we'd become friends. While the other two TAs — young, polished, and ambitious — were careful about what they said to me, Carla was always refreshingly honest. She'd done her fieldwork with gangs in Los Angeles, which gave her a certain toughness and clarity.

"Interesting?"

"You were a little combative up there."

I felt a little combative, maybe out of anticipation of Suzanne's voicemail, but I hated being so transparent. "Was it that obvious?"

"To me. Maybe not to the students. But it was fine. I loved it. What kind of fool buys hundred-dollar yoga pants?" She purposefully did not look at the other TAs as she said this.

I went into my bag and pulled out my phone. "I need to check this. But I'll see you all on Wednesday. We should start thinking about what we want to put on the midterm."

I walked out of the lecture hall and read the text from Eva that I had ignored: "Please CALL me immediately after class."

I was perplexed at the emphasis on CALL, but before I did, I listened to Suzanne's voicemail. At first, there was just static. And then I heard her, though I couldn't make out what she was saying. Her voice sounded like it had traveled through a cave before making it to me. She was animated, her words moving up and down in emphasis. There were other people whom I couldn't recognize. At least two. A conversation. Some more static. And then, as if she had stepped out of the cave for a second to get some air, her voice finally cleared: "You know Raj." Just as quickly, she became muffled again, and remained so for the next two minutes. I listened to the entire message again, hoping that I had missed something the first time.

You know Raj. Three clear words among hundreds of unclear others. Not knowing what came before or what came after, and unable to sense Suzanne's tone, the words could mean anything. Without thinking it through, because I was sick of thinking through everything, I sent the voicemail message back to Suzanne and added a note: "I think you may have dialed me by mistake."

As I walked back to my office, I saw Emily Baker's smiling face on a bulletin board. For the past few months, there had been posters all over campus announcing Emily's imminent arrival. She and I had attended graduate school together. In the very first class of the first year, she had said something so incisive about Marx that I knew instantly we were on two different tracks. She'd gone on to distinguish herself in graduate school, had gotten a job at Princeton, and published a highly regarded book based on the fieldwork she'd done in Haiti. The book — on what Emily called "Haitian epistemologies" — had informed how Eva and her NGO approached helping the Haitians after the earthquake a few years back.

As if that weren't enough, all the while Emily had been making a name for herself as a poet, too. Last year, she'd published a book of poems with a simple blurb on the cover from Toni Morrison: "Emily Baker has the poetic sensibility of Emily Dickinson and the grace and power of Josephine Baker." She'd gotten the cover review of the *New York Times Book Review*, which I had seen but could not bring myself to read. And she'd won a major award that came with a $50,000 check.

The school had chosen the poetry collection for our annual all-campus read, and now there were posters all over campus with Emily's smiling, confident face, announcing the public reading she was going to give this Thursday evening. She'd cut her hair since I'd seen her last. She looked severe, but also, with her piercing eyes, quite beautiful.

I'd followed her career, trying hard not to feel so much envy. When her poetry volume had appeared in my mailbox at work, I had initially flipped through it and then set it aside, grumbling something about the pretentions of the craft. But one afternoon a week or so later, I'd bought myself a large cup of coffee and sat down with the slim book. I remembered her academic writing as being typically obtuse, but the poems were clear and bold. The first section — "Black and Middle Class" — had poems about her parents and the bookish, warm childhood they had provided for her and her sister Tracy in

Sacramento. In the second section, the work turned more directly to the title of the book: *Dear Tracy*. Poems about the sisters growing up together, and how much their teachers had marveled at Tracy's schoolwork. Tracy was a year younger, and more sensitive, and Emily had always felt the need to protect her. Around sixteen, Tracy had pulled away from Emily, her family, everyone. A year later, during the summer before she was supposed to go to college, Tracy disappeared. At first, the family feared that she'd run away. A week after she left, they received a postcard confirming their fear: "I'm fine. Don't come searching for me. I'm on my own now."

The collection is a meditation on sisterhood, guilt, and loss. In one particularly heartbreaking poem, Emily sees a homeless woman she's convinced is Tracy. When it turns out not to be her, Emily brings her dinner anyway. They talk, and at the end of the night, Emily doesn't know what to do, and so she drives to her bank, withdraws as much money as she can from the ATM, hands it to the woman, and says, "Can I come see you again?"

By the time I'd finished the book, my coffee was cold. And whatever envy I'd felt for Emily was replaced by a sheer wonder at her talent to look into the thingness of things and not flinch. She was able and willing to explore head-on the fact that her sister had left, seemingly rejected Emily and her parents without any explanation. I'd have trouble asking the questions Emily was asking about the possible reasons Tracy had turned away from her family, and answering them in this very public way.

I walked past the poster and called Eva.

"What is going on, Raj? Why didn't you just tell me what happened this morning?" Eva's tone was less angry and more bewildered, as if I were Neel and I'd flooded the bathroom floor during a shower. "I had to tell Leslie that we hadn't talked because you got in late and left early. She knew you hadn't told me."

"I'm so sorry. It would have taken too long to talk through it."

"We didn't need to talk through it. I just needed the information. Raj, I told you your jokes would get you in trouble."

"This wasn't like the other times," I said. "What did Leslie say?"

"She said you were thinking about other things and that maybe you were trying to connect with the guy."

Leslie's unwillingness to give me a supporting hand the night before hurt all the more because she knew me well enough to be right.

"Can we talk about this tonight?" I asked. I didn't want to have the conversation right then, with students walking by. "I have to get to office hours."

"Please, let's talk now," Eva said. "The students can wait."

I stopped in front of another bulletin board, Emily once more staring at me. She had on glasses with stylish purple frames. "What do you want me to say?"

"I don't know, Raj. I can't believe you said that aloud."

"I can't either. I really can't." I'd been thinking about how best to make this all go away. Call Bill right now, apologize profusely, and then send an email to the committee and the

Blacks, doing the same? That would smooth it all out. I was very experienced at apologizing. "It wasn't an insult, though. The guy knows the difference."

"I'm sure he knows you didn't mean it as a slur. But you know better than I do that your intention is not the problem here. No one on the committee is going to care about that."

"Is that what you're worried about? Them?" I was trying to push this away from me, which I had no right to do.

"I'm worried about us," Eva said. "Please don't turn this on me. You know that I'm worried about you."

"I know, I know. And I appreciate it. Can we talk about this tonight?"

"I just wish you hadn't said it. That's all."

"I can't tell you how much I wish I hadn't either. But my experiences are closer to Bill's than anyone else's on the committee. So if anyone has the right to say it — and I know none of us do — wouldn't it be me?" This line of thinking was going nowhere good. But I was trying to give myself some wiggle room within this straitjacket of stupidity I'd strapped myself into.

"No."

And I had no quarrel with that. Bill and I were not the same people with the same experiences and the same problems. But I could think of any number of big and small moments when I had been on the receiving end of racist taunts. I didn't know Bill, and Bill didn't know me, and yet I sensed that we had both experienced the despair and wretchedness of feeling out of place. That was all I had wanted to talk to him about — or not. Maybe as we were warming up close to the net, hitting balls back and forth. I had only wanted to connect, but I had tried to do so in the worst way possible. I'd not meant for those words to leave my mouth.

"What are you going to do?" Eva asked. "Are you going to get in touch with him?"

"I have his number and his email. I don't know if it's best to write or go see him."

"Maybe both."

"I really messed up. I know I did. And there's no excuse for it. But that place has been screwed up for a very long time, and they just don't know it."

"I know," Eva said.

"Can we talk about this more tonight? I should get going."

"OK." Eva hung up the phone.

When I got back to my office, Dan was still there.

"Jesus, man. I have office hours."

"If someone comes, I'll get dressed."

"I'm going to grab a quick lunch. Students will be here when I get back."

Dan made a big show of gathering his things. He put on his jeans and slipped into his shoes. "You know squatters have rights."

"Go home, Dan. Talk to Julie." I was more than happy to tell someone else to face up to his problems.

As I walked out the door, my phone buzzed. Suzanne had texted: "PLEASE CALL ME. I want to explain." I put the phone away and headed out. When I returned ten minutes later with my sandwich, a student was waiting for me. There was a time when I loved office hours, having students come in and engage with the ideas I had presented in class, pushing them further than we'd gotten in the lecture. But now, more often than not, they just wanted me to repeat what I'd already said. Maybe because hardly any of them took notes anymore. Where, in years before, they listened to what I was saying and then translated it by writing it down in their notebooks, now they didn't have to do that. They simply took their picture and then asked me to explain what I'd already explained.

At least the student waiting was the diligent, careful note taker from my morning class. If I had to talk to one of them, I was glad it was one like him, someone who seemed to have been paying close attention. He had come up to me after class a couple of times to ask for clarification on something I'd said during my lectures. It had been clear that he was working through whatever I'd just said, but both times he'd seemed nervous and cut the conversations short.

Now he was dressed in basic ironic chic: skinny jeans, a button-down checkered shirt, and Top-Siders with socks. But there was something entirely un-ironic and stiff about his bearing. His eyes were set back in his face, and it seemed that smiling was labor for him; his look conveyed that everyone was inevitably going to disappoint him.

"Hi, Dr. Bhatt," he said, reaching out his hand to shake mine. It was clammy. "I'm Robert. From your morning class."

Robert? So formal. "C'mon in, Robert," I said, opening my office door.

He noticed the empty bookshelves before sitting down, as

if he were confused about where he'd ended up. "This place is pretty empty."

"I like clean lines," I said. "And nothing to carry if I need to make a quick exit." He didn't respond. "My books are at my home office," I added. "Do you mind if I eat?"

I hated to eat in front of students, but I was starving and I sensed that this was not going to be a quick conversation. There were two types of students during office hours: those who left as soon as their questions were answered and those who hung around to chat. It seemed like Robert had no one waiting for him.

"Please," he said.

I unwrapped the sandwich. "Here is the one genuine benefit of French colonial rule in Vietnam: the bánh mì." The grilled beef in the soft baguette, layered with jalapeños, cucumbers, and mayonnaise, was perfect.

"It smells good," he said.

I couldn't tell if this was courtesy or if he wanted me to offer him some. He was eying the sandwich like he hadn't eaten all day.

"You want some?" I asked, expecting—hoping—that he would say no.

"Sure," he said. "I'm starving."

I was so hungry, I knew the whole sandwich wouldn't even have been enough for me, but I reached into my desk drawer, found a plastic knife, and cut it in two. Robert picked up the slightly bigger half and took two consecutive bites.

"Where'd you go to high school?" I often asked students

this on their first visit, to break the ice, and also to get a sense of their lives.

"Northern California."

"Where?"

"A town called Martinez."

"Martinez! I grew up near there. Did you know it's Joe DiMaggio's hometown?"

Nothing.

"Jeff and Stan Van Gundy?"

More nothing. There were plenty of women at the Tennis Club who had the same immobile expression on their faces that Robert wore now. But theirs was from Botox.

He continued eating, and finished his half sandwich before I'd taken a second bite of mine.

Perhaps Robert's family lived in the biggest house in Martinez, but they probably didn't. I had known it to be a forgettable little place, with endless neighborhoods of drab tract homes built when stucco was in vogue. That's what Robert reminded me of: drab, white stucco. I'd read all sorts of studies about why children needed boredom in their lives to make them more creative. I got the feeling that Robert had been plenty bored growing up, and somewhere in the midst of a long, hot summer day, he had taken a magnifying glass to a colony of ants, or kicked a cat or two. He probably thought accepting my sandwich offer was the polite thing to do.

I had to stop myself. I realized that I was making assumptions about this young man I knew nothing about. I took another small bite. Maybe I had low blood sugar.

"So what's up, Robert?" I asked, trying to shift my thinking. "How can I help?"

"Do you like teaching?"

I chewed my food. God, I wished I hadn't chased Dan out. He would have rescued me. Whereas I stayed in conversations I didn't want to be in, Dan just cut them off. "We need to end office hours early today," Dan would have said, without waiting for a reply.

"I do."

"Why did you become an anthropologist? You could have become a historian, a novelist maybe. Even a lawyer. All the Indian kids in the dorms want to be doctors or head up to Silicon Valley."

I wiped my mouth with a napkin and finished chewing. There isn't one Indian kid who wants to make films or hasn't figured out exactly what she wants to do? What made Robert an expert on that entire swath of the student body? "Do you have a specific question about the class?"

"No," Robert said. "It's all pretty self-explanatory. Structuralism. The raw and the cooked. Your lecture last week on dirt was pretty spot-on, though." He fiddled with his hands before he continued, as if he wanted to be careful about what he was going to say next. "It wasn't just an abstract theory. Well, it was pretty abstract at first. Of course, I'm not Hindu or Jewish. But as you went on, I realized I know that feeling." He lowered his voice slightly as he said this, as if he didn't want anyone else to hear. "I felt out of place growing up. And I feel it on campus all the time. What you were saying made sense." Enthusiasm was appearing on his face, replacing the apprehension he had when he first walked in. "It kind of hit close to home."

The compliment felt nice; I certainly could use the confidence boost. Whatever damage I was wreaking in the rest of my life, here I seemed to be making a small difference. Maybe I'd judged Robert a bit too harshly; it could be that he was just a little awkward. And who of us isn't?

"I'm glad you found something useful in the lecture. And to your question about why I became an anthropologist — I like people." I was settling into the conversation more. I didn't have it in me to shuffle him out. And wasn't this kind of engagement what I wanted from students? "I like talking to them. I like hearing about their lives. That's what an ethnography is. *Ethnos* is 'life.' *Graphy* is 'to write.' Life stories. The stock-in-trade of anthropology. Doing fieldwork can be really exciting. And I had an anthropology professor in college whom I loved. He was pure charm and erudition."

"Is that what you're trying to be? Charming and erudite?"

What was up with this kid? He didn't seem to have a filter. Or maybe this was all in earnest and he didn't have the nuance to know how to ask certain types of questions. Given what I had said myself not twenty-four hours earlier, I felt some empathy for him.

Before I could answer, Robert continued: "You do a pretty good job of it in class. I was expecting it to be boring, but you've kept it lively. I've taken my share of large lecture courses. It's no easy thing to keep two hundred students engaged. But here's what I don't understand. In anthropology you take what people say as evidence for the arguments you're making. I say one thing and mean another all the time. If you were interviewing me, I would probably tell you all the things you wanted to hear, and not what I actually thought and felt."

"That's a smart point. But that's why I would spend more time with you. And try to read between the lines. *And read beneath the lines.* I'm not just taking everything at face value. But sure, there are clear limits to the method. But there are limits to all methods. We recognize that and work from it."

"Biology doesn't have limits. Chemistry. Engineering."

"I can't speak for the sciences. But there are plenty of scholars who would argue against that. Argue against the idea that a lab is a perfect place of objectivity and equity. How many times have you heard of one study debunking another that had been gospel only a few years before? Coffee is healthy for you one year, bad the next. I keep drinking it no matter what."

This line of argument seemed to satisfy him; he nodded his head. If only defending the discipline were always this easy.

He rubbed his forehead with his fingers. They were long and lean and quite graceful. "Do you think they pay you enough for the work you do?" he asked.

Where before his eyes had darted around, this time he looked straight at me. And the slightest mocking smile curled up on his face. I worked at a large public university. All of our salaries were public information. For all the fancy degrees I had, it embarrassed me how little money I made. I was sure that Robert had been snooping around online.

"Are you here to discuss my salary?" I asked, trying my

hardest not to let the anger and humiliation I now felt appear on my face or in the tone of my voice.

"I guess I was wondering if you feel you're being properly paid for the hard work you do. My father has never been paid what he deserves, and I've always felt sorry for him. He's worked so hard his whole life. And he has nothing to show for it." His voice seemed to crack a tiny bit. "I know it sounds a little weird, but he reminds me a lot of you. You both have a similar sense of humor. A little self-deprecating."

To avoid having to respond immediately, I took another bite of the sandwich—a bite that happened to include an enormous jalapeño pepper. I tried to chew it slowly and swallow, but my mouth was on fire. I could feel sweat forming on my forehead. I couldn't figure out if Robert wanted to connect with me or if this was some elaborate way of mocking me. That last bit about his father was perplexing. Did he see me as a father figure as well as an object of his pity? I swallowed the pepper and took a long sip of my water before I answered.

"Robert, I appreciate your concern, but if there's nothing else you're wondering about the class, I think we're done here. I'm sure there are students waiting in the hallway."

I got up from my desk and walked into the hall. "I'll be just another minute," I said to a student, then I went back and sat down.

I expected Robert to apologize for having overstepped. But instead he reached down for his backpack and stood up. "Thank you for your time and for sharing your sandwich. That was an interesting lecture today. Something that calls for a further discussion."

When he walked out, I noticed that I had spilled a dollop of mayo on my shirt. I wrapped up the rest of the sandwich, tossed it in the garbage, and tried to wipe the mayo off.

Another student walked in. He had a shock of blond hair and was dressed in a sweatshirt and shorts. He was wearing the same tennis shoes Federer wore in his matches, with the laces untied.

"Go ahead and sit down," I said.

"I can't stay. I have practice. But I wanted to come by and let you know that I won't be here for the midterm. We have an away match. When can I take it after I get back?"

I didn't know this student, but I had a pretty clear sense of his life. His tennis skills had been celebrated since he was a kid and now he was convinced that he was headed somewhere big on the court, only to end up with a decent consolation prize: a job in finance after graduation, hired by an older former college tennis player, followed quickly by marriage, kids, an affair, another kid. Right then, as he stood in my office with no perspective, it must have all seemed so open and unknown and possible to him, as if soon enough he'd be wearing his own namesake tennis shoes and some other kid would stroll into some other office wearing them, their laces also untied.

"You've known the date of the midterm since the first day of class," I said. "You couldn't have come to see me any earlier?" It was a genuine question.

"Things came up." He was staring at the grease spot on my shirt.

"You can take it before," I said. "But not after."

"But I have other stuff going on."

"So do I. Be thankful that I'm letting you take it early."

He was speechless, as if this were the very first time anyone had ever said no to him. "I'll talk to my coach."

"Feel free," I said. "I'm sure he can write out some kind of exam for you. But for my exam, I'm the only one you need to talk to."

We agreed on an earlier date. He left.

I closed my door halfway, reached into the garbage can, and removed the sandwich. It was, after all, fully wrapped. For the next ten minutes, I sat there, finished eating, read *ESPN* online, and felt good about pushing back with the tennis player. I had a reputation for being overly accommodating to students' needs.

As office hours were about to end, one last student walked in. This one I also recognized from my large lecture class. He reminded me of myself when I was in college, though he was taller, more handsome, and far more self-assured. So, in fact, he was nothing like me, but for our shared Indianness. He always sat in class with a pretty young woman, whose ethnicity I couldn't quite make out.

"I'm in your anthropology class. My name is David."

I was about to ask if that was short for something. I didn't think this new generation of Indian Americans had gotten in the habit of Americanizing their names.

"It's just David," he said. "I get that confused reaction from other Indians all the time. My family is Catholic. That's actually why I came to see you."

He had a very inviting smile; it would be much easier for

him to navigate the world. A good smile can soften any situation. But as he sat down, he became more serious.

"I was a little taken aback by the last thing you said in class today, about how India fills an absence for Christians, and Westerners more generally."

I sat up in my chair, to signal that I was paying full attention to him. In turn, David also seemed to straighten his back.

"Maybe 'taken aback' isn't the right phrase. It actually upset me, more than I first realized."

"Why?"

"I'm Catholic and Indian, but born in Los Angeles. So I guess that statement was confusing for me."

Here was the type of conversation—full of ideas and mild arguments—I longed for in office hours, and which I seldom was able to have these days. So often, students seemed to treat the ideas I presented to them as static, meant to be regurgitated on an exam and nothing more.

"I can see that," I said. "But when I make a statement like that, it's not meant to include everybody and every experience. I have to try and speak to some general experiences about why there has been such a consistent interest in Indian life throughout American history. Today I tried to argue for one way of understanding that interest. But there are always exceptions. You're an exception."

David nodded. I couldn't tell if he was buying this argument or not.

"But are you arguing that Christianity is empty?"

"No, no. I'm arguing that for those Americans who turned away from Christianity, India filled the hole left behind."

David glanced at his phone. It was buzzing.

"I'm so sorry. I have to take this. But if it's OK, I'd like to come back on Wednesday so we can talk about this more. I should have come in earlier."

"Do come back," I said. "Let's talk through this. It's worth a longer conversation."

David got his things and walked out.

At 12:30, I headed to another class. And at 2:00, I had yet another. These classes were smaller, forty students each, and because they were more advanced, there was a lot of conversation and back-and-forth with the students.

I was about twenty minutes away from being done with the second class when I took a sip of water and examined my notes to see what else I needed to cover. There were too many voices in my head — the things we'd been talking about in class, Robert asking me about my salary, Suzanne asking me to apologize to the Browns. There were administrative emails I had to respond to, letters of recommendation I had to write. I opened my mouth to resume. The students took notice and readied themselves to write down whatever I was going to say. But nothing came out. The words and the ideas were there, in my head, in my throat, but that's where they stayed. It was as if a muscle tissue had grown over my mouth; I usually had plenty to say. The students waited.

Then someone in the back started talking about the essay they'd read. And then another student added something else. I let them all talk among themselves.

At 3:15, when I finally got out of my third class, I felt like a bus had hit me. I had talked straight through three, seventy-five-minute sessions, minus those last twenty minutes. Over the course of the day, I had taught nearly three hundred students. Most of them had been engaged and interested. Some of them less so. I felt completely depleted.

As I walked back to my office, my right knee suddenly sore for no apparent reason, I saw Josh Morton again. This time, he was in shorts and a T-shirt that read YALE SWIMMING. His hair was wet. He was clearly in peak physical shape. If he had taught at all today, he had probably had one class, a small seminar with ten or fifteen fully engaged students. I bet if one of them had asked him about his salary, he would have proudly revealed the numbers. He got paid a lot more to do a lot less, at least when it came to teaching. That's all there was to say about that. With my shoulders hunched and my lower back sore from being in front of the classroom, I felt like I was literally aging faster than him, my step getting slower with every passing day. If indeed we were all living in a state of insecurity, I had to imagine that anyone with the freedom and opportunity to take a long swim in the middle of a workday might be able to manage that insecurity a little better than a prison guard working in a lockup in Tennessee.

When I pulled into our driveway, I sat for a minute, collecting my strength for the evening.

In the kitchen, napkins, forks and knives, and glasses for water and milk were laid out on the table. There was a pot on the stove. Set tables and family dinners were important to Eva, and I appreciated that. But the late afternoon sun was beating through the window, and as much as I liked the idea of it, I didn't want to sit where the heat had accumulated through the day.

Eva walked into the kitchen.

"I appreciate your willingness to try," I said.

"One of these days, we'll all sit, talk about the day, and eat our meal."

I started walking out of the kitchen.

"Can we talk now? You've been avoiding me all day."

"I just need a moment to change and gather myself a little. I've had a long day of teaching. I haven't been avoiding you."

"Some days we talk on the phone five times when you're at work."

I got a bottle of wine from the pantry and uncorked it. Eva took two glasses from the cupboard and held them out. I poured.

From the back of the house, I could hear Neel bouncing off the walls, slamming and opening doors, his body somehow too big for the space. Arun, who was much less prone to being hyper, had been swept into his older brother's lead. The boys had started back at school several weeks before, and things weren't going well for Neel. And when things weren't going well at school, things weren't going well at home.

"They're fine," Eva said.

"Let me go check."

"Stop, Raj. We need to talk about this. This affects us all."

"No!" Arun shouted at the top of his lungs. He had become an expert at screaming foul at most everything.

"Go ahead," Eva said, lowering her voice in resignation. She was trapped between the bad behaviors of all of the boys in her life.

We walked into the living room. There were toys everywhere and remnants of school worksheets Neel had started and then abandoned. I liked a neat house and so did Eva, but with these two boys, that was a state of being we wouldn't return to until they left for college. Neel, especially, had a particular gift for speeding up entropy.

"You want to go?" I asked. "I need a minute and then I'll be there."

And again a scream, this time a little different. Eva took one more sip of the wine, set her glass down, and headed back. I tried my best to tune out what was going on in the bedrooms and concentrate on my wine.

"He took it," I could hear Arun cry. "He took it."

"I don't have it," Neel yelled back. "You asshole."

Well advanced in his use of curse words, Neel had a tendency to torture his younger brother. And so it was hard to believe that he had nothing to do with the disappearance of whatever had gone missing.

I wanted to let Eva handle it, but I couldn't pretend nothing was happening. I've never been able to drown out the noise. I went to Arun's room, where the battle lines had been drawn. Both boys were in their underwear and their hair was tangled. The floor was covered with Legos.

"I didn't take it," Neel said, turning to me. From the day he was born, there'd been something in his bright brown eyes, some sense that he could see *everything* and that there was never enough time for him to process it all. Now those eyes were pleading with me to believe him.

Neel was a big, strong boy, with smells and hair just around the corner. He'd grown out of his baby phase quickly, while Arun had lingered in his. Arun was smaller and sweeter, qualities he sometimes used to his advantage.

"What's the *it*?"

"A Lego guy," Neel said. "Darth Vader. And I didn't take it. But I know you don't believe me. You guys never believe me. You always believe this little shit."

Arun was distraught and confused.

"Language, Neel," Eva said.

"I don't care. You won't believe me no matter what I say."

"Neel, I think you should go to your room," I said, trying to keep calm. Separating them was the first step toward deescalating the moment.

"I'm not going anywhere," Neel said, starting to cry, too.

"Please go," I said. "Let me try and figure this out."

He finally left. Eva followed him.

For the next twenty minutes, as I helped Arun clean up his room and find Darth Vader, Neel raged across the hall about all sorts of things that didn't need raging. Dinner, his brother, his room, the curtains, what he could and could not watch on television. All of it accompanied by so many tears. I thought about all the friends I had who had kids this age, and I couldn't imagine any of them went through what we went through on nights like this. And we had these nights so often.

I took Arun into the kitchen after we cleaned up. Eva had made a stir-fry and I got us two plates of it.

"I'm sorry your brother is so upset."

"It's OK."

Kids' brains are sponges; I didn't want Arun's to be saturated by this chaos.

I watched as he slowly and methodically made his way through dinner, taking small bites and chewing thoroughly. In the corner of his plate, he set aside a pile of mushrooms.

"Want them?" he asked.

I did. They were my favorite part of the meal.

Then we headed for a bath. Arun removed his underwear and got into the warm bath water. I soaped him up and then he went completely underwater to wash it off.

"All done," I said. "You want to get out?"

He didn't respond. He got onto his belly. His sweet little bottom bopped out of the water like the top of an apple. I reached over and pinched it.

"Stop," he said sweetly.

"How was school? Are you liking it?"

"It's fine. Recess is fun. And I've been playing the recorder." He continued to rock back and forth in the water.

"Do you see your brother during the day?"

"At recess sometimes. He walks around by himself."

I felt sad thinking of Neel by himself in a playground full of laughing children.

"But then I go and play with him," he continued. "He's always nice to me at school. He gives me some of the gummies in his lunch after I've finished mine."

"Let's get out and draw a little," I said. "Maybe we can make a little note for him."

He got himself dressed and I pulled out some coloring pens. I could spend hours coloring. It gave me an activity to concentrate on while I let my mind wander. There was something meditative about it. Maybe that's why Bill Brown kept those beads around his wrist.

"Superheroes or chickens?" Arun asked, holding up two different coloring books.

"You pick."

He took the chickens. I opened the other book randomly, found the right shade of green among the pens, and started coloring in the Hulk. As I worked, I thought about what I should say to Bill, whether I should email or call or reach out to him in person. The longer I waited, the more nervous I would be in talking to him; I knew that I needed to take care of it as soon as I could. And yet, when I pictured the start of the conversation in my mind, I felt anxious. What exactly would I say? What if he refused to see me at all?

"Get out," Neel yelled across the hall.

Arun was gone and I hadn't even noticed. Lately, I'd been losing some of my sharpness, particularly at the start and the end of the day, leaving me with a precious few hours of clarity in the middle. There were many things I found difficult about parenting, but close to the top was having to go through the stresses of my everyday life and somehow put them aside in the evenings, turning my full attention to the needs of the children.

When I stepped into Neel's room, Arun was hanging on to Eva's leg, saying, "I want Mom too."

Eva shot me the look that she reserved for giving up on things.

Neel's room was a special kind of messy. Whenever we cleaned it, his stuff was back on the floor in a matter of minutes. He had a tendency to pour all of his concentration into one thing, fully and intensely, at the expense of everything else. If he wanted one specific Lego out of the hundreds of stray pieces that littered his room, he would rifle through everything until he found the right piece. But he would never go back and unrifle once he'd found what he was searching for. The mess stayed. Still, at the end, without fail, he would have produced some remarkable car or building, something that he would have envisioned entirely in his head and then executed with his hands. In some ways, this trait had been there right from the start. He had literally torn through Eva, intent on getting out of her belly and into the world, no matter the mess he left behind. As the years passed, this behavior had evolved, and Neel's hyperactivity and his quick shifts between intense focus and wandering attention had led to a diagnosis of ADHD, and the attendant prescriptions to manage it. His room was a reflection of everything that was going on inside his head.

On one wall he had a poster of Chris Burden's *Metropolis II*, a kinetic sculpture of a massive cityscape with roadways and cars that the boys had been mesmerized by for hours when we took them to see it at LACMA. On another wall was a poster of Ganesh, drawn in colorful street art. Of all the Indian stories I'd shared with the boys, the story of Ganesh was Neel's favorite. I'm not sure what he liked about it exactly — maybe the fact that Ganesh was the beloved son of Shiva and Parvati. Or maybe, strange as it may seem, that Shiva had chopped his son's head off when he didn't recognize him after returning home from a long trip, and replaced it with an elephant's. I think Neel appreciated the ingenuity. On the bottom of the poster, in ornate lettering, it said, *The God of Removing Obstacles*. As he got older, Neel would have more and more obstacles along the way, and the idea that Ganesh might be watching over him — as shaky as my belief in the gods may be — felt comforting.

"Get out," Neel said again. "Or admit that I didn't take your Lego."

Arun walked up to Neel, twisted his upper body a full ninety degrees, and landed a significant left hook into Neel's belly. Neel instantly folded over, cried out.

"Arun!" Eva yelled, her anger bringing him to tears.

Neel did not retaliate, which showed more restraint than we often gave him credit for. He easily could have crushed Arun.

It was as I was standing there, with the boys screaming and crying, unable to control the situation as it worsened, wishing desperately that I could spank them into submission, which of course I would never do, that I suddenly remembered the headless man.

"Arun," I said, "come with me right now."

I thought he would object, but knowing he had pushed things too far, he walked out of the room.

"Let's go," I said. We walked through the house and out to my car. I opened the door, reached in, and removed the Lego man I had seen the previous evening. I hadn't noticed then that it was Darth Vader's body.

"Is this what you lost?"

Arun's body stiffened a little. He examined the Lego. I wondered how he was going to react. "I'm sorry."

I wanted to get mad at him. But while he wasn't innocent in this instance, he so often got caught up in Neel's hurricane, it was hard to punish him for behavior he observed in his brother all the time.

We walked back into the house, and into Neel's room.

"I'm sorry," Arun said, unable to look up as he talked. "Darth was in Dad's car."

Neel was buying time, figuring out how best to respond. He had been unfairly accused of doing something he hadn't done. He now had some power to punish Arun and to punish us for not believing him. He took a step toward Arun, and my body stiffened, afraid that he was going to retaliate for the earlier punch. But Neel's body seemed to be loosening.

"It's OK," Neel replied. He leaned in and gave Arun a big, enveloping hug. Neel could pivot from one emotion to another very quickly. As intense as his rages could be, he also knew how to forgive and forget quickly.

I went into my bedroom for the first time since I got home. I sat in my reading chair, my head hanging. And as I was sitting there, Neel walked in. He was in his frayed boxers, the ones he refused to change for days on end because he found such strange comfort in them. Why did he descend into this chaos so often? Why didn't that beautiful boy, Neel's better nature, not appear with more frequency? Wouldn't that be better for us all? We would scream less; he would get the things he wanted. And perhaps we could even sit down for a meal together at the table that Eva always set. I didn't know what to say. Neel stood by himself in the middle of the room, wanting to be rescued, his face puffed up from all the crying and raging.

And then I heard the words "No one wants to be with me" come out of his mouth. I got up and grabbed him and brought him close. I held him tightly. "No one wants to play with me at school," he said. He broke into a deep, wailing sob, head buried in my chest. I ached for him.

"Come," I said.

"I don't want to shower," he said, giving me a sly grin through the tears. His unwillingness to shower was one of our long-standing disagreements.

We both got into the hot double shower. I shampooed his hair, and he insistently soaped himself, once and then twice. After, we put on pajamas and went into his room, where Eva had left a plate of dinner for him, along with his math homework. He ate, listened to a book on tape, and did his fractions. Then he drew in his sketchbook while I cleaned up. We crawled into his twin bed together, though there wasn't enough room for both of us. He smelled like shampoo, and as he entered the hazy space right before sleep, he kissed me and bundled himself in his blanket. I walked out.

Usually Eva fell asleep with Arun, but when I came out of

Neel's room, I noticed that he was in his bed alone. I went and touched his soft cheek and then covered him in the blanket that he'd already kicked off.

In the kitchen, Eva was sitting at the table, finally eating her dinner. There was a stack of bills next to her and the half-empty wine bottle.

"He seemed better after the cry," she said. "Maybe he just needed to get it out."

We were both all about the hope of the next day. I poured myself another glass of wine.

"I'm completely at fault here, and I'm trying to figure out how best to fix this," I said, turning to the conversation that I knew she wanted to have. "But it's more complicated than that. In this instance, the fault is mine. But there's a larger problem at that place, and for that they're at fault too. They all are. I always feel like I'm on the verge of breaking some unwritten rule that no one thinks to tell me exists. And the constant questions about India. I can't deal with it anymore. I was just happy that finally there was going to be someone else kind of like me, someone I wouldn't feel I had to prove myself to, someone I could feel comfortable with. And I totally screwed that up."

"I get it. And I understand why you're frustrated. We talked about the problems with the TC before we joined."

"And, ultimately, I wanted to join as much as you," I said, guessing she was going to bring this up. "Maybe even more."

One afternoon, several years earlier, the two of us had driven to the TC for our membership interview. After years of moving between small apartments, we now had a mortgage and two young kids, and were discussing joining a ten-

nis club. We were becoming domesticated very fast, simul-
taneously hopeful and terrified at this new turn in our lives.
Eva, who had wanted to return home to California perhaps a
sliver more than I did, had been taking the move a little harder
lately. She had liked her old job. She'd liked how quickly the Q
dissected Manhattan; our annual visits to Flushing to watch
rowdy, muggy tennis; the sheer mixedness of people walking
down most any New York block, a marked contrast to how
she'd grown up.

"What are we doing? We leave the city and suddenly we're
staid suburbanites, joining a tennis club?" she asked from the
passenger seat as we exited the freeway. "Let's forget this. I'll
call Leslie and tell her we're not coming."

Eva was concerned about propriety; she followed through
on any promise she made. And so either she was being overly
dramatic or she genuinely didn't want to do this interview.

"Are you kidding?" I asked. "Leslie worked so hard getting
things together for us, having people write all of those letters
of recommendation."

"Pull over," she said, her voice strained.

I drove into a neighborhood with big houses and lush
yards, and parked. We had about ten minutes of wiggle room
before we needed to be at the TC. "Are you having a panic attack about joining a tennis club?"

"I'm having a panic attack about all of this," she said, pointing to the houses. "About coming back here. About raising our
boys in such a decidedly homogeneous place."

"You don't have to tell me."

"I miss our old life. I certainly don't miss not having Neel and Arun. But I miss getting falafel on the street. I miss the simplicity of getting just enough groceries that I can carry in my arms. The crisp fall days. Though I think in the time we were there, we actually had about four of them."

"I miss the subways," I said.

"Yes. And I miss the walking. Sixth Avenue went on and on and on. For my whole life, I've been moving forward. I needed to get out of here, and I did. And I love being back. That we don't have to worry about parking. I love how much easier it is with the kids. That we didn't have to go through some elaborate lottery system to get them into elementary school. That my parents are here whenever we need them. But part of me feels that in coming home, I've also taken a huge step back." We sat in the car for a long minute. I could see Eva's mind churning between her misgivings and her sense of decorum. "Maybe we can go through with the interview, since they're waiting for us, and then postpone joining until we're ready. In a couple of years."

"That sounds like the right middle ground."

If I'm being honest, I was relieved. While I wasn't quite ready to admit it to Eva, I had come to realize by then that I really wanted to join the club. I thought I would play my best tennis on those pristine courts. And that pool looked awfully nice.

I started the car before Eva had a chance to change her mind. "Let's just get through the interview."

Leslie and Tim were waiting for us in the parking lot when we arrived.

"We were worried you guys weren't showing," Leslie said,

smiling to cover what might have been genuine worry. She hooked her arm into Eva's. "I'm so excited. You and the boys are going to become as attached to this place as we are."

We all entered the clubhouse smiling. I remember that whatever nervousness I might have felt dissipated the moment we walked in. Everyone was very welcoming, as if we were the guests of honor at a small, intimate party, arriving right at the crest. A few people on the committee knew Eva from childhood. They gave us warm hugs. Someone asked about her parents.

"I think now that they have grandchildren, you'll see them here more and more," Eva had said.

They offered us wine, and a minute later we all sat down with glasses in our hands. They asked us the same basic questions then that the current committee had been asking this latest crop of potential members. Eva talked about her familiarity with the place, how after years of being on the East Coast, she was ready to be home. And when it came time to talk about our interest in tennis, I had answered, "I played a bunch in high school, but I've been away from the game a bit. I can't wait to get back on the court." I wondered if they got this answer a lot. So I added, as Valerie Brown had, "And Eva and I had our first date on a tennis court."

After the interview, the four of us went out for dinner.

"You two were perfect," Leslie said enthusiastically. "And Raj, you sealed it with that first-date-on-the-tennis-court thing. Is that true?"

"Partially," Eva said. "We weren't actually playing. Big spender here had gotten us nosebleeds at the US Open."

"I wanted us to be able to talk," I replied. "There was plenty of room up there. And a view of the city."

"Well, it clearly charmed the men *and* the women in the room, which is hard to do," Leslie said.

We got our letter of acceptance very soon after. Eva and I privately gloated that we must have been at the top of the list. By then, she'd set aside her reservations. After joining, I took a few lessons with Richard to jump-start my game. And we went a lot. I went a lot. At some point, it seemed that I knew more people there than Eva did.

Now, years later, as I sat sipping my wine and thinking back to that evening, I tried to pinpoint why, despite my reservations, joining the TC had been so alluring. It was something I'd been thinking a good deal about recently as I sat through the membership meetings. It was hard to peel away the layers, but when I saw that well-shaded jewel box for the first time — the clubhouse and the pool and the tennis courts — it felt like I was returning to a kind of safety.

In the decade that passed between our arrival in America and my departure for college, my parents worked very hard in order to move us from apartment to condominium to house. By the time we made it into the house, I felt settled and rooted and protected. But that feeling dissipated the second I stepped out the door. With my parents at work and my sisters figuring out their own way, I traveled to and from school alone, first with a key around my neck, and later with it hidden in my pocket. My English was improving, but still far from perfect. To get to the first school I attended, I walked down our street and through a dark tunnel that went underneath a freeway.

Every morning and every afternoon, I ran the length of the tunnel as fast as I could, hoping desperately that no one took the time to notice me. There weren't many other Indian families around back then, and so I learned to navigate among the black and white kids, doing my best to lie low until I worked things out. During this time, the one person who helped me the most was my fourth-grade teacher, a black woman in her fifties named Mrs. Holmes, who paid careful attention to my work and to me. Maybe she'd noticed how confused I must have seemed in class. From the start of the year, she was liberal with her praise and encouragement and attention, which provided me with the backbone I needed to do well in school that year and for years after. On the last day of school, she gave all the children hugs. When she came to me, she added a kiss to my forehead and a whisper in my ear: "I'm so proud of you."

Two years later, when I tested out of that school, I always had a bus pass to take me to the better schools farther from home. There were two rules to riding the bus: pay the fare and never, ever make eye contact with anyone. Eye contact was a threat. And if someone thought you were threatening them, then you lost something—your glasses, your backpack, your dignity.

Junior high school was an ecosystem full of tribes and factions. One afternoon as I sat on the bus, I felt something on the back of my head. I was about to turn around, but I caught myself. I ignored it. Soon, more things landed on me—chips, rolled-up pieces of paper, spitballs—accompanied by laughter. When I'd first gotten on the bus, I'd noticed several kids from school in the back, and they'd noticed me. They weren't in any of my classes; most of the black students were tracked separately. Perhaps I was wrong, but I assumed these were the kids who were throwing things at me. As my stop neared, I wanted to pull the cord to signal to the driver to stop. But I didn't want to announce that I was getting off. I was hoping that someone else would pull it, and then I could just run off the bus.

Someone else did. The bus slowed down. I grabbed a hold of my backpack, but kept it hidden. When the bus came to a stop, I shot out of my seat and raced to the front door. As I stepped off, I checked to the right. The kids had all rushed out the back door. For a second I thought about getting back on the bus, but the driver closed the door.

I started walking away as quickly as I could.

"What's the hurry?" one of them said. "You don't like chips?"

They came after me and I took off running, the sound of their footsteps getting closer and closer. I ran and ran, hoping I'd see someone I knew. At one point, I felt a foot kick mine. At full speed, I wobbled, my arms flailing. If I fell, I'd have to accept the beating, from them and the hot concrete sidewalk. Somehow, I regained my balance and kept going. By the time I finally stopped, in a neighborhood I didn't recognize, my chest burning, I was completely lost, but at least they'd given up their pursuit. From then on, whenever I saw one of those kids at school, smiling at me, I knew it was a reminder: I would never be safe. For some years after, I assumed they had gone after me because I wasn't black. That picking on a brown boy had no consequences. But later, I knew that it was more complicated than that. In flexing their power over me, they were perhaps flexing a bigger power they didn't have, and knew they would never have. My time on these buses, in these neighborhoods, in these schools, was limited. Soon I would leave and go on to better things. Perhaps they sensed this and tried to beat the freedom out of me.

During that time, going back and forth to different schools, I tried to stay invisible. But I could never shake the feeling of exposure.

What did this have to do with joining a tennis club? God, everything and absolutely nothing. Maybe all these years later, I wanted to feel protected, wanted my children to feel protected.

"I've been thinking a lot about why I was more comfortable joining the club when you were so unsure about it," I said to Eva as she finished her dinner. "I have these great memories of being at the Bombay gymkhana, of my parents spending time with my dad's work friends over dinner while all the kids ran around, going in and out of the pool, drinking sodas we weren't supposed to have. Maybe I thought that joining the TC would cure me of all my exhausting nostalgia for that time. Or maybe I was excited to be part of a group. Though I knew I wouldn't be fully accepted. I don't know if I know this now, in retrospect, or knew it when we first joined. Or maybe I just liked the game so much, the feel of the racquet in my hand, the sound of the ball bouncing on the hard court, the pain in my heels after a strenuous match. Maybe that was enough to overlook everything else." I couldn't understand how I had been so hopeful. "I've been avoiding you today because I'm embarrassed. About the fool I made of myself last night. But I'm also embarrassed for thinking that joining the TC would mean that I actually belonged to the TC. Was that just incredibly naïve?"

Eva placed the fork and knife on her dinner plate and put her hand on top of mine. "We don't have to go anymore."

She'd liked growing up there, swimming and running around through the long days of summer; she'd wanted to share that with our kids. And she had — the kids loved it. And I loved so much of it too. I looked at her now, her eyes a little glassy. Maybe she didn't want to go anymore because of me. Not because I felt uncomfortable, but because she did, with me. I pushed the thought away; I didn't have it in me to explore that too deeply today.

"No," I said, "we're not going to get driven away. I'll take the boys swimming after school tomorrow. If someone wants to say something, they can. But I think they're all too scared." I felt emboldened. "And I'll call the Browns tomorrow."

"That's their name?" Eva asked, her mood lightening.

"Yes. The whole thing is absurd. I'm absurd."

"How did Suzanne respond?"

"Who cares about Suzanne? You know she dialed me by mistake today?" I put my phone on the table between us and hit speaker.

Eva listened to the voice message without saying anything, paying close attention, as if she were trying to crack a code.

"Who's she talking to?" she asked when the message ended.

"I don't know."

"'You know Raj.' What does that mean?"

I had been asking myself this question all day. There was such certainty in Suzanne's voice.

"She's either just finished explaining what a horrible racist I am or the exact opposite. Either way, I sent it back to her."

"What?" Eva asked. "The message? Are you serious?"

"I'm not going to keep something that wasn't meant for me."

"What did she say?"

"She asked me to call her. I'm not going to."

"I'm not a big fan of hers. You don't owe her anything."

Eva finished her dinner, pushed her plate aside, and started working through the stack of envelopes on the table. I sat with her. She did all the bills, and all she asked in return was that I keep her company while she wrote the checks. The farther in she got, the sharper the look of worry that developed on her face. She didn't have to say anything. We had become people we didn't think we would become. We had two different credit cards that were close to being maxed out. We lived in a town where the cost of living was very high, and we simply didn't have the salaries to keep up with the Joneses or the Blacks, though we also had no interest in keeping up with them. We just wanted to live in our house, buy some organic peaches when they were in season, maybe go on vacation every couple of years, replace our aging minivan.

"I can pull some more money out of the Do Not Touch account," I finally said.

"But we'll be back to this soon enough. If one of us lost our job, I don't know what we'd do."

"Sell this house, go on the road," I joked, trying in vain to get her to relax.

"That may not be so off base," she said.

I finished my wine.

"Go on to bed," she said. "I'll be there in a few minutes."

"Are you sure?"

"You've had a long day."

I leaned down and kissed her on the head, then went and crawled into our bed, a queen that my father had bought for me when I started graduate school. He hadn't been one to buy much for his adult kids, but he'd splurged on the bed; he thought it was important to sleep well.

I stayed awake for as long as I could, waiting for Eva, but I didn't make it all that long before falling asleep.

I wasn't sure what time it was when I got up in the night, but Eva was with me and I could feel the warmth of her thighs in my hands, the smell of wine on her breath. In our early years together, it had seemed perfectly fine to luxuriate in every corner of our bodies for hours. But now, so many years in, with kids sleeping in the next room and our muscles changing, lovemaking felt nearly too intimate to bear. Somehow these late-night, half-asleep moments allowed us to be free and uninhibited. When we finished, we held on to each other tightly as we fell into a deep sleep.

Tuesday

"WHAT HAPPENED?" Eva asked, stepping into the kitchen in the morning, clearly surprised by the tranquil scene before her. I had woken up early, made the kids' lunches, and fried them each an egg. They were showered, eating, and watching a cartoon on an iPad.

I shrugged my shoulders. "I have no idea."

"I slept very well last night," Eva said shyly.

"Maybe we can get to bed early tonight," I said.

Neel brought his empty dish to the sink. "What're you two whispering about?"

"Nothing," I said.

"It has to be something."

I pointed to a little plate with his medicine and various vitamins. He quickly took them with a glass of water.

When they got into the car without my having to plead, I wondered if the fight between the boys, and the crying after, had in fact been therapeutic. Maybe that's how I would consider moments of peak chaos in the house from now on.

We were just pulling out of the driveway when I heard a shriek from the back seat. "Wait. I have to get something." And before I could object, Neel was already out of the car, heading back inside.

"Are we always going to be waiting for him?" Arun asked.

Through the rearview mirror, I saw the soft, gummy smile of a child just out of baby teeth.

"Maybe. When you're older, are you going to remember all the times you were waiting?"

"I think so," Arun said. "But it's OK. He needs his things."

Neel returned with my old iPod, which he'd found a few days earlier in a drawer full of wires. He'd attached it to a small, portable speaker. I had no idea what was even on it, but as he played songs on our way to school—"Wild World," "Kashmir," "Lose Yourself," never letting any one reach past the minute mark—I was drawn right back into my emotional life from a decade earlier, when I'd first learned to download music.

As we got close to their school, he happened upon Biggie, who always reminded me of our time in New York.

"Can we listen to this one through?" I asked. "It'll get us right into the parking lot."

We blasted "Juicy" out of that little speaker. The kids were smiling and bobbing their heads in the back seat. I was doing the same in the front. I felt as if we were engaged in an act of moderate civil disobedience.

Their school was public only in name. The few kids who

walked were accompanied by their parents; I couldn't remember one time when my parents had walked me to school. Most of the students, though, were delivered in cars. There was a drop-off line, a queue of fancy cars and a teacher shepherding the students out and into the playground, to run around before school started. I got into line. No tunnels or buses for these kids.

"Who's picking us up?" Arun asked.

"I am."

"What're we going to do?"

"Whatever you two want." I turned to the back seat and squeezed both their hands. Arun seemed perfectly happy. Neel was forlorn; his mood crashed as soon as we'd pulled into the drop-off lane. "Have a great day."

The two of them got out of the car. Arun bounded away, but Neel lingered, as if he didn't know where he was going. He turned back to me and lifted his right arm slightly into an invisible sling, with his hand tucked under his chest. Then he slowly put up his middle finger. After Neel had learned the wide-ranging implications of the gesture, he'd made it his own, using it to convey that we were making him do something he didn't want to do, but that he was going to do it anyway. There was so much concentrated existential angst in that nubby little finger. I gave him a thumbs-up, and as I did, I saw a parent look at Neel, and then at me, with disgust on her face, as if Neel's behavior were going to rub off on all the other kids.

As I pulled out, a white Tesla pulled in. There must have been twenty different parents who owned that car, but of course it was Suzanne dropping off her boys. We saw each other and I quickly turned away. I could see from the corner of my eye that she was lowering her window.

"Can we talk?" she mouthed. "Please."

I nodded my head and pointed to the parking lot. I could only avoid her for so long. I parked my car, got out, and waited. She walked over a minute later.

"Hi," she said, uncharacteristically tired. "I'm so sorry. I hate these phones. Can we go back to no phones at all?"

I didn't say anything.

"I just wish you could have heard the whole conversation."

"So do I," I said. "I'd really like to know what 'You know Raj' means."

"Mark called me right after they got home from the meeting on Sunday night. He was livid, and I could hear Jan chirping in the background. They wanted to meet immediately. They said they'd drive to my house, but I said it was too late, I needed to be with my kids. The younger one won't fall asleep without me. So we agreed to meet in the morning, at Francine's, for coffee. That's when I must have hit the call button."

"What exactly are they so mad about?" I asked.

"Mark feels responsible for bringing their friends into what he kept referring to as a 'hostile environment.'" She used air quotes. "Mark said that if you'd said what you said at the hospital, and you worked there, you would have been fired. He wants you to apologize to the Browns. And to them."

I laughed, taken aback that Mark and Jan were going to spend their social conscience capital against me. "I'm happy to talk to the Browns. I was already planning on reaching out to Bill. But that's my business. You can tell Mark that he won't be hearing from me." I was surprised by how quickly this was moving. I'd known, of course, that there would be blowback from the TC, but I thought it would percolate for a few more days so that I'd have some time to strategize on how best to proceed. "But why are you upset about this? You said on Sunday that the committee wanted me to apologize too."

"Because Mark and Jan are trying to expel you from the TC," she said. "Apology or no apology."

"They don't have the power to do that," I said. "No one does." I was trying to project confidence, but I knew they would find some way to circumvent the rules, or create new ones if they really wanted to.

"That's true, they don't. But that's not going to stop them from making plenty of ugly noise. I know you only heard that one sentence in the message. I wish you could have heard the other things I said. They don't know you very well. *You know Raj.* That's why I said that — I was trying to give them a sense of who you are. That you weren't being offensive. That you were joking around. They're trying to make this into something it's not. They're trying to make you into someone you're not. I'm afraid it's all getting a little out of hand."

I looked away from her as the last of the kids went into their classrooms. I didn't know what to say. It seemed too absurd that we were in front of a school where our children were given everything they could possibly need and more, talking about my expulsion from a tennis club because a bunch of white people think that I'm racist.

"I appreciate you telling me," I said. And I did. I appreciated that, at the moment anyway, she seemed to be on my side. "Mark can do whatever he wants, but he's going to get a fight from me. And now I need to get to work."

Suzanne had a confused expression on her face, as if she'd finally arrived at a situation that she couldn't fix or order through her own sheer will. I got back in my car and drove away.

The three days when I wasn't teaching I balanced between grading endless piles of papers and writing. I still held on to the idea that I was going to write something smart and get my career back on track. I had a doctor's appointment today, and then I would go home and sit at my desk. I'd checked out a couple of new books of ethnography that had gotten some buzz, and I wanted to read how this newer generation of anthropologists were writing before I dived back into my own work.

As I was driving, my phone rang. I didn't recognize the caller, but it was a campus number. I picked up.

"Raj?" The voice was deep and gravelly.

"Speaking." It was a response I'd heard my father use for years whenever he'd picked up a phone.

"It's Cliff. Cliff Turner. Are you on campus today?"

Cliff was the department chair, an old-school anthropologist who had done his original fieldwork in West Africa, and in the decades that had followed, had maintained deep ties with the communities that were the basis of his dissertation. He was a beautiful stylist in his writing, well read, and a genuine guy who never led with himself or his many accomplishments. As he neared retirement, his books could fill a small shelf, but he was most famous for an essay he'd written about the male circumcision ritual of a West African tribe, which had the most artful, poetic descriptions of young boys, en route to manhood, in profound pain. A man who could make poetry out of pain was my kind of guy.

This was the first time in the nine years that I'd worked for him that Cliff and I had spoken on the phone. Our communications were always either in person or via email.

"I'm not," I said and then added, "but I can be."

"Could you? If you don't mind. Perhaps sooner rather than later."

Cliff seldom made demands of me. And because he didn't, and because I admired him, I wanted to go see him as quickly as I could. I was wearing jeans, an old white T-shirt, and my flip-flops. It was far too slovenly for the office. But it would have taken me too long to go home first to change.

"I have an appointment now. But I can be there right after. Say ten?"

"That's perfect," Cliff said. "I appreciate it. I'll be in my office."

Driving to the doctor's, I kept thinking about what could be so urgent with Cliff. Good news could wait. Bad news had to be delivered immediately, in person. Maybe the university had run out of money to keep me. There was always talk of budget cuts.

The worry about Cliff compounded the worry I'd been feeling already about my doctor's visit. A week earlier, I'd gone to my internist for my yearly checkup, and had left thankful that my nagging cough had revealed nothing and that new medical guidelines had kept the lubricated gloved fingers away for one more year. But the doctor had examined the mole on my left heel, one that Eva had asked me to point out to him, and said that I needed to see a dermatologist about it. My internist generally had no affect, but in a rare moment of mirth, he said, with a grin on his face, "When in doubt, cut it out."

When I'd called the dermatologist's office, the receptionist found me an appointment right away. At first, I'd assumed that they just had plenty of openings, but then I started to wonder if the description of the growing mass on my foot was alarming enough to get me in as quickly as possible. And once that thought had entered my head, the anxiety I felt about the mole became outsized.

I'm not a fan of doctors' offices. Who is, besides drug reps? But this one seemed innocuous enough as I stepped in. The walls had photographs of attractive women who I assumed had benefited from some of the skin treatments the office offered. There were orchids on the side tables and a tumbler of cucumber water. I filled out some forms and waited.

"Rajesh Bhatt?"

A young woman in scrubs had opened the door into the waiting room and called my name. She did a double take. I followed her to an examination room, feeling pretty good about myself. Maybe the casual chic of jeans and a T-shirt could be a new style for me.

"Professor Bhatt. I had you for Intro to Anthro a few years ago."

My shoulders fell.

"Did you graduate already?" I glanced at her name tag.

"I did," Kimberly said. "I got my degree in biology and then started working here. I'm a nurse's assistant."

Is that all it took to be a nurse's assistant? She seemed competent, but if somehow she ended up with a scalpel in her hand, I was going to run out of there as fast as I could.

We walked into a room and she closed the door behind her. What word would best describe being in an examination room with a young former student of yours? Awkward? Fraught?

"So, the note says you're here to have a mole checked."

"That's right."

"Anything else?"

"If the doctor can, I would like a full body scan. Per a request from my wife."

When I had originally made the appointment, I had asked to see a male doctor, because Eva had warned me about the exploratory nature of a full body exam.

"That's easy enough," Kimberly said.

She pointed to a clean, folded hospital gown. "You can strip down to your underwear and put this on." She didn't make eye contact as she said this. "The doctor will be right in."

"What grade did you get?" I asked, acting out my nerves. "In my class."

"An A-minus," she said proudly. "I was happy with it. It was a challenging class."

"That's good to hear. If you're going to have to give me a shot, I'm glad I didn't fail you."

At this, she smiled. "I'm an expert with needles. You won't feel a thing."

And then she left. I was glad to say goodbye.

In the harsh light of the doctor's office, as I got out of my clothes, my body felt old and dry and ashen. I wished I had taken a shower before coming, but I had been too busy getting the kids ready.

A few minutes later, the doctor came in. Barely in his mid-thirties, he seemed not to have lost his baby fat. Kimberly followed behind. "I understand Kim here used to be a student of yours."

"Yes," I said, wanting Kim to disappear.

"That's why I don't practice where I went to school," the doctor said with a silly grin on his face. "How awkward is this?"

I avoided Kim's eyes. Clothes don't offer much protection, but a hospital gown is basically tracing paper. I couldn't hide my protruding belly or my chest, which wasn't nearly as lean and muscular as I liked to imagine.

"Well, let's check you out," the doctor said cheerfully. Perhaps he thought he was displaying positive bedside manner. To me, he just sounded like a kid playing doctor.

He pulled down my gown so it was hanging around my waist. Kim now had an iPad and was scrolling through it with some purpose, doing her best to pretend that I was not nearly naked.

I have seen plenty of muscular forty-four-year-old bodies and plenty of soft ones. Mine was what it was: the result of too much work and not enough time in the gym. I played a lot of tennis, and that mitigated the worst of it. And anyway, I had convinced myself long ago that Indian men were genetically incapable of strong, defined bodies, despite a fair amount of evidence to the contrary.

As promised, the doctor checked everything. He pulled down the back of my boxers and, using a wooden stick like a tongue depressor, pulled apart my cheeks and took a quick peek. When he got to my groin, which he kept covered, I stared at the wall in front of me.

"I hope you don't find anything down there," I said. I had to say something.

He lifted my scrotum with his cold, gloved fingers. It felt like he was down there for a long time, checking, separating, tugging. "All pretty normal here," the doctor finally replied. "So let's see this mole."

I sat down on a reclining chair and he took a close look at my heel with a lighted magnifying glass.

"Kim, you want to come take a gander?"

Kim walked over to my mole.

"Do Indians get skin cancer?" I asked. I had always figured that one advantage of being brown was freedom from this particular bit of life's nastiness.

"The last guy I had in here was Saudi," the doctor said. "Had something on his heel as well. It was much larger, the size of a quarter. So no, you aren't immune."

I felt my stomach fill with bile.

The doctor studied the mole again through the magnifying glass. "I don't like the look of this," he said.

This was a phrase you never wanted to sense a woman thinking as you undressed in front of her for the first time, or hear from a doctor examining any part of your body.

"The heel is a pretty popular place for these things to grow. You say it's been getting bigger?"

"I think so. But it's been so gradual that I can't tell."

"We should cut it off and get it tested."

"It's all yours," I said.

The second I said this, Kim came forward with the iPad and asked me to sign a consent form. A minute later, the doctor gave me an injection to numb my heel. Despite the numbing, I could feel it tug as he sliced the mole out.

"It should take us about a week to get the results. I'll call you."

"So what happens if it's bad news?"

"We cut out about four millimeters from that area and graft it with skin from elsewhere. Your thigh, probably."

I wanted him to say something reassuring about the mole he just removed. Maybe that, judging from others he had cut out, he could tell it was probably benign. But I knew he wouldn't. I looked at Kim, whose eyes were full of youth and pity.

After they left, I put my clothes back on and walked out of the office.

In the parking lot, I sat in my car, which had warmed from the rising sun. Here it was: I was a middle-aged man waiting for my biopsy results. This is how the downward spiral truly begins. I had thought it was when my regular doctor told me that I needed to get my cholesterol under control, or when my students had begun to compare me to their parents. But no. This was it. Now on my arms I noticed little spots that I hadn't seen before; I checked my face and my neck in the rearview mirror.

My skin was going to betray me after all.

As I started the car, my phone rang. It was my mother. She'd memorized my teaching schedule, and if I screened her call when she thought I should be free, she would call back until I picked up. She didn't believe in leaving a message or texting. She did believe that I was forsaking her if I didn't answer the phone every time she called.

I now visited her less and less because it was hard for me to be in that house, picking peaches and plums off the trees my father had tended with such care. And she didn't visit us because she didn't like being away from the bed that they had stopped sharing in his final years, but which she now slept in religiously. In lieu of actual visits, we talked on the phone often. Sometimes daily. My sisters Swati and Rashmi took turns visiting her on the weekends, and so I saw these calls as my particular duty, one I had come to enjoy. Sometimes we talked for thirty seconds, sometimes for my entire drive home from work.

"Hey, Ma."

There was silence on the other end, like there always was when she had something on her mind.

"What's up?"

"Well, since you asked," she said. "There's something I wanted to tell you about."

"What is it?" I tried not to sound annoyed. I wished we didn't always have to go through this back-and-forth.

"There's this man," she said. "In our group. He's new. He cooked a chicken biryani that everyone liked. You know, we've been vegetarian at our functions. But he had come the first day with this dish, and no one said anything, but one by one we all had it, and soon the bowl was empty. He had added a bit of saffron. What kind of man thinks to add saffron?"

Several years after my father's death, my mother had started socializing with a group of Indian retirees, all of them figuring out how to grow old in a country they still considered foreign.

"And so now everyone is bringing new dishes," she said. "Not me, of course. We're eating fish and chicken. But no beef." She talked about food for a while. And then: "Well, the second time he came, he sat next to me at dinner. He was very friendly and chatty."

Here I could sense her voice dipping. "I'm sorry your mother is talking about these things. She shouldn't."

I knew the widowers often paid attention to my mother. She liked the attention, but didn't like that she liked it. She had grown up with the idea that proper Hindu women were supposed to be objects of desire only for their husbands and that their own desire back should be muted, nearly inarticulate. I knew she wasn't comfortable saying anything like this to my sisters, but she felt OK talking to me. She considered me her sensitive son, or more precisely, she thought that because, as a child, I had been infused with more American culture than my siblings, I wouldn't judge her for expressing an interest in men other than my father.

"It's fine. Continue."

"But now he keeps calling me. The first couple of times I picked up and we talked."

"What did you talk about?"

"First, the biryani. He said not being stingy with the saffron is the key."

Growing up, my mother used to make a small tin of saffron last for a couple of years. I knew nothing about this guy, but it was hard for me to trust a man who had loose hands with saffron.

"Then we talked about Bombay. He lived there with his family. Quite close to us, actually."

The mention of the "us" gave her pause. I knew she was thinking about my father.

"Where?"

"Near Kemp's Corner."

"It's a small world," I said, wanting her to feel at ease.

"Yes. Well. Now he calls every day."

"And?" I asked.

"I don't want to talk anymore."

"Why not?"

"I'm not sure. At first, it was fine. It was fun to talk to someone new. But now I feel a little trapped, like I have to wait around until he calls. He doesn't like leaving messages."

But neither do you, I wanted to remind her.

"Well, if you're tired of talking to him, then the next time he calls, tell him to stop. You can be nice about it. But firm. If that doesn't work, I can talk to him. Or maybe it's just going to take some time to figure out how to have these types of conversations. How to set your boundaries."

She didn't respond.

"How does that sound?"

"Good," she said tentatively.

My mother was in her late seventies, still healthy and strong, with some years ahead of her. But she was unmoored from the family life she'd had for nearly forty-five years. Not long after my father died, she'd noted that, having gone from being a daughter straight to a wife and mother, she was now on her own for the first time in her life. She'd said that with anticipation, but I think the freedom could be hard for her to navigate.

"This is all perfectly normal," I added. "To want to talk to someone and then to decide you've had enough. You have the right to change your mind."

"Yes, you're right."

Her voice was lighter; I was glad to have helped her solve her problem. That feeling of utility was not one I had much of in my life these days.

"But otherwise, you like spending time with all those people?"

"Oh yes, it's wonderful. We've been going on these widows' walks. Women-only hikes. I get exercise and my money stays in my pocket."

After my father died, my mother had filled her days at an Indian casino. It got to the point where she was going three or four times a week. My sisters and I had tried to get her to stop, but after months of heated arguments, we finally dropped it. It was easier not to talk about it. She went, and we knew she went, but it seemed that she was going less than before, and I guess that was the middle ground we had reached. Maybe now she wasn't going at all.

"A win-win," I said.

"How are you?"

This was a signal that our conversation was coming to an end. She meant the question, and there was a time several years ago when I would've answered it honestly. But now, I knew that she wasn't as able as she used to be to process emotional problems that had no easy resolution. I wasn't doing well, but telling her that would force her to confront the fact that she didn't know how to help me. So I lied.

"All is well," I said.

"Good."

And then she hung up abruptly, like she felt vulnerable.

I pulled out of my parking spot and drove onto the street. The doctor's office was in a building adjacent to the main hospital in town. As I drove past, I slowed down. It had recently gotten a facelift and now, with its liberal use of glass, appeared more tech office than hospital. I drove around the block, returned to the parking spot I had just left, and walked the hundred or so yards to the entrance.

The lobby was big and bright. On one wall there was a large directory, with the various specialties, the names of doctors, and their office locations. Under Cardiology, I found William E. Brown, MD. His office was on the fifth floor. I walked over to an elevator and stood next to a shrunken, elderly woman leaning on a cane. When the doors opened, I held them so she could go in first. She stepped in, turned around, and faced me. The doors remained open.

"You coming in?" she asked, her voice firmer than I would have expected from that infirm body.

I wasn't entirely sure what I was doing. I couldn't just show up in Bill's office and ask to see him. He was a doctor seeing real patients with real problems. And I was terrified that he'd have me thrown out of the hospital, though I knew that likely wasn't a rational concern. He would be well within his rights to do so, but it seemed out of character. Still, as long as I didn't actually see him, I could pretend that he wasn't furious with me.

The elevator doors began closing. I placed my hand in between and they opened up again.

"Make up your mind," the woman said, this time with the sharpness of an elbow.

I looked down at my T-shirt and jeans and then at the clean, bright lobby behind me. I turned around and quickly walked away. I'd email Bill and set up a time to have coffee.

"What an asshole," the woman said as the doors closed.

I made my way out of the hospital with my head down, hoping that Bill wasn't going to walk by. As I stepped outside, thinking it was safe, I saw Mark Black walking toward me, alongside two colleagues. They were all men, wearing ties and white doctor's coats, laughing. One was Indian. Mark hadn't noticed me yet, but I knew that if he spotted me looking away, he would think I was avoiding him. And so in the second that passed, I kept my eyes on him, and he turned from his colleagues and saw me. He didn't break his stride as we approached one another. He resumed his conversation, and as he went by me, looked my way, smiled, and said, "Nice to see you, Raj." I wanted to go home and crawl under the covers. But I couldn't. I had to talk to Cliff, and I had a feeling that conversation would bring still more chaos into my midst.

When I reached campus, all the spaces near my building were already taken. Each successive parking lot I drove through was full, until I finally found a spot on the top floor of a parking structure, under the bright sun. As I walked to my department, I was sweating in the late morning heat, and my heel burned from where the doctor had made his incision.

I snuck into my office for a minute to gather myself. I didn't like using the overhead fluorescent lights, so it was usually dark except for a single lamp on my desk, which had inspired the majors who took a lot of my classes to dub my office the Bat Cave.

When I'd first moved in, there had been an old desk lamp that must have been purchased secondhand in 1968. It was heavy, grey, and did the job well. But eventually it started making a crackling sound. The department secretary, in what had seemed then like a generous gesture, insisted that I could use her discretionary funds to pay for a replacement. At the campus bookstore I found a sturdy lamp, something that might have been used on a partner's desk in a 1950s insurance company. I'd grown attached to it over the years; the lamp felt like the one thing that I actually owned in my office, though of course I didn't. But at least I'd picked it out.

Today, though, when I reached to turn on the lamp, it was gone. Dan liked pulling little pranks on me. Often, when I left the office to use the bathroom, he would open my browser so that it looked like I was shopping for hemorrhoid cream or something to help with constipation. I texted him: "I want my lamp back." And then: "Showered yet?" Then I opened up his browser and left it up on a popular dating site.

I went to see Cliff. Right before I knocked on his door, I peeked into the secretary's cluttered office. Mary had worked in the department for well over twenty-five years, her closet now filled with the ethnic clothing she'd asked various faculty members to get for her while traveling the globe doing field-work. Some days, she wore an Indian salwar kameez, on others a long Guatemalan skirt. Today she had managed to make an intifada scarf look marmish.

Mary made the department whistle and hum. She knew how to get nearly any expense reimbursed. She could arrange for your classes to be when and where you wanted them. And so we all overlooked her quirks. Like the way she went through everyone's garbage to make sure we were recycling; or that for department lunches she always ordered Chinese food from one particular place because she liked taking home the chow mein; or that she gathered donations from the faculty herself for her gift during Staff Appreciation Week, guaranteeing we all felt obligated to leave a generous sum.

Now I saw that my lamp was lighting up her desk. Magnificently, of course.

She looked up from her work.

"I borrowed your lamp," she said.

"I see that."

"The light is really soft. Soothing."

"I know."

"You don't need it today, do you?"

"Well . . ."

"You can use the overhead lights. I'll put it back tomorrow morning."

She turned back to her work. She was daring me to say something, but she knew I wouldn't. She had boundaries with the tenured members of the department, but with grunts like me, not so much. I knew that if I complained, she would find small ways to torture me, and she knew that I knew that. She would heavily monitor my use of the supply closet, or say that I was making too many photocopies, or place a TA in our office. It was her version of a prison shanking. A stern look was really the only recourse I had available to me, as pitiful as that was.

I knocked on Cliff's door.

After I'd left my first teaching job in a shadow, Cliff had done me a solid. My advisor from graduate school and Cliff were old friends, and Cliff had offered me a lectureship. "Considering your qualifications, I'm sorry we can't offer you something better," he had said when I first came to his office. He was being kind. I had a fancy degree and extensive teaching experience. But what I didn't have, and what the university valued the most, were publications.

For all his unforced erudition in everyday conversation, for his charming streaks of self-deprecating humor, Cliff was a remarkably bad speaker in front of students. He had a slight stutter when he was nervous, and teaching too many students at once made him nervous. In contrast, I could give lectures in my sleep, but I hadn't written much of anything. So there we were. I admired Cliff's brilliance, and he admired my ability to convey the brilliance of others to students.

"Come in," Cliff said.

I walked into his office. There was a department rumor that once, some years back, the office had been used in a movie about a distinguished professor. It was larger than everyone else's, and Cliff made full use of the space. There must have been three thousand books neatly ordered on the bookshelves, and he had read every last one of them. Once I had flipped through the top few books on a stack of volumes — *The Collected Works of Max Weber* — that sat on his desk. There were check marks and notes throughout them all. I knew the Weber hits on bureaucracy and the Protestant work ethic; Cliff knew the entire discography intimately. He made a habit of knowing the B-side of things.

I liked his office for the books, and for the smell. It was against university regulations, but Cliff continued to smoke a pipe when he was by himself. For a while in college, some friends and I had taken to wearing sport coats and Doc Martens and smoking pipes as we biked to class. Since then, I'd loved the smell of loose tobacco; it reminded me of those brooding days, riding high on my own intelligence and the freedom of college.

"Thank you so much for coming in, Raj. I appreciate it. Please sit."

I did. Cliff switched from his reading glasses to his regular glasses. He was in his mid-seventies, with matching white hair and a beard, and I suspected that he was going to teach and write until the day he died.

"How are classes going?" he asked.

"Fine," I said. "Same as ever. But if you're asking about them, maybe I should be worried."

I could see that he was trying to find some judicious way of proceeding with the conversation. He had taken on the chairmanship only because no one else in the department would. It was not a natural fit for him. He had no leadership skills and very little desire to deliver bad news to people. He did his best work alone.

"A student, or a group of your students, has filed a complaint with the dean's office about some of your views in class. And the dean's office sent me this."

Cliff turned his sleek Apple screen—his one nod to the twenty-first century after a lifetime of figuring out the twentieth—so that we could both see. The browser was open to a hectic, full site, packed with articles and banners and ads. I didn't recognize it, but right up top there was a headline: "Anti-American Professor Spews Hatred of the West." There was a video embedded in the story, and Cliff clicked to play it. At first, the footage was grainy; it was hard to make out. After a few seconds, though, it zoomed in and the picture became clearer. It was me. Lecturing. I recognized the red Lacoste shirt I had worn the day before. I looked kind of fat, which made me sad.

He turned up the volume. "Americans have been so obsessed with these gurus not only because they fulfill our Orientalist desires, but also because they offer an alternative to the culture and religiosity of Christianity. They offer a counterpoint to the emptiness of Christianity and Western life." And to ensure that I wasn't misquoted, the slide saying the same thing was lit up behind me.

The article had been posted that morning at six eastern time. There was no byline. I quickly scanned the story. There were quotes from anonymous students about my belligerence in class, my so-called rants about anthropology as a form of colonialism. I scrolled down farther. There were already two thousand comments.

My body felt hot. My heel was on fire.

"Please don't read those comments." Cliff placed his warm hand on mine. The gesture was alarming in its intimacy. "It's the gutter."

"Is the student who complained to the dean the same one who took this video?" There were so many students taking pictures and videos of my lectures, I couldn't begin to guess who it might be.

"I don't know," Cliff said. "I learned about all of this a few minutes before I called you this morning."

"What did the student complain about to the dean?"

"He — and I'm assuming it's a he. It may not be. The person thinks you're stereotyping Christians, and white people more generally. 'Reverse racism' and 'religious discrimination' are the specific complaints. He says you keep saying that white people stereotype others. When, in fact, it is you who is stereotyping them."

I had wondered when this type of accusation was going

to come my way. It wasn't a huge surprise, given that lately students had become more and more vocal about the source of their injuries. And now that it had come, I had two initial thoughts. Had I actually been stereotyping these students? I didn't think I had been, but I worried that no matter what, this was not going to turn out well for me.

"Cliff. It was a lecture on Orientalism and Orientalist desire. Bread-and-butter Edward Said. I've been giving some version of that lecture forever. Careers have been made on the idea. I'm just the messenger."

"Raj, I have no question about the content of the lecture or any of your lectures. I have already explained this to the dean's office."

"So what now?"

"The dean has to follow a certain protocol when complaints are filed. They want to see your complete file. And your evaluations."

Now my back was soaked. Digging always led to dirt. "The evaluations are stellar," I said. "It's the only thing I have going for me."

"It's not the only thing. But yes, they're stellar. I'm hoping they'll clear all this up. For now, go on with your day. I'll have Mary send your file over to the dean, and I'll be in touch if anything more comes up. I'm sorry I didn't tell you this over the phone, but I thought we should do it in person. If it was just the student complaining to the dean, it'd be easy to handle. But I worry this publicity will blow up the issue still more. We're in a different world now. I don't recognize it."

"I teach tomorrow," I said.

"For now, come in as usual. Let's assume that as quickly as the story has grown, some other story will replace it. That's what often happens with these things. We'll figure this out, Raj."

When I stood up, I felt something wet at my feet. I saw that the Band-Aid the dermatologist had placed on my foot was soaked in blood. I gingerly walked out.

I went back to my office and, with the lights off, turned on my computer. I took a tissue and pressed it against my heel, and then typed my name into Google. One of the first hits led me to the same site that Cliff had just shown me: *Freedom Now*. I scanned the headlines; for a moment I considered that this all might be a joke, a satire of a conservative site. The biggest headline read simply, "Jews and Hollywood." It was accompanied by a photo of Steven Spielberg. The story about me was sandwiched between "The Racism Behind Black Lives Matter" and "WWARD: What Would Ayn Rand Do?" I couldn't believe that people actually went to these sites. The tone was angry, but the primary mode was one of bewilderment. All of the articles were, at their heart, about how the country had changed into what it was today. The writers of this site seemed incredibly alarmed — threatened — by a more diverse nation, with a changing workforce and a changing set of voices. In the most literal of ways, the world didn't look the way it used to, and these people didn't like that. They didn't like me.

I went to my story; it was barely two hundred words. "Professor Raj Bhatt is part of a new generation of activists dressed up as so-called scholars. As you can see in this video, which an intrepid, vigilant student in his class sent to us, the use of 'scholar' to describe this man is a stretch at best."

I had known, the second Cliff warned me against it, that I was going to read the comments. He may have some Buddhist ability to tune out what people thought of him, but I certainly did not. "Go home, Haji" was the very first comment. And they rolled on from there, one after another. "Terrorists with fancy PHDs r still terrorists." "No1 wants 2 hear u and ur stupid accent. Ur jokes rnt funny." "Vans? You kidding with those? Aren't you guys always barefoot?" "Perv."

After a while, the commenters stopped writing actual words and instead left a chorus of two emojis: a white middle finger and a dark-skinned man in a turban. It started with a few people but spread to readers across the country. I had people from Arizona to Maine flipping me off. I couldn't believe they all cared so deeply about what went on in my classroom.

Before I clicked out of the article, wishing I had listened to Cliff, I scrolled down one more time, either to inflict a little more punishment on myself or maybe out of a desperate hope that there was one defender out there among all the flame-throwers; I couldn't be sure. One name caught my attention. In lieu of symbols, "BigBen24" had left a charming haiku. Big Ben? There were many Bens in the world, and surely plenty who went by Big Ben. But considering the history I shared with the one Big Ben I knew personally, and his love of a particular phrase that appeared prominently in this haiku, my gut told me this was him.

. . .

I started college in the fall of 1990.

I drank too much those first months, and between hang-overs and exams, I watched bombs as they rained down on Baghdad. It was my first taste of freedom and my first tele-vised war.

That Halloween, still unsure of who I was and where I be-longed, I dressed up as Saddam Hussein. I wore dark green pants, a pine-green half-sleeve shirt my mother had bought me at the start of school, and a pair of combat boots I had borrowed from Art Chu, a handsome Korean-American guy who had an-chored the defensive line on his high school football team. Art lived down the hall in my dorm, and he and I had become best friends in the six weeks we had known each other. In an act of intimacy we both laughed off, he held my chin and drew a bushy mustache on me using a thick black marker. And just so there was no confusion, I pinned a sign on the front of my shirt that read *Hi, I'm Saddam Hussein.* Dumb costume? Absolutely. But I liked that part of me didn't care, or more precisely, didn't know to care. It was an altogether more innocent time.

It was a warm, still California night, the smell of upturned earth heavy in the air. Several of us from my floor had arrived at a Halloween party at one of the nicer fraternities on cam-pus. I'd gotten tickets from a guy I'd met in my medieval his-tory class, John. Once inside the crowded house, everyone scattered, including Ursula, a girl from my dorm whom I had taken to and who was now dancing with another guy. Reared in a large Catholic family, she could barely afford college. She was Carmen Miranda for the night, with a hula skirt and a hat she had made with wax fruit. She told me she was going to re-

turn the fruit to the drugstore after Halloween for a full refund. She had long fingers, long legs tanned amber, and an ex-
quisitely long neck; she looked like a tropical heron.

I went through the house and into the backyard. I wasn't
entirely sure what I was doing there. A few minutes later, John
walked onto the deck.

"Glad you could make it, Raj."

John wasn't dressed up, but as he figured out my costume,
he gave me a knowing nod.

"How's the plague?" I asked, referencing our last history
lecture.

"Still black," he replied.

He asked if I wanted to see the rest of the house. I said sure.

"It's hard to tell with all these people here, but this is one
of the better houses on campus. We get hefty donations from
the alumni."

In the kitchen, he told me they had a cook make them
lunches and dinners during the week. "We have to fend for
ourselves for breakfast and on weekends, but the pantry is
completely stocked." He introduced me to several guys who
were members of the house. After meeting the fifth or sixth
guy, I realized that John was trying to recruit me. I felt the sudden boost of confidence that came with being desired. Maybe
I didn't need Ursula after all; if I joined the frat, I'd have girls
lining up for me.

John and I maneuvered past large groups of people and
made our way upstairs. The mood up there was more laid
back. In every room, there was a different small, individual
party going on. I was leaving behind the kids and settling in

for a night with the adults. We walked into a room where several people were sitting around drinking. There was a bottle of Jack Daniel's, cans of Coke, and an ice bucket on the table. In the dorms, we only drank cheap beer; the bottle of whiskey seemed extravagant, a sign of what awaited me if I played my cards right.

"Cuba libre?" John asked.

I must have looked perplexed.

"Rum and Coke?"

I'd had two or three beers already and wasn't sure that liquor was a prudent decision. But I didn't want to say no to John.

"Of course."

He made us two drinks, and we went into his room.

All the other rooms had two beds, but this one was a single, the décor a bit more postcollege than the others. There was a large, framed Ansel Adams photograph of Half Dome on the wall, a full bookshelf, and a small couch. There were two women in the room, one dressed like the white-robed Princess Leia and the other like Pocahontas in a little brown suede bikini top, a matching suede skirt, open-toed moccasins, and a feather in her hair. John kissed Leia and introduced her as his girlfriend. She was much prettier than Carrie Fisher, less sisterly. I wished Art and the others could see how quickly I had ascended.

But not five minutes later, Ursula walked in with a muscular guy with dirty-blond hair and no costume. I already disliked him for his sinewy arms and the confidence it took to show up to a Halloween party without a costume, but I couldn't help but be thrilled at the sight of Ursula, despite that. We nodded to one another but didn't let on that we lived on the same floor. John introduced me to Pavel, another member of the house, and Pavel introduced Ursula to us all. And so there we were: John and his girlfriend, Pavel and Ursula, Pocahontas and me.

Ursula and I stayed quiet as the others talked about people we didn't know. I took long sips of my drink so I had something to do with my hands. I was tipsy enough without it, but paradoxically, the more I drank, the less out of control I felt. And the more I hated Pavel.

"So, Pavel. Is that a European name?"

"It's Czech."

Things were worse than I thought. Not only did he have Ursula on his arm, but Prague was the hip place to be. Everyone seemed to be going there for the summer and coming back with stories of cheap beer and flowing wine.

"That's cool," I said and took another long sip of my drink. I thought about going to the bathroom and never coming back.

"I've been introducing Raj to the guys in the house," John said to the group.

"What do you think?" Pavel asked me.

"It's a nice place. We've been going to a bunch of parties this term and some of the other houses are pretty disgusting. But I don't know. I'm not sure fraternities are for me." Truthfully, I just didn't want to seem overly eager. While the principled part of me hated the idea of frats, I had loved walking around with John, feeling the effect of being his guest in this place.

"What's wrong with them?" Pocahontas asked.

"I guess I'm not that big into group activities."

"That's how I felt too," Pavel said. "That's how I still feel sometimes. But the perks are great and the alumni contacts are amazing. The big companies don't expect much from the students on this campus, so they don't come and recruit. You know who shows up to the job fairs? Insurance companies and car rental places wanting to hire branch managers. You need something else to move you along."

I didn't want to like what Pavel was saying, but it made sense. Maybe a frat would give me more options than law school.

"I agree," John said. "I don't like every guy here and some of them don't like me, but that doesn't mean we can't be helpful to one another. Everyone's civil; we don't have to be best friends. You should think about it."

I could see how they could help me. But I also saw how they thought I could help them. I'd been surprised by John's interest in me in class, but while I guessed not all of the brothers were so forward-thinking, John must have realized just how white the house was. I would darken it a little — not too much — and they would look a whole lot more welcoming and open-minded than the other fraternities.

I thought about how I'd explain a fraternity to my parents. I assumed they didn't know much about them, but then they always surprised me with how much they gleaned from their preferred information sources: snippets of TV movies, *20/20* reports, and the *Wall Street Journal*. My father may have correctly determined that fraternities were clusters of binge-drinking, oversexed, burly white boys. Though he'd never spoken in explicitly moral language, I knew he thought that most white Americans were too susceptible to alcohol, too enchanted by the allure of the easy life. He wanted me to do better, rise above. If I pledged, I could just say I was boarding in a big group house. Or I could tell him the truth and emphasize the networking benefits. He would appreciate the utility of that as much as I did.

"I have an idea," John said. He asked Pavel to help him, and they stepped out of the room, returning a few moments later with a small, round Formica-topped dining table. "It's been a while since I've played quarters."

"I'm not playing," Leia said immediately.

"C'mon," John said. "We should give Raj a bit of what he thinks us dumb frat boys do all the time."

He winked at me. I felt like I'd said too much.

For the next hour, we played quarters, drank still more, laughed, and listened to Bob Marley. The pairings around the table were clear. John and Leia kissed and joked between turns, and Pavel whispered to Ursula. I wanted to make a pass at Pocahontas, but I didn't know how.

After a while, Pavel got up and opened the mini-fridge. "Hey, Raj," he said, "we're out. Could you go a couple doors down and get some more from Steve's room? Tell him I sent you."

I sat there for a second, not sure what to do. It seemed a normal enough request, but it didn't feel right. He was treating me like a pledge already, asking me to do the dirty work that pledges do. But there weren't any other pledges around; I was just the brown kid he was asking to go fetch him some beers. Him, the especially muscular blond guy in the room.

When I hesitated for a moment, Pavel said he'd go. But I knew that if I didn't, I'd feel as if I'd been ungracious, unwilling to do just this one favor, so I told him not to worry.

The booze hit me as soon as I got in the hallway, and I stumbled, dizzy. I didn't want to go into a stranger's room and ask him to give me beer. But I moved toward Steve's door anyway. There was a similar party going on inside. Because so few people had commented on my costume all night, I'd forgotten I had it on. As this roomful of people, none of whom I knew, turned to look at me, I became aware of two things: one, that my costume might be in poor taste, and two, that it might, in the minds of others, align me, the only brown guy in the room, with a Middle Eastern dictator. I felt freakish, grotesque.

"Saddam Hussein," I said, pointing to my sign. "But it's just a costume. Obviously." One of the brothers made an exaggerated attempt at laughter. "Pavel asked me to get some beers from you guys. He said I should ask for Steve."

The laughing guy pointed to the back of the room. I walked through the group of people, opened the refrigerator, and grabbed two six-packs. One of the guys, who I assumed was Steve, looked at what I'd taken.

"That's too many," he said. "Put one back."

I did as he said and quickly left. I wanted to go back to my dorm, but I thought I should see the night through. I walked back to John's room; Pocahontas was the only one left.

"Where is everyone?" I asked.

"A song came on and they all went downstairs to dance," she responded, a little dazed and fully drunk.

I turned toward the door.

"Where are you going?" she asked. "Come sit with me."

I went and sat next to her, trying not to stare at her suede top, trying not to think about Ursula, wherever she'd ended up.

"I guess it's just us Indians," I said.

She didn't smile, or even seem to get the joke.

"I love your bushy mustache," she said, turning to me and tapping her fingers right above my lips.

Before I realized what was going on, she leaned in and kissed me. I lay down on the couch and she got on top of me, her feathers beautifully disheveled. I was drunk enough to lose myself in the pleasure of her.

But sometime later, a voice called into the room: "Ann?" And then louder: "Ann!"

There was a guy at the door who had the distinct, surprised expression of a boyfriend. And while there were plenty of guys wearing football jerseys downstairs, this guy looked like he actually belonged in one.

"Who's this?" he asked in a calm voice.

"Ben? What are you doing here?" Ann sat up and tried fixing her hair. "I don't know what's going on. He just started kissing me," she said.

"No, no," I said right away, turning to Ann. "Please tell him."

She glanced at me but didn't say anything. She looked as scared as I felt. Ben took a big step toward me.

"I think I'm going to take off," I said, getting up from the couch.

"You're not going anywhere," Ben said in the commanding tone of someone who's caught a stranger in his house.

"No, listen," I stammered. "I didn't know that Ann was attached. I wouldn't have done anything if I had known."

"I told you to sit down," Ben said.

I tried again to leave, but Ben blocked me at the door with his substantially larger shoulder.

"Where the fuck do you think you're going?" he yelled.

He took another step toward me, and I darted behind him. I ran down the stairs, but I could hear footsteps behind me. I made it to the front door and thought I was in the clear, but someone kicked my feet and I fell onto the grass, which was wet from spilled beer. In seconds, Ben was on top of me, kicking and punching. I was too drunk and scared and confused to fight back. I could see a crowd gathering in the yard, though no one intervened. Ben landed a hard kick to my stomach, leaned down, and said, loud enough for everyone in the yard to hear, "No sand niggers allowed!"

"Shut up, Ben," John said, pushing him aside. He'd just made his way to the front yard. "What the hell are you doing?"

"He was fucking with Ann."

"That's your problem and hers, not his. He's my guest."

John helped me up. My pants were wet, and my lip was bleeding. I saw Ursula in the crowd, clearly embarrassed. I wasn't sure if it was for me or for her.

"C'mon back in," John said. "I'll help you get cleaned up."

I looked at him, then over at Ben. I bit at my cut lip, doing all I could not to let the tears come. I had never hit anyone before, and now I desperately wanted to know what it felt like. But I realized what a mistake it would be to get into a fight in front of this crowd. There was no one there who would have my back. I assumed Art Chu had wisely made his way back to the dorm already.

"I'm good," I said to John, and walked away.

Two weeks later, when Ben and I went in front of a three-person university judiciary committee, he showed up wearing his number 24 football jersey, thinking somehow that it would help him. It probably did. He was clear and forthright when speaking to the committee. Yes, he had said it. But it was because of my costume, because I was dressed as Saddam Hussein. In the heat of the moment, with the alcohol, the crowd, all the news on TV, and the emotional toll of the night, he'd been overwhelmed, confused. "I would never say something so deplorable to a fellow student like Raj Bhatt. But Saddam is our enemy. I was so upset thinking about all the innocent people he's killed. I shouldn't have said what I said, but we're at war with an evil, evil man, and at that party, coming face-to-face with a representation of that evil, I was overcome by my love for this country, for freedom."

"Even if he was saying it to my Halloween costume," I said to the committee, "I think Ben was less upset that I was dressed like a dictator who has killed countless innocent Kuwaitis than he was by the fact that Saddam was making out with his girlfriend." I don't think the committee, or my eighteen-year-old self, understood the full implications of my suggestion that Ben was angry because Ann's white body was on top of my brown body.

Ben and I had to leave the room while the committee deliberated. He seemed comfortable and nonplussed, sure that there weren't going to be any consequences for his actions. When we were called back in, the committee gave Ben a stern warning to watch what he said. But nothing more. With that, I received a warning of my own: not all invitations should be accepted. There were some groups I would never belong to.

Ben walked up to each member of the committee, shook hands with them, apologized profusely, and thanked them for their time. After seeing how easily they accepted his apology, I just walked out.

I never stepped into a fraternity house again. For much of my freshman year, I'd been drunk at least three nights a week. But when I returned for my sophomore year, I became deeply involved in my classes, never earning anything less than an A-minus for the rest of my college career. I fell in with that crowd of pipe smokers. We wore tweed jackets ironically and Doc Martens in a nonfascist way. We read Gramsci and Fanon, and reserved Friday afternoons for drinking expensive beers. Though I'd not known this when I entered college, this was who I had wanted to be. A thinker of sorts.

As I was getting ready to graduate, I heard through the grapevine that Ben had been accepted to Georgetown Law School. It took me some years to understand that I had gone to college with a lot of Bens: guys who could spend four years drinking too much and not studying enough, kicking around whomever they wished along the way, without ever endangering their future prospects.

Was "BigBen24" the same Ben? Maybe. I could imagine him having come across the article in between depositions. If it was, his haiku suggested he still lacked a certain imagination. "Hey there sand nigger / Mount that big camel now please / Iraq awaits." I sat in my dark office, clapping out the syllables. He'd missed the final one.

I texted Eva. "Talk?"

"Running into a meeting. Everything OK?"

"Yep. Chat later."

I waited a few minutes — Eva was disciplined and put her phone away during meetings — and then sent her the link to the article, adding, "Don't read the comments."

I heard the key in the door. I fumbled around and quickly closed the browser on my computer. I wasn't quite ready to talk to Dan about the video. He walked into the office and found me sitting in the dark.

"You know the university can see your surfing history," Dan said, switching on the overhead light.

"Of course," I said, getting up from my desk, smiling off his joke.

He looked me over, once and then once more. However outwardly bad I might have seemed to Dan, it was nothing compared to how I felt. Even though so many years had passed since that night, I still felt nauseated every time I thought of it.

"If you don't mind me saying, you look like shit," Dan said.

He noticed my bare feet. I shifted my foot slightly so that he wouldn't see the bloodied bandage.

"I don't think I've ever seen your toes before. They're perfectly nice, but flip-flops seem a little comfortable for work, don't you think?"

"After Monday, I don't think you get to comment on how anyone else dresses in this office," I said. "I wasn't planning on coming in. I needed to grab something. How was class?"

"Same old." Dan noticed my empty hands. "What did you need to grab?"

Dan would have understood the absurdity of the couple of days I'd just had. He might even have given me some much-needed perspective, or at the very least, made some joke about racist Mercury being in retrograde, which would have made me laugh. But I felt a little too vulnerable about it all to share with him now. I would later.

"These," I said, slowly turning both my middle fingers toward him, before leaving the office and heading to my car.

I made one stop on my way home: a store in town that sold overpriced modern furniture. I walked in and was greeted by a severe, very tall saleswoman.

"Can I help you find something?"

"Do you have desk lamps?"

She pointed to the back. I found about ten of them, all lit up, all sleek and metal and perfect. As I'd walked into the store, I'd decided I would splurge and spend a hundred dollars. Good light didn't come cheap.

Clearly, I'd underestimated the extent to which that was

true. The first lamp I saw was $600. Sure, the lamp was beautifully designed — three pieces of smooth metal, seamlessly attached and producing even, soft light. But still. The next few were less expensive, but not by much.

"Good light isn't cheap," the saleswoman said.

"Indeed," I said.

"Let me know if you have any questions," she said.

I nodded and continued checking out the lamps. I could go to a hardware store; a lamp would be so much cheaper there. But I couldn't let go of the vision of walking into my office with something new and sleek, something fancy. I needed to treat myself.

I picked the cheapest one — $250. The body was silver, and the light emanated from a structure the size of a large blooming tulip. I liked the lamp well enough. Not $250 worth. But I was determined not to walk out of the store empty-handed.

My phone rang while I was finishing up at the cash register. The saleswoman pointed to a sign on the counter: NO CELL PHONES PLEASE. I walked several feet away, sat down on an Eames lounge chair, put my feet up, and answered the phone.

"Is this for real?" Eva asked.

"Which part?"

"The comments."

"I told you not to read them."

"The comments are the story. Who took the video?"

"Some asshole in my class. They've also filed an official complaint against me with the dean's office."

"For what?"

"Reverse racism."

"Oh, Raj. This is crazy."

"One group thinks I don't like black people and another thinks I don't like whites. How did I get here?"

Eva didn't answer.

"Did you read all the comments?"

"A lot of them."

I wondered which ones had stood out to her.

"There are over three thousand now," she said.

I almost felt a sense of pride. No one had ever paid this much attention to me.

"Did you read the haiku?" I asked.

"I missed that."

"I think that guy Ben from college wrote it."

"Ben?"

"Halloween." I had told her the story years ago.

"Ah," she said, remembering. "You think it's the same guy?"

"I do."

"Are you home?"

"I'm headed there. I'll get the kids and then I have a match tonight. Busy day?"

"It's OK. I'll be home by five thirty."

I wanted to tell her about the biopsy, but I could see the saleswoman hovering in my peripheral vision. "I'll see you tonight."

I hung up the phone. The saleswoman was several feet away, her face now bright red.

I looked at her, smiled, and walked out with my expensive lamp.

• • •

That afternoon, when I went to pick up the kids from school, Neel's teacher and the principal were waiting out front. The principal, Mr. Forman, assumed that running an elementary school meant maintaining an insistent seriousness at all times. He was married to Neel's teacher, and during the school day, they scrupulously tried to keep their distance. Now they were standing a few feet from each other, not saying a word.

"How are you?" I said as I headed to the playground.

"Can we talk for a moment while the kids are still playing in the yard?" Mr. Forman asked. "We'd both like to discuss something with you."

I followed the two of them into his office, going through the possible list of things that Neel could have done. He could be impulsive and demanding at home, but while Eva and I were always waiting for some of these behaviors to appear in class, they never had. His teachers had mainly said that he started answering questions before they'd finished asking them and that he had trouble staying on task. It was the latter issue that had led to his ADHD diagnosis.

Maybe I had no reason to be nervous. I wondered if I should have more faith in him; it could be positive news. Perhaps Neel had done well on a test and they wanted to congratulate me on the fact that my son was well on his way to winning a Fields Medal. I wanted to believe that was just as likely as anything else. But nothing about this week suggested good fortune was coming my way.

Once we were in his office, Mr. Forman sat down, then gestured for me to do the same. Mrs. Forman remained standing.

"We had an incident in class today," Mrs. Forman said.

She shared her husband's seriousness, which she conveyed through careful articulation.

"Before you continue, I do want you to know that Neel has always had some trouble transitioning to the start of classes," I said. "He loves school, but he's never been great with transitions."

"Today in class, the boy sitting next to Neel noticed something he was drawing," Mrs. Forman continued, as if she had not heard me. "And it must have disturbed him deeply because he took it from Neel and brought it to me."

"Took it without his permission?" I asked.

"Took it because it was very disturbing."

It was never the best idea to snatch something away from Neel.

The teacher reached into her blouse pocket and placed a folded-up piece of binder paper in front of me. I opened it.

It was a pencil drawing of two skyscrapers in flames. Next to them was a series of dollar signs. Below, Neel had written, in his poor penmanship, "Time to get paid / blow up like the World Trade."

I repeated the lines to myself. They sounded so familiar, and yet I couldn't place them.

"Neel is a wonderful boy. Smart, energetic, creative." Mr. Forman prepared to deliver the shit part of the sandwich. "But it goes without saying that this is very concerning for us all. In this time in particular."

"And what time is that?"

"There are sensitivities."

"It's a kid's drawing," I said, "not a Hezbollah manual."

"I completely agree," Mr. Forman said. "But you also need to understand my position in a situation like this. I have to keep the whole school in mind ahead of the needs of any one student."

"Keep the school in mind? Do you think this is a threat?"

"Absolutely not," he said.

I was trying hard to resist the urge to get up and walk out. I focused instead on the words on the page, letting them run through my head. Finally, some synapse connected in my brain. Unwittingly, I laughed.

"Is something funny?" Mr. Forman asked.

"No, no," I said. "I couldn't remember where I knew these lines from, but I finally did. It's a song lyric, something he heard in the car this morning. Christopher Wallace. You know, the Notorious B.I.G.? The rapper. Anyway, it's just a metaphor." I realized I was actually proud of Neel; he'd pulled the most interesting lyric from the song. The little fuck. "Perhaps it wasn't the most judicious thing for him to be listening to adult rap lyrics," I said before the principal could lecture me on proper parenting. "But it was the morning, and the kids were talking to each other, and I didn't think he was listening that closely."

"That's his special gift," Mrs. Forman said. "Just when you think he's doing something else, not paying any attention at all to what you're saying, you realize that he was completely tuned in all along."

"It's not a threat," I said. "He was just doodling. I promise we'll listen to Bach and Mozart in the car from now on."

"Well, it's my responsibility to figure out what to do with all this," Mr. Forman said.

"What else is there to do?"

"I need to think through the options."

"It seems to me that there are only two options," I said. "We see this as a kid's drawing and leave it at that, or you decide to make an example out of Neel."

"We need some time to think this through."

I got up to go. I still had the paper in my hands. Mr. Forman reached out for it. Maybe he needed it as evidence.

"Can I have that?" he asked.

For a second, I thought about crumpling it up. It was, after all, my son's property.

"When you're done with it, I'd like it." I imagined keeping it safe, framing it, and giving it to Neel as a high school graduation present, a token of his early foibles.

I walked out of the office and went to get the kids. I'm not sure why, but I felt exuberant for the first time all week.

"Can we go to Scrappy Art?" Neel asked when he got in the car. "I need some stuff for an art project."

"Can we just swim instead?" Arun asked.

"I'm sick of swimming," Neel said.

"How can you be sick of water?" I asked.

"I didn't say I was sick of water. Just treading in it."

I didn't want to go to Scrappy Art, but since Neel seemed excited to go for a school project, I obliged. Arun would likely complain to his therapist years later that Neel always got to choose their after-school activities.

Scrappy Art was a place in town that sold all sorts of random donated things — old trophies, ribbons, broken clocks. In essence, clean junk. Their business model relied on the idea that the things you didn't need, the things you might normally throw into a landfill, could be repurposed into art. One man's trash, as they say. Neel was a hoarder and he loved stuff. He was also very bad at keeping track of time. If I said five more minutes, he heard fifteen. And so half an hour after I told him it was time to go, the young woman behind the counter had finally rung up all the scraps Neel had gathered.

"This is amazing," she said. "What are you going to do with the bowl?"

"It would make a perfect belly," Neel said.

"Oh, definitely," she said, as if they were on the same artistic wavelength.

The junk he bought — old pipes, buttons, a cigar box, screws, used corks, and on and on — cost me $20. Arun bought himself a used basketball trophy and a stack of baseball cards.

On the drive home, both kids were happy in the back, working through their treasure of junk and discussing their possible uses. I kept glancing back at them, so content now. Eva flashed in and out of their beautiful little faces. Of course, just then I felt the burn on my heel, as if to remind me that all happiness is fleeting — I could go at any moment.

"What's the matter, Dad?" Arun asked.

He and I looked at each other through the rearview mirror. My eyes were moist.

"Nothing, sweetheart," I said, quickly turning away. "You two keep playing."

I brought the kids into the house and Neel went to his room with his booty. We wouldn't see him for the rest of the evening. When he got into a project, he fully got into it.

While the kids were in their rooms, I cooked my go-to meal: chana masala and rice. The kids loved it. And I loved the idea that the food was infusing them with some ineffable Indianness that I hadn't otherwise provided in our day-to-day lives. Regardless of any other cultural shortcomings, I was very proud of how skilled they'd become in Indian buffet lines.

When dinner was ready, I brought large bowls to the kids, and they happily sat in their rooms, ate, and worked on their projects. Or more precisely, Neel worked on his project and Arun sat beside him, watching and fiddling around with a small box of stray Legos. I changed into my tennis clothes and waited for Eva to come home. When she did, she dropped her handbag on the floor of the kitchen as if it were full of bricks.

"Why are they so quiet? Are they watching something?"

"They're eating and doing Scrappy Art things. We should budget going there every week."

I didn't tell her about the mole. I knew she would have allayed some of my concern, but subconsciously, I think I wanted to continue worrying about the mole so that I had less energy left for worrying about my job. I made her up a dinner plate, poured her a glass of wine, and as she finished her first long sip, I told her about Neel's doodling.

"Jesus," she said. "What is going on this week? Let's just try get through the rest of it without any more drama."

"Trust me, I'm trying," I said. "Let's talk to him when I get back."

"Who are you playing with?"

"I don't know. I'm assuming they're going to stick me with a stinker. I'm not expecting a welcome party."

It was interclub season. The various clubs around town, public and private, played against one another. On Wednesday nights, it was the A league: college-level players and middle-aged roosters strutting around. Tuesday nights were the B's, like me, all of us playing under the assumption that we were just an improved backhand away from the A's.

I assumed that word of Sunday night had spread as it always does at the TC: each member of the committee had told one other person about what had happened, insisting they not tell anyone else. In turn, that one person had told one more person, extracting the same promise not to divulge. By now, it was likely that half the club knew. But still I wanted to get on the court. Hitting that ball back and forth would give me some semblance of peace, even if only for an hour or two.

"Are you nervous?" Eva asked.

"About the match?"

She shook her head.

"I think you're more nervous about me going than I am."

"Maybe," she said. "Maybe."

After all these years and all these matches, after the kind of bad day I'd had, I still got excited as I neared the court. This time, I would play better than I ever had before. This time, I would move to all the right places at exactly the right time. This time, I would levitate, just for a moment, as I whipped a forehand across the net.

It was the first time I had been to the TC since Sunday evening. While some ineffable thing had changed for me, the place was still sunny, the huge oaks and magnolias were still resplendent, the greens of the leaves matched by the deep greens of the court. The place was continuing on as it always had. As I walked through the parking lot, I saw Stan getting out of his car. I assumed he was going to walk behind me without saying a word. I kept my head down and carried on.

"Want to hit?" he asked, now walking a few feet behind me. I was happy to be surprised.

"Sure."

"You have any balls?"

I reached my hand into my tennis bag.

"A few."

"That's all we need."

We found an empty court and stood several feet from the net on opposing sides, hitting the ball back and forth slowly. Usually we would chat during this part of the warm-up, something about the Lakers or the Turgenev he'd just finished. But neither of us said anything. Gradually, we stepped farther and farther back, until we were both at our respective baselines, hitting the ball with decent pace. Stan knew how to warm up properly before a tennis match. His strategy was to wear out his opponent with his consistency. He'd told me once that early in matches, he did everything he could to return every shot. He wanted to let his opponent know that he would always be there.

When I played poorly, I used my arms to hit everything. When things fell into place, I used my feet and my body to generate power. With Stan, I was stroking the ball beautifully, and the pop coming off the sweet spot of the racket was blocking out all the other noise in my head. I even forgot about the pain of my heel. The game had always allowed me a break from the everyday stresses of life. That was how I'd first started playing, really.

Two years after we'd arrived in the country, my parents bought a condominium in a brand-new complex. After living in a nearby apartment that was beyond cleaning, the newness was important to them. The complex had sixteen buildings with four units in each, most overlooking a swimming pool and a small clubhouse. Our second-floor unit was on the far side, overlooking a seldom-used tennis court. I can still remember the condo's cost: $88,000. Back then, it seemed like an enormous amount of money.

The first year we lived there, the place was full of young families and recently married couples, swirling with excitement and energy at having bought into a desirable building. Everyone decorated their balconies with flowers and plants, and there were lots of potlucks in the clubhouse. My parents made friends with the Iranian, Sikh, and Jewish families who lived close to us. I learned to swim properly in that pool. The whole place was tucked behind a gate with a security code; inside, we felt secure.

But after a few years, the place and the people changed. Families moved out, divorces were finalized, and the people who moved in didn't always stay for long. There were a few boys my age, and we would roam around together after school and in the summers, swimming, playing catch, and keeping track of who had moved out and who had moved in.

One afternoon, three of us had broken into one of the apartments that we'd been monitoring for months. Looking through the windows, we could see the place was empty, but somehow the back patio door had been left unlocked. We walked right into the master bedroom; there was a mattress on the floor, made up with sheets and a few pillows. Next to it was a neat stack of *Playboy*s. We stayed there for an hour.

A week later, riding the confidence from our previous break-in, we entered another apartment, whose former occupants my family knew. Reza Faruki had left Iran after the 1979 revolution with a wife and young child. A few weeks earlier, my father had bought some of their furniture: a few coffee tables, a dining room set, and Reza's beloved stereo system, with its enormous speakers. My father had never been the type to have friends. Though he'd never said it, he implied that the needs of the family and the demands of work left little time for anything else. And yet, I could see my father's affection for Reza, and how Reza returned that affection. In late middle age, it seemed that both men had found pals.

"Why are they selling this to us?" I remember asking. "Don't they need somewhere to eat?"

"They need to move," my father had said, the disappointment clear in his voice. And then added, "Quickly."

I knew there was more to the story.

I led my friends to Reza's old apartment, hoping that the front door would be unlocked.

It wasn't, but when I pushed it, it opened. Before we noticed anything, we instinctively plugged our noses.

Overtaken by the stench, and the immediate absence of more magazines, my friends walked out. But I lingered in the living room.

The layout of the apartment was the same as mine: living room, dining room, and two bedrooms down the hall. But it was now nothing like the warm apartment I'd seen when my family had visited. The carpet was haphazardly cut up, as if someone had taken a knife to it. There were only a few stray pieces of furniture left, and the walls were discolored.

Every time we'd come over, Reza had handed my father a Michelob and then taken great pride in choosing a record to put on. Cat Stevens, Miles Davis, Ravi Shankar, the Rolling Stones.

"Bhatt," Reza had once asked my father, "what did you listen to in Bombay? Miles was the *thing* in Tehran."

"A little Miles," my father had responded, taking a sip of the beer. "A lot of Coltrane."

My father seemed like a different man with Reza. At ease. A bit playful. It gave me a sense of what he might have been like before the stresses of work and raising a family had shaped his life.

Now, many of those records Reza had handled so carefully lay shattered on the floor. I walked through the living room, stepped into the kitchen, and opened the fridge. There were a few Coke bottles, some milk, and an open can of tuna. I grabbed a bottle, opened it, and took a big, greedy gulp, and then another. I walked down the hall, drinking, and peered into one of the bedrooms. I nearly dropped the cold bottle from my hand.

Reza was asleep on the bed, facing away from me. He was wearing pajama bottoms and a white T-shirt. It was four in the afternoon. I had led my friends up here because I was sure that he and his family were long gone. I saw him stirring on the bed, shifting in his sleep. I stepped backward and ran out of the apartment as fast as I could. I stopped only to throw the unfinished bottle of Coke in a bush, then kept running all the way home.

I never told my parents; I felt I'd seen something I shouldn't have and was worried about getting into trouble. But that moment haunted me: a warning about what happens to men when they can't keep their lives together.

I spent more and more time at home after that, gazing out at the tennis court from our kitchen window. It was usually empty, but once in a while a couple would come to play, and I would watch them. The woman was the better player. They would hit for a while, then meet at the net and maul each other, his tongue reaching deep into her mouth. I wonder now if my earliest interest in the game was born from a kind of erotic charge.

Sometime later, a man started coming to the court, with a little shaggy dog and a frayed leather travel case filled with faded balls. He would serve out all the balls and then go to the other side, gather them, and serve them out again. He was methodical. Ten in the corner, ten down the T. I started going to the court, shyly hanging around on the side. Not long after, I started chasing balls for him. I can't remember now whether the dog's or the man's name was Teddy. Let's say it was the man's. One day I showed up and Teddy pointed to his things. There was an old aluminum Prince racquet in his bag.

"For you."

"I can't." Even my twelve-year-old self knew not to accept a gift right away.

"Of course you can. A boy needs a racquet."

Teddy showed me the western grip for a forehand and a backhand. This was the first and last private tennis lesson I would receive until I took one with Richard, but I saw Teddy on most Saturdays and Sundays after that. I went from collecting balls to hitting them back.

One Saturday, Teddy didn't show up. He was absent again on Sunday.

"Go play with someone your own age," my father said.

When I saw a woman walking around the complex with the dog, I went up to her.

"Teddy's not been feeling well," she said. "He'll be out there again soon."

But he never came back. I moved on to skateboarding. A few years later, when my parents started earning more money, we moved into a house. I took up playing again at the public courts nearby with a group of older, encouraging Filipino men. They made me much better, tougher, on the court. Whenever I showed meekness by hitting a ball with no real pace, one of them would crush it back and say, "Don't Gandhi the shot." It was effective. During matches, when I babied the ball over, I'd mouth the phrase to myself to get my adrenaline pumping.

Despite their coaching, I went on to play unremarkable tennis on my high school team, and then in college and graduate school, when I started reading Marx and Weber, I let it slip away. Tennis was not a part of any of my social circles. I was embarrassed for loving it so much.

I didn't step back onto the court until we joined the TC. Now I was playing the best tennis of my life. I was getting to balls quickly; there was torque and ferocity in my forehand and backhand. After a wrist injury, I'd added a piercing backhand slice to my game that bailed me out when I wasn't fast enough to set up for the Lendl backhand I'd emulated in high school. And now, using an open stance, I could whip my forehand pretty well, even as I knew that I was tearing my elbow to shreds. There wasn't a drop shot I couldn't chase down, and I often salivated when I saw one coming my way.

In this strange country of my mid-forties, I was playing better than I had in my teens. I knew that as the years passed, that would not continue. But for now, I felt strong and athletic on the court. In the middle of a match, waiting for a serve that I would return flawlessly, everything slowed down. The ball was twice its normal size. These hours on the court had become vitally important to me. I wasn't going to let Mark or anyone else threaten my peace.

Our team captain — an anesthesiologist by day — came up to the court where Stan and I were hitting with a can of new balls. "You two stay on the show court," he said. "Good luck."

"Are we the lambs?" Stan asked the captain.

"Of course not," the captain said, failing to disguise his disingenuousness. "We don't do lambs." Any excitement I'd felt about the match deflated. Sometimes when the opponent's best players were too good, the captain sacrificed the first line and placed the better players lower down so that some of those matches could be competitive. We were playing a club from across town, which traditionally had not had solid tennis players. But this year they were much better.

Their number one team walked over to our court. I'd played one of them before. A few years back, I'd come across a book called *Use Your Head in Tennis,* published in the early 1950s. While it professed to be all about tennis, it was actually about manners. It had these witty chapter titles: "Service with a Smile," "When You Are Overmatched," "Middle Class Tennis." My favorite line came under the heading "Don't Be a Murderer": "There's at least one in every tennis club: the slam-bang, neck-or-nothing player who hits every ball as if he wants to batter it to smithereens." The perfect description for this guy. He either hit the ball to the fences or hit screamers just inside the line and out of reach. Stan's shots were so consistent, if this guy's game was off, we'd maybe have a chance.

His partner, though, was different. We hit some warm-up ground strokes to break in the new balls. He was calm, his body moving forward gracefully with each crisp shot he hit. It was clear he could hit the ball better at thirty percent than I did at one hundred and ten. If I posed any challenge, he would turn up the strokes to fifty and blow me off the court. After we joined the TC, I encountered this kind of player more and more, who had learned the game from pros as a kid, played plenty of junior tennis, his parents driving him from tournament to tournament, buying him shoes and tennis clothes that I still felt were too expensive for me to buy for myself. He had probably played in college, and now, in adulthood, his game was effortless. No matter how hard I worked on the court, I was never going to catch up to someone like that. And the TC was full of them: men whose work lives had never conflicted with their love of the game.

I had been hitting the ball well during warm-ups. I felt the same way when the match started. Whatever was happening off court I could atone for on it. But before I knew what was happening, we were down 0–6, 1–5. As expected, Stan had been consistent. But no matter how many times I told myself not to Gandhi the shots, I had. Over and over again.

The only levity in the match arrived during what turned out to be the last game. I was about to serve when I heard squawking above me. Sometimes hawks flew high overhead, doing a mating dance, maybe, or simply mocking all of us below for the fact that they could fly and we couldn't. This time, the bird was much lower, and less graceful. A duck. It landed on the service line on my side, the majesty of its green feathers matching the court. It inspected me, then Stan, and then our opponents.

With any other duck, I might have stepped toward it and made a threatening gesture with my racquet. But I knew it was best not to fuck with this particular duck.

Every couple of weeks, this duck or one of its flock made its way to the TC. Adjacent to the club was a massive property, well over forty acres, with flowing gardens, multiple ponds, and an enormous Spanish-style villa in the middle of it all. The owner had made her money—*lots* of it—in television. I had never seen her in person, but I liked that she was there. And because I liked her, and liked that she, an African-American woman, was the biggest landowner in town, I respected her ducks.

"Hey, sweet thing," I said, walking toward the duck. "We're almost done here."

My opponents looked at me like I was crazy.

The duck waddled to the side of the court and hopped onto a bench. It only flew away when I double-faulted into the net, ending the match. I couldn't remember the last time I'd played so poorly. Given that we were at the number one line, and that I knew we were the team's sacrifices, I'd wanted to do well. And so of course I'd hit one nervous shot after another.

I placed the game balls, still bright yellow, back into the can and shook hands with my opponents. When I turned to do the same with Stan, I saw that he'd already grabbed his racquets and walked away. Our opponents pretended not to notice.

I made my way from the court, past the swimming pool, and toward my car. I didn't want to hang around for the beers we usually had after our matches. But Leslie was walking toward me as I was attempting my escape. When we got close, she leaned forward and gave me a kiss on the cheek and then a hug, with the same intimacy she always held between us. I felt relieved, especially after the shunning from Stan.

"Nice match?" she asked.

"We lost," I said. "So no. I tell my kids it doesn't matter if you win or lose. But that's horseshit. You here to play?"

"No. The kids have a joint lesson with Richard."

For Leslie, the week was moving along as it always did.

"We should all play again soon. It's been a while."

"Yes, let's do that," I said.

"You good otherwise?" she asked, now with concern in her voice.

"What's up, Leslie?" I was in no mood for small talk.

"I hear you spoke with Suzanne."

I nodded my head. I hated that the two of them were discussing me.

"It was an unfortunate moment," Leslie said. "But I wonder if a simple, easy chat with the Browns might put all this to rest. I can see why you wouldn't want to talk to Mark and Jan. They're insufferable."

"I regret doing it," I said. "It was stupid. I shouldn't have had so much wine. And I truly don't give a shit that Mark and Jan are livid with me. That's a badge of honor. But in regard to the Browns, I don't see how what happened between us is anyone's business but ours. Why has everyone suddenly decided they're experts on race relations? The sins of this place run pretty deep."

"What sins?" Leslie asked.

Leslie could be both keenly aware and completely ignorant.

"I'm sorry, but there's not going to be any big public apology from me. If I apologize to the Browns, they'll be the only ones who know about it, and I'm certainly not apologizing to anyone else."

"Fine, suit yourself," she said.

In all the years I'd known her, this was the first time Leslie had snapped at me. I knew that smoothing everything over was the easier way to go. And I didn't like the idea of her, or anyone else, being mad at me. But being liked, I'd learned, had its costs.

"Are you coming to the meeting on Friday?"

"Absolutely," I said.

"I'll see you there." She walked away.

I was about to head to my car, but I turned back to the pool. Children in pools were like little colonists in training. They weren't happy unless they occupied every last inch of water. There were about five couples talking and drinking poolside. I knew them, but Eva and I didn't socialize with them. A few of the dads were working the barbecue. It was unusually crowded for a Tuesday evening. I went and found an empty lounge chair away from them.

I took off my tennis shoes and shirt and walked over to the deep end. I dropped in feet-first and tried to think what might happen if somehow my body gave up and I didn't rise from the bottom. The cool water covered me, and when I hit bottom, I crouched and lunged up. After a few seconds of beautiful silence, I heard the laughter and splashing of the kids. There were at least ten of them in the pool, and now that I was in the water, I could see a slight film of dull muck on the surface, the collected formula from all the sunscreen their parents had insistently lathered on them, swirling together with their grime and escaped pee.

I swam over to the far end. There was no hard-and-fast rule, but once an adult started swimming laps at one end of the pool, the kids knew to keep out of the way. I wasn't much of a swimmer, but I had barely broken a sweat on the court and wanted a workout. I didn't care that I was in my tennis shorts. I got into a rhythm. I tried to see how far I could swim without coming up for air. I loved the peace of swimming underwater.

In the last few years of his life, my father had insisted that the family go on vacations, to make up for all the ones we'd never taken as children. One year, we went to the cold Alps, another to warm Kauai. On that island, away from their regular lives, my parents actually talked and laughed together for several consecutive days. Our first full day there, we all went down to a beach known for easy, calm snorkeling. My mother had bought herself a very modest swimsuit — essentially a dress — and my father wore a pair of swim trunks with little elephants on them that must have been at least a decade old, but were still in perfect shape. The two of them sat on the beach under an umbrella in low chairs. I went into the warm water right away and struggled for a while to breathe through the snorkel. But then it clicked, and I floated for the next hour, watching the schools of colorful fish, the occasional ray, wanting to get out of the water to tell my family about it but not wanting to miss a thing.

Finally, I went back to the beach. "You have to come in," I pleaded to my father. I was in my early thirties, high off the idea of *experiences,* and annoyed that my father didn't govern his life in a similar way. I thought he was too passive.

"You go ahead," he said.

"Please. Just this once."

I fitted a snorkel and mask on him, shared my newfound breathing lessons, and watched as he stepped gingerly into the water. He put his head under and tried to figure out how to work the little tube. I realized then how seldom he put himself in situations where he didn't know exactly what he was doing. I swam away so that he could work this out in private.

Several minutes later, I looked back toward the shore. He had just pushed his feet off the sand and was slowly but surely swimming toward me. Though it was hard to see his face through the mask, I knew there was wonder in his eyes. Wonder at the fish, wonder that he was underwater, and wonder that he was floating in the air. I motioned for him to come toward me. He put his thumb up and gracefully swam out. I had never been in the water with him; he was a smooth swimmer, piercing the ocean ever so slightly as he moved. As a kid, I had learned to swim by myself. I'd always assumed he didn't know how, because he'd never go in the pool with me. When I'd asked him to come in earlier, I figured he'd just stay near the shore.

The two of us swam farther and farther out. There were hundreds of fish, deep blue, red. We saw two turtles, one enormous, the other a little smaller, leisurely circling just below us. It was the longest stretch of uninterrupted time my father and I had spent alone together as adults. He died soon after.

As I swam in the pool now, the memory of that afternoon carried me through my laps. When I stopped to rest, I grabbed a hold of the side and looked around. While I'd been under, the entire pool had emptied of children. Every last one of them. There was still plenty of daylight and the air was very warm, but the kids were all jam-packed into the hot tub and some of the parents were guarding the edge, as if to ensure that their children would not get out. I felt a sudden chill come over me. Maybe it was all just a coincidence. They were warming up in the hot tub before they sat down to eat.

I got out of the water. I hadn't brought a towel, so I went into the bathroom, pulled a handful of paper towels, and dried myself with them. Despite a liberal use of the towels, my body still felt damp. Outside, I put on my tennis shirt and my shoes. As I was tying my laces, there was a small jailbreak from the tub: a few kids jumped into the deep end of the pool. By the time I got up and was heading out, the rest of the kids had returned to the cool water. On the other side, none of the parents looked my way.

As I walked from the car to our front door, the sky was orange and pink from the sunset. Inside, the house was surprisingly quiet. I rummaged through the fridge, made myself a peanut butter and jelly sandwich, and headed to our bedroom. I needed to get out of my wet shorts. As I left the kitchen, I noticed a thick, coiled snake right outside our back door. It didn't move, but every few seconds its forked tongue slithered out of its mouth.

I quickly walked down the hall. The kids' doors were open, but the lights were out. Eva was in bed, reading.

"They're both asleep and it's barely eight," she said, smiling. "What are we going to do?"

"Come. You need to see this."

We walked into the living room. Eva stopped when she saw the snake, then leaned down to get a closer look.

"The rattle is missing. But that's definitely a rattlesnake."

"Are you sure?" I asked.

"I can feel it," she said, pointing to the prickly hair on her arms.

Uncoiled, the snake would have been several feet long, as thick as a baguette. It was full and mature.

"What now?" I asked. I'd grown up on the sixth floor of an apartment building in Bombay. In matters of wildness, I deferred to Eva.

"We have to kill it," she said. "If it thinks this is its new territory, we're in trouble. It'll start laying eggs."

"Kill it?" I asked. "Are you kidding? Let's call animal control and have them do it."

"It'll be gone by the time they arrive. We have to do it now."

"Maybe it'll just go away."

"It won't. It's *here* now."

As we were discussing its future, the snake slowly uncurled and slithered away, as if it knew that its life was under attack. We watched it head into a thicket of Mexican sage to the left of where it had been resting, and we rushed out another door to the yard to see if we could find it. It was gone.

We went back inside. Eva checked in on the sleeping kids and then went into the bedroom. I could sense her agitation.

"We should've killed it," she said. "The kids can't go in the yard now. I'll always think it's lurking. I wish you hadn't waited."

"Waited?" I asked.

"Never mind."

"Say it."

"You deliberated about what to do. We should've gone outside right away."

"I didn't sign up for this. You were the one who wanted a house with a little land. This isn't my childhood. If it were, we'd still be living in a small apartment in an overcrowded city."

Eva stared at me.

I walked into the living room to get myself a pour of something warm. I quickly turned and went back to the bedroom.

"It's returned."

"In the same place?" she asked, jumping out of bed.

I nodded. This time, we both went outside immediately and armed ourselves with gardening gloves and a shovel. Eva was in her pajamas and had slipped on her rubber boots.

"We have to cut its head off," Eva said, making practice lunges with the shovel. "That's the only way."

"You want to do it?" I asked.

"I was hoping you would. I'm sorry about what I said inside. Please help me with this. I'll never feel comfortable being back here if we don't kill it."

I took the shovel.

"One quick stab," Eva said. "No hesitation."

"What if it jumps at me?"

"That's why you're using a shovel. You can keep your distance."

I walked up to it. My instincts — fight, flight, and preservation — were turned up way past ten. My head was telling me to do it. I had to do it. And yet, I suddenly felt unable to kill this living creature. Why should killing a snake that was threatening my family bother me? And yet it did. I gripped the shovel hard. And then I loosened my hands. I always hit a tennis ball much better when I held the racquet lightly in my hand. I readied the shovel. If I didn't get a proper strike the first time, the snake would leap right into me. It was facing us now, aware of the danger, prepared to strike the second I moved toward it. The skin was a deep shade of olive and rust.

"I can't do this," I said, stepping away. "I'm a Hindu. We don't kill things." I was only half joking.

Eva took the shovel without looking at me or saying anything. And she clearly went through the same thought process I just had. She walked up to it, got herself ready, then walked away. She handed the shovel back to me. "I'm a Catholic. We don't kill things either."

We laughed nervously as the snake's eyes shined in the porch light. I was holding the shovel and Eva was right behind me. Then, in one swift motion, she snatched the shovel from my hand and, with one forceful blow, took the head off the snake, letting out a shriek as she stabbed. The snake hissed and its fat body convulsed. Eva let go of the shovel and it fell to the ground.

"What the hell was that?" I asked, nauseated. In all the years I'd known Eva, I'd never encountered this violent reaction to danger. I hoped that, given different circumstances, I would have the same impulse to protect my family.

"I have no idea," she said, somber. She had teared up. "Can we clean this up in the morning?"

"I'll get rid of it," I said. "You go inside."

I got a couple of garbage bags and scooped the head into

one. I had to use the other bag as a glove to pick up the body. It was heavy, and while I'm no herpetologist, I knew the bulge in the midsection was a sac of eggs. Without thinking too much about it, I gathered everything up and threw it all into the garbage can outside. I washed the blood and the bits of guts from the ground with a hose, then went into the kitchen and got some dish soap and a sponge and carefully scrubbed the ground.

When I got into bed later, I thought Eva would be fast asleep.

"What did you do with it?"

"I put it in the outside garbage can."

"Maybe we should bury it tomorrow."

I didn't want her to know that it was carrying eggs, though they were the very reason she'd needed to kill it.

"No. It's pretty mangled. Let's leave it."

"Do you wish we lived somewhere else?" Eva sounded re-signed, as if she were certain that I was going to say yes.

"No," I said, feeling a little unsure about my answer. "I just don't want to deal with snakes."

Wednesday

As I drove to work, I turned on the air conditioning. We'd taken a hopeful turn toward cooler weather earlier in the week, but now it was warm again. I dialed my mother to check in on her gentleman caller.

"How're the boys?" she asked.

"I just dropped them off. They're fine. Neel got into a little trouble at school yesterday."

"What kind?"

Before I could answer, she continued, "Do you know how many times one of your teachers complained that you couldn't sit still?"

She'd said this to me before as a catchall when we were having trouble with Neel. I didn't know if it was true or not.

"And what did you say to them?"

"That it was their job to keep you occupied."

"I'm sure that went over well."

"It was fine. You grew out of it. On your way to teach?"

"Yep. Any more calls?"

"No, but he usually calls in the afternoon. After his yoga class. He says he feels most at peace to talk to me."

"He sounds like a piece of work."

"No. It's good that he exercises."

Despite her concerns the previous day, it seemed that she was actually looking forward to the call. I hoped her misplaced guilt wouldn't deter her from the pleasures of a new friendship.

"Exercise is important," I said. "I'm glad you have a new friend. Just keep getting to know him however it feels comfortable to you and you'll be fine."

There were a few seconds of silence as she processed this. I knew she wouldn't say anything more on the topic, so I moved on.

"Who were our neighbors in Bombay?" I asked. I wanted to ask her about Reza Faruki, but for some reason was nervous to come out and do so.

"The Dastoors?"

"Yes! Their apartment always smelled like fish. They were a quirky family. I remember how much the son liked cake. And what about here? The Farukis."

"They didn't live as close as the Dastoors. You don't remember them? They lived several buildings away. Why are you asking?"

"No reason," I said. "The Faruki dad popped into my head yesterday. I was wondering what happened to him."

"I don't think he was quite prepared for the hardship of

coming to this country. His father was high up in the military in Iran. From what I gathered, they had lived a very comfortable life there. He'd never held a job before coming to America. And working at Radio Shack was probably not what he had envisioned when they moved here."

"I remember their apartment. All those beers and Cokes in the fridge."

"For a while there, he and your father became fast friends. Your father wasn't the type to have friends. He didn't have time, or maybe he didn't trust the idea of a friendship. But he always liked walking over to Reza's for a beer and a chat after work. He tried helping him when he lost his job. Tried to find him something new."

"Did you keep in touch?"

"No."

I finally told her the story of going into his apartment.

"Why didn't you tell us then?" she asked, sounding concerned, even alarmed.

"I thought you'd get mad at me for going in there."

"Of course we wouldn't have been mad. I wish you'd told us." She paused. "Though we never told you what actually happened to him. And we probably should have. It was just too much, and you were so young."

My mother was skilled at speaking in a variety of emotional registers, but nervousness was rarely one of them. Hearing it in her voice now was making me anxious.

"When you saw Reza, his wife would have already left with their daughter. After he was fired from Radio Shack and couldn't find work, she went and got a job at that Kmart near us, in curtains and bed linens. She knew her way around fabrics. But he refused to let her take the job, saying he would find one soon enough. The idea of her bringing in the money, and the possibility that he might never find another job, terrified him, though he'd never admit it. We went over there one evening to help them work through it. He was overly cheerful, insisting that everything was going to be fine. That he had some solid leads — which he didn't. We tried convincing him that women work in America too, but he wouldn't listen. And so she took the job anyway. And she found an apartment for herself and the little girl. That's when he sold us all that furniture. He kept saying he didn't have any use for it anymore. We didn't need it, but knew he wouldn't accept money from us otherwise, and we wanted to help. We were really worried about him. And then a week or two later, he killed himself."

"Wait, what? What do you mean?" All this time, I'd assumed Reza was living out his life somewhere. I was probably one of the last people to see him alive.

She didn't respond.

"How?"

"I don't remember."

I think she did, but wanted to spare me the details. "In that apartment?"

"No."

"Why didn't you tell me then?"

"He was such a decent man, and you were so young. We didn't want to scare you."

"Did Swati and Rashmi know?"

"Yes."

I wasn't sure what disturbed me more, Reza's death or the fact that my family had kept the circumstances from me.

"Don't think about him too much," my mother said. "It was a sad situation."

"Indeed." I had reached the campus and needed to get off the phone. "I have to go, Mom. I just got to work."

"OK, Raj," she said. And then, in a softer tone: "It wouldn't have made a difference."

"What?"

"If you'd told us then. Reza was very depressed, and we couldn't have offered him the help he needed. We didn't know how to help him."

"Right. OK." I wasn't sure what to say. I just wanted to get off the phone. "I'll talk to you later. Let me know if that man starts to bother you again. I can have a chat with him. But he sounds fine."

She hung up, and my mind circled back to Reza, to the deep despair he must have felt as he lay there in bed, knowing that he had nowhere to go, and no family to support or be supported by anymore. Maybe I was having a particularly shitty week, but at least I had Eva. She and the boys were still by my side, and I knew they weren't going anywhere.

I parked and walked to my building, my new desk lamp in hand. I was still several feet from the entrance when I saw the sign.

Every morning, there was a different flyer taped to the glass in the main door, announcing a talk or a club meeting or a film showing. Neel hated school now, but I knew that he'd thrive once he made it to college; there would always be something for him to do, some new taste to develop, some new source of dopamine, at any hour of the day. If radio stations were still around then, I could see him filling the 1–4 a.m. slot with nineties hip-hop.

Usually I glanced at the flyer on the door and walked right through. Lately there had been a surplus of talks with "anthropocene" in the title, a word I knew but didn't fully understand. And before that, it was "affect." Everyone was giving papers on how much "affective labor" everyone else was doing. For a while, the hipper, younger scholars were stylishly barking for a return to the "aesthetic." I predicted that "boredom" would be next.

Regardless of the buzzword, as soon as the advertised event had ended, the flyer went down. On the bulletin boards spread throughout campus, there was a clear warning that only "authorized persons" could add or remove flyers. It was a rule that students followed with surprising fidelity. Except this time.

Someone had taken the turbaned-man emoji that had been so prevalent in the comments section of the story about me — I'd started to call him Haji, because it was so similar to the clichéd image of the bearded, screaming Middle Eastern man ubiquitous in recent American war movies, always being mocked by the troops — blown it up to fill an 8½ x 11 piece of paper, and carefully taped it to the glass. My first instinct was to assume it was some mildly anarchist kid, sick of how only certain people got to post certain things. It couldn't possibly be targeted at me.

But what if it was?

Someone had to know that I came through this door at about the same time every Monday and Wednesday morning. I turned around and searched behind me. There were some students walking in the distance, but no one close by.

I looked back at the flyer. The color gradation was set as dark as possible. I saw my reflection in the glass and then moved over so that my face was superimposed on Haji. Certainly this was no noose or swastika; it was an emoji, one of countless images available on all Apple devices. I was about to reach out and rip it down. But instead, I took a photo with my phone, to keep as evidence.

I didn't know what to do next. Maybe I should call the campus police to make sure no one took it down while I went upstairs. The effect of it was far more powerful when you came upon it as I had. But what would I say to the police? How would that conversation go? The flyer was meant for me and me alone, and yet I knew that someone else, someone removed from all this, wouldn't see it that way. I'd tell them someone was taunting me. And how do you know it's meant for *you*? they would ask. If it was on your office door, that might be different. But this is a door that hundreds of people go through each day. What is so offensive about it? You don't even wear a turban.

I made my way upstairs.

I walked up and down the hall, not knowing what to do or

whom to talk to. I knocked on Cliff's door. No answer, which wasn't a surprise. He wrote at home in the morning and came to the office at ten thirty.

I went to my office, removed the desk lamp Mary had returned, and plugged in my new one. I was going to get productive work done under this new soft light. I had to.

I turned on the computer and checked in on my new online presence. Six thousand comments. Not too shabby, but I wasn't the hottest story on the internet. The story about how Jews had founded and now controlled the major Hollywood film studios had north of ten thousand comments.

I closed the tab and worked through the driest, most uncontroversial lecture in my files. I could introduce it in class by saying we were going to back up a bit, get some background context that I felt the students needed, and then I'd tell them about kinship patterns among the Nuer. Basic, uncontroversial Evans-Pritchard. Today and for the rest of the term, I wasn't going to say a single memorable thing. My job now was to become profoundly boring and unremarkable.

I had written the lecture, and created the accompanying PowerPoint slides, several years earlier. But I hadn't read it in a long time. As the years had passed, I'd let some of these basic ideas go, incorporating them into other, more complex lectures. Some of the slides had photographs of the Nuer that Evans-Pritchard had taken during his fieldwork in southern Sudan. The people were all minimally dressed. I'd explain how these photographs represent the gaze of the anthropologist on the native, but no matter the context or the explanation, the images would float away on their own and someone would surely accuse me of displaying exploitative, racist images of Africans. As I went through and removed all the photographs, I wondered if this kind of second-guessing was going to be my reality in the classroom from now own.

Just as I was finishing, Dan appeared.

"Three days in a row," I said. "I could get used to this." He was dressed in ironed khakis and a tucked in, light green gingham button-down shirt. "You getting ready to sell a house?"

Dan closed the door behind him.

"I may be on the dating scene soon," Dan said. "Need to adjust and think ahead."

"Stop."

"You never know. Her silent treatment is deafening. I'm sorry I'm here again on your day. I don't have anywhere else to go."

"I'm glad you're here. Did you see the email?"

"Of course."

Cliff was very diligent about sending department news to the whole faculty. A new book. An email. A fellowship. An email. An impending clusterfuck. An email. Cliff thought the department ought to know what was going on.

"It's horrific," Dan said. "I'm sorry. And the comments. Please tell me you didn't read them."

"Every last one," I said. "I can't help it. I keep refreshing it to make sure I don't miss new ones. It stopped stinging after the first thousand. Now I just want to be the most hated man on the internet."

"I would have read them too."

"Did you see that flyer downstairs? At the main entrance?"

"What flyer?"

I took out my phone and showed it to Dan. He looked at it closely.

"Holy shit," Dan said. "You need to show this to someone right now. Who's doing all this?"

"I don't know. I don't think Cliff knows either. Somebody in my class complained to the dean's office. But I don't even know if it's the same person that sent in the video and put up the flyer."

"Is Cliff here?"

"No. I'll talk to him after my morning class." I gave Dan the once-over again. "Seriously. Why are you dressed so well?"

In the gingham shirt, Dan looked very much the patrician he actually was, but didn't want to be. He had gotten through Choate without being inappropriately touched, drank his way through Haverford, and had done his dissertation fieldwork in Costa Rica because the surf was so consistent.

"I don't know," Dan said. "Maybe the not-caring shtick is getting old."

Dan made wisecracks about everything. The fact that he hadn't about the article made me feel even more worried than I already was. We'd had plenty of conversations about how neither of us had any protective layering in our jobs. I wondered if Dan was trying at least to dress the part of someone who took his job seriously. Because he thought my job was in jeopardy, through some sort of associative logic, that might mean his was too.

"You going to be here all day?" I asked.

"Yep," Dan said. "Lunch?"

"I'd like that." I didn't want to be alone.

I grabbed my satchel and the old lamp and walked to Mary's office. She noticed the lamp in my hand.

"I returned it," she said.

"And I'm returning it back to you. Enjoy." I put it down on the floor next to her desk and walked out without waiting for a response. I wasn't feeling good about much of anything, but it did feel good to give back the lamp. What was mine was mine, and what was not was not.

Cliff's door was still closed.

As I headed to the lecture hall, I was sure that students were either staring at me or going out of their way to avoid me. Usually I had to maneuver past skateboarders, students on their phones, and indifferent, slow walkers. But now there was a clear, unobstructed path in front of me.

I'd left my office a little late and got to the lecture hall just as class was supposed to start. I didn't want to linger onstage for too long before I began talking. I would give my lecture and go right back to my office.

When I walked in, things were quiet. And somber. I reached the front, got my notes ready, and scanned the room. In the back left-hand corner of the lecture hall, the seats were oddly empty. A small pod of students was missing. Robert, my salary tracker, was not in his regular seat. I checked my watch: I was five minutes late. I saw my TAs sitting together in the front row. Carla shrugged her shoulders. Normally the chatter wouldn't die down until I was a few sentences into my lecture.

"What's going on today?" I asked aloud, knowing very well that most of them had probably seen the video online.

No one replied. If I was being paranoid, I'd say that they were avoiding making eye contact with me. And who's to say I wasn't being paranoid? I eased into Evans-Pritchard and theories of kinship.

"Who do you consider your kinfolk?" I began. "Blood relations? Friends? Community?"

It was an interesting enough question, but for the next hour, I kept my talk as dry, clinical, and unremarkable as I could. Plenty of charts. Discussions on matrilineage and patrilineage. The second I was done, the students left the hall as if they'd heard a fire alarm. It was just the three TAs and me.

"Were you actually trying to be boring today?" Carla asked.

"Did I succeed?"

"Exceptionally well. Is this because of that stupid article?"

I shrugged my shoulders. "I guess. No more thought and analysis and critique for me. Just anthropology straight out of the 1950s, further sanitized for today's viewers."

We headed to the exit. When we stepped out of the hall, the first thing I noticed was how quickly the morning clouds, still overhead when I'd walked into class, had burned off. The sky was blue and brilliant.

The next thing I noticed was the crowd of roughly forty students gathered right outside the lecture hall. I recognized some of them from the class that they'd just skipped. A lot of them had signs: *Christian Hater. Not a Safe Space for All of Us. #FireDrRaj.* It was the nickname some of my favorite students had given me over the years; a term of endearment and respect rolled into one. I'd loved it when they'd called me that. To see it used as a weapon was unnerving.

"What the fuck?" I said, louder than I'd intended. During the lecture, I'd started sweating whenever something I was saying didn't seem to be going over very well. Now, I could literally smell the stink on me.

"What's going on, Raj?" Carla asked.

I was about to respond when, to the left of the crowd, I noticed Robert. He stood there, signless and expressionless. I couldn't figure out if he was there as a protester, witness, or passerby. He didn't say anything, didn't pay attention to anyone around him. He just stared at me disapprovingly, as if he were trying to reject me before I could reject him further.

"Professor," one of the protesters from the crowd said, "why do you hate Christians so much?"

I turned to Carla, who was as perplexed as I was with the question.

"I don't hate Christians," I said, addressing the crowd. "When did I ever say that?"

"You say it all the time."

I recognized this guy from the class. He was a soft-looking kid with a friendly face and a big, overgrown beard. I didn't have the strength that morning to talk to all of these students — or through them, as the case may be. From what I could tell, none of them had been listening all that carefully in class. They'd tuned in for a few key phrases and run with them, completely omitting any sort of context.

I started walking away without saying another word. But as I walked, the whole group moved with me. Robert followed along. I couldn't see Carla anymore, or the other TAs. Despite the fact that I was in a safe public place, with the protesters and plenty of other regular students passing by, I suddenly felt incredibly alone. I picked up the speed of my step.

"You can talk all day in class, but you can't stop and talk to us now?" another student asked. "We're the ones paying your salary."

It was hard to know whether to be touched or offended that so many of my students were concerned with my yearly take. Maybe I should just embrace it. Maybe Robert could be my own personal union leader. As I looked around at the rest of the crowd, I supposed they wouldn't be fighting the good fight with him.

I kept walking. If I could only make it to my building, I could leave all this behind me.

"Man up and talk. Look at us. We're waiting for you to talk to us."

It was the bearded kid again, but this time his voice had the menace and swagger that come from having several dozen people supporting him. *Man up?* I knew the smarter, wiser thing would be to keep walking. But, of course, I stopped; I was too weak. I turned to the group. They all stopped as well.

When I'd first seen them, before I'd read their signs, they'd seemed like a bunch of kids waiting to get into an alternative hip-hop concert, languid, milling about before the show started. But now, there was something different about them. The crowd was mostly young men, but there were plenty of women too. And they were entirely white. Before, there'd been some distance between them and me. Now, as I'd walked and stopped and the crowd had swayed along with me, they were quite close. Most of them were still in front of me, but several were behind. I was surrounded.

"What do you want from me?" I asked, my tone quiet and questioning, hoping that talk would get us through.

"We want you to stop making offensive, unfounded statements in class," the bearded kid said. "We want you to treat us with respect. You're living in the West, teaching in the West. Maybe you could at least *try* to act like you don't hate *it* and *us* so much."

There was a murmur of agreement from the crowd.

"I don't hate the West at all," I said. "I'm a product of it. Like all of you." I heard some sounds of disagreement. I continued: "But criticism, dissent, is one of our core values. That's what I've been trying to teach you this term. Parts of America are admirable, other parts are not."

"Why don't you critique the Africans that sold the slaves as much as you critique the whites that bought them?"

The beard was clearly the spokesman. Every time he said something, the rest of the group backed him. I tried to come up with an answer that wouldn't lead to more questions. I shouldn't have stopped walking; I'd have been safely in my office by now, admiring my new light, arguing with Dan about whether we were going to have Korean tacos or chicken salad for lunch.

"We can't talk about these issues in this kind of conversation," I said. "That's what the classroom is for. I saw that many of you weren't there today. Come back next week. Let's talk through this. Let's figure this out."

"Some classrooms may allow for discussion, but yours doesn't," the beard continued. "All we hear are your half-baked ideas. We don't get to talk. All we get is you, spitting on the graves of our ancestors. *You don't respect us.*"

I looked at him and all of the students behind him. I took one step away, trying to signal to the crowd that I was done and needed to be let through.

"Don't walk away." This time, a big, tall student I didn't recognize was speaking. "You stay here and you listen to us." There was a threat in his voice.

Right then, I didn't know what would happen if I walked away. I'd felt a vague sense of fear when I first saw the crowd, and that had only grown more acute. There was no one here to protect me, to come to my defense. I thought at least Carla would have stayed behind. I tried to find a quick exit. I wanted to run, but if I did, I'd never be able to enter that classroom again. I saw Robert. Will you please tell your friends to let me through? Even pleading with my eyes was humiliating. No matter. He just stood there with a blank expression on his face.

There was a slight opening in the crowd, and through it, several feet away, I noticed that the bulletin board where I'd seen the flyers for the Emily Baker reading on Monday was now covered with Haji flyers. But these were different from the one I'd seen earlier. Now they had a diagonal line across the face.

I suddenly felt disoriented, as if my synapses were short-circuiting. I could see everything that was happening around me, and yet I couldn't piece it together.

"I treat you with plenty of respect." My voice was louder than before and rising with every word. "I come into the classroom ready to work. But so often I don't get anything back from you. You're lost in your phones, completely uninterested in anything I have to say."

I pushed past a few students and went up to the bulletin board. Before I quite knew what I was doing, I was pulling down all the flyers, crumpling them up, and yelling: "You can't do this. This is not OK. You have to leave me alone!" I couldn't believe what I was doing. I kept telling myself to stop, but I couldn't. My voice kept rising. "You have no right to mob me like this. No right at all. I'm so tired. So tired of all of this." I'd had my back to the students. When I turned around, they'd all gone silent. "You want me to respect you? Fuck that. Not when you behave this way. You have to respect *me*."

Robert was still there, now with some concern on his face. The beard had finally stopped talking. I wanted to walk up and slap him. My ears were ringing and I couldn't think straight. I had scraps of paper in my hand. I released my fingers and they fell to the ground. My left hand moved instinctively to the front pocket of my jeans. At the bottom I felt a wet spot.

I walked back to my office. As I did, I checked over my shoulder. Most of the protesters were still in place, but the beard and a young woman were behind me, following. I entered my building and waited for the elevator doors to open. The two of them caught up. I did my best to breathe in and out, deeply. Perhaps my mother's saffron-wielding friend was on to something by starting his day with calming yoga.

They got in the elevator when I did. The beard's earlier look of confident defiance had softened, perhaps unnerved by my freak-out.

"What are your names?" I asked.

"I'm Alex," the beard said. "And this is Holly."

Holly seemed like a nice enough young woman, her dark roots showing through her blond hair.

"Alex and Holly," I said, "I'd appreciate it if you would leave me alone."

"Why won't you talk to us?" Holly asked. "You have office hours, right?"

I had expected her voice to be mousy, but it was strong and direct.

"They're canceled today."

"But you're here," Holly said.

"No, I'm not," I said.

The elevator doors opened. I walked to my office, with Alex and Holly following behind. My hand was too unsteady to get the key into the slot. I stopped, turned around, and faced the students. "I'm not going to say this again," I said, my voice livid. "Office hours are canceled. Please leave." As I said this, Cliff stepped out of Mary's office. We made eye contact. Alex and Holly didn't budge. I put the key in the lock, opened my door, and quickly closed it behind me. I couldn't stop my body from shivering.

"What's going on out there?" Dan asked, sounding worried.

There was a knock on the door. And then another.

"Please leave," I could hear Cliff say. "It's time for you to leave now."

Several seconds later, a knock. "Raj, it's me."

I opened the door and Cliff came in. Inviting him into my office, empty of books and any sign of a lifetime spent learning, made me feel pathetic.

"Cliff, I need some help," I said.

"Dan, can you get a glass of water?" Cliff said.

Dan left the office and came back with a small water bottle. I drank it quickly.

"I'll be right back," I said. Without waiting for a response, I left my office and went to the bathroom down the hall, stepped into a stall, and locked it. I checked my jeans. I had never been so glad in my entire life for the glorious deep blue of new 501s. I placed my hand on my groin and felt the wet spot again. It was just a little, but I had lost control right before I started ripping down the flyers. I straightened myself up, stepped out of the stall, washed my hands, and went back to my office.

"What happened?" Cliff asked.

"A group of students were waiting for me when I finished class today, gathered for a protest."

"Protesting what?" Cliff asked.

"Me. They say I hate white people and Western culture. There must have been, I don't know, fifty of them? A hundred? They were fine at first, but then they got aggressive. I may have lost my temper for a moment." I tried remembering as clearly as I could exactly what I had said. "I feel embarrassed about the whole thing." But it wasn't just embarrassment that I felt. Sadness was now working its way through and settling into my body. It was the sadness of having openly admitted what I thought I'd done a pretty decent job of keeping enclosed.

Respect me. At some point, I'd been on an upward trajectory with my job. Not a rising star, but someone with a little shine. But that was all gone. And as the years went by, and I walked around the campus unnoticed, I had lost some sense of myself. And my sense of self-respect. I hadn't realized how deeply I felt that.

"Are you all right?" Cliff asked.

"I don't know," I said. It was hard to keep my thoughts straight. "But I have to prep for my afternoon classes."

"We'll figure out your classes," Cliff said. "This is unaccept-able. Dan just told me about the flyer downstairs."

"They're also up near my classroom."

"You're going home," Cliff said.

"I'll teach your classes," Dan said. "I'll take care of it. You go."

I wanted to thank him, but all I could muster was half a smile. This serious, responsible Dan scared me.

"Everyone simply needs to cool down," Cliff said.

"From the look of it, I don't think anyone is cooling down," I said. "What's going on, Cliff? I just want to teach my classes. Do my job. I'm a very small cog in this machine."

"I know," Cliff said. "I know. Let me call the dean right now. This is ridiculous. I'll be right back."

He opened the door.

"Does he have time to see us now?" I could hear Alex say.

In a raised voice, Cliff said, "If the two of you don't leave this department immediately, I'm going to call the campus po-lice and have you both arrested."

"This is a public university and this is a public space," Holly said. "We have a right to be here."

Dan went and closed the office door. "You want me to get us some food?"

"I can't eat," I said. "This is bad, Dan."

"Yeah, it is," Dan said, sounding genuinely concerned.

"Can't you just lie?" I asked. All I wanted was for Dan to make light of the moment.

"It's going to be perfectly fine," he said with a forced smile.

"I'm sure parents are calling the dean right now, complaining about what I'm teaching their kids. That fucking video. The judgment has already been made. I'm going to be the scapegoat for everything people hate about liberals and colleges and professors." If they needed a cliché to go after, wasn't Josh Morton the better choice? "This is a shitty job with too much teaching and no power. But I need this shitty job. I can't lose it."

"You're not going to," Dan said, trying hard to sound reassuring. "Let's just see how this goes. And the silver lining: you're done teaching for the week. It's already the weekend for you."

"Does this mean I don't have to grade the one hundred essays sitting on my desk at home?"

"I give you permission to toss them in the garbage."

"Are you sure you want to teach my classes? I can cancel them."

"It gives me something to do. I can't sit here for the rest of the day."

I took out two documentaries from my desk drawer. "Show these. I save them up for a rainy day when I'm totally sick of teaching."

"Which one for which class?"

"It doesn't matter."

"I'll take care of it."

There was a knock on the door, and then Cliff walked in. "I've left a message with the dean. But if you're ready to go, I can walk you to your car. Maybe we can get some lunch if you'd like." He picked up my bag. "Come on."

I was expecting Alex and Holly to be waiting still, but the hallway was empty. We went down the elevator. As soon as we stepped out, we heard the loud buzz of conversation. Perhaps a quarter of the students who'd protested in front of my class were now seated in an orderly circle on the floor. When they saw me, they all stopped talking. Several of them had lit candles. Whereas before they seemed angry, now they were subdued and purposeful. They were holding some of the same signs, but Alex and Holly had a new one: *If Gandhi Could Do It, So Can We. #HungerforRespect.*

Holly yelled out loud, for my sake and theirs: "We won't eat until that man is gone from this university!"

I couldn't believe it. I'd assumed some planning had gone into the protest in front of my class, but now I realized something much larger and more organized was afoot. These students had gotten together and planned a big, loud protest as the setup for a more strategic strike to get rid of me. I didn't think I was worth the trouble.

I started smiling.

"What's so funny?" Alex asked. "Does our hunger make you laugh?"

"Not at all," I said. "I'm just happy some of you were listening during my classes."

"Gandhi belongs to us as much as you," Alex said.

"You're absolutely right. That's the smartest thing I've heard in a long while. And please, you can use him all you like. But remember that he was a man of extremes who held his convictions very tight."

"We're not in class," Alex said. "We don't have to listen to your bullshit." At that, he turned to Cliff: "It's a disgrace that you've employed this man. We demand you fire him right now. Do the right thing."

Cliff didn't bother to answer. We walked out.

"We're going to need some help here," Cliff said once we were outside. "This is a fine act of thuggery."

"At least now we know their demands." I wanted to make a demand of my own: to rewind the week to Sunday morning so that I could start all over. "Am I going to be all right?"

Cliff was perplexed. Was I asking about my emotional, psychological state? If so, he was ill equipped to help me with that.

"I mean, is my job going to be OK?"

At this, Cliff's face perked up, as if I had asked him how Hegel fits into modern intellectual history.

"Of course your job is going to be OK. By the time you come back to your classes next Monday, this will all be in the past tense."

Cliff was not a cheerleader about anything. His tone was always calm and even-keeled. But I got the distinct sense that he was trying to wish a reality into existence by visualizing his desired outcome.

"I think I'm just going to head home," I said. "Can we take a rain check on the lunch?"

"Of course. Take it easy for the rest of the week. I'll be in touch as soon as I hear from the dean."

I walked to my car and sat inside for a few minutes, staring out the windshield. As I was about to drive off, I saw Robert, about fifty yards away, watching me. Had he been there all along? There was something menacing about him, but there was also something in his empty eyes that reminded me of another young man his age whom I had met years earlier, while trying to immerse myself in a clash of two seemingly different cultures.

In the early aughts, I had landed in Ahmedabad for a year of dissertation fieldwork. I was born in the city and had spent my first eight summers there before we emigrated. In the years since, I had remembered those summers through soft evening light. My father's father—a successful attorney, driven by childhood poverty, his reputation built on smart lawyering and the six months he'd spent as a political prisoner in a British jail—had an enormous rambling house, and in the summer it would be filled with roughly fifteen cousins and their parents. There were green parrots and brazen monkeys in the trees surrounding the house, talent shows on Sunday evenings, cricket matches in the gully outside, and when the heat was blazing, we would all sleep on the rooftop terrace, awakening to a cool morning breeze and peacocks perched on the ledge. If bad things were happening, in the world or in the house, I was not privy to them.

As I got older, I intellectualized the city, seeing it as a cultural hotbed that had been entirely overlooked. Gandhi had spent much of his adult life there, using it as his base for the final decades of his life. Local industry was dominated by the Sarabhais, an old family that had started in textiles and moved on to manufacturing pharmaceuticals, dyes, and pigments. Unlike Bombay and Calcutta, Ahmedabad had no colonial architecture, and both Louis Kahn and Le Corbusier had designed major buildings there. Their love of concrete had trickled down into the design of single-family homes throughout the city. In the mid-1950s, Charles and Ray Eames had visited as Nehru's guests and helped set up India's first design school. One of the Sarabhai heirs had traveled to New York, met John Cage, and they'd talked Indian music and philosophy. Drawing on that exchange, Cage concluded that silence was the best way to out-Stravinsky Stravinsky. Decades of rich modern history, and all the while, hostility between the city's Hindus and Muslims had simmered, but had never overwhelmed the place as it had elsewhere in India.

When I had originally planned my fieldwork, I envisioned writing an ethnography of the city. Bombay got all the glamour love, Delhi the historic love, and Calcutta the intellectual love. No one ever talked about Ahmedabad. I would call my dissertation *The Life of an Unknown Indian City*.

But in February 2002, roughly six months before I was set to arrive, the city convulsed in rioting. A train carrying Hindu passengers returning from a pilgrimage had been set on fire, killing nearly sixty people. The moment had triggered violence across the state of Gujarat, particularly in Ahmedabad. Muslims had killed Hindus on the train, and now Hindus killed Muslims on the streets, both groups pointing back to hundreds of years of mistreatment by the other. The stories of rape, of women being sliced up with dull knives, and of families being burned alive were too much to take, because of the brutal acts themselves, but also because these were *my* people engaging in acts of violence and trying to justify them by saying that they had been victims of Muslim violence for too long. If my family had never moved to America, and I had grown up in Ahmedabad, would I have been right there in the middle of it? I'd like to think that I'd have condemned it. But who knows? By the time I arrived, my research had transformed; now I planned to write a requiem: *The Life and Death of an Unknown Indian City.*

I'd already made my return-to-my-roots trip in college. I took a lot of moody pictures of old Ambassador cars, insisted on eating street food, and visited with cousins who had moved on from the lives I'd thought they still lived. I earnestly went through my grandfather's dusty bookshelf, bringing back with me his copy of Emerson's *Essays,* Nehru's *The Discovery of India*, and a tattered three-volume set of *Capital.* I liked the idea of my grandfather as an exceptionally well-paid Marxist.

On this trip, I was all business, wanting to maintain a scholarly distance from everything and everybody. I was going to figure out what had caused the death of the city I loved. I wanted to develop an unsentimental view of the place. By talking to Hindus and Muslims—poor ones, rich ones, and those in the middle—I wanted to determine how they could live side by side for so long and then turn on their neighbors with such swift anger and violence.

For the first several days after I arrived, I stayed with my father's friend from childhood. He was a very successful surgeon whose house had more servants than occupants. He couldn't understand what an anthropologist did, and he became obsessed, during mealtimes, with asking me how much money I would earn at the peak of my career. It was his only yardstick for what I would become.

When I was ready for a place of my own, he insisted I stay in an apartment he owned. I wanted to refuse the cook and the housecleaner who came with it, but I didn't; ultimately, I liked the convenience. "It's very safe," he kept saying. "The whole building is Hindu. Don't worry about what happened in February. It was just a few bad boys." He also put me in touch with people all over the city I could talk to. After two months of fumbling around, doing interviews that made no real sense to me, I was ready for a break. Eva was flying in. I was going to pick her up at the airport, and from there we'd take the next flight to Jaipur, far from the leering eyes of my neighbors, who would surely have something to say about the fact that we weren't married. From Jaipur, we'd start an extended vacation through northern India, then head down to Goa for Christmas on the beach.

But before I picked her up, I had to do one more interview. I had been trying to arrange a meeting with this particular man for a while, but he'd been hard to pin down. Anand Mehta was a local official, and my father's friend had set it up, insisting that I needed to speak to him if I wanted to understand what had happened in Ahmedabad over the past decade. We agreed to meet in the restaurant at the Holiday Inn; it was one of the better hotels in town. I often went there in the afternoons, to get away from the heat, have a pot of tea, and transcribe my notes from the day into my laptop.

I had expected someone older, but the man who walked in was in his early thirties and dressed in a way that suggested he had the means to keep the difficulties of Third World living at bay. He walked in without much fanfare, but the reactions of the hotel staff made clear that they recognized him as a man of import. He arrived with a young man who couldn't have been older than twenty-one, who stood to the side while we talked.

"It's so nice to meet you," Anand said, sitting down. "What will you have?"

"I just ordered us a pot of tea."

"Perfect."

He placed his cell phone on the table. It was much fancier than mine.

"Were you born in the States, Raj?"

"I was born here in Ahmedabad, but we lived in Bombay," I said. "We came here in the summers. My family moved to the States when I was eight. I live in New York now."

"Good," Anand said. "Good. So we can actually talk. Like people who understand one another."

The tea arrived, and I noted that the teacups were more delicate than usual.

"How's Zabar's?" Anand asked.

"You know it?"

"I did an LLM at Columbia."

This eased some of the tension that gripped my body. There was often a divide between the people I was interviewing and me. They saw me as irreversibly American, and I couldn't con-

vince them — through a bit of Gujarati here and a nod of understanding there — that I was closer to them than they assumed. But Anand was different. He knew my world and I
knew his. Maybe after all this time, I had finally found someone who would speak to me honestly.

"Zabar's is still great. It's turned me into a fan of all kinds
of fish."

"We're not so different from the Jews, especially when it
comes to our relations with Muslims," Anand said. "But I can't
understand their love of fish. And pastrami. What exactly is
pastrami?"

I wasn't sure if it was a rhetorical question or not. "I don't
exactly know, but it sure is tasty."

Anand's face tightened, as if I had betrayed my Hinduness
through beef consumption. His disapproval reminded me that
I wasn't here to have a friendly conversation. I took out my
digital recorder, placed it between us, and turned it on.

"Maybe we should start. I'm sure you're busy." I explained
a little of what I was doing and why I wanted to talk to him.

"You want to know what's happened to Ahmedabad? That's
both a complicated question and a fairly simple one. You spent
time here when you were young, correct?"

"Yes, the summers. With my grandparents."

"I'm sure you remember this as a sweet, gentle place. My
favorite thing to do when I was growing up was to go to the
night market at Law Garden. We'd eat and have ice cream afterward and run around. Everything felt safe. Some vendors
were Muslim. And some customers. But mostly, we all kept to
ourselves. They lived in one part of town, we lived in another.

But then something happened. Our lives began overlapping. We were told that we had to live in the same neighborhoods, to get along, even though we never had before. So now, the city is going through a natural change, something all cities go through. We're returning back to our normal, separate lives."

He spoke with the confidence of someone who could create neat, comforting narratives out of all sorts of conflicting data.

"But does this so-called natural change always occur with so much violence?" I asked.

"The violence was unfortunate," Anand said, taking a sip of his tea. "But we know where to lay the blame for that."

There was no change in his manner when he said this. It was as if he were talking about his favorite bagel spread at Zabar's. He was laying the blame for all the violence that had occurred in February at the feet of the Muslims.

"Do you think there is blame on both sides?" I asked. I opened my notebook. "According to some accounts, there were nearly eight hundred Muslim dead compared to two hundred fifty Hindus."

"No," he said. "Just one side is to blame. It's always been one side. How is it that a majority Hindu city like this is named after a Muslim ruler? Is that fair? We've been welcoming for centuries. But I think our patience finally has run out. Those Hindus on the train were coming home from pilgrimage. They were happy in their faith. Do you know what it's like to be trapped in a burning train compartment? If you want numbers, I've got numbers for you. Long-term numbers tallied over many centuries." Anand stopped and held my gaze. "They deserved everything they got. And more."

Anand was spewing pure gold. I was already thinking about using him as the opening vignette for my introduction. The Columbia University–trained fascist. As hard as it was to sit and listen, I desperately wanted him to keep talking.

"Do you agree?" Anand asked.

Recently, I had watched Indian political and public life harden into something ugly. And it was always jarring to return, to see family and friends, and people who looked and seemed so familiar, standing on the wrong side of things. A cousin I had grown up with had told me that at the height of the rioting, he had purchased a machete, which he'd used to patrol the streets near his house at night. "If one came at me, I wasn't going to stop and have a discussion," he'd said.

Anand could easily have been a boy I'd known as a child, playing cricket together in the hot afternoons. Something about his slickness made me sick. It wouldn't have surprised me if he had personally lit the fires that had burned so many alive, though I knew he'd have someone else to do his dirty work. He would go far in politics.

"I'm trying to get as many views on this as possible," I said. Telling him I disagreed with him would have made me feel better, but it wouldn't have helped me do my job.

"I know what I must sound like to you," Anand said. "But I'm simply trying to keep my children from being subjected to the kind of fear and uncertainty I've had to endure. I want them to feel safe when they're walking to and from school. They shouldn't have to be afraid."

I took a sip of tea and subtly checked the recorder, hoping it was still on.

"Did you get what you needed?"

"Definitely. This has been very helpful. If you have the time, I'd love to hear more. This is a great help in understanding what's been happening here, and how the public feels about it."

"I could talk for hours," Anand said. "But I think I've been fairly clear. We've experimented with living together. That experiment failed. Now it's time to move on to something new. Or something old, as the case may be."

I glanced at my watch.

"Are you late for something?" Anand asked.

"No," I said. "I have to leave for the airport in half an hour to pick up a friend."

"A friend?"

If he didn't approve of me eating pastrami, he was certainly going to take issue with the fact that Eva was white and American and we were unmarried.

"Yes, someone from back home."

"What time does he land?"

"At five."

"Babu," Anand said to the young man who had been waiting in the wings. "Take this gentleman to the airport after we're done with our tea. And if his friend has any trouble getting through customs, please help him."

He spoke to Babu in rapid-fire Gujarati, while he had talked to me in perfect English.

"No, no," I said, "I'll take a taxi. I need to stop by my apartment first to pick up a few things."

"I have some work I need to take care of here. Babu will take you wherever you like. Just tell him."

I reluctantly agreed. It would be a relief not to feel that yet another taxi driver was overcharging me.

"Are we finished?" Anand asked.

Before I could answer, he took a sip of his tea and checked his phone. It had buzzed a few times during our conversation. He didn't seem interested in me anymore.

"I don't want to be rude, but I have to make a call," Anand said, holding up his phone.

"I have plenty for now. And I should probably get going in case there's traffic."

I got up and reached into my pocket. Anand just shook his head.

"You have my mobile. Call me anytime you need anything while you're here. Doctorji is an old friend. He does all our work." Anand pointed to his belly. "He took out my appendix. I would do anything for him."

"I'll be in touch," I said.

A few minutes later I was riding to my apartment in Anand's clean and very new Mercedes sedan. I sat in the back seat as Babu maneuvered through the streets.

"So you work for Anand?" I asked in Gujarati.

Babu nodded and looked back at me through the rearview mirror. "Yes, sir."

"What do you do?"

It was an innocuous question. "I'm his driver, sir," he said. I hadn't noticed much about him before, but now, through the mirror, I could see that his cheeks were hollowed out, his eyes dim.

"How long have you been doing that?"

"Many years. Anandji has been very generous to me and my family. I don't know where we would be without him. I support my whole family with this job."

He was very proud of this fact.

"So what does Anand do?" I asked, curious about what Babu knew of his boss's dealings. Anand's official title was Sub-Minister of Law, but I didn't understand what exactly that meant.

"He's an important man," Babu said. "A government minister."

"A minister of what?"

"I don't know, sir. Is this the right way to the apartment?"

"Yes," I said.

When we reached my apartment, I picked up my packed suitcase and we continued on to the airport.

"So, were you with Anand during the riots?"

I saw him through the rearview mirror, but his concentration purposefully remained on the road ahead. Maybe I was sensing something that wasn't there, but I got the distinct impression that Babu had seen things he wished he hadn't. A foot soldier in a dirty war.

He didn't answer my question.

As we neared the airport, I said, "I'll be fine. You can go once we get there." I felt weird enough having accepted this favor from Anand, as if doing so were excusing his horrific views.

"No, I have to stay."

"Just tell Anand that you dropped me off safely."

He drove the car right to the main entrance of the terminal. Despite the signs, he parked, got out, and opened the door for me. People turned to stare. I felt like a movie star.

By the time we got inside, Eva was already there waiting, her suitcase next to her. She looked beautiful despite the exhaustion of traveling halfway across the world. I hadn't seen her for two months, and that first glimpse made me realize just how much I had missed her. I turned to Babu and gave him a thumbs-up. He saw Eva, and for the first time since we met, he gave me the slightest hint of a smile. As I walked away, he didn't move.

"I'm so glad to see you," I said to Eva, walking up to her, grabbing hold of her hand. The warmth felt nourishing.

"The flight came in early and I made it through customs and baggage claim without a problem."

"Let's go find our flight and get out of here."

"Who's that man?" Eva asked. "He looks like he's waiting for you."

I turned around and saw Babu still there. I motioned him over, and as he tentatively walked toward us, I thought about how best to introduce Eva.

"Babu, I want you to meet my wife," I said in Gujarati.

He smiled, and without missing a beat, so did Eva. He began talking to her in a mix of Gujarati and Hindi. He was welcoming her back to India and explaining that things had changed since she left. I couldn't believe it. With her olive skin and brown hair, Eva looked vaguely ethnic. But still. I'd spent two months trying to convince people that I was Indian, and they had looked at me skeptically every time.

"We have to catch a flight," I finally said.

Babu stopped and waved to us.

We both said goodbye and walked toward the departure gates.

"What was that?" Eva asked.

"I'm not entirely sure. He may think you're my *Indian* wife."

"Excellent," Eva said. "The Indian part." She smiled at me sheepishly. I had missed her terribly.

"I wonder if there's an Indian Vegas for us to visit," I said.

Babu and Robert seemed like similar young men: sorrowful faces, unsure and scared of what they'd already seen and what their lives were going to become. I didn't know Robert at all, but I got the sense that his affiliation with Alex and Holly was by happenstance. When I'd seen them together earlier, Robert had been on the outskirts of the group. And the grievances Alex and Holly had been shouting about didn't match up with what Robert had said to me in my office.

My one big regret from that entire year of fieldwork was that I had not spoken to Babu more, that afternoon in the car and maybe sometime after. I should have probed and asked him how he felt about the violence in Ahmedabad. Had he participated in it? But I was scared for him and didn't want to compromise his relationship with Anand. I knew that Anand would have fired Babu on the spot if he'd said anything that contradicted his boss. Still, when I was back in New York the following year, struggling to write my dissertation, trying to home in on a thesis that got Ahmedabad from the magic of my childhood to the gruesome killings that had changed the city, I kept thinking that Babu held the key. I didn't think that men like Babu — poor men, with few options for upward mobility — hated their neighbors because they were a different religion. It seemed far more likely that it was because people like Anand had convinced them that they were poor because Muslims had taken the livelihoods that rightfully belonged to them.

I brought together my findings, worked through my argument, and eventually finished my dissertation. And yet, I'd always had this nagging feeling that I hadn't gotten to the heart of the questions I set out to ask. Thinking about Babu now and trying to figure out what was going on with Robert, I was starting to make some of the connections I hadn't made then. Maybe this is why my career had stalled. I had come up with some decent explanations for why Ahmedabad had been engulfed in flames — the religious tensions, the economic uncertainty, and the politicians who'd turned a blind eye and let hundreds die. But I'd not been able to figure out how this local story connected to something bigger. Now, strangely, the protesters and Robert were helping me get there. I didn't want to get too far ahead of myself, but how far were we from our own moment of communal violence?

Sitting in the car, I thought about the rest of that trip, the time I'd spent traveling with Eva. We'd started by splurging on a hotel in Jaipur that had once been a castle. Then we rode camels in the desert near Jaisalmer. In Goa, we bought some hash from an Israeli and watched a sun that never quite set. Eva and I were good travelers together because neither of us was interested in seeing the sights. We liked meandering through the days, eating dinner at five one night and nine the next. And I particularly appreciated that she never asked me questions that forced me to give answers I couldn't give. Why was there so much poverty in India alongside so much wealth? How could anyone just ignore the beggars? What's up with the cows?

I asked her to marry me on a beach in Goa.

I was by no means the first member of the broader Bhatt clan to marry a non-Indian, and as such, my family's interest in tradition had greatly waned. Still, I insisted on a full Indian wedding.

"Don't you want one of those church weddings?" my father asked when I called them with the news. "I've vowed never to go to another Indian wedding, and it would be bad form if I didn't come to yours."

In hindsight, I probably wanted an Indian wedding so badly because I thought that small bit of tradition and ritual might soften the acute sense of loss I felt about the city of my perfect childhood summers. And I wanted to replicate a photo from my parents' wedding reception where my mother is wearing a sari and my father is wearing a suit, both with enormous garlands around their necks. My father had just returned from a trip to America, and that suit was a signal of where he had been and, from this vantage, a sign of where he was headed. For me, the photo has always represented their youth, before good and bad decisions aged them.

"She doesn't want to wear a sari," I said to my parents when Eva and I first visited them after getting engaged.

Eva shot me a pleading look. "I didn't say that."

"Let me rephrase. She doesn't want to be one of those white women in a sari."

"Well," my mom said, leaning in closer to Eva, "if she wants to wear one, she'll wear it well. And she'll certainly look better than you did in a tuxedo. Remember when you went to the prom? People must have thought you were a waiter."

Unlike my father, my mother had been excited to put together an Indian wedding. When my two sisters had gotten married, my mother had treated the whole thing as a utilitarian affair: she needed to get her daughters married. But now, with their lives feeling a little more settled in America, she relished taking her future daughter-in-law shopping for clothes and jewelry. And of course, I was the lone son.

"But remember," my father had said, "it doesn't have to be so long. There is nothing in any religious book that says how long the wedding needs to be. Tradition is simply a guideline, a suggestion. And I would suggest something short and sweet."

In the photo that now sits on the mantel above the fireplace, there is Eva's immediate family and mine, with the two of us in the middle. I am wearing my bespoke Indian salwar suit, which I had bought while I was in India, and Eva is wearing a deep orange wedding dress, the color a match for the sari she'd worn during the full, unshortened ceremony. Both of us have garlands of flowers around our necks and huge smiles on our faces.

I was thinking about the smell of those flowers as I started the car, backed out, and drove away. I had a few hours to kill before I met Eva at the boys' school for a meeting with the principal to talk about Neel's drawing. I decided to take a walk on the beach. The day had only gotten warmer — the ocean breeze would be welcome.

We went to the beach all the time, but I seldom went by myself. As much as I enjoyed the water, I didn't like being at the beach all that much. The sand got everywhere, and while I found the salt water cleansing, I was uncomfortable with the depth of the ocean. But today a change of scenery seemed like just the thing.

I drove to one of the more secluded beaches in town, parked my car, and began walking on the sand. It was a Wednesday afternoon, and besides a few sunbathers here and there, the place was empty. I found a spot at the point, in the shade of secluded cliffs and an overhanging tree. I took off my shoes and sat down, leaning against a rock. The ocean was calm and glassy, and for a few minutes I gazed out at it, trying my hardest to empty my mind of every possible thought. I had purposely left my phone in the car.

I lay down on the sand and closed my eyes; the sound of the crashing waves suddenly became louder. When I opened them, I saw a small crew of sandpipers digging their long beaks into the wet sand, searching for food. I closed my eyes again and felt sleepy. I couldn't remember the last time I'd napped in the middle of the day. What did it matter now? I didn't have to be at the school for a while. I let myself drift off.

Sometime later, my shaded spot had moved into the sun and I felt hot and itchy in my jeans and half-sleeve shirt. My forehead was sweaty. I checked my watch. Somehow, well over an hour had passed.

The beach was still empty. Out in the water, two glistening gray bodies eased themselves out of the waves and back under. The dolphins were much closer to shore than I had seen before. I watched them come out again; they seemed to be swimming away, but then, when they appeared a third time, they were back to where they'd started. They were circling, beckoning me. I decided it must be a sign.

I looked down the beach; no one was there. I took off my shirt, then my pants and boxers. I didn't have a towel. I left the clothes in a neat pile and ran toward the ocean. If I'd had on swim trunks, I would have waded gradually into the cool water, but doing without, I just ran straight in. I went under, swam several yards, then surfaced, my lips tingling from the salt. Farther out, I saw the fins emerge from the water again.

I didn't know if there was danger in getting too close to them, but I swam out about fifty yards, the farthest I had ever been. Below me, the ocean floor might have been fifty or sixty feet deep. I treaded water. The dolphins reemerged, now much farther out. I turned around, and by the time I made it back to where I could stand, I was exhausted. I started to get out, the black hair on my body wet and clean, and noticed two women walking toward me, down the beach. They were well into their seventies, I guessed, but they were moving swiftly. For a second I considered staying put until they passed, but I didn't even break my stride. I saw them do a double take, clearly noticing me emerging fresh from the froth of the ocean, just as I'd emerged from my mother's belly.

Perhaps at some other point in my life — at some other point in the week — I might have picked up the pace and run to my clothes. I didn't want to seem like a creep. But as the week had slowly chipped away at me, the idea of stripping down didn't seem so strange. I walked out of the water, and as I passed in front of the women, I turned to them. I smiled and they smiled back. I figured it'd be a good dinner party story for them — they'd always remember the man who emerged naked from the sea on a warm Wednesday afternoon.

I used my boxers to dry myself off, and put on my jeans and my shirt. I removed as much sand from my feet as possible before putting on my socks and shoes, and I ran my fingers through my hair to comb it.

When I got back to the car, there was a text from Eva. "Are you close?" She had sent it at 2:45, which is when I was supposed to have arrived at the school. It was now 2:55. I drove over as quickly as I could, but by the time I got there and parked, Eva was waiting for me outside.

"I'm so sorry," I said. "I lost track of time. What happened?"

She reached over and removed some sand from my ear. "Did you go swimming?" she asked, perplexed.

There were wet spots on my shirt.

"I did." She had a neutral look on her face; I had no way of guessing how the meeting had gone. "What happened?"

"It's fine. He's not suspended. I'm actually glad you weren't there. You would have lost your shit. I tried to keep the peace so they wouldn't suspend him. That would have set us back weeks, if not months."

"I'm glad you did. Does he have to do anything?"

"No. We just need to have a conversation with him about appropriate behavior."

I was relieved that at least one of the week's disasters had been averted.

"God, I hate that man," Eva said. "He's constantly quoting other people; I never know when he's speaking for himself. I swear, if he quotes Martin Luther King at me one more time, I'm going to scream."

I really liked it when Eva let the hate fly.

"Didn't you teach this afternoon?" she asked, turning back to my wet shirt. "Why were you at the beach?"

I was about to explain when I saw Suzanne walking toward us. With all her PTA duties, she was at the school often. "I'll tell you once we're done with this awkward conversation," I whispered.

"Hey, you two," Suzanne said, her eyes studiously staying on Eva, not me. "Everything OK?"

"Fine," Eva said. "Fine."

I could see that she wanted to keep walking.

"I heard Neel might have had some trouble. Please let me know if I can help in any way."

"Neel is a bright kid," Eva said. "He gets bored in class waiting for everyone else to catch up."

Though her tone didn't reveal it, I knew Eva was pushing back at whatever Suzanne was not saying in her offer to help.

"He certainly is," Suzanne said. "I've been in the class. He's always done with his work well before any of the other kids. My son included. The school needs to do a better job of keeping him engaged."

This generosity loosened Eva up a bit. It loosened me up too.

"What did the note say?" Suzanne asked. "I know I shouldn't ask, but I've been dying to know. Jackson said the teacher took something away from him."

"It's sitting in the principal's office," Eva said. "He insisted on keeping it. I'm sure he'll let you see it."

"No, no," Suzanne said. "I'm sorry I even asked." She finally looked at me. "Leslie told me you two had a chance to talk."

"Sounds like there are a lot of conversations happening all around," I said.

"I just wanted to know what Leslie was thinking in relation to all this," Suzanne said. "That's it."

"And what's her take?"

"I don't know," Suzanne said. "What I do know is that Mark is coming to the meeting this Friday. I told him not to, but he's insisting. And he hasn't been shy about telling others what happened. It's the most involved he's ever been at the TC. He seems to be developing a diversity curriculum all on his own. He sends us more and more articles and books to read every day. I wonder if he's read them all himself."

I wondered what books Mark wanted them all to read. *The Fire Next Time*? *Beloved*? Maybe my old favorite, *Invisible Man*. I'm sure he'd suggested smart books—he could do his research like anyone else—but the irony of his newfound role as great educator on the long history of American racism was not lost on me. I hoped that was true for the rest of the committee too.

"Am I still invited to the meeting?" I asked.

"Of course. You're a member of the committee. He's not."

"I'm very interested in hearing what Mark has to say."

Without saying anything else, Eva started walking away, and I followed. I looked back at Suzanne for the slightest second; she seemed a little hurt at being abandoned without warning.

"Why do I hate that woman so much?" Eva asked, her voice almost loud enough for Suzanne to hear.

"I don't know," I said. "Maybe she means well but doesn't know how to say it. I can't figure her out."

"When did you see Leslie?"

"After my match last night." I wondered if she'd been a little tense with me because things had been tense between her and Eva. "Are you two having some kind of fight?"

Eva shook her head. "I'm taking a small break from her. We're just in different places right now. Or maybe we've always been in different places. She likes not working, and spending Tim's money. I like my job and what we do in the world — and I don't have that much money to spend. I don't know. It may end up being a long break."

School wouldn't be out for another half an hour. We took a walk down the street to get a cup of tea.

"I went to the dermatologist," I said as we walked.

"And?"

"And he was worried about that mole on my heel."

"When did all this happen?"

"Yesterday."

"Jesus. You need to tell me these things."

"I was going to, but I didn't want to worry you. What if it's bad?"

"It won't be," Eva said.

Why did everyone have so much false confidence in my life except me?

"You don't know that."

"I don't. But why don't we wait to worry about it until we have something to worry about."

"I don't know how to do that."

"When are you supposed to hear back?"

"Early next week. I have no idea why it takes that long."

We went into the coffee shop and got iced teas. As I was putting sugar in mine, I turned to Eva. "I'm a little scared."

"I know," she said, grabbing hold of my hand. She'd had a few biopsies herself.

"Not just that." I told her about the protest and my screaming. Just thinking about it made me feel embarrassed all over again for losing my composure. "I went to the beach after to wash off the muck."

"This is insane," she said, sounding both incredulous and concerned. "Are you OK?"

"I'm fine. I just want the week to be over."

She got back in line, bought two huge chocolate chip cookies, and we went to pick up the kids. Arun came running toward us; Neel was more circumspect.

"You're both here and we get cookies?" Arun asked, sounding confused as he took an enormous bite.

"What did they say?" Neel asked.

Eva and I looked at each other.

"Everything is fine," she said. "Let's just not draw in class for a while, OK?"

"Fine." Neel gave us a sly little smile.

Eva drove the boys to the TC, and I followed in my car. When we got there, it was mostly empty. Eva had parked near the bottom courts, and I parked next to her. The kids had already gotten out and run off with their cookies to play Ping-Pong. Eva was rummaging in the back of her car for swim things. She kept a swim bag there — with suits for all of us, towels, and a few bags of almonds — for unplanned visits like this.

She walked on ahead to the pool. I stopped to watch a doubles match. Four A-level guys. The ball made a crisp, clean sound as it popped off their racquets. All four players were constantly moving their feet, even when the ball wasn't coming toward them. I badly wanted to be invited to a game like this. The TC was filled with all sorts of different, parallel, hidden social hierarchies and cliques. The old families, the new ones, the ultrarich, the ones with two working parents, the out-of-work parents who pretended they weren't, the Christians, the liberals, and on and on. It was one large, shifting flow chart of alliances that everyone could see but no one could fully map. But I'd always assumed that play on the court transcended this. If you were good and you weren't an enormous dick, you got invited to the better matches. Even if you were a dick, but you had game, you still played. There were rules within the matches, but also rules on how the matches got set up. If you were lower on the hierarchy, you didn't insist on punching above your weight.

But as I watched the match, and all of them pretended I wasn't there, I questioned whether good play could take care of everything. Between what had happened at the pool the night before and what Suzanne had said, I was sure that Mark had been in touch with various club members and instructed them to shun me, that if enough of them did, maybe I would get the hint and realize that the TC was not a place where I was welcome anymore.

The kids were already swimming when I walked into the pool area. Usually Neel was up in Arun's grill, but now they were gliding around each other gracefully. I changed and got in with them while Eva swam some laps. I loved watching her swim.

"One lap?" I asked.

"Sure," Eva said.

We raced the length of the pool. I swam as hard as I possibly could, but she was already done and waiting to do another when I got to the end. She always beat me.

I took turns raising Neel and Arun over my head and throwing them toward the deep end. After a while of that, we warmed up in the hot tub and waited for the pizza we'd ordered to be delivered. We got out to eat, then went right back into the hot tub. As we were sitting there, the gate opened. Leslie's two girls walked through.

"Do we have time to get out before she gets here?" Eva asked.

I shook my head.

"She's just so smug about her well-behaved girls."

A minute later, Leslie walked through the gate. She saw us and, realizing that we might have noticed her hesitation, came straight over and started talking, as if we'd hung out a few nights earlier for a barbecue and a swim.

"A quick after-dinner dip," Leslie said. Then she lowered her voice. "The girls are driving me absolutely crazy."

Leslie's girls had already jumped into the pool. Neel and Arun joined them.

"Is Tim coming?" Eva asked as Leslie stepped into the hot tub.

"He's traveling for work. I'm not sure I even know where he is. Des Moines. Boise. One of those."

"I haven't seen him here in a while," Eva said.

"Funny, I haven't seen him at home for a while either," Leslie said. "He comes home from these week-long work trips and then gets mad when I need a little break away from the kids. They're depleting me. These lovely girls. I don't know what to do."

I could see that Leslie wanted to talk to Eva.

"I'll go swim with the kids," I said, getting out of the hot tub.

"What was up with chatty Leslie?"

We hadn't had a chance to talk about it since we got home from the TC. The kids had to be put to bed.

"Oh, I don't know. I guess Tim has a new job, and he's gone a lot. And it sounds like maybe he took a pay cut. I'm not sure. Anyway, she seems lonely and a little stressed out. I get it, but when I think about everything we have going on, it's a little hard to empathize."

A few minutes later, we turned off the lights. Eva drifted to sleep quickly. I picked up my phone. I had two new emails from Dan.

The first one's subject line: "Assuming you've seen this?" The body of the email only had a link. I clicked through.

While the story that had come out on Tuesday morning had been on a smaller, lesser-known website, this second one was on a site with a much bigger following called *Mansfield*, named after the editor who had started it. I had graduated into wider cultural relevance, and with that came the sort of exposure that would put my job in still greater jeopardy.

Over the past year, *Mansfield* had grown many, many times over in readership and influence. Jack Mansfield, the young editor who ran it, had graduated from Berkeley with a degree in classics and a pure, uncontainable anger toward the left. He'd gone to Berkeley to please his liberal parents, and during his time there had rejected everything they believed in. He'd built his platform attacking universities, which he thought were dens of intellectual laziness, sexual freedom that oppressed those who were unable to participate, and anti-whiteness. His particular object of ire was tenure. At least in this, I was safe. But, of course, it also meant that I, inherently, was not safe.

As the editor's star power had risen, he'd been interviewed by the *New York Times*, where he'd said proudly, "When we put our fucking gun sights on you, your life is ruined." He understood that a video clip could be judge, jury, and executioner all in one, no matter its veracity. Where *Freedom Now*, the first site I'd appeared on, dog-whistled, *Mansfield* was explicit in its distaste for most anyone with a background distinct from its founder's. One story asserted that the death penalty acted as a deterrent to crime in black communities; another argued for the importance of a "Museum of White American History and Culture," to be built on the National Mall.

The link led to a page that didn't have any story, just a video, with the headline "Have Our Universities Finally Gone Nuts?"

I clicked. The video buffered and I appeared on-screen, walking through campus, avoiding eye contact with the students around me. And then I say, "Fuck the Christians." There's a subtitle for this, as if my English isn't clear enough. I stop in front of the bulletin board, tear down the Haji flyers, and scream, "Respect me!" I look out at the students and the camera. I'm crazed, unhinged. And then a message appears on-screen: "This is Professor Raj Bhatt. He has a lot of fancy degrees, which he thinks give him the freedom to say all sorts of nasty, unfounded things about our great United States of America. You're spending your hard-earned money so that your children can get educated. But instead they're being abused, ridiculed. Your children are being radicalized, told to hate themselves and their history. Isn't it time for us to examine what our youth are exposed to day in and day out in the Liberal University Complex?"

I watched the video one more time and turned up the volume a little more. Eva woke up just as I began groveling for respect.

"What is that?" she asked groggily.

I started the video again.

"Holy shit," she said, once it was over.

"I'm fucked, Eva. They spliced all this together. I actually said I don't hate Christians. But it's not going to matter. I tore down those flyers. I look insane."

"You just have to explain to Cliff what they've done. He'll know that they're targeting you."

Eva was describing the world as it should be: Cliff and the dean's office and the university would see that I was being unfairly attacked, and they would stay in my corner, fighting for what was right. But I had a clear sense that, even though the video was doctored, they were not going to be able to defend me. The edges may have been spliced together, but at the center of it, I was still screaming like a madman. I could explain the reasons why, but it was ultimately my responsibility to be the adult in the group.

"I'm sure you're right," I said, and kissed her on the forehead. "Go back to sleep."

A minute later, I could hear her faint snoring.

I opened the second email from Dan. It was another link, this time to a Twitter page with the hashtag #FireDrRaj. There were hundreds of tweets, presumably from the many hundreds of students I had taught in the past, outlining all the things I had said and done that had offended them. "He stares too much #FireDrRaj." "He has a thing for blondes. Ew #FireDrRaj." What would Kim, my former student turned dermatology assistant, write? "He needs to work on his hygiene. Yuck #FireDrRaj." And then there was this one, as if they had peered into my insecure, underpublished heart: "Where's the book? #FireDrRaj."

The scope of the hashtag widened as the tweets went on. Now students from all over the country were using it — anyone who had a gripe against a professor. I had become a proxy for every allegedly bad professor in America.

"I think I'm done," I said, hoping Eva was still awake.

She didn't respond.

I didn't see myself surviving this. Even if the university wanted to defend me, there was going to be too much backlash from parents who didn't want their children in a classroom with me. I had never felt so exposed. Not only was I pretty certain I was about to lose my job, but my cry for respect — which, as ridiculous as it looked in the video, represented my most fervent and private frustrations about my career — was being broadcast for all the world to hear. My deepest insecurities had become public property, something that could be shared among strangers.

I put the phone away and tried to fall asleep, knowing that if I didn't, the next day would be even longer and more miserable than it was already going to be. I don't know how much time passed. Eventually I must have drifted off, but I awoke not long after and saw Eva reading something on her phone. I didn't think she'd taken the video very seriously. Maybe, as she'd fallen back to sleep, she'd finally realized the gravity of the situation.

"What do you think?" I asked.

She was flipping back and forth between stories on her phone. I couldn't see what she was reading. Why had she turned the volume off in the video?

"It's insane, right?"

She turned to me as if she had just realized I was awake. Without saying anything, she showed me her phone so I could see. At first, the details in the photo were unrecognizable. I stared at it for a few more seconds. It was a city street with nearly every building collapsed, looking like it had been carpet-bombed.

"Southern Mexico," she said. "Earthquake. There are already a hundred dead and it only shook two hours ago."

Eva returned to her phone and then she was gone. She would be for the next several days, figuring out how to get the right help down there.

I turned away from her, pushing my face into the pillow. All week, I'd felt like my life was crumbling. Now that an entire region was, in fact, crumbling, in the most devastating way, I felt foolish.

There was little I could do to control what was happening at work. But I knew one thing I could do to make things better elsewhere. Tomorrow morning I would call Bill Brown and put at least one part of this whole thing to rest.

Thursday

"Hɪ, ʀᴀᴊ."

"Twice in one week? I didn't peg you as the phone type."

I was in the kitchen, cleaning up after Eva had left with the kids for school. She wouldn't be back until late into the evening.

"I loathe the telephone," Cliff said. "In fact, I loathe most forms of communication. Except texting, which I now do with my children. I don't think we've ever had a better relationship."

In the near decade I had known Cliff, this was the most he'd ever revealed to me about himself. As little as I knew about him, though, I'd always imagined him to be a caring, present father.

"I wish we could have department meetings via text," Cliff continued. Then he sighed. He had something to say to me that he didn't want to say.

"Is this about my star turn?" I asked.

"I'm afraid so."

"When did you see it?"

"Just now."

"I feel really bad about it, Cliff. You've known me for a long time. You know I never lose my temper like that. But they were pushing and pushing. I should have known one of them would have a camera on. I walked right into the trap." My voice suddenly cracked. I wanted Cliff to rescue me from all this, to say that it was going to be OK.

"Can you come in again this morning? I'm sorry to keep doing this."

"Of course."

"The conference room at ten."

I hung up the phone and wondered why he wanted to meet in the conference room. He had never asked me to do so before. But then again, we'd never needed to. Trying not to think about it too much, I went to my computer and checked in on the dark, ghostly version of myself that continued to appear online. The mob calling for my firing grew with every passing minute. There wasn't much I could do to stop them, it seemed to me; but I knew I had to do something. I had to feel like I was working in some way to fix the problems I was facing. I switched over to my email.

"Dear Bill, if I may. I'm so sorry that I didn't write earlier." I sat for five minutes, trying to decide what to write next. I couldn't find the right words to convey my apology. I wanted to tell him about myself, give him a sense of where I was coming from, without trying to justify my behavior. It was a difficult balance to strike in an email. The nuance of what I wanted to say seemed easiest to communicate in person. I wished I had been brave enough to talk to him when I went to the hospital.

I finished cleaning the kitchen, took a shower, and got dressed in a button-down shirt and a thin, navy-blue corduroy blazer. It wasn't as tailored as Bill Brown's, but I liked how I felt when I put it on. I didn't wear it nearly enough. I was always afraid that I would mess it up, afraid that people would know that I liked wearing the jacket. I hated for people to think I was vain.

The landline rang. For a second I couldn't figure out what the sound was, we so rarely used that phone. I went and picked it up, readying myself to say that we weren't interested. I was hoping it was someone telling me that my computer had been infected, or the IRS demanding that I send them money. I needed an excuse to yell at someone.

"Hello."

Nothing. Usually there was a second or two delay before a marketer came on. We had been getting solicitations for cruises lately. Eva and I were not cruise people, but sailing away sounded pretty good at the moment.

"Hello," I said again. I was about to hang up, but I wanted the pleasure of refusing the solicitation.

"Why do you hate Christians so much?" a deep voice asked.

"What? Who is this?" Throughout the week, the increasing swirl of craziness had remained outside our home. Now the line of safety had been breached, and I felt scared.

"It's a simple question."

"Don't call here again," I said, about to hang up.

"You married a Christian, didn't you? She certainly looks like one. Do you hate her too?"

"Who the hell is this?"

The caller didn't say anything more and a few seconds later hung up. I was in the living room, looking out the window at the blooming yellow roses right outside. There was a sudden bang on the glass and a blur of brown. The phone fell out of my hand. A bird had flown into the window, bounced off, and flittered away. Sometimes the smaller birds didn't survive the impact, but this one seemed to have done fine; my heart was still pushing up against my ribs.

I locked every window and sliding door in the house. But really, how much danger could any of them actually keep out?

When I got to campus, I took a hopeful turn through the parking lot near my office. Sometimes, midmorning, I could get lucky with an orphan spot. And sure enough, there in the corner, under the cover of an enormous tree, I found one. I'm not big on signs, but this I would take. A shaded spot so close to my office? Maybe things would be OK after all.

I entered my building and walked toward the elevators. When I had left campus the day before, the forty-plus group waiting for me after my lecture had dispersed. Now, only four students remained, all sitting on the floor on top of sleeping bags, haggard and exhausted. Alex and Holly, plus another young man and woman. A hunger-strike double date. Alex was surprised when he saw me. Or maybe he was just surprised that I was dressed up.

"Have you been here all night?" I asked. They were there to protest me, to get me fired, but they were still my teenage students, who, if things were different, would be coming to my office hours to talk about how they were struggling to adjust to college, to figure out where they belonged in such a big place. Whatever they thought of me, my instinct was to engage with them. They had wanted to talk yesterday, but their approach had done nothing to open a space for that. Now, with the clarity of a new morning, I wanted to try to work through what specifically troubled them about what I'd said.

"We have," Alex said.

"Go home. Eat something. Get some sleep. And then come by and we can talk. I'll be in my office all day. This has gotten out of hand."

The anger and conviction were gone from Alex's eyes, replaced by fatigue.

"We'll go home—and we'll eat—once you leave this university," Holly said.

"Are you sure?" I asked Alex.

"Yes, I'm sure," he replied, his eyes saying what his mouth wouldn't.

I stepped into the elevator, and as I waited for the doors to close, all four of them stared at me.

"They're in the conference room," Mary said when I knocked on Cliff's door. I'd been hoping Cliff had misspoken.

"They?"

"You'll see," she said, smiling. She seemed to be taking pleasure in all this. I couldn't understand why.

"Mary," I said, feeling ready to voice all of the things I normally would be too embarrassed to say aloud, "do you dislike me?"

She looked genuinely perplexed. "Raj. Why would you think that? I don't dislike you." Then she lowered her voice. "Not any more than any of the other overpaid and underworked members of this department."

"I wish I were overpaid and underworked."

"You come in two days a week. Two days, Raj. That's it."

I hated being lectured by Mary. Despite all the years she had spent working with academics, she still didn't understand that a majority of the work was done outside the office.

"I'm just disappointed that you've never brought me back anything from your fieldwork. Clothes and jewelry from India are my favorites."

"I'll bring you back something next time." An empty promise. I wasn't going to be doing any fieldwork in the near future. "But in the meantime, I know someone in town who makes Indian-inspired jewelry. I'll get you some."

"I think every week should be Staff Appreciation Week." She gave me a wink. "They're waiting for you. Everything is going to be fine. The department needs you."

I was responsible for a large chunk of teaching in the department, so in that she was right. They did need me. But despite my gripes, I also liked teaching here. I needed them as well. And thus my nerves as I walked down the hall.

The conference room, a totem to the long, illustrious history of the department, was dominated by an enormous table with twenty austere wooden chairs around it. One large wall was filled with framed, 8 x 10 photographs of every faculty member who had earned tenure in the department over the four decades since its founding. The first thirty or so portraits were of serious, unsmiling white men, many of them with crew cuts and thick, black-framed glasses. The more recent additions were women and two nonwhite men. On the other large wall were framed covers of the books published by the faculty through the years.

Cliff was seated at one end of the table, along with a woman who taught in the English department. She was in her early fifties and had close-cropped brown hair. Once I had heard her give a talk on *Tristram Shandy* that was funny, incisive, self-deprecating, and ultimately just brilliant. She possessed a rare talent for making the eighteenth century come alive. She had made me want to read the novel, though I never did. She gave me a warm smile when I opened the door.

"Raj, come in," Cliff said.

The two of them had been talking, but their conversation ended abruptly as soon as I appeared.

"Let me introduce you to Cynthia Wood from the English department. She's now the associate dean, and she's in charge of this little issue we have."

I was reaching to close the door when someone came walking in behind me: Mr. Insecurity, with a friendly nod, as if we were old friends.

"Sorry I'm late," Josh said. "Why is parking so hard on this campus? We need a faculty-only lot."

"I'm sure you know Josh Morton," Cliff said, ignoring Josh's entrance. "Josh's new research is on cyber witch-hunts. He got in touch with me the other day and has generously offered his help with all this."

"It's such a pleasure to finally meet you, Raj," Cynthia said. "You know, I happened upon your remarkable essay on second acts long before I knew you were here. God, it was terrific. I'm glad I was done with my second book when I read it. Did you actually write it as an undergraduate?"

My belly felt hollow from regret. For the first time in I don't know how long, someone was giving me a bit of intellectual respect, something I had stopped receiving from my peers and colleagues long ago. "I did. I was so much less self-conscious then. Not worried about what others might think. What I should have written about were the difficulties of finishing the first book."

"Oh," Cynthia said, "you've already written the first book. It's perfectly outlined in that essay. Let's talk after all this is over."

That didn't sound like someone who was getting ready to fire me.

"Well," Josh interjected. He didn't seem like the type of guy who dealt well with not being the center of attention. "I've been following your case online since I heard about it. You don't need me to tell you how bleak it is. These days, we have to be careful about what we say and when."

"Wait," I said. "I want to be clear about something. There are two videos out there. One of me lecturing on Monday, which is a lecture I have been giving for the past decade without a prob- lem. Students have often pointed to that lecture as the best part of my class. And then the other one, of me leaving class yesterday, which I'm guessing is the reason for this meeting today. The first one is real. The second one is completely doctored. I didn't say 'Fuck the Christians,' on or off camera."

"Isn't that your voice?" Josh asked.

For someone who considered himself a cyber expert, Josh should have known the tricks of the trade of online harassment.

"Of course. But I didn't say those words in that order."

Cliff was relieved. Josh looked like I had ruined the speech he had written.

"You don't think I'd say something so stupid on camera — or even off it. They took words I said and spliced them together. I promise. If you get a hold of the video, I'm sure somebody in media services can show you the digital stitching. They've edited several minutes down to ten digestible, inflammatory seconds. I admit I went a little crazy with the posters, but they were horrible. Look at them."

I took out my phone and showed them a photo of the Haji flyer. Cynthia and Josh were not as horrified as I would have hoped.

"Well, whatever the method, unfortunately, it's out there," Josh said. "You can't unmelt butter."

My god. These were the insights that had gotten him that Audi and an endowed chair? I was certainly envious of his accolades, and his job security. But he was an idiot.

"No, we can't," Cynthia said. "But how can we show that it's, you know — margarine? Cheap margarine at that."

She looked at me and shrugged her shoulders, as if to apologize for having to go on with this horrible metaphor.

"I think the ideas these students are spouting—that any discussion of racial and class inequality is anti-American—are big, pernicious, and nearly unstoppable at the moment," Josh said. "We hear all these stories about students being too liberal on campus. Insisting statues be torn down and axing Homer and Humbert Humbert from the curriculum. But they're not the real problem. The problem is the conservative students, caught up in whatever they're hearing from their angry parents and all this hateful noise online, staging witch-hunts across the country." Josh stopped and turned to me. "I'm not suggesting you're a witch."

"Thanks for the clarification," I said, appreciating the levity.

"It's impossible to contain something like this once it's out on the internet," Josh said. "The question is how best to minimize what has already happened to you. That's the only thing we can control."

I didn't want to admit it, but Josh's sense of this seemed right. Cliff and Cynthia nodded their heads in agreement.

"You have to lie completely low from now on," Josh said.

"Trust me," I said, "I want nothing more than that. If I could, I'd disappear."

"Our primary concern is for you and your sense of security on this campus," Cynthia said. "The dean's office and the president's office have already had plenty of calls from parents and media outlets. And we're dealing with it. But we need a strategy for how to deal with the few remaining, die-hard protesters downstairs. They've cleverly set up their own sense of well-being as a weapon. The worse they feel, the more powerful they get. I don't know how long this hunger strike will last, but they're clearly trying to force our hand. One of the students from the group has approached the dean's office, though. He would like to talk to you. Would you be interested in that?"

"I've actually been trying to talk to them, but they won't engage," I said. "I'm assuming it's that guy Alex who's downstairs now?"

"Alex?" Cynthia asked. "I don't know. Whatever his name, he says he wants to talk, and perhaps get some sort of an apology." Cynthia herself seemed apologetic at having to convey this last bit of information.

I looked over at Cliff, who seemed to be my only real ally in the room.

"An apology?" I asked. "Shouldn't they be apologizing to me? This is a hit job. I don't mind them calling me Haji, or whatever they're calling me. But after being dragged through the mud, do I have to beg them for water to clean up?"

The bad metaphors were piling up thick and high.

I looked around the room and then again at the wall of mostly somber white men. The committee at the TC was asking me to apologize to an African-American man, and now my bosses were asking me to apologize to a group of white students. They were different situations—one the absurd machinations of the leisured, the other a debate about education and knowledge. In one, I understood where my fault lay; in the other, I did not. Apologizing in the way they both wanted meant I was taking a hit for them. But not apologizing meant that I might not have a job or access to a place that I had come to love. Either way, I wasn't going to like where I ended up.

"Forget the apology for now," Cynthia said. "But would

you at least consider talking to them? You're welcome not to, of course. We would understand completely. But it might be helpful."

"Just to, you know, to stem the tide a little," Josh said. "These students just want to be heard. They feel ignored."

I'm not sure what I had expected from this meeting when I'd walked in. Perhaps a conversation. But it was clear that the three of them had already decided what they wanted from me. This is what Cynthia and Cliff must have been talking about before I arrived.

"I can't say that I can empathize with what you are going through," Cynthia said. "You're in a horrible, horrible situation. And sadly, we don't have any past experiences to lean on here. You don't have to talk to this student. We're just trying to figure out how to de-escalate. You saw them downstairs. They're taking this hunger-strike thing seriously. We can't control the media, if you can call these right-wing garbage dumps that. But we might be able to control what's going on here."

"I'll have to think about it."

"Of course," Cynthia said, her tone suggesting growing impatience. I couldn't tell if, after the obligatory friendliness when I had first walked in, this was the real Cynthia. She did, after all, represent the needs of the university and not me. "We want you to think about it. But understand there is only so much that I can do. Only so much the university can do. At some point it's going to be up to you. I'll do my best to help, but there are limits. You're going to have to help yourself too."

I had wanted Cynthia to like me, because it meant that I

was more likely to keep my job. But it was clear now that her primary responsibility was to bring the hunger strike to an end. She would like me as long as I helped her to do that.

I stood up.

"There's one other thing," Josh said. "Just so all the facts are straight. You have a PhD from Columbia. Your first job was at a pretty good institution. All very serious, admirable credentials. Why did you come here for such a clear drop in rank?"

I looked at Cliff, thinking he might say something so that I wouldn't have to. He didn't.

"There were some complications at my old job," I said.

"What kind of complications?" Josh asked.

"I had a disagreement with a colleague."

"A disagreement?"

"I don't think that's relevant to what's going on here," Cliff interjected. He knew the story.

"I'm only trying to get all the information," Josh said. "If they learn that you left a previous job out of conflict, they'll say that you're prone to conflict. We need to get ahead of things."

As reasonable as that sounded, I had a feeling that what Josh really wanted was gossip.

"Yes, Josh. I did have a disagreement with a colleague. But the nature of that conflict is irrelevant at this point. I left because I couldn't do the job, and they finally called me on it. I had to produce a book, and I couldn't. I have all sorts of reasons why. But ultimately, promise is only realized in work. Promise followed by further promises means nothing. I'm a middle-aged man with one small publication to my name. The years have passed and I haven't done what I set out to do. I failed, Josh. That's why I find myself in this situation. Because I failed."

When I looked up, Cliff had a sweet, parental expression.

"I really appreciate you sharing that with us," Josh said, concern now covering his well-exfoliated face. "You know, I write in my book that engaging in insecurity is the key to our security. I'd be happy to give you a copy. It might help you work through some of this."

There was an awkward silence in the room. "Thanks for the offer, Josh, but I think I'm fine on my own," I said. "I don't think we really see eye to eye. So far as I can tell, the key to insecurity is insecurity."

Cliff and Cynthia smiled. They seemed equally tired of Josh's clichés. For a second, knowing that all three of us thought Josh was an idiot was enough to get me through.

"Let me know if you want to meet with the student," Cynthia said. "But again, no pressure."

"I can be there with you if you like," Josh said.

"I'm fine," I said.

As Josh and Cynthia began walking out, Cynthia shook my hand. "Let's be in touch about your work. There are some funds in the dean's office for special projects. Maybe we can knock off some classes so you can spend time developing your ideas."

"Thank you," I said. "And I don't mind talking to the student. Go ahead and set up the meeting. Is noon today too early? I can't promise an apology, but I can certainly listen to him. I think it must be that bearded kid, Alex, who did all the talking yesterday."

"Thank you, Raj," Cynthia said. "I'll email him right now. He'll be there."

"You can use my office if Dan is going to be there," Cliff said.

"I'll check," I said. "But I'd prefer to use my own."

Using Cliff's office would make me feel like I was playing grown-up.

I was sure Cynthia had just played me with the promise of funds that would probably not materialize. She didn't seem to be the slick administrative type, but maybe authenticity was her strong suit. I was actually curious to talk to Alex. I wanted to understand what was going on with him. An anthropologist's habit, I guess.

Cynthia and Josh left; it was just Cliff and me in the room.

"You don't have to talk to him," Cliff said. "I should have said that when Cynthia was here."

"I want to."

"Are you sure you want to do it alone?"

"Maybe I'm being naïve, or maybe I trust my ethnographic skills too much, but I think I should talk to him one-on-one. If it's the two of us and him, he might think we're ganging up on him."

"I'll be down the hall if you need me," Cliff said.

I sat down in my office at noon, and a few minutes later heard a knock on the door.

"Come in, Alex."

In the time that had passed since the morning meeting, I had done my best to be mindful, to clear all the noise from my head, to put myself in a place where I could listen to what

Alex — I was so sure it was him — had to say. I wanted to understand what it was the protesters actually wanted, beyond all the silly slogans. It was my scholarly instinct to dig beneath. But also, I trusted my ability to talk through our problems and find some solution that didn't involve them insisting on my firing.

But the second the door opened and Robert walked through, the mindfulness disappeared. I didn't know Alex, and there was an ease in that. But with Robert, despite his inappropriate interest in my salary and his general awkwardness, I thought we'd made some small bit of a connection. He'd always been engaged in class. And I'd given him half a sandwich I'd wanted for myself. The idea that he was actively involved in this, and not just an observer, felt like a betrayal.

"Alex is downstairs. He feels pretty weak."

"Then maybe he should eat," I said, the words coming out with a sharp edge.

"Yes. That's what we all want, don't we? To put a stop to all this. To do the right thing." His tentativeness from Monday — the looking, the looking away — was replaced by a newfound confidence. His sentences were now declarative, his spine more upright. And yet, these upgrades seemed temporary. I knew Robert was a strange bird. He was a fairly bright kid, but also a bit of a loner, not that good at picking up on social cues. He seemed like someone who needed guidance, and he had turned to me for that. Over the years, I'd had my share of students who'd wanted to forge a similar bond with me. But none who had pushed the boundaries quite as he did.

The confidence I was sensing now had to be coming from

Alex and Holly, and from *Freedom Now* and *Mansfield,* all of whom had given him a way to articulate his frustrations, mostly by giving him someone to blame. And I was that someone. I wasn't sure if I'd be able to convince him that I wasn't the enemy.

"Should I close the door?"

"Open is fine."

Cliff stuck his head in.

"All good?" Cliff asked.

"Perfect," I said, trying to sound professional. "Robert, do you know Professor Turner, the department chair?"

"I'm happy to meet you, sir," Robert said, standing up and shaking Cliff's hand. "Are you teaching next term?"

"I am," Cliff said. "A seminar on the anthropology of adolescence."

"I'll be sure to take it."

Cliff nodded and left.

"So, you wanted to talk to me?" I asked, trying my best to remain calm.

"I did," Robert said.

"Before we start, I want to ask you something. Did you take that video of me on Monday?"

"Yes," Robert said without hesitating. "I've been recording you on and off since the start of the term. The truth is, I couldn't keep up with the complexity of your lectures. It always seems like you're saying pretty straightforward stuff, but when I go back and listen to it, I can hear the layers. I mentioned your lecture on dirt on Monday. During the class period, I wasn't sure why you were spending all this time talking about Hindus and pork and beef. But I wrote down the ideas. I recorded them and went back and listened. It didn't sink in until a day or two later. I was by myself at a party, watching all these guys having fun. They didn't want anything to do with me. I've never had a group of friends like that before."

Robert paused and looked down. I hoped that if the ideas from my class were still resonating with him, then maybe we'd be able to talk through this after all.

"But there was something different about you on Monday. You were so much more animated than usual. You weren't reading from your notes. You were talking like you were hanging out with a friend. And so toward the end of the lecture, I started taking a video like I do sometimes. My dad wanted to know how my classes were going and I thought I'd send it to him. I came to see you after class because I was excited. I wanted to talk about the ideas. About anthropology. But then you got mad at me when I brought up your salary. I know it was wrong of me to dig around for it. I wish I hadn't done it."

I thought of myself as being a pretty decent judge of people, an astute reader of emotional tremors, but I couldn't figure out how genuine Robert was being. His face gave nothing away.

"I was embarrassed when you rushed me out of your office like that. I really like what you've been teaching us. I can't wait to come to class, more so than any other class I've taken here. It gives me a way to make sense of the world. I've liked being a part of the conversation. But I made one mistake and you shut me out."

Listening to Robert, I was reminded of what an intimate encounter teaching could be. I pushed students to question their assumptions about themselves and people culturally different from them. I pushed them to open up. But I expected them to stay on their side of a boundary that I drew.

"I don't mean to shut you out, Robert. On the contrary, I've enjoyed having you in class. And salary aside, you were asking incisive questions on Monday, the kinds of questions I appreciate. Maybe I overreacted a bit in the moment, but I've moved on. I'd like to continue the rest of our conversation."

Robert appeared to be considering this. But then:

"I don't know. When I got home that night, I watched the video I'd taken of class and those last lines of your lecture kept echoing in my head. I was offended. And I guess I wanted to shame you like you'd shamed me. I have some friends from high school who have been sharing articles from *Freedom Now* on Facebook, and it seemed like something they might pick up on, but I guess I assumed they wouldn't respond. That's why I sent that email to the dean's office too. I knew they'd listen to me. But the next thing I knew, I heard back from the editor, saying that my story was live, and I heard back from the dean. I didn't think it would come to all this."

"So why are you here now?" I asked. "You've already got plenty of videos of me. You want to take more?" I could hear the edge in my voice, but I couldn't help it. I knew I needed to be the adult in the room, but I was tired of the role. I was the one whose livelihood was in danger.

"I didn't take the second video. And I didn't set up the protest. That was all Alex and Holly. They're in the same discussion section with me, and I'd heard them complain before about how biased your class is. You teach anthropology, but all

you do is tell us what's wrong with the discipline. The anthropologists weren't colonists. They were scholars studying the
differences between people. And there are differences—just
look at you and me. When the first story came out, I sent it to
them. I didn't think they even knew who I was, but they wrote
back right away. Alex is part of a group of students across the
country pushing universities to return to a more traditional
curriculum."

I wondered if Robert had reminded me so much of Babu
because Anand Mehta was not so different from Jack Mansfield. Both men were deeply invested in the principle of separate but equal. And both of them had found good foot soldiers,
men who were happy to hide behind the security of a group. I
couldn't sway the headwinds, but maybe I could pull one lost
soul out of the gale.

"Robert, there's a difference between hating the West and
criticizing it from within. It's like I said yesterday: there's a
long history of criticism in America. You know Bruce Springsteen?"

"My parents listen to him. I don't."

"He's spent most of his career criticizing America, but that
doesn't mean he doesn't love this country. He's an American
icon. The power of dissent is a rich part of who we are. Robert,
I respect your opinions, and I show that by critically examining your ideas. That's what we're here for. My job is to show
you that ideas are meant to be broken apart and studied. If
they're not, they solidify into something nauseating and dangerous. If you remember nothing else from this class, I want
you at least to remember how I've taught you to think. And

hopefully I've created a classroom environment that allows you to critique my ideas as well. But just because you don't like my ideas doesn't mean you can get me fired."

We sat there without saying anything for nearly half a minute. Robert shuffled in his seat. Sometimes in class, when I asked a question and no one answered, I would let the quiet build in the room. After enough discomfort, someone would eventually speak up. But Robert didn't.

"I'm not sure there's anything else for us to talk about," I finally said.

"But there is."

I waited.

"Just apologize for your derogatory comments about Christianity. You're attacking us for our backgrounds, for being white and Christian. How is that any different than when people attack you for being Indian?"

"Robert, I think it's time for you to leave."

"Say it," Robert said as he stood up. One last-ditch effort. "This could all be over."

"You're asking me for an apology, but giving you one would mean admitting I did something wrong. I have no problem with apologies. I make them all the time. But I'm not going to apologize for saying something I have every right to say."

He walked out.

I waited for a minute and went down the hall to Cliff's office. I closed the door behind me.

"How did it go?"

"Not very well. A little strange, actually."

"He seemed like a normal enough kid."

"He put on quite the act when you came into my office."

"And what did he say after I left?"

"He admitted that he took the first video and complained to the dean's office, but the second one is the work of our friends downstairs. I think it's his relationship with them that's got him mixed up. Mostly he seems like a loner, going through normal adolescent stuff. These other students are telling him that people like me are the reason his life isn't what he wants it to be. Maybe he's finally found a group that will take him in."

"How did you leave it?"

"He said that I needed to apologize for what I said in class. I think he was hoping that I would apologize on the spot so that he could take a trophy back to his new friends." Everyone was asking me for apologies, and yet they seemed to be more and more meaningless, a bandage that wasn't up to the task of healing the serious wounds festering below. "Thank you for all your help with this, Cliff. I know it's the last thing you want to be dealing with. You should be home writing." I tapped on his desk. "I'm going to head home myself. Text me if anything else comes up."

"Don't go yet," Cliff said. "Please sit." He pointed to the empty chair. "I'm sorry all this is happening."

He took out his can of tobacco and prepared a pipe. When he was finished, he placed it on his desk, opened a drawer, and took out a brand-new one. "Interested?"

"Sure," I said, sitting down. He prepared mine, and we both lit up. The office filled with fabulous, fragrant smoke. I leaned back in the chair.

"Do you know how long I've been married?" Cliff asked.

"I don't."

"Fifty years. Does that seem like a long time to you?"

"It's longer than I've been alive."

Cliff nodded. "We have two wonderful children and seven grandchildren. My son and daughter-in-law just had their fourth. I don't know how they get anything done. But they do it all." He patiently blew out some smoke. "When I met my wife, I was with another woman, my high school sweetheart. We'd grown up together in a small town in Oregon. Our families knew each other really well. But the woman who would become my wife was from San Francisco and offered me a bigger world than I'd ever had access to before. I was scared of giving up the security of such a familiar life, but I worked up the courage to break up with my girlfriend. When I did, she told me that she was pregnant. It was so sudden, I thought she was saying it just to keep me, and I stormed off, but not before saying some pretty mean-spirited things that I didn't think I had in me." Cliff leaned toward me, even though his office door was closed. "It turns out that she *was* pregnant. She moved to Portland and went ahead and had the baby, but didn't tell me. I had moved on to a new life. And then, right after my wife gave birth to our first child, my ex-girlfriend sent me a photo of our five-year-old daughter. She had named her Agnes. A perfect name. Her mother said that she simply wanted me to know about my daughter. She didn't expect anything. To this day, Agnes doesn't know who I am. I follow her life from afar and I still send her mother money. Agnes is an Episcopal priest. I suspect she got the priest's demeanor from her mother."

Cliff seemed almost serene as he told me this story. At the beginning of the week, just talking to him on the phone had felt too intimate. Now this.

"No one knows about this except her mother and me. You're the first person I've ever told. My wife doesn't know. My children don't know. There are plenty of things husbands keep from their wives, parents from their children. But what kind of man keeps this kind of secret from his family? I've lied to them and I've been completely absent from my daughter's life. Sometimes I think about sitting in on one of her services, but I'm not sure I ever could."

I don't know why I had assumed that all of the books he had written, and all the honorary degrees he had received, had made Cliff immune to secrets and tragedies. But sitting there, smoking our pipes, I felt really touched that Cliff trusted me enough to bring me into this corner of his private life, and as if he were trying to tell me something, that there was a lesson in all of this for me.

"Are you going to see her?" I asked.

"I don't think so." He relit his pipe.

"Do you want to?" I asked.

"I do," Cliff said. With his layers of wrinkles and a beard on his face, I couldn't tell what he was feeling.

"You should, then."

He shook his head. "We've all found stability in our lives. She has, I have, my family has. This would wreck all of that. If they find out after I die, that's fine. I guess I'm not who they think I am. I suppose we're never the people our loved ones think we are." He paused and smiled. "That's a little dark, isn't it?" He took another drag from the pipe, but he had smoked through the tobacco. "Why don't you keep that pipe. It's a nice one. Though I wouldn't want to start you on a bad habit."

"Thanks," I said, standing up. "Among bad habits, this is a good one."

"Raj," he said as I got to the door. "I want you to know that I think you're a core part of this department. You've had plenty of reason to be bitter and angry. And yet, you've shown up. I appreciate that."

"Thanks," I said. "I like teaching. And I like teaching here. I don't want to stop. I can't afford to stop. I'll wait to hear from you."

"Yes. Hopefully sooner rather than later."

I walked out of the office but lingered in the hallway for a moment, his words echoing in my head.

I didn't know Cliff that well, but he'd always been straightforward when he wanted to tell me something. Still, like so much of his writing, the implications of his words generally gained more meaning the further I got from them, illuminating some corner he'd not directly intended to illuminate. Perhaps he'd told me the story to make a connection, sensing that I needed a friend, signaling that I should feel safe in being honest with him in return. But it also posed the idea of a double life. Who or what was my Agnes?

I went into my office, grabbed my new desk lamp, and with the pipe in my back pocket, took the elevator down. I tried to prepare myself to face the protesters. The doors opened, I took a deep inhale as if I were about to dive into a cold pool, and walked out. For several seconds, no one saw me.

Robert had rejoined the group of hunger strikers. Sitting there with the two couples, he was the fifth wheel. And about twenty feet to the right of them was a whole new group of students. I recognized some of them from my classes. David, the handsome Indian student who had come to see me in office hours earlier in the week, was among them. My heart sank. A brown Catholic kid who thinks I'm being insensitive to Christians? I was screwed.

The second group of students was gathered around a table filled with Styrofoam containers. While the hunger strikers sat nearby, this other group stood and piled plates with food. I noticed a platter of thick samosas.

A few of the students looked my way, and one of them tugged at David's arm. David turned to me. "Professor Bhatt! Please come join us. We were hoping you were around today."

I walked over to them cautiously. Together, this racially diverse group was perfect for a poster of a college that did not exist.

"The South Asian Student Association usually has a mixer once a term," David said. "This time, we figured we'd do it here. We have some tasty food. Have you had lunch? Please eat with us."

David smiled. It was hard to contain my own.

"We have plenty for everybody," he said, loud enough for the whole hall to hear. "You don't have to be a part of our association. We accept everyone."

The protesting students just sat there, stone-faced.

The smell of the Indian food was overwhelming. Had I not eaten in more than twenty-four hours, I would certainly have broken down. But I think it's safe to say that Robert, Alex, Holly, and the others didn't have the same Proustian ties to samosas that I did.

One of the students handed me a plate with rice, palak paneer, and chicken tikka masala. Maybe I was hungry, or maybe the food was just great, or maybe it was the joy of eating among friendly faces. Whatever the reason, I finished half the plate at an unreasonable pace. The rest of the students eating lunch formed a little circle around me, taking turns telling me which class they'd taken with me and how much they'd enjoyed it.

"How's the vest?" one of the students asked. "I miss it."

One term, I had worn a slimming orange down vest nearly every day I taught. It became my security blanket.

"The zipper broke. I need to get it fixed. I love that thing."

"Bring it in next time," a young white hippie said to me. He wasn't wearing shoes, but his feet were remarkably clean. "I know how to fix those things. And I still owe you for all those eggs."

"Were you in that class?" I asked.

He put out his hand to shake. "Simon. Egg Man."

Now I remembered. Simon was in a small seminar I had taught on literature and ethnography. The students were all very smart and engaged, and at some point, as we were talking about the use of point of view in ethnographic writing, the topic had turned from a figurative conversation on chickens and eggs to a more literal one. Our chickens at home were laying far too many eggs then, and so over the course of the term I would bring in a dozen or so to each session. The students who wanted them would take a few. Simon was always willing to take the extras. After a few weeks, we started referring to him affectionately as the Egg Man.

"Of course, Egg Man! How are you?"

I said this louder than I had intended. And as I did, self-conscious about my exuberance, I looked over at the other group. Robert was staring at me. He seemed hungry, tired, and haggard. "Please come and eat," I said.

"Yes, please," David added. "We have plenty."

Without waiting for a response, David and the other students began putting together plates of food, as if they were a finely tuned assembly line at a food bank. They made five heaping plates, and with respect and solemnity they placed them on the floor in front of the students. I watched them. One group on one side, the other group on the other, with so much nourishing food in between. I watched Robert as he considered the plates of food. He had to be starving. He looked up and noticed me watching him. "Please eat," I mouthed to him.

"Thank you," Alex said. "But no thank you. We appreciate the thought."

"We'll leave it here in case you change your mind," David said. I finished eating my food, mainly so as not to offend David and his group, but I had lost my appetite.

"Thank you all," I said to David, Egg Man, and the others. "I can't tell you how much I appreciate this."

"See you in class on Monday," David said.

I nodded and walked away, the lamp in my hand and my belly full.

. . .

When I got back to my car, I realized why my convenient parking spot had been available during prime time. My front windshield, along with some of the hood, was covered in white, wet bird shit. These weren't the polite droppings of sweet birds; they were marking their territory, and clearly I was in the wrong place. The flock above squawked down at me.

"Please stop," I pleaded, louder than I'd intended, looking up at the birds in the tree and the blue sky beyond.

Right then, a woman walked by on a nearby pathway.

"Raj?"

The voice was familiar, but I couldn't place it. Nor did I immediately recognize her face, despite the fact that I had been staring at it for months.

"It's Emily. Emily Baker."

She walked up to me, looking like she had been on a decade-long yoga retreat. Her face was clear and lively, her body long and toned, and she was dressed in clothes that had probably come from some expensive little shop in SoHo. She gave me a big, genuine hug.

"In all this time, I never imagined someday I'd find you yelling at a tree."

I pointed to the car.

"Ah. If one dropping is considered good luck, I would go get a lottery ticket." She gave me a second hug, this time holding me tighter. "I'm so glad to see a familiar face. How did I know that you'd end up in a beautiful place like this? How are you?"

"I'm OK," I said, wanting to sound upbeat and confident.

"You know, a job, kids, a mortgage. The middle-aged holy trinity. You?"

"I'm fine. I'm here for this reading, and I just did a seminar with a group of faculty."

"How was that?"

"Atrocious. I didn't realize just how insane academics can sound when they're trying to make sense of poetry. Some woman was going on and on about how I was writing in the tradition of Wallace Stevens. I fucking hate Wallace Stevens."

Years ago, I had envied Emily's Athenian opinions, the way they emerged from her head fully formed and well armored. But now I appreciated the clarity.

"Have you seen the campus?" I asked. "It would be fun to show you around."

"I'd like nothing more."

I put my lamp in the trunk and we walked out of the parking lot. As we did, she locked her arm in mine, the gesture a little more intimate than I had expected.

"The campus itself isn't that collegiate, but there's a great path leading to the ocean. Shall we do that?"

"That sounds perfect," Emily said. "So I confess, I'd heard through the grapevine that you were teaching here. I was hoping to see you at the seminar."

"They don't invite lecturers to those things."

"Ah," Emily said, without sounding condescending. "I told the guy in the English department who invited me that we were in graduate school together. He asked if I meant the guy in the news. Are you in the news?"

I took my phone out of my pocket. The second video was

already open. I'd watched it at least ten times. I handed it to her. She cupped the phone to shield my screen from the sun. When she finished watching, she handed it back, a mischievous smile on her face.

"Bad evaluations?" she asked.

I chuckled. If only. "I lost my shit. I tore down the posters and screamed at the students, but the video is doctored."

I went to the photos and showed her the one of the flyer. "They stapled these over posters for your reading," I said, with some added needling enthusiasm. "For once, I had higher billing than you."

Emily examined the photo closely. "This is really messed up. But you must have done something to warrant all this. Something smart, I'm sure."

"I said something in class that some students took offense to. Now I'm having to defend myself for parroting Edward Said."

"Last year I taught a seminar on African-American poetry and the students complained that the syllabus wasn't diverse enough."

"You should have added some Stevens."

It was Emily's turn to chuckle. "Being on a campus these days is depressing me," she said, sounding resigned. "If given the opportunity, I'd quit teaching in a heartbeat. I'm so over it."

"But you have a perfect job," I said.

"Trust me, the only perfect job is no job at all."

Our conversation was flowing, so I didn't want to disagree. But there was a clear difference between her job and mine.

I looked ahead and saw Josh Morton about fifty yards farther down the path. I watched as he noticed me and started to turn away. But then he saw Emily and quickly straightened up. As we got closer, I said, "Let me introduce you to a grade-A jackass."

"Raj," Josh said, smiling. I don't know why I'd not noticed before how straight and white his teeth were. His vanity was exhausting. "I'm glad we were able to meet this morning. I'm working closely with Cynthia to monitor the situation. All this is going to blow over in no time, don't you worry."

"That's good to hear," I said. I paused, drawing out the moment. I knew Josh wanted an introduction to Emily, and I loved not giving him what he wanted, if only for a few seconds. Finally: "Emily Baker, this is Josh Morton. Josh teaches here and is a bit of a campus celebrity. And Josh, this is my old friend Emily, who was always the smartest student when we were in graduate school together. I imagine she's still the smartest person in any room she enters."

Emily shook hands with Josh. "Raj is probably right about that," she said, laughing.

I bet Josh wished I wasn't there so he could talk shop with someone at his level.

"I'd love to send you a copy of my book," he said. "I think you'd find it very interesting. I'll have my publisher send it out immediately."

"That would be great. Do send it." Emily turned to me. "Raj is going to show me the ocean before I need to head to my next appointment. It was nice meeting you."

Josh was clearly waiting for an invitation to join us. Neither Emily nor I said anything.

"I'll see you tonight at your reading," Josh said. "I can't wait to hear you read. And Raj, please be in touch if you need anything. Truly, absolutely anything." He looked me in the eye to emphasize the offer.

"For sure," I said, wanting to enjoy this moment a little longer. "I appreciate it."

As we walked away, Emily asked, "Is that the guy who wrote the insecurity book?"

"The one and only." I didn't know what I would do if she said it was a smart book.

"It's a stinking piece of shit," she said.

"Thank you," I said, and then repeated, louder and with glee now spilling out of me, "Thank you!"

"You didn't always teach here, right?" Emily asked.

"Nope."

"Is this a better job?"

"No. Decidedly worse."

"What happened?"

My eye fell on a young man effortlessly skateboarding, as if the wind were ushering him along.

"It didn't work out," I said.

"You don't have to tell me."

"It's not some huge secret," I said. "The work wasn't going that well. And we wanted to move back to California."

"I can understand that," she said.

"What about you? Congratulations on all the amazing success. Truly. I'm tired of being envious, so I'm just going to be happy for you."

She skipped a couple of beats, which surprised me.

"It's amazing and it's not," she said. "I hate doing these public events. But I can't say no to the money, or the fact that the university bought five thousand copies of my book. My god. When the book came out, I was hoping to sell maybe five hundred. I have a career that's doing better than I ever could have imagined. And a husband who can't deal with any of it. He keeps saying that our kids are poorly behaved because their mother is constantly distracted."

"You have shitty kids?" I asked, trying to hide the small bit of delight I was feeling.

"I have the mother of shitty kids," she said wearily. "And I'm the mother. I've tried my very best to be there for them. My husband thinks that we've always concentrated on my career and that it's time to turn to his now. He wants me to quit my job — my fucking job at Princeton — so we can move to the Bay Area and he can break into Silicon Valley. He thinks Facebook is on its way out because too many people only post about the exciting things in their lives, that it isn't real enough. He wants to replace it with a platform where people are more honest and call it Truthbook, where you can see the good and the bad."

I must have looked confused. Couldn't he have tried at least to make it sound like less of a direct rip-off? Truthteller? TruthNow? TruthLeaks?

"I know. It's insane. I don't want to know the truth about people. I prefer the lies. He says he's sitting on a unicorn. I feel like I'm being rammed in the back by one, over and over again. So yes, job, kids, and a mortgage for me too. But I don't know how long that's going to last."

I admired Emily's willingness to be completely unfiltered

about what she felt and said. Was that why she'd become such a feted poet? "Maybe your husband is on to something. You could post that as your status update."

She grimaced, unable to mask the stress her husband was causing.

We stood at the end of the dirt path, the start of the beach. There were about twenty students on beach chairs and towels, doing their reading. A few were in the water, surfing.

"This is where these kids study?" Emily asked. I remembered she had been an undergraduate at the University of Chicago: very cold or very hot, depending on the time of year.

I pointed to a dolphin out past the waves. Several more breached the surface.

"You're kidding me. Let's go back. This is depressing me."

We headed toward campus.

"What are you working on next? More poetry?"

"No," Emily said. "I've written all the poems I'm going to write." She quickly checked her watch.

"Are you expected somewhere?"

"The library," she said, sounding tired. "I'm supposed to meet with students before my talk. I needed a little break and this was perfect. Thank you so much."

"I'm sorry I can't make it tonight." I hadn't been planning on going, and now I couldn't because Eva would be home late. But it had been so nice catching up with Emily, now I regretted missing her event. "My wife is working and I need to be with the kids."

"Don't worry at all. It's going to be miserable. I'm miserable at this."

"I'm sure you're not," I said. "I bet they'll be blown away. I certainly was. As I expected, your first book was smart. But this one — it's something else altogether. Heartbreaking and hopeful at the same time. I'm sorry you and your parents have had to go through so much. There was so much love, so much humanity, in the way you wrote about Tracy. I feel her absence now too."

"I appreciate you saying that," Emily said, her shoulders relaxing, as if she were fully letting down her guard. "It means a lot coming from you. I know we haven't kept in touch, but I always enjoyed being in class with you. You made such thoughtful comments, while everyone else was peacocking. I'm so glad I ran into you. Stay in touch this time. This is already the best part of my trip. And please get that car washed."

We hugged and she walked off, disappearing into the mill of students all around.

I got in my car and tried to use the wipers, but all they did was smear the droppings across the windshield. No rose-colored glasses for me; I was seeing the world through streaks of shit. I drove straight to a car wash and got in line. When it was my turn, I stepped out.

"Regular or extreme wash?" the attendant asked. He was a young, skinny white kid wearing an oversized sweatshirt. He looked at the windshield and then at me. A large smile spread over his face. He pretended to shoot a skeet gun, and without waiting for my answer, he wrote *Extreme* on a piece of paper and handed it to me. "You can pay inside. We'll work extra-hard on this one." I went into the store.

"Anything else?" the young cashier asked, taking the slip from me.

"Do you sell lottery tickets?" I asked, remembering what Emily had said. Maybe bird shit really would bring me luck.

"How many do you want?" she asked, barely acknowledging my presence.

"Just one. I feel lucky."

"I'm sure you do," she deadpanned.

How many guys like me, thinking they were the lucky ones, did she encounter a day?

She rang me up for the car wash and one ticket. I took it from her, fished a coin out of my pocket, and scratched. Somehow, I matched three numbers and looked up at the cashier, trying to remain expressionless. And then I scratched the prize. Did a ten-dollar payout on a one-dollar ticket mark luck? I certainly thought so. I felt a slight uptick in my spirit as I handed her the ticket.

"I guess you are lucky," the cashier said, allowing herself the slightest smile and handing me a ten-dollar bill. "You want this or ten more tickets?"

I froze. It was a difficult philosophical question. I hadn't even considered getting more tickets; I knew that I'd just scratch and scratch and be left with nothing. But what if luck was a real thing? I was seldom at the receiving end of it.

"Can I have nine tickets?"

The cashier watched me indifferently as I scratched ticket after ticket. After the first few, I still thought my chances were pretty high, but by the end, I was a lot more heartbroken than

I'd expected. I handed the cashier the nine tickets to throw away.

"Next time, quit while you're ahead," she said.

I wondered if her father had also mailed her photocopies of quotes from the *Wall Street Journal*.

"I think you're right."

I walked out to my clean car.

I felt unusually happy whenever I got into my car after someone else had washed it. For the first hour or so, before the dust and grime made its way back in, life seemed ordered, contained. But it amazed me how little time it took for the dirt to reappear on the floor, for the back seat to be filled with empty water bottles.

I checked to my left before pulling out of the car wash. I noticed a car parked a little ways away. I couldn't be sure, but the man in the driver's seat bore a striking resemblance to Robert. Had it been an old beat-up Civic, I would have thought it was him. But what could he possibly be doing driving, of all things, a candy-apple-red Mini Cooper? I knew he couldn't afford it.

As I drove away, I kept checking my rearview mirror, sure that the Mini was following me. It was there every time, hanging a couple of cars back.

I had to pick up the kids, but I still had an hour or so to kill before school got out.

I stopped at a sporting goods store to buy some tennis balls. I parked and looked around; I didn't see the Mini. I checked my phone to see if there was a note from Cliff. My school account had at least fifteen emails from nonschool addresses that I didn't recognize. The first one I opened had the subject line "We're Coming For You." The body read: "This is our country. There's no place in it for people who hate us. Go home. You're not welcome here anymore." I so badly wanted to delete it, and all the others festering in my inbox. But I knew I should save them to show Cliff, and maybe also to the police, who I was thinking should be involved in this whole mess. I checked one more time for the Mini, got out of the car, and hurried inside.

My first job in high school had been at a store like this, and I'd loved it. It made me feel sporty and athletic, a feeling that carried over to the present, as I examined the weights, the new tennis racquets, the golf clubs. I palmed the footballs and basketballs. I grabbed several cans of tennis balls and headed to the register.

I walked past the gun section on my way to the checkout. In all the times I'd been in the store, I'd never paid much mind to the guns. I had no interest in them; I hated that they sold them. And yet, the gun section was a little like the porn section in a video store — back when video stores were still a thing — shameful yet inviting.

Once, a couple of years back, we'd had a young man come pounding on our front door, yelling, in the middle of the night. He was obviously high on something. We called 911, and until the police arrived and arrested him, Eva locked herself and the kids in the bedroom while I watched him through the thick glass of the door, clutching a cricket bat in my hand.

A few days later, when I spoke to the sheriff about what to do if something like that happened again, he suggested I buy a gun, to give myself some time before the police got there. The message I read into that: ultimately, I was responsible for my safety and the safety of my family. Others could help, but in the end it would fall on me.

I knew all the information about guns and how they escalated violence, but still, the fear from that night, that sheriff's advice, stuck with me. I thought about the phone call I had received that morning. Whoever he was knew my landline; I assumed he knew where I lived, too. What would happen if he showed up at our house? Weren't these the sort of extenuating circumstances that justified bending my moral compass a bit?

At the register I paid for my tennis balls, but hesitated before leaving the store. I went back to the gun counter.

"You need something to shoot those balls?" the young man behind the counter asked. He was wearing a cheap button-down shirt, maybe one he had taken from the back of his father's closet. But there was something keen and bright about his manner.

"I'm just looking." I couldn't believe I was there.

The salesman explained that the handguns would require a background check, but a BB gun or a basic single-shot rifle could go home with me today. I assumed that they were less capable of doing major harm, and yet the ease of access to these guns was frightening. "Check them out. Full refund if they're not good for you." He pointed to a rifle. "This one here is perfect for squirrels and warning shots and maybe coyotes if they get too close. That's all you need sometimes. A warning shot."

He removed it from the case and placed it in front of me. I hadn't mentioned why I needed one.

"My dad uses it for gophers," the salesman said. "It gets a little messy, but it keeps them out of your lawn. And the fruit trees. You don't want them getting to those trees that you've grown and nurtured for years."

He was a good salesman. He knew all the right man buttons to push.

"Can I use it for snakes?"

"Of course. Just aim for the head."

Half an hour and a brief tutorial later, I was driving to pick up the kids with a rifle, a box of bullets, a desk lamp, and several cans of tennis balls in the trunk of my car. As I stood at that counter, a gun had felt like a perfect fix. I'd felt out of control all week, and as much as I knew it was really a sign of the opposite, the gun gave me the feeling of wrestling the control back.

I decided to call my mother.

"Everything OK?" she asked. "You don't usually call at this time."

If I told her that I'd bought a gun, she would hang up, call my two sisters, and the three of them would be at my doorstep by nightfall, wanting to solve all of my problems. I appreciated this about them. But I was far too old for the Bhatt sisters to be holding my hand.

"Why wouldn't it be?" Before she could answer, I continued, wanting to turn the conversation away from me. "Any more calls from the saffron man?"

"Yes, we've been talking. And we're going to have lunch next week."

I didn't say anything. I was a little uncomfortable talking to my mother about going on a date with someone who wasn't my father, no matter how happy I was that she seemed to have found someone to keep her company. But also, to be honest, I was disappointed that she didn't have a problem that needed fixing.

"But I'm not even sure it will be next week. By then, I'll probably have changed my mind anyway."

"I'm sure it will be wonderful. I'm glad you're doing it. It's important to get out."

"Is Neel doing better?"

"He's fine. He's already talking about Thanksgiving. Both boys are."

"Speaking of which, Swati suggested that this year we get the whole thing catered. There's a new Indian place in Berkeley we could order from."

"And?"

"And I think it's something to consider."

I looked forward to Thanksgiving more than any other holiday because my mother spent days and days cooking beforehand. I spent the entire day eating — idli sambar for breakfast, fresh samosas to snack on, three kinds of vegetables instead of the turkey, molasses ladoos throughout the day — and still came away with a cooler full of leftovers. But I knew all the work exhausted her; she deserved a break.

"That's a great idea," I said. "This way you can just relax the whole time, spend time with your grandkids."

"I'm so glad," she said, sounding relieved. "I'll tell her to go ahead and order it."

I hung up and went to pick up the kids.

When I got to the front of the car line at school, Neel and Arun ran up. Neel banged on the trunk. I reached for the button to pop it open and let them dump their backpacks in, but then stopped myself, remembering the contraband in the trunk.

"Just bring your stuff in with you," I said, lowering the window, trying to sound breezy.

At home, the kids took showers without too much prodding. Since our blowup earlier in the week, they had been doing things before I had to insist. Once they'd changed, they both sat at the dining table and did their homework while I made them snacks before dinner. Eva would get home after they'd fallen asleep. Whenever she was out, the three of us bachelored it a bit, eating in front of the TV, finishing pints of ice cream. They also listened to me a lot more when she wasn't around — no extra parent to appeal to when I played bad cop.

Neel came into the kitchen to get some milk.

"What's for dinner?"

"I don't know yet. Any preferences?"

"I like whatever you cook."

I was removing eggs from the fridge. A thin omelet with goat cheese sounded delicious. We could at least start with that and then move on.

"The phone light is flashing."

Before I could tell Neel not to touch it, he pressed the button and a voice came on that I didn't recognize. "Welcome home, Christian hater. How was your day?"

I slammed the stop button.

"Who was that?" Neel asked, worried. "What's a Christian hater? Are you a Christian hater?"

It had been a different person than the one who had called that morning.

"Nobody," I said. "A recording. They're trying to sell us things."

Neel was skeptical. He had never been very gullible. He'd finished with Santa Claus early and hadn't even entertained the possibility of a tooth fairy. "It didn't sound like a salesman."

"I'll listen to it later," I said. "Go ahead and get back to your math."

"Are you cold?" Neel asked, now sounding concerned. "You're shaking."

"I'm fine. I just haven't been feeling well today," I said. "I've had kind of a crummy week."

"That's probably my fault," he offered, his head down.

"No, no," I said, running my fingers through his thick hair. "It's just some stuff at work."

Neel returned to his math, unconvinced. I hated that the kids were being affected by this mess now too.

I made the omelets and gave them to the boys. "Start with these." Once they were eating, I turned my attention to other things.

I didn't have an exact plan for the gun. I went out to the car, making sure the kids didn't see me bringing it into my bedroom, still in an enormous shopping bag, and locked the door. The salesman had helped me load it. I felt safe with it in my hands, but I didn't feel safe with it lying around. Where could I put it so the boys wouldn't find it — where Eva wouldn't find it—until I had a chance to explain things? I carefully shoved it deep under the bed.

"Hey guys," I said, walking out to the living room. "I need you not to go into our bedroom tonight."

"Why?" Neel asked, inquisitive as usual.

"I'd like one room where your Legos aren't spread out," I said, then immediately felt bad for turning blame on them. I softened my voice. "It's just for tonight. Promise?"

Both boys agreed.

They went back to their eggs and their work, and I spent the better part of the next hour making them more food, helping them finish their homework, and cleaning up the kitchen. After dinner they went out to the backyard to shoot baskets. I monitored for trespassers as casually as possible.

As soon as it was dark and the kids were back inside, I closed all of the curtains in the house, careful to get all of the corners too, so that no one could peek in. I stood at the front door, watching the cars drive past, checking to see if any of them slowed down in front of the house. I didn't see any Mini Coopers.

By the time Eva got home, at 9:30, both kids were fast asleep. When she's out late, I often stay up watching basketball on my laptop or maybe a Swedish murder show. But I wasn't in the mood for either. I'd been sitting in our bedroom in the dark. When Eva walked in, I could sense her fatigue.

"Long day?" I asked.

"Brutal. Why are you in the dark?"

"I was reading and just turned off the light," I said, lying. I needed a few minutes to gather myself.

"Can you take the kids tomorrow? I have to be back at work by seven."

"Of course," I said. "Leave whenever. I've got nothing else." That last line lingered in the air. The truth had a way of smelling up the place.

Eva sat down on the edge of the bed, her shoulders slumped. "They want me to fly down next week."

"You should. The kids and I will be fine."

"There are four hundred dead so far," she said in a matter-of-fact tone. She peeled off her clothes and left them on the floor, as if she'd shed dead skin. "Neighborhoods reduced to rubble."

She got up and went to take a shower. When she came out several minutes later, the light from the bathroom shone into the room. I was still just sitting, but I'd moved the rifle next to my chair so that it was in plain view. I could see on her face that this was one step too far in an already long week.

"What the hell is that, Raj? Please tell me it's a toy you confiscated from the kids."

"I bought it today," I said, already sensing that no reason was going to be convincing enough for her. "It's for shooting small animals. The gophers have been bad this year. And of course, the snakes."

Eva looked at me as if I had revealed myself for exactly who I was: someone who cracked easily under pressure. She quickly got dressed. "What's the matter with you? Are you OK?"

"No," I said, "I'm not. I'm the pariah of the TC, my career is and has been in shambles, I'm the target of bigots across the nation, and now some of them are calling our house and threatening us. Oh, and also, my doctor won't call me back to tell me whether or not I have cancer. So, no. I'm absolutely not OK. Nothing is OK, Eva."

I could feel tears gathering in my throat. I swallowed and tried to push them down.

"The doctor will call you back," Eva said, her voice softening. "But what do you mean, people are calling our house? What are you talking about?"

I caught her up on the meeting, the conversation with Robert, the phone calls, the car I was sure was following me. "They know where we live."

"Then let's call the police."

"And tell them what? I've gotten two calls about my alleged anti-Christian bias? They're not going to do anything."

"But at least they can take down a report."

"Sure. We can do that. But what about Robert? There's something about this guy, Eva. Something about the way he keeps staring at me. It's so easy to find out where people live on the internet. I just don't feel safe." I showed her the emails I'd gotten that afternoon. "This is not an empty threat. We need to protect ourselves. I want to be able to protect you and the boys if anyone comes here after me."

"But you're the one with the gun," Eva said.

"If someone were to come to our door right now, threatening us, wouldn't you prefer me to have this? It could take the cops ten minutes to get here. And it would be too late by then. This will help me keep us all safe." I picked up the loaded gun and held it out to her, as if it were a ceremonial sword. "Just hold it for a second."

"Don't point that thing at me," she said, sounding genuinely terrified. She took a step back.

"Relax, I'm not. I just want you to hold it. To see what it feels like." How, in a matter of hours, had I come to sound like a guy who sends a yearly check to the NRA?

"I don't want to. You know there's nowhere in this house we can keep that. The kids will find it, I just know it. Neel is a bloodhound. I don't even want to think about them finding it. If something were to happen to them because of that, there wouldn't be any going back for us." Her voice cracked as she said this.

"I'll keep it from them, I promise. I'll get a safe. But I need this right now. I'll get rid of it as soon as everything calms down again."

"Get rid of it now," Eva said. "I'm not going to be able to sleep if it's in the house, and I'm exhausted, and I need to get up early. Can you go put it in the car or something? And then come to bed. We both need some sleep."

I took the gun out to the hallway. I wasn't ready to give it up. I leaned it against a shelf filled with books, many of which Eva and I had inherited from our parents and grandparents. Old copies of *Ulysses* and *The Discovery of India*, Marx and Kipling, my father's well-worn editions of the *Upanishads* and the *Meditations* of Marcus Aurelius, both with check marks and underlinings throughout. I removed the *Upanishads* and walked into Neel's room, kissed him on the cheek, and checked again that his window was locked. I went across the hall and did the same with Arun.

And then, book and gun in hand, I went down the hall and opened the back sliding door into the yard. It wasn't a full moon, but it was close, and it cast silver light across the lawn. I left the book on top of our picnic table and walked the perimeter of the property. Where my hands had trembled with the shovel and the snake, they were calm and steady now. There were all sorts of noises — a passing car, a rustling in the bushes, wind in the trees, coyotes howling in the distance. Of course, I knew rationally that Robert, or whoever was calling me, wasn't going to show up right at that moment. But then the week had made a mockery of reason.

After a full lap, I went inside, poured myself a hefty bit of scotch, and took it out back. I sat on top of the picnic table under the porch light. I flipped through the pages of the *Upanishads,* lingering on the passages my father had marked. Maybe I'd find some advice on how best to move forward when you argue with your wife about a gun and the world seems to be closing in on you. His typical counsel — be neither happy in victory nor daunted in defeat — wasn't cutting it, no matter the crazy returns it had somehow gotten him on his investments. There had to be something more practical in this book, though nothing was leaping out at me. Maybe it was the scotch moving too quickly to my head, or the fact that the language was so abstract and arcane, but none of the passages made much sense. I closed the book and finished my drink.

When I went back inside, Eva was asleep. I carefully placed the gun in the farthest part of my closet; I wasn't going to leave it in the car. It seemed easier for someone to break into that.

I got under the duvet. The sheets were warm and the pillows were cool. I looked over at Eva, whose face was tense, even in sleep. I knew that I would lie to her in the morning and say that I'd left the gun in the car.

Wanting to put the thought from my mind, I checked my phone. There were more emails from strangers and none from Cliff. There were also three emails from Robert, all sent within minutes of one another. The first one had the subject line "On Durkheim." It was a video of me giving a lecture on religion a few weeks back. He had written a note: "This was a great lecture." The next email was simply titled "The Walk." It was a video of me walking around campus. I didn't know when it was taken. And the last one: "The Poet." It was taken earlier in the day, right after Emily had noticed me in the parking lot. We had hugged, not just once but twice. The hugs were quite intimate. Then she'd locked her arms in mine and we'd walked away, both of us animated, clearly happy in each other's company. I looked over at Eva.

I couldn't figure out which of the last two videos unnerved me more.

Friday

WHEN I WOKE UP, with the bright morning light streaming through the bedroom window, Eva was still fast asleep. No
one had knocked on the door in the middle of the night, no
one had broken in through the windows. I got up and looked
in on the kids, both of whom were still deep under the covers.
I opened the curtains in the living room. Everything outside
was green, clean, and unthreatening.

As I was making my coffee, I heard a steady, rhythmic beat
coming from the back. It was 6:30, but next door one of the
farmhands was already out doing his rounds. His job was to
walk around the edges of the field, banging on a white plastic bucket. Apparently, it kept the crows from picking off the
blueberries. He often started this early and spent the better
part of the day traversing the property, beating. "How does he
do it?" Eva asked. She had come into the kitchen.

"I don't know."

She went to the pantry to pack the kids' lunches.

"You should take a shower and go," I said. "I'll take care of everything here." I thought about showing her the video of Emily Baker and me in case Robert posted it. I had nothing to hide, but taken out of context, I knew it would give her pause.

"And you're going to return the gun today?" Eva asked, giving me an intent stare.

"Yeah, I will. I never should've bought it. But you know it's just a basic rifle. It would have been useful with that snake."

"We didn't need a gun," Eva said with a grin. "I took care of it."

She left the kitchen and returned twenty minutes later, dressed and ready to go.

"I have an idea," she said, standing close to me, taking a sip of my coffee. "What if I go down to Mexico next week for work, and afterward you fly down and we go somewhere far from the earthquake? Just a couple of days at the beach in the warm water. My parents could watch the kids. We both could use a little downtime."

"I'd love a break," I said. "That sounds great."

"Perfect. I'll search for hotels. It'll give me a distraction at work. Maybe I can look into Tulum if it's not too far. Someplace kid-free." She poured her own tumbler of coffee. "I'll probably be able to pick up the kids after school. We've done most of what we can do from here. But I'll let you know if I can't."

I had a regular drop-in tennis game I liked to play on Friday afternoons, but I wasn't about to ask her to leave work early for that.

"OK. If you can't, I'll figure something out. I have the membership meeting at five. I'm sure the kids can hang out while I'm in it, if work gets too busy."

"I should definitely be there by four forty-five. You don't need to worry about the kids running around while you're in the meeting. I'll keep them down at the pool. You'll have plenty on your plate. Nervous?"

I shook my head, feigning confidence. But I didn't need to pretend with her. "A little."

"I know you think it's cheesy, but just speak from your heart. You're pretty effective when you do."

Eva left, and I finished making lunches for the kids.

"Mom still saving the world?" Neel mumbled when he walked into the kitchen, rubbing sleep from his face.

"The earthquake is bad," I said. "But she's probably going to pick you both up this afternoon."

"Tell her I need a little extra time after school today."

"For what?" I asked.

"An art project," he said cryptically.

Arun was still asleep, so I went to his bed and got under the covers.

"Hi, Mom," Arun whispered.

"It's Dad."

"Do we have school?"

"It's Friday. One more day."

"And then we can play video games?"

"Then you can play video games."

Arun would have been perfectly happy to stay in bed, with

the covers over him, for the rest of the day. I could see why. I had slept so poorly myself, I could use a full day to calm my mind.

Later, as I waited in line to drop the kids off at school, I saw Leslie, whom I had no interest in seeing. She waited for Neel and Arun to get out before walking up to the driver's side of the car.

"I'll see you tonight?" she asked.

"Of course," I said.

"Mark has been emailing us. A lot."

"So I hear," I said. "It's going to be fine. I'm actually excited to talk to him. He's been so busy talking to everyone about me, I'd love to hear what he has to say in person."

I had a plan for the meeting. I was going to force myself not to interrupt Mark as he lectured me. I was going to keep calm. And then I was going to unleash everything I wanted to say to him — and to the committee — without ever losing my cool. Anger would only hurt me.

But that was all for later. There were more pressing tasks at hand.

It took me well over an hour to write the email. At first I addressed it to Cliff, Cynthia, and Josh, in that order. Cliff was my immediate boss, even if Cynthia had a higher position in the hierarchy of the university. And obviously Josh came third. But at the last minute I had a change of heart and put Cynthia first. She was the one who was going to make whatever decision needed to be made.

Once the salutations were settled, I turned to the note. I decided to be as straightforward as possible:

Yesterday evening, I received a series of emails from Robert, the student who took the video of me in class, and whom I spoke with yesterday. They included more videos, which I am forwarding here. I will let you draw your own conclusions, but it is clear that he's developed an inappropriate interest in me. The woman in the third video is the poet Emily Baker, who gave the Campus Reads talk yesterday. She's an old friend of mine from graduate school.

I sent the email and then checked in on my ever-growing online presence. The first video and article had tracked well over ten thousand comments. I couldn't believe that many strangers were taking time out of their days to spit on me.

I usually devoted Fridays to writing. Most weeks I spent hours struggling over an essay, a small project that at some point I was confident in, but this week I couldn't look at any of it. I did a cursory check on the pages and pages I had written on Ahmedabad; for the first time in a long while, I felt that I might be ready to return to them, make some real sense of what had happened to that city. I wondered whether the deadly splintering among neighbors that I had seen there was starting to mirror the slow-moving splintering I now saw in my life here, both places enamored with their own sense of harmony and openness.

I worked for an hour or so, then checked my email. Nothing. I couldn't believe it was taking them so long to respond.

I went out to the yard. I needed some distance from my phone. I watered and overwatered everything. I'd hated gardening when I was a kid and my dad had made me help him, but as an adult, it gave me a sense of accomplishment, as if I had finally come into my own, tending steward to my own land.

I handled with particular care our large pot of bougainvillea. At some point, a seed had migrated from the fig tree on the other side of the yard, and now there was a large fig branch growing inside the bougainvillea pot alongside the magenta flowers. I loved that a seed could travel across our lawn, with the aid of a bird or the wind or some other force, and root itself deeply enough in this new place to start producing fruit. I was watering it when the drummer walked by again, just on the other side of our fence. Despite being home so much, I had never seen him up close. He was probably in his fifties, but he looked older from years spent in the sun, his forehead the texture of an old leather football. When he saw me, he raised his index finger to signal he'd be right back. About one hundred yards away, a group of men and women were picking fruit. He walked toward them and I continued my watering. He returned with a small bucket that he held over the fence. I grabbed a hold of it. It was full of fat, freshly picked blueberries.

"*Niños*," he said with a smile on his face.

"Thank you. They'll love them."

He continued on with his drumming, and I finished watering.

When I got back inside, proud of the time I had let pass without checking my email, I took a quick peek. Still nothing.

Over the next few hours, I was tethered to my desk, sure that an email would arrive imminently, while I had the space and clarity to respond. I made lunch. I checked my email. I cleaned the house and folded some laundry. I checked my email again. Nothing. Still.

The only message of any sort that I'd received was a text from Eva, confirming that she could pick up the kids from school. She'd run some errands with them and meet me at the TC around five thirty. At least that meant I'd get to play a little tennis.

Every Friday afternoon, a revolving group of players gathered at the TC. One was in his eighties and in remarkable shape, but most were middle-aged. All had pretty decent games. Richard, the pro who was on the membership committee with me, was always there, pairing people up for doubles matches. We'd play a set and then rotate around.

I left the house not long after two thirty, with my tennis bag in one arm and the rifle in the other. I carefully placed both in the trunk of my car and went back into the house to get my swim things and a change of clothes. I had planned to return the gun before playing tennis, but even with so little to do, I still got going too late.

I drove to the TC and parked my car at the far end of the lot, in the shade. I took one more look at my email. I was trying my hardest not to read into their silence. I decided to send Cliff a text: "Haven't heard from you. Assuming all is well and Alex and Holly are finally eating a proper meal. Did you see those videos I sent you?"

I had a few minutes before the other players would start arriving. I called my mother. She picked up before the first ring.

"Still on for lunch next week?" I asked. I guess her date was affecting me more than I wanted to admit.

"He was supposed to call today, but he didn't," she said, sounding a little disappointed, before changing course. "Are you going to play tennis?"

"I am." I was usually the one to switch subjects so quickly.

"Enjoy. Your father never took time to enjoy things. I'm glad you are."

I hesitated before hanging up.

"What is it, Raj?"

She'd always had a knack for sensing my tremors.

"Nothing." I considered how much I wanted to share with her. As often as we talked, I was seldom fully honest about any problems in my life. I was her only son; I wanted to be confident and unblemished. But maybe what I was being was dishonest. "I've had a tough week, Ma. I'm pretty tired." I gave her a rundown of all the terrible things that had happened in the past five days. The only thing I didn't mention was my fear of being fired. For her, having a job was the best and greatest defense against chaos. Anything could be managed as long as there was a monthly check coming in.

"That does sound tough," she said, clearly worried. "I'm glad you're going to tennis. The exercise will make you feel better. Get on that court. I always feel so refreshed and clear-headed after my hikes. In a better state of mind to make decisions."

"Could we all just move in with you?" I joked.

"Hot meals every night, and your mother in your business all the time." She laughed. "I'll come visit you soon."

We said goodbye and hung up. I got out of the car and saw that someone had pulled in a few spaces away while I'd been on the phone. A red Mini. And Robert was in the driver's seat, staring at me.

I walked toward him. "What the hell are you doing here?" I asked, with equal parts anger and bewilderment. He opened his door and stepped out. In the days that had passed since we'd first spoken, he'd come to look even skinnier. His face was gaunt. We were standing close to each other. He had me by at least two inches, but he seemed shrunken, slumped from his hunger strike. "How long have you been following me?"

"I haven't been following you. I know you're a member here. I assumed you would arrive sooner or later."

"How do you know I'm a member?"

Robert didn't respond.

"You followed me yesterday to the gas station," I said, feeling relieved that my suspicions were true, that I wasn't descending into unfounded paranoia. "I saw your car. Did you follow me home too? Are you the one who's been calling me?"

"No," he said, confused. "What calls?"

"Please tell me you weren't in my yard last night," I said, now feeling righteous. "Because if you were —"

"What would you do?" he snapped, a bit of light in his eyes.

I tried counting my breaths to calm down. I didn't know what to do. I didn't know what he would do. I thought of the gun. I had my car keys in my hand; I could pop the trunk with the click of a button.

"I don't understand what you want. Why are you taking these videos of me? Why are you sending them to me?" I softened my tone, trying to remember that this was a young man, a student. "What are you trying to say to me?"

He thought for a moment.

"You've challenged us in class constantly," Robert said. "And I appreciate that. For so much of this term, I felt like I was a part of something when I came to your class. That you valued what I was saying. I don't feel that way anymore, but maybe I want to. I guess I thought you might like those other videos. That's how I see you, unedited."

"I'm glad you felt welcome in my class, and I'd like for that to continue. But you can't follow me around like this. It's completely inappropriate. We could have had this conversation in my office."

He looked around as if just realizing that's not where we were. "This is a nice place. I wish I'd had a place like this when I was growing up. The tennis courts near my house were covered in weeds."

"I've always wanted to play on grass," I said, trying to bring some levity to the conversation.

He smiled tentatively. "I'm not sure I'd feel comfortable in a place like this, though. It's too fancy. I'd always be nervous about what I was wearing and whether I was saying or doing the wrong thing." He paused for a few seconds. "Aren't you? There must not be a lot of people like you here."

That certainly was true, but I didn't appreciate the assumption that his discomforts were mine.

"I'm actually fine," I said, knowing that he might not take that well. "I'm pretty comfortable here."

"How can you afford all this?" he asked. Not surprising. He

seemed always to lash out when he felt shut down or rejected. "I know you don't want to talk about your salary, but I don't get how you're keeping all this together."

"I think it's time for you to leave, Robert. Come see me on Monday if you'd like. We can talk more." I could see a few men assembling on the court. The better players would arrive first; I wanted to make sure I got a good game. I also wanted Robert to leave.

"I don't have to go anywhere," Robert said like a petulant child. "This is America. I have the right to peacefully assemble."

I shuffled the keys in my hand, wanting to get my tennis bag. How well hidden was the gun? "Indeed it is," I said. "But this is a private club, and nobody has *invited* you here. As a member, I have the right to ask you to leave. So please leave."

We had no security guard or anything of the sort. The place policed itself. If you weren't invited, you didn't come in. I doubt that, in the history of the TC, anyone had ever had to be asked to leave.

I popped the trunk. There was my worn Babolat tennis bag and, next to it, the rifle. Not very well hidden. I grabbed the bag and closed the trunk as fast as I could. I looked at Robert, who was eying the back of the car. He had obviously seen. "I'm going to go play some tennis," I said, turning away.

He got back into his car, and I headed to the courts. I noticed Richard standing nearby; he'd been listening to the exchange. I wondered how much he'd heard.

"Grade dispute," I said, trying to lighten the mood.

I thought Richard might laugh at the joke, but he didn't crack.

"Raj, why don't you take my place?" Phil, one of the better regulars, asked when I got to the court. "My knee feels weak."

Without considering it, I ripped open my bag, pulled out a racquet, and did some cursory stretching.

"I'm good to go," I said, signaling that I didn't need any warm-up. While none of these players seemed to be avoiding me, they weren't openly friendly either. I hoped my play would take care of everything.

Despite all the noise in my head, I hit a crisp first return. But it was a struggle to stay focused on the game while I could see Robert's car, still parked in the shade. He'd started the engine but hadn't gone anywhere.

I lost the first game; I wished I'd taken the time to warm up properly. It was my turn to serve, which required more warming up than any other shot; it used every part of your body, each muscle working as a separate lever in a complex, sequential machine. And yet, I waved off offers to take some practice serves; I couldn't slow down, not today. The first serve I hit bulleted to the court to the right of us. I had no idea how I'd done that. I tried again, with the same result, and double faulted the first point. And the second. I could sense my partner and opponents growing impatient. Winning or losing didn't matter here. But getting in a proper game did.

Richard was watching me. He motioned to toss the ball higher and farther to my left. I finally got one in, spinning it so that it traveled along a high arc and landed right in the middle of the service box. The guy returning it stepped in and crushed the ball back. It was past me before I'd taken a step. And then

I double-faulted the fourth point. I turned to Richard, but he turned away.

In the changeover, I saw the backup lights go on in Robert's car. He swung out and drove away. Some semblance of focus returned to me. For the next several games, I played as I'd envisioned myself playing when I ran onto the court. I wasn't sure it was enough to make up for that terrible start, though.

When we were done with our set, I checked my phone. There was a message from a number I didn't recognize. I was about to listen to it when another call came in. It was Cliff.

"You playing?" Richard asked, annoyed.

I stuck up my index finger to signal that I needed a minute. I answered the phone.

"I got your email," Cliff said. "Can you talk?"

"Sure." I couldn't tell from his tone what he was going to say. "I just got finished talking to Robert."

"Are you on campus? Is he?"

"No," I said. "He followed me to this place where I play tennis." I didn't want Cliff to know I belonged to a tennis club. Even though I was pretty sure Cliff wouldn't judge me for it, I felt guilty about the life of leisure it suggested. "As you may have noticed, he likes following me around."

"You play tennis?" Cliff asked. This had always been the hallmark of his writing: the artful digression.

"I do."

"Why don't I know that? We should play."

"That would be great," I said, trying not to sound impatient with this tangent.

"What happened with Robert?" Cliff asked.

"I just had a mild shouting match with him. That's what I've become. A shouter. I asked him to stop following me."

"Those videos are completely inappropriate. It's bad enough that he took them, but to send them to you like that is beyond the pale."

I appreciated Cliff's clarity.

"I want a restraining order placed against him. I think he was at my house last night."

"We can certainly look into that," Cliff said. "I did a quick check of his records. He's a junior who has taken three terms off at different points during his time here. He's been on and off financial aid. Mostly on. His grades are substandard. Academically, he's unremarkable."

"He's been following me in this nice car. How does a kid like that afford it?"

"It's not his. His roommate's girlfriend just reported it missing. He took the keys yesterday when she was staying over. I'll let the campus police know that he came to see you."

At that, Cliff paused. By now, I knew the pregnancy of that pause.

"What else?"

"I'd have preferred to do this in person," he said, now sounding resigned with having to deliver the news. "Cynthia asked me to tell you that you should take the next couple of weeks off. Dan will fill in for you. We need to let things cool down."

I knew this was coming. And yet I still felt blindsided.

"Am I out of a job, Cliff?"

I thought he would respond immediately: Of course not, you've got nothing to worry about, this is temporary. But he provided none of these assurances.

"Let's take this one day at a time," Cliff said. "If it was up to me, you'd be back here on Monday morning. But Cynthia is managing this now."

I needed the job. Not only for the money and the health insurance, but because it gave me a place to go week after week, year after year, spending my time among students, a majority of whom appreciated what I was teaching them. I was a pretend intellectual who stood above all the glittering gold around me. Without the job, I didn't know who I would be.

"Please help me with this," I pleaded. "I need this job."

"I'm doing all I can," he said. "I'll be in touch if anything else comes up."

I hung up the phone and looked around, feeling dazed.

"You want to step out for a set?" Richard asked.

I shook my head and ran back onto the court. I could barely feel my legs. I'd thought playing would take my mind off the conversation with Cliff, but there was nothing quite like worrying about how you were going to pay your mortgage, and what you were going to do with the rest of your life, to ruin a set of tennis.

At a quarter to five, I stopped. I put my tennis bag away, grabbed my change of clothes, and headed to the shower, no energy left for the conversation ahead, after days of being jacked up for the fight with Mark.

I walked into the bathroom, which was empty, and stripped

down. I turned on the shower and checked my email while the water warmed up. Nothing interesting. I listened to the voice message.

"This is a message for Raj Bhatt. It's Dr. Brewer. You came to see us earlier this week. It's about three o'clock on Friday. I'll be here for another few hours. Please give me a call at the office."

I was naked. My mouth filled with bile. Good news came from the nurse, bad news from the doctor himself. That's how it worked, right? I dialed the number, and the longer the phone rang, the worse I felt. Finally I reached the answering service. I asked that the doctor call me back immediately. Then I got into the shower and turned the water to cold. I needed to cool off. I tried convincing myself, as I dug deep into my scalp with shampoo, that there was some rule that doctors couldn't give test results in voicemail messages.

I got dressed, walked out of the bathroom, and went to put my tennis clothes in the car.

Years earlier, when I was first starting to teach, a friend had given me a useful piece of advice: on the first day of class, when the seats are packed, arrive a couple of minutes after the scheduled start. It created a sense of anticipation. I wanted to make an entrance.

I walked into the clubhouse several minutes after five. Everyone turned to me, and I flashed back to stepping into that frat house room years earlier. What would my name tag say now? *Hi, I'm Raj Bhatt and I so wish all this had turned out differently.*

In all the other meetings we'd had, Suzanne had arranged

for a large cheese plate and brought along several bottles of wine. Neither the cheese nor the wine was anywhere to be seen this time, as if the conversation required a certain purity of mind that the light consumption of dairy and alcohol would impair. Everyone had arrived already, and after that initial glance, none of them looked at me again. I hoped they were trying to signal that the meeting wasn't that big a deal, that they were merely engaged in everyday conversation, too distracted to wave hello. All of the seats on the two couches were taken. One lone chair remained, which felt entirely appropriate. I took my seat on the witness stand.

Suzanne looked at me as if this were the last thing in the world she wanted to do. "Thank you all for coming," she began. "As you know, we're here to make some decisions about all the wonderful couples we've met in the past few weeks. We have fifteen couples and five open spots, so some difficult decisions need to be made. But before we get to that, we have other business that requires our attention. Mark is going to be here for the first ten minutes. He has asked to address the committee."

Mark was in his scrubs. In all the years I had seen him around, he had exuded a forced formality. He never did anything without purpose. And there was such clear purpose to showing up in scrubs. What he needed to say was serious enough to pull him away from the real work of making hearts beat — as if the collective heart of the TC needed salvation. If I'd had any inkling that he was going to show up like this, I would have gone out and bought myself camo fatigues; obviously, he was ready for war.

"Thanks, Suzanne," Mark said.

He had not yet made eye contact with me. I locked in on him.

"Many of you know that Jan and I are deeply involved in some philanthropies around town that we hold near and dear. Even though we didn't have much growing up, I was raised with the idea that service is as important a virtue as anything else. It is the single most important value we have instilled in our children. I've been working at the same hospital for my entire career. Years ago, when I got the job offer, I accepted on one condition—that I could have a gap year of sorts. During that year, I traveled with a group of doctors to sub-Saharan Africa where we tended to the basic health needs of the population. Then I spent some time working at a hospital in the Bronx where I treated early cases of young men dying of AIDS. Both those experiences were extremely formative. They taught me that we must always strive to do better for the people around us. Years later, I heard of a young senator from Illinois who wanted to help us find that more perfect union, and I sent him as much money as I could. I'm sharing this not to pat myself on the back, but because I want you to know exactly where I'm coming from. That you all understand that I only want what is best for us."

Mark had a stirring speaking voice. I'm sure he could deliver one hell of a eulogy, or give an inspirational speech to his residents about the healing power of touch when administering medical care. Now he was playing lawyer, giving his opening statement. Had the speech not been all about me, I might have been more willing to weigh the good with the bad.

There was plenty of good. But as it was, I had been biting my tongue so hard that I was leaving teeth marks. Each time he brought up a new point, started tugging at a new heart-string, I wanted to refute it. It took every last bit of my self-control to keep my mouth shut. I hoped the committee had noticed that two of the three examples he had given to dem-onstrate his selfless largess were about him saving black folks.

"I cannot tell you how many applications we got for the jobs that Bill and Valerie Brown now have. Hundreds upon hun-dreds of the very best doctors from across the country and the world. Bill and Valerie beat them all out, and not just because they're a couple. They're at the top of their game individu-ally. Both are brilliant clinicians, and both maintain serious re-search projects. The work Bill is doing is going to revolution-ize cardiovascular care. We did not sacrifice quality in getting them here. I begged them to come and told them that this was the place for them, professionally, personally, and socially." He paused for effect and purposefully made eye contact with each of the committee members but me. "Let's be honest. We're not a very diverse community here — in this club, in this town. And we need to change that. Fast. The world is changing and progressing rapidly. And I don't want us to be lagging behind, wondering what happened. And so for all these reasons, what happened last Sunday evening was truly horrifying. It shook me to my core. And it should have shaken you all as well. It was completely unacceptable."

He finally turned to me. "Raj, I'm going to need you to do the right thing and apologize to the Browns. They don't deserve what they got from us on Sunday evening. We trusted you to represent this club. We gave you that opportunity, and you abused it."

"I'm happy to apologize to the Browns," I said, looking right back at him. "I have every intention of doing so."

Despite his confidence, Mark seemed surprised that his speech had been so effective. "I'm very happy to hear that."

"You need to know that the second those words came out of my mouth during the interview, I wanted to find a moment with the Browns to say sorry. I was horrified. I'm not going to make any excuses for myself. The responsibility is on me. It's certainly not who I am, and I feel particularly bad because I put the Browns in such a terrible position. They seem like a wonderful couple." It was my turn to eye the other committee members. "But what made me so angry that evening, an anger that has only grown in the days since, was how quick most of you were to tell me how you thought I needed to handle the situation. As if I wouldn't know that I had made a mistake myself. As if you were all infallible arbiters, when in fact there have been countless instances since I've joined this club when I have been on the receiving end of someone else's stupidity, and I have never gotten an apology. It happens almost every time I come here — maybe even every time, and often more than once. So where's my apology? I'd love an apology for the fact that this club is almost entirely white and none of you have really done anything to change that. That now that Mark has discovered diversity, your first move as a membership committee is to consider the expulsion of one of the club's only brown members. Maybe an apology for every time

I've been asked to teach people about India and Islam and everything in between. Or for every time a member has tried to connect with me by saying that they didn't come to places like this when they were growing up, assuming that I didn't either. For every time a guest has assumed that I work here, or that I've been told that Indian accents are cute, and then been asked if I could do one. I'd love an apology for every time someone has spoken to me in one way and the rest of you in another." To their credit, everyone in the room, with the exception of Mark, was listening attentively. "Or for all of the times I've been followed here by a cop, because of course a brown guy in a shitty car headed to a tennis club is only interested in blowing it up. An apology that I can't report that cop because I'm afraid that they won't show up to my house the next time I need them in the middle of the night." I took a deep inhale, nearing the finish line. "And I'd definitely like an apology for every time someone has called me Kumar and you've all stood by in silence."

I felt like I was back in the bathroom, naked, facing down my mole of mortality. "Listen, I like you all. You're my friends. But you don't see what I see. You don't feel what I feel."

No one said anything for several long seconds.

"I think you're mixing up some issues here," Mark said in an imperious tone. "You have some grievances, but this is neither the time nor the place for them."

"This is exactly the time and place for them. *We did not sacrifice quality in getting them here.* What the hell does that mean? Let me tell you. You're saying that you usually have to sacrifice quality when you hire black people. It's easy for you to turn to me and insist I apologize so that you can go back to the Browns and say, 'See, there's no race problem here! We handled the race problem!' You haven't. The problems here are much deeper than me and my stupid mouth and my one terribly offensive joke. This place is essentially segregated. It has existed for decades, and if we went through all the records, we probably could count on one hand how many nonwhite members it has had. I joined thinking that I could change that a little. I'm not saying that by doing so I was sitting down at the lunch counter or refusing to move to the back of the bus. But still."

"You're pretty far out of line here, Raj," Mark said. "How can you say that I haven't done anything to change this place? That's exactly what I was trying to do and you screwed it up."

"You're right. If the Browns don't want to join the club, I'm sure a lot of that will be on me. But what I'm saying is, even if that had never happened, if they'd had a perfectly placid interview and accepted an offer to become members, I bet they still would never have felt like they truly belonged here."

As I said this, I caught some movement outside one of the clubhouse's large windows. I was sure that Robert had just walked by.

"Raj?" Suzanne asked, following my eyes. "Is everything OK?"

"It's fine," I said, trying not to reveal my worry.

"I urge this committee to act," Mark said. Clearly, he hadn't given much thought to what I'd said. "To do what's right for us all."

"Oh, come on," I said. "This is a membership committee meeting for a tennis club. You're not speaking in front of the

UN General Assembly. Let's cut the formality. Where do you want us to go from here?"

"I move for your family to be removed from this club," Mark said.

I laughed out loud. "Mark, my kids are third-generation members. And I don't think you're in any position to kick someone else out of the club. But I guess if you want to, you're welcome to try. That is, of course, unless you're off to save Africa again."

Mark just stared me down. Then he stood up. "I'm not going to sit here and listen to this. I've said my piece. I'll leave it up to the rest of you to make a decision." He turned to the group. "When I was on my way here, I believed we could work this out. I don't know Raj, but I thought he would be reasonable. Clearly that's not the case. For the integrity of this club, I urge you at least to remove him from this committee. It's a crucial gesture we have to make."

There was that phrase again. *Know Raj. You know Raj.*

As Mark walked out of the clubhouse, I saw Robert again. This time, he peered through the window, but didn't seem to realize that I was inside. He was definitely searching for me.

With Mark gone, it was just the five of us again. Before all this started, we had gotten along quite well. Now, no one was looking at anyone else, the tension in the room high and uncomfortable.

"Let me just say," Suzanne said, calling us to order. "I told Mark not to come today, but he insisted. As the chair of this committee, perhaps I should have barred him. I didn't, and now I'm actually glad he came. We needed to have this conversation. And we need to keep having it." Suzanne then addressed me directly. "It's difficult to hear what you've just said, Raj. And I'm going to think long and hard about it." She turned back to the rest of the group. "But for now, Raj is right. This whole thing is between him and Bill Brown. It's none of our business. We need to move on to the work we've come here to do."

I thanked Suzanne with my eyes and a slight nod of my head.

"None of our business?" Leslie asked. "It certainly is our business. It concerns all of us and the long-term integrity of this club. If word spreads — and word always spreads — that we did nothing, then who are we? We need to act as a group."

To Leslie's credit, she was looking me right in the eye.

"In terms of what you just said," Leslie continued, "I don't recall you sponsoring any families to make this place more to your liking. And you've had ample opportunity. I don't think you can place all the blame on the rest of us. Don't Tim and I get some credit for bringing you in?"

I couldn't believe what she was saying. Leslie and I weren't just casual friends. We had shared meals many times, in our house and theirs, laughing and stumbling through our middle years. It was hard to stomach that the TC might be more important to her than that.

Now it looked like that membership might be revoked. If this were a vote, it was one for expulsion and one against.

"Here's what I don't understand, Raj," Richard said. "You said this horrible thing on Sunday, and a few hours ago I heard you telling a kid, a teenager, to get out of the club. In all the years I've worked here, I've never heard someone speak to any-one like that. What's going on with you? We've spent a lot of time together on the court. I've seen you become a much bet-ter player. But I don't recognize the man I've seen this week. You seem, I don't know — you seem unhinged."

Considering how long we'd known each other, why did Richard assume that I was in the wrong in the conversation he'd overheard?

"That was a student of mine who's been stalking me. There's a little movement on campus to get me fired because a group of students think I'm anti-American or something. While some of you have decided that I'm racist, they feel the same, but in a different way. At the risk of sounding self-pitying, it seems everyone has chosen this week to point out my fail-ings."

"Do we need to call the police?" Suzanne asked, concerned.

"It's fine. He's somewhere outside right now, and I'm go-ing to have to deal with him once we're done here. But to your second point, Richard: I'm not unhinged. In fact, I feel quite the opposite. I'm being clear and honest for the first time in a long while, saying exactly what I mean. This here is who I am."

"Some of the guys on the court were saying today that you're bringing a negative energy."

I shrugged my shoulders. "I'm sorry they feel that way."

"Listen, I don't really care what you say or what you don't say," Stan said. "I just have one question."

I waited.

"What's happened to your game? You played horribly on

Tuesday night. I've never lost that badly. I was so embarrassed. So far as I'm concerned, if you get your game straight, everything else will take care of itself."

I couldn't tell if he was joking. He sounded serious. He probably was. He was pretty consistent in what he deemed important.

I looked around the room and then out through the large window. I needed to go out and deal with Robert.

"I'm going to go," I said. "I'm not sure if you had intended on taking a vote regarding my standing on this committee. But it seems like it's a two–two split. And I'm happy to break the tie and vote myself off. But if you don't mind, my last act would be to suggest that you put the Browns at the top of our acceptance list. It's important that they decide whether they want to join or not." With that, I stood up. "I've really liked spending time with you all. And I'm sorry it had to end this way."

I walked out. Two for and two against, numbers that were nearly too hard to bear. Half this group, people I thought were my friends, voting against me.

I stepped out of the clubhouse, into the part of the day that I loved the most. There was still over an hour of soft sunlight left.

I saw Eva about to enter the small gate leading to the pool, a large canvas swim bag slung over her shoulder. Arun was close to her, Neel several feet behind. Talking to Robert. The two of them stood no more than half a foot apart; Robert was handing Neel his football.

"Say thank you."

I could hear Eva say the words to Neel, who, football in hand, mouthed appreciation under his breath.

Robert said something to Eva that I couldn't make out, but she had a smile on her face, the one she used when she wanted to be friendly, even when she had no time to be friendly because the kids were begging to get in the pool. I wished she would just keep moving. Get through the gate and start swimming, so I could deal with Robert on my own.

He stepped toward Eva.

I took off toward them.

I didn't know where Robert had gone as I played my second set. But given the way we'd parted, I knew that he'd likely returned angry. I was pretty sure he knew who Eva was; certainly there was a photo online somewhere with all of us together, enjoying a sunny day at the beach. "Dad," Arun yelled as I approached. "Are you going to swim with us?"

"I am," I said.

"This nice young man was complimenting Neel on his throwing arm," Eva said.

"Hey, Robert," I said.

The look on Eva's face shifted slightly.

"Is this your family?" Robert asked, a put-on chumminess to his tone. "Your sons? They're handsome." Robert tapped Neel's upper arm and kept his hand there for a second. "And this one has quite the gun here. You gonna play football?"

"I'd like to," Neel said.

I kept my eyes on Robert's hand, his long, pale fingers. He squeezed Neel's shoulder just slightly. I wanted to snatch Neel away, but I also didn't want to spook Robert with any sudden moves.

"They're lucky to be able to run around here," Robert said, finally removing his hand, then turning to Eva.

"Yes," Eva said, barely eking out a smile. "We count ourselves very fortunate."

"Can we get in the pool?" Neel asked, impatient to swim.

Usually we were vigilant about standing watch before we let them go in the water. But I wanted to get them away from Robert.

"You two go on ahead," I said. "We'll be right there."

Neel and Arun ran off toward the pool, surprised at this new freedom. I felt a small bit of relief seeing them go, relief that immediately turned to anger. Anger that Robert had followed me here, that he had touched Neel and felt comfortable doing so, that no one who saw Robert coming into the TC would question his right to be there, that he was the one who'd started this whole ridiculous process that had put my career, my livelihood, and now my family in jeopardy.

"So, you're taking a class with Raj?" Eva asked, trying her best to lower the tension she must have read on my face.

Robert was surprised.

"He's told you about me?"

"Yes. That you're a smart student."

"Now that's a complete lie," Robert said, annoyed. "There's no need for false flattery."

"She's not flattering you," I said. I'd had enough of him. I needed him to leave. "You are smart."

"I know flattery," Robert said. "You were really friendly

when we were first talking, but the second you heard my name, I saw fear on your face."

"Listen," Eva said, "I'm not scared of you. That's not what this is about. You haven't been very kind to my husband. The protests at school and the stories online have made us pretty jittery. I'm just being extra-protective of my kids. You can understand that, can't you? You can understand how you've made us a little uncomfortable?"

"I don't know why you're so worried about me. I'm not the one with the gun in my car."

He and Eva both turned to me. Now there was fear on Eva's face.

"Did you think I didn't notice?" Robert asked, suddenly defiant. "Tennis racquets and a rifle. Real cool."

"What do you want?" I asked Robert. "Why are you still here?"

"What do I want?" It had been a long week, and Robert seemed addled—hungry, I was sure, and alone—his new group off somewhere without him. "I want this. The beautiful wife, the house, tennis on the weekends, kids who look up to you. I want this, and I'll never have it, and I don't get why you do."

Robert shoved his hands in his jacket. Neel and Arun were both on the diving board, about to drop into the deep end. They were good swimmers, but still, I was nervous that they were alone in the pool. I took a step so that I was now in between Eva, who was closest to the pool, and Robert. I considered what to do next, and realized that Suzanne and the rest of the committee were right outside the clubhouse, watching us. Robert saw them too, and without another word, turned around and walked toward the parking lot.

Eva quickly went to the pool, and I followed her, unsure what to think. Was he going to his car to leave? Or was he going to come back? I knew I'd locked my car, but it wouldn't take much to smash the window and pop the trunk.

"Get in the pool, Dad," Arun said.

"I will," I said, my voice sharper than I'd wanted. "I will in a minute, sweetheart."

I sat down on a poolside chair. My heart was racing and I wasn't feeling well. I wasn't going to be able to get in the pool until I knew that Robert had left. I walked back to the parking lot just in time to see him backing his borrowed Mini out of his spot. As he started moving forward, he aimed the car right at me. He crawled along and then picked up some speed. When he was about twenty feet away, he straightened out, and eyed me as he slowly drove past. I watched his car until it turned onto the road. I headed back to Eva and the kids.

As I walked past the pool, I could feel my breath getting shallow, an acute feeling of nausea taking hold. It felt like the flu was coming on, which didn't surprise me. For years, whenever we went on vacation, I would be hit with a bad cold on the first day, my body signaling that it needed a break. And if ever I needed a break, it was now. I sat down again, hoping a moment of rest might help.

"Is he gone?" Eva asked. She had gotten the kids out, I guessed as a precaution in case Robert came back; they were standing next to her, water dripping off their shorts.

"Yes," I said, my voice feeble. "They can go back in."

"Come in with us," Arun said to Eva.

"I will, sweetheart," she said, her eyes still on me. "You OK?"

"I'm fine," I said, certain I was about to throw up. "Fine. Go in. I'll be there in a minute."

Eva removed the tunic she was wearing, placed it on a chair, and dived gracefully into the pool.

Obviously I wasn't fine. My chest felt like it had just caught on fire. I looked up at the bright sky and then at the illuminated hills behind us, hoping that the passing seconds would return me to normal. Arun was on the diving board, getting ready to jump in, his swim trunks hiked up to his belly button. Neel was waiting in the water, anticipating the splash Arun was about to create. I labored to catch my breath. My head felt heavy, as if my body could no longer bear the added weight, and I slumped to the side of my chair, which gave out. I could feel the hot, wet asphalt on my cheek, and I began to fall into a deep sleep, only to be pulled back for a few more seconds by Eva's frantic screams. But then I let myself go.

My shirt was off and I was hooked up to a machine that made all sorts of beeping sounds. There was an IV in my right arm. And now there was someone standing above me.

"Hey, Raj. Are we going to play that doubles game soon?"

Bill Brown, in a white doctor's coat, prayer beads still on his wrist.

"Just as soon as I get out of here," I said in a weak voice.

"How do you feel?"

"Exhausted."

"You should. You've had a heart attack. Not a bad one, but

bad enough. For me, even the mildest attack is a cause for alarm. You're a little too young and too fit for something like this. Do you have any family history of heart problems?"

I thought of my grandfather. We'd just returned to Bombay for the start of school, after a long summer with him in Ahmedabad, when he died of a heart attack. The first time I ever saw my father cry was when he heard the news. Years later, not long after that trip we went on to Kauai, he succumbed to his own faulty heart.

"My father and grandfather both died from them," I said, scared of saying this aloud, scared of recognizing that I was next in line.

"That's certainly family history," Bill said.

"Am I going to be OK?"

I didn't want to ask the question.

"You will be if you take care of yourself. Indian men have four times higher risk of heart disease. I've seen way too many of you in here through the years. Of course you know this, but you have to be careful with sugar and red meat. Did you grow up a vegetarian?"

"I did."

"Are you still?"

"No."

"Maybe it's a good idea to go back to that. It can't hurt."

I nodded my head.

"Did you save me?" I asked.

"I was the cardiologist on call. It took me a few minutes to figure out why you were so familiar. I'm sorry the paramedics had to cut open your nice shirt. You were in bad shape. You gave your wife quite the scare."

He tilted his head to the side of the room where Eva was standing. I could see she'd been crying.

"Go ahead and talk," Bill said. "I have to check on another patient. I'll be right back."

The nurse helped me sit up a bit and gave me a small glass of water. She was a beautiful older woman, her silver hair tied back. The deep wrinkles on her face looked like the map of a country I'd like to visit.

Eva walked up to me, trying to pull back her tears.

"I thought you were giving the quake victims too much of your attention," I said, joking. I could vaguely recall the details of the attack: slumping over in the chair, Eva's frantic commands to stay awake, the paramedics walking over.

She stood next to the bed and tapped me on my arm, a little harder than I'd expected. She was about to say something, but started to cry. There were so many things I found graceful about Eva, but her crying was not one of them. Her face was a wonderful mess.

"It's fine," I said. "I'm fine."

"You scared me. Really badly."

"I'm sorry."

She took a tissue out of her pocket and wiped away her tears.

"I know you've had the week from hell. Sometimes it feels like all of our weeks are crazy, though. That we're hoping that somehow the following week will be better, mellower. I'm running one way, you're running another." Eva squeezed my hand. "Let's slow down. Maybe I can pull back on my work."

I knew that we couldn't afford for her to do that. And besides, she was better at her job than I was at mine.

"The kids saw it?"

"I'm afraid so. Arun is freaked out. Neel has gone mute."

"Are they here?"

"They're with my mom."

Bill walked back in.

"I'm going to call and give them an update," Eva said, stepping out of the room.

"So what now?" I asked Bill.

"We'll keep you overnight. I want you to get some rest. And we'll do some tests. Hopefully there isn't a major blockage in there." He read the chart in his hands. "You've had quite the busy week. A skin biopsy too?" I could feel myself getting tense; the last thing my heart needed was more tension.

"What does it say?" I asked.

"It's clean."

"Good clean or bad clean?"

"There's no bad clean," Bill said with a smile. "You're fine. All you have to worry about is your heart."

I felt in my heart what I felt in the rest of my body: broken and tired and relieved.

"How's that stress level?"

"Maybe a little high since we first met," I said, feeling pathetic that I had let the stresses of the week threaten my life.

"We'll get all your blood work back and try to see the whole picture," Bill said, looking up from the chart. "But your family history plus stress is not an ideal combination."

"I've had a pretty bad week." My voice cracked as I said this. Bill placed his warm hand on mine.

"I would worry less about your skin and more about your heart," Bill said. "I've seen what stress can do to how the heart functions. Just walking down the street here, or even in a big, mixed place like LA or New York, watching people watch you, listening to their questions, and figuring out the right answers, can calcify arteries. You know what I mean?"

"Yes," I said. "I think so."

The warmth from his hand traveled through my body, as if he were restoring some life force within me merely through touch. If my purpose was to give a decent lecture now and again about purity and danger, then Bill's was to be a doctor. He saved lives for a living. He made hearts beat again. My god. It was bad enough that I had debased Bill when I just thought of him as a kind, smart man. But to do this to a man with the gift of life seemed an unforgivable crime.

It was time to do what I should have done days before.

"I'm sorry, Bill. From the bottom of my damaged, ill-beating heart, I apologize. It was a stupid, stupid joke. I meant no harm or insult. I was desperately trying to connect with you in a place where connection has been hard to find. Most days, I feel like I don't belong anywhere."

"I know that feeling very well," Bill said. And what he said next had so much more weight because he was a doctor and he was wearing a white coat and he had just restarted my heart:

"But I've learned to make nowhere the somewhere I live. And I like it. I've settled in. And now with a job I like, in a city where I'm not constantly fighting to find a parking spot or worrying about shoveling snow, I have some more free time. And I'm thinking maybe I'll join a nice club, and that maybe there will be a club within a club."

I nodded my head in agreement.

"We're straight," Bill continued, returning to a more professional voice. "Let's just get your ticker back on track. That's our main goal."

"I'm so sorry they asked you about Tiger."

"Val and I had a good laugh about it in the car. I didn't want to say it, but I did have a class with him. Introduction to African-American History."

"You're kidding."

Bill shook his head. "With a professor who was an expert on MLK."

"What was he like?"

"Like a guy who was an expert on MLK." Bill winked. "Tiger was fine. The place was full of overachievers, so you tried not to make a big deal about it. He was actually a little dorky. We were friendly enough with each other. Both of us these light-skinned young black men playing these very white country-club sports. But I got the sense that he wasn't trying to make friends. Or to make some black guy connection. He went by Tiger then. Completely un-ironically. Who does that? And like his namesake, he didn't travel in a pack."

The nurse walked into the room and asked for Bill.

"I'll be right there," Bill said to her and then turned to me.

"Get some sleep. I'll be back in the morning. And I'm serious about doubles."

"Just one more thing."

"Sure."

"On Sunday night, when you and Valerie were driving out of the parking lot at the TC, did you see me?" I asked.

"I did. Valerie wanted me to stop. But I didn't want to." He paused and bit at his lower lip. "I was mad at the whole situation. I wasn't mad at you. Or maybe I was and I just needed a moment."

I wondered if the week would have been different if Bill had stopped. Maybe not that much. And I suppose it was a week that needed to happen. But what effect would that one little apology, given with the hope of acceptance, have had on the contours the week ended up taking?

Though Bill was assuring me that my heart was fine, that I was stable, I still felt a weight on my chest. Through luck, circumstance, history, whatever — here we were: me with my shirt ripped open, hooked up to a machine that monitored my cautiously ticking heart, and Bill in his white jacket and his beads and that sweet watch I coveted. Where did we fall on the long arc of history? On a gradual climb up? At the peak, looking at the long drop below? Or maybe we were a small uptick, as if we'd leaped into the air as high as we could.

"I'll see you soon, Raj," Bill said. "Get some rest."

The God of Removing Obstacles

As i was getting ready to leave, Eva placed her hand on my arm, pulling me back.

"What else am I going to do?" I asked her. "I can't stay at home all day anymore."

Three weeks had passed since my heart attack. Bill had released me after two nights in the hospital with a prescription for rest, a stern warning about the dangers of stress, and a promise to hit some balls. That first evening home I'd sent Cliff a text, and five minutes later he'd called.

"What in the world happened?" he'd asked, the concern reaching straight through the phone.

"I'm fine. Just a little tired."

We'd talked for a few minutes, and by the end of the conversation, he'd told me to take the term off. "We'll figure things out here. Take as long as you want."

I had been waiting for this offer for years. A sabbatical. I could take a proper look at what I had written on Ahmedabad. Or I could dig into the difficulties of second acts again. Maybe Cynthia was right — a book was hiding in there.

But first, I had turned to more immediate things. While Eva was at work and the kids were at school, I spent my time in the kitchen, transforming it into a laboratory for good health. Quinoa, beans, and turmeric in absolutely everything. I wanted us to give up meat. Generations of my ancestors had been fine without it — though, according to Bill, it hadn't been enough to help their hearts in the end.

My mother had come to visit, and I'd made her cook with me the whole time. It was so relaxing that I started daydreaming about opening an Indian food truck — or, perhaps more practically, an Indian food sedan. But after a few days of teaching me recipes she knew only by feel, avoiding the topic of my heart attack, and playing with the boys when they returned from school, my mom was tired; she needed a break. The morning before she planned to leave, she dropped the boys off at school and spent the day at a nearby casino, returning home about half an hour before I needed to pick them up.

"Tea?" she offered, joining me in the kitchen.

"Please." I sensed she wanted to talk about something before she left.

She reached down below the stove to get a small pot and moved around the kitchen swiftly, mixing water, milk, tea, masala, and sugar. There was very little frailty in that nearly eighty-year-old body.

Before she took a seat, she went to her purse, pulled something out, and placed it on the table between us. It was a stack of bills, maybe forty or fifty of them, all held together by a dirty rubber band. I looked down at Benjamin Franklin's sad eyes.

"I'll pay the taxes on it, but why don't you put it in the kids' college fund." She took a careful sip of the tea and added, her attention in the cup, "Or spend it some other way. Whatever will help relieve some of your stress."

I tapped the stack with my fingertips. I knew this was coming from a place of concern. But it made me feel a bit like a child, unable to take care of my own needs.

"I'm set," I said, pushing the stack a little closer to her.

"How old are you?" she asked.

It could have been a rhetorical flourish, a setup for what she was going to say next, or it could have been a genuine question. She'd never really tracked my birthday. More than once, she'd gotten the month right, but not the day.

"Forty-four."

"You know how old your father was when we came here?"

"Forty-seven."

The number had a near-mythic quality in my head. He'd essentially started over at that age: a new place, a new job, a new life.

"You were too young to remember this, but the years leading up to the move were difficult for us, and particularly for him. He'd had a bout of typhoid. He didn't think he was getting anywhere in his job, even though he'd just gotten a pretty decent promotion. And he was nervous about your future in India, yours and your sisters'. He kept saying that was why he wanted to come here. But in reality, he was desperate to shake things up. And so he picked us all up and we moved. I wanted to come as much as him. Maybe I was having my own middle-life crisis. Is that what you're having now?"

"Maybe," I said, smiling. "Maybe."

"Give yourself a break. You're doing fine. You have a far more open, honest relationship with Eva than I ever had with your dad. The kids are a challenge, I know. They're meant to be a challenge. That's their job." She took a sip of the tea. "And there are plenty of jobs around. If this one is bad, go do something else. Go work for Google. They're always hiring."

I couldn't remember her ever being so clear and direct with me.

"It's all a gamble, isn't it?" she continued. "All of it. You make decisions. Decisions are made for you. Sometimes you get lucky. And sometimes you take a lot of losses before you hit a jackpot." She pushed the bills back toward me and gave them a tap. "I know you take after your father, always trying to be so calm and even-keeled, even when things get crazy. But I don't think that's right. You need to celebrate the victories and mourn the losses. And then you can move on."

"I miss him," I said. "Even more than after he first died. He's been on my mind so much lately. I need him to guide me through these years."

"I miss him too. You know that he and I didn't always get along very well. We fought a lot. But I still miss him and the life he and I built together." Her eyes were a little glassy. "You're doing just fine without him, though. Maybe I am too."

She left the next day.

In the days that followed, the conversation swirled around in my head. I appreciated her confidence in the progress of my life, but clearly I hadn't been doing fine. And as the days stretched into weeks, I missed the routines I realized I had come to love. The commute to school, the nerves I felt as I stepped into a full classroom, which disappeared roughly five minutes in. I missed the students, the ones I had gotten to know and the new batch that would come in at the start of every new term. I missed helping them understand a school of thought they had no sense of before.

I appreciated all the concern, from Eva and my mother and Cliff, but I longed for normalcy. And I wanted to return to this one particular classroom, with this particular set of students. If I didn't go back in there, they would always remember me as the guy who went nuts after lecture one day. I wanted to try to explain myself.

"Maybe end class early today," Eva suggested.

"I'll be fine. I'm going to take it completely easy. I promise. What time is the show?"

"Five," she said. "Let's meet here and go together."

"OK."

Eva hugged me, as if I were being deployed for war. "Please be careful."

"I promise to keep the screaming to a minimum," I said, a smile on my face.

I got in the car and headed to campus. I'd missed this ride, when I would rehearse the witty things I was going to say in class. At the entrance to my building, there were no announcements on the glass door. The hallway inside, where the hunger strikers had struck, was strangely antiseptic, as if it had been scrubbed clean. I took the elevator up.

Before I went to my office, I checked to see if Cliff was in. The department knew I was coming, but I wanted to say a quick hello to him first. We'd spoken on the phone only that one time.

"He's on his way," Mary said, standing up from behind her desk. "How're you feeling?"

"Fine," I said. "It's all fine. I just have a flair for the dramatic."

She rummaged through her messy desk full of papers and found a single key. "We've had an office open up. Since you've been sharing all these years, we were thinking that maybe you should have it."

I had assumed my sympathy gift would be a little succulent on my desk, or maybe an orchid if Mary was feeling generous. To me, the real prize was that I'd had a bit of a break, and I still had my job.

But now, here was my chance to get the office I'd always wanted. I could bring in some books, buy a rug, maybe splurge on an overpriced Eames chair. I already had the perfect lamp to light it all up. It would be the office of my dreams.

"That's very nice of you," I said. "But I don't want to abandon Dan. What would he do without me? Or, more precisely, what would I do without him?"

Mary smiled, as if she'd known I would say that. "I'll let Cliff know you're here."

I left and walked down the hall. I found Dan at his desk. When he saw me, he sprung up, surprised, even though I'd told him I was coming in. He stepped toward me, unsure of what to do with his tall body.

"What the fuck, Raj?" he said in a tone of mock exasperation. "We're too young to be having heart attacks." He gave me a tentative hug.

"It's all right," I said, pulling him in closer. "You can't crush it."

"Is it OK?" He placed his paw on my chest.

"It's fine. I'm supposed to take it easy. Maybe we can start taking afternoon walks." I wasn't sure how I would feel being back in my office. But it was comforting to be back, my desk just as it was when I left. "Thanks so much for teaching my classes. Are they paying you for it?"

"They are," Dan said. "You should have heart attacks more often. Everyone around here has been so friendly to me, it's like I'm the one who had it. I think they're all feeling a little guilty. I'd take advantage of it if I were you."

"I think I will. Let me know if you have any ideas. How are things? Back home yet?"

"In fact, that's where you've had the greatest impact. Julie has never been kinder to me because now she thinks I'm going to have a heart attack too. And yes, your classes are fine. Nothing out of the ordinary. Though I think I'm boring them. Are you sure you want to be back in there?"

"I'm not. But I think I have to."

"Returning to the site of the original trauma?"

I raised my middle finger. I had missed him.

There was a faint knock on the door. We both looked over.

"Welcome back," Cliff said, subdued.

In the time I'd been gone, he seemed to have aged a little, the gray in his beard leaning toward white. I wanted to give him a hug, but it seemed like too intimate a gesture. Perhaps feeling this as well, he remained just outside the door.

"I'm so glad you're OK," he said.

"So am I."

"What have you been up to besides rest?"

"Nothing. I'm bored senseless."

"I'm glad you're here. But you're still welcome to change your mind."

"Let's see how today goes." The closer I got to the start of class, the more nervous I felt. And I felt self-conscious about being the subject of the conversation. "I should probably do some prep for class."

"Yes, yes," Cliff said. He turned to leave, but stopped. "Young Spielberg is on an indefinite leave of absence from school. And the Mini is back in safe hands."

"Where is he?" I asked.

"Back home, I suppose."

I thought about the last time I had seen Robert, his face layered with hurt, confusion, and anger as he drove past me at the TC. Though I never wanted to see him again, I worried about him.

Cliff left, and Dan and I went over the material he had covered in my absence.

"Between these three and your own classes, you must have been exhausted at the end of the week," I said.

"Actually, it wasn't that bad. I'm so sick of managing my own time."

I found the lecture I wanted to give and started going through my notes.

"You nervous?" Dan asked.

"A little."

"What're you going to say?"

"I've no idea," I said. "I tried writing something down, but it felt too forced. What if I freeze?"

"You won't," Dan said. "I've seen you lecture. You're good."

After I read over my notes, I walked down the hall to Mary's office.

"Do you have contact information for all the students?"

"What's the name?" she asked.

"Robert Edwards."

It sounded like the name of a Puritan preacher.

Mary typed the name in and turned the computer screen toward me. There was one number, which I put into my phone.

"Are you going to call him?"

"I don't know." All I had wanted was for him to keep his distance, but still I felt compelled to reach out.

I went downstairs. Usually I made myself instant coffee from the department kitchen, but this time I went to the campus café and got a cappuccino. I didn't put any sugar in it; I didn't want to dilute the boost I got from the strong flavor.

I walked past the bulletin board that had been plastered first with Emily Baker's face and then with the Haji man. No trace of either. But there was a flyer for a talk called "Discourses of Race and Animalness." Below the description for the talk, this gem: "A vegan reception will follow." It wouldn't have surprised me if the flyer was performance art. But despite my instinct to mock the reception, I appreciated the lively conversation the talk might lead to. The speaker and the organizers and the university were interested in ideas and new ways of thinking, and that was the electricity that would keep this place — and others like it — lit for a long time. I had spent most of my adult life on a college campus; it was where I felt the most comfortable. And so in my own way, I would do what I could to fight the Jack Mansfields who wanted to shut those conversations down.

I took out my phone and dialed the number that Mary had given me.

"Robert?" I said as the ringing stopped.

"Who's this?" he asked, his voice flat.

"Raj Bhatt."

"Hey, Raj," he said, his tone unchanged.

I was less surprised by his comfort in calling me by my first name than by the sense that he wasn't taken aback by my call.

"How are you?" I asked.

"I'm OK. Back home. Taking a break from school."

Over the phone, the bite was gone from his voice. He sounded despondent.

I didn't know what to say next. Robert had made me miserable. He had tried to get me fired, pushed me to buy a gun, and contributed a lot to the stress that had brought on a heart attack that could have killed me. But over the past few weeks, I'd tried to work through the things he'd said to me. I had tried to understand his pain. I had some ideas, but they were nothing more than that. Part of me felt sad for him. This kid—and he really was only a kid—seemingly unloved and untethered, needed someone. And that someone wasn't Alex and Holly. I thought about David and his friends and their Indian food. I wished they could have plucked Robert away from the hunger strikers.

"I want to apologize to you for how I lost my temper, Robert. It wasn't appropriate for me to yell at you the way I did." Before he could reply I said, "And I also wanted to tell you again, because I know you didn't believe me before, that I think you're a bright student. Before everything got so crazy, that's what I'd gleaned from our conversation. You should concentrate on school. And the work. Take classes from as many different people as you can, and after all that, you can decide which arguments make the most sense to you." I hoped his mind was still open. "But these ideas you're getting from your friends Alex and Holly, from so-called news outlets like *Mansfield*—you need to stay away from them. That stuff is poison. It's telling you that you and I are completely different kinds of people based on the color of our skin. We're not."

"You know I'm not in your class anymore," he said, a sharp edge back in his voice.

"Yes, that's true. You don't have to listen to me, and ultimately you need to figure all of this out on your own. You'll have to decide what kind of person you want to be. But I hope you keep in mind some of the things we've talked about." I was about to end the call right there, not wanting to argue with him. "But let me be clear about one thing. Stay away from me and my family."

I waited for a few seconds, but he didn't reply, so I said goodbye and hung up.

Eva hadn't wanted me to call him. But I'd needed to say this last thing to him. I texted her. "Just had a brief chat with Robert on the phone. All good. Heading into lecture." Right before I sent it, I added a Haji emoji.

In the past, I'd fantasized about what I'd say if I knew I was giving my last lecture. Would I talk about the things that were important to me? What advice would I give? Whom would I invite? I was certainly hoping this was not going to be my last, but my entrance into the lecture hall had an elegiac quality to it. I lingered for a moment, looking at the students seated there, with their laptops and phones, talking away. And then I made my way down the aisle, between rows of chairs. I instinctively tapped my fingers on my chest, a tic I had developed over the past few weeks.

As the students saw me, I felt their murmurs tick up. *Holy shit. It's him.* I got up to the podium and scanned the class. There were nearly two hundred students, and they were all looking up at me. I don't think there was a single one who had expected to see me. I had their attention in a way I'd never had it before. I turned and waved to my TAs, who seemed just as shocked as the students did.

There were so many of them I recognized, not by name but by their faces. I saw some of the group that had surrounded me outside the lecture hall during that first, awful protest. Several turned away, I suppose out of embarrassment or anger. I couldn't tell which.

I saw David. I gave him the slightest nod, and he nodded

back. Then I went into my bag to get my notes and buy myself a bit of time. I took some deep inhales and visualized the students listening with rapt attention. I needed to get myself some of those prayer beads.

When I looked up, I saw Alex and Holly sitting toward the back, where they usually sat. I hadn't even considered whether they would still be in the class or not. I was still mad at them, and all the other students who'd helped start this whole mess. I gave them a warm smile. All I could do was make my case as clearly as possible. What else was there to do? My heart couldn't take any more yelling.

"Hi, all," I said. "It's nice to see you. I'm sorry I've been away. But I've missed you." Mostly, I had missed the buzz I got from standing in front of all these people. "It seems that I've become a bit of an internet star. I'd be lying if I said I've never had an interest in stardom, but this was not the variety I had in mind."

Some of the students laughed nervously.

"In case some of you have been living under a rock, you can Google me. But not now. Later. And if you want a laugh, see what they're saying about me. It's a little heartbreaking." I was looking out toward the students, but not making eye contact with any of them. "A lot has happened since I was here last. I understand that some of you don't agree with the kinds of things I've been teaching. And you're well within your rights to disagree." What I said next I said with some purpose: "But I've earned the right to be here. To say things that I have thought through carefully over many years. All sorts of people, from all over the country, have had the chance to weigh in on what should have been a conversation between us about the material I've been teaching. But I would like to keep that conversation going. Here. In this lecture hall. At the risk of sounding romantic about it all, there is no better place I know than the classroom for us to work through big ideas, and to discuss what we agree and disagree on. I hope you see that things got a little out of hand. But I'm here and I'm excited to get back to work. Do any of you have any questions?"

The room was silent. Perhaps more so than I ever remember it being.

Finally, a young woman up front said, "We heard you had a heart attack. Is that true?"

"I did," I said.

"Because of what happened?" she asked, concern in her voice.

"Partly from that. But there were other things going on in my life." I tapped my chest twice. "But it's good now. Pumping blood, feeling stuff. Doing what a heart does."

I waited to see if there were any other questions. I looked right at Alex and Holly, inviting them, but neither said anything. I didn't bother trying to read the expressions on their faces.

Then I turned to my notes and began: "I want to talk a little today about structuralism and the Frenchman Claude Lévi-Strauss, who did not, contrary to popular belief, start a jeans company."

"Hurry up. We need to get to school."

Neel had never uttered these words before, and maybe he'd never utter them again. But for the moment, he was excited.

The school was having its annual art show, and he had been working on something for weeks and weeks, using all the bits of junk we'd been getting at Scrappy Art, taking it with him every morning, stuffed in his backpack. For the past week, he had stayed after class on three different days. All this from a kid who was never shy about telling us, in both words and gestures, how much he hated school.

The art show was in the gym, and when we walked in, the place was already packed with students and their parents and grandparents.

"Go ahead," I said, nudging Arun and Neel. Lately they'd been sticking very close to me. "Check out what your friends have done."

They took off. Eva and I wandered. The first-grade class had painted self-portraits, which all looked essentially the same. There was a section with interpretations of Van Gogh's *Sunflowers.* I wondered if the art teacher had told the students about the ear.

"Do you have any idea what he's done?" I asked.

"Nope," Eva said. "Every time I ask, he says 'art.'"

Through the crowd, we saw Leslie. I hadn't seen her since that day at the TC. She was waiting for us to signal, to take a step toward her. I turned away.

"Hello," I heard behind me.

Suzanne. I hadn't seen her since the heart attack either.

She was there with her husband Jack, a square-jawed, handsome man whom, despite my better judgment, I liked. Unlike his genre of guy, he actually asked questions whenever I saw him in the hot tub, and listened as I answered. Often he had follow-up questions. The rest just talked and talked about stuff they knew nothing about.

Eva gave Suzanne a warm smile. I could sense that Suzanne wanted to say something, but she seemed nervous.

"How are you feeling, Raj?" Jack asked.

"Much better."

"You've got us all scared straight. I know it's not what you would have wanted, but thanks for that. No more red meat for me."

"The burgers are killers," I said, smiling at the idea that this was simply an issue of bad fats.

"I'm glad you're feeling better," Suzanne said, her eyes moistening. "It was terrifying seeing you on the ground like that."

"It was terrifying being like that. If Mark hadn't stormed out of the meeting, he could have made himself useful."

She cracked a smile.

"The Browns accepted," she said, offering up the information with a certain amount of satisfaction.

"That's good news," I said, my tone perhaps more subdued than she'd been expecting.

It was great news, the outcome I had wanted when they'd first walked into the clubhouse. But I wished I hadn't sullied it. I wished it hadn't been sullied. I liked the idea of Bill and me hitting tennis balls in the evening light after a long day of work. I liked the idea of us on that court. And yet, I couldn't see myself returning to the TC. I hadn't talked to Eva about it, but she probably sensed that that part of our lives was over. There was no going back.

"We should probably go check on our little Van Goghs," Eva said, gently moving us away. "We'll see you soon."

"Of course," Suzanne said.

We saw Neel and Arun in a corner. When we walked up to them, I didn't see at first what Neel had created. I was too focused on him and Arun standing next to each other. Neel had his arm around his younger brother's shoulder, and they were both looking up at Neel's work. Neel had about a foot on his brother, and they had the same broad shoulders, which they'd inherited from me, which I had inherited from my father. They would fight and they would make up and we would yell at them and fall asleep with them, and soon enough they would go off to college. And all throughout, they would remain perfect. I couldn't get enough of them.

Arun stepped forward and touched Neel's art. I finally looked at it.

On a pedestal was a large mass, roughly three feet by three feet, made from all sorts of junk — plastic spirals from the bindings of folders, pieces from trophies, buttons, parts of old telephones, swaths of cloth, and on and on. I didn't recognize it at first, but then, through all the scraps, something appeared. Someone appeared. I don't know how Neel did it, but it was uncanny how much the sculpture looked like the poster of Ganesh in his bedroom. Eva and I moved in closer. He had used beautiful, large silver buttons for Ganesh's eyes and that huge salad bowl he'd bought for the big belly. He'd created Ganesh's most prominent feature, his elephantine trunk, entirely out of empty Adderall prescription bottles, with his name and dosage on each of them. He had asked for the empty bottles to store pennies and buttons and little Lego pieces. I had assumed that they'd disappeared into the bowels of his bedroom.

Eva and I turned to each other, the tears already pouring down her face. I imagined that she, like me, was most struck by the trunk. Seeing all those pill bottles, I was hit with the fear of exposure. We'd had our challenges with Neel and we did our best to keep it in-house. But our fears were not his fears. We squeezed the boys on their shoulders. Neel had the biggest smile I think I'd ever seen on his face.

"What is it?" a nearby grandmother asked. It was kind of her to do so.

Neel pointed to the title he had given it: *The God of Removing Obstacles.* "We have a Ganesh in our house and I wanted to make another one. You know, my interpretation. The base is papier-mâché, and I kept adding all the various pieces." He spoke with such confidence and self-assurance.

The old woman looked at Neel and then at us with joy on her face. "It's quite the thing."

Without realizing it, without being able to stop myself, thick tears had begun streaming down my face as well. Would Neel and Arun remember sometime later in life that the first time they had seen their father cry was at a school art show, thankfully away from all their friends? It would, eventually, be a good memory for them. At least I hoped so.

I was crying for this fearless and true thing Neel had created. A Ganesh of his own making. And I was crying for the boys, whom we tried to shape and mold, and who would one day come to love and hate all that shaping and molding, before they left us and shaped and molded themselves. They were also tears of rage. I still had not fully pieced together the week I'd had and what I'd learned. All that talk about belonging and membership had broken me, just like something else had broken my father, and his father before him. I kept thinking that I would arrive at some place where all of it might make sense, where I might feel some sliver of comfort. I'm not sure that place exists. Not for me. Maybe not for any of us. And yet, being close to the boys, and their big, beating hearts, I also felt a distinct sense of clarity. About a world, though increasingly darkened and frayed, I could now see and parse with greater precision. And with the recognition that, of all of the places I had been, right here was exactly where I wanted to be, standing in perfect, unsullied silence.

Acknowledgments

So many wonderful people have helped make this book:

These past many years, my colleagues in the Department of Asian American Studies at UC Santa Barbara have provided an ideal, generative place to teach and write.

I want to thank the partnership between PEN America and the Civitella Ranieri Foundation for the remarkable gift of time and daily Italian lunches in tiffins. My thanks particularly to Dana Prescott, Diego Mencaroni, and Lily Philpott.

Many people have read, commented on, and been sounding boards on different iterations of this book. My deepest appreciation to them all: Falu Bakrania, Ryan Black, Lacy Crawford, Joe Crespino, Elizabeth England, Farrell Evans, Keshni Kashyap, Brian Lockhart, Bakirathi Mani, Keith Scribner, Josh Sides, Sumant Sridharan, Rajiv Vrudhula, and John Weir. And thank you to Terence Keel, Lisa Park, and David Pellow for the conversation, drink, and fortification.

To my summer dinnertime friends: I'm so grateful to be stumbling through these years together.

A big, hearty thank-you to my agent, Seth Fishman, who read this book quickly when I first sent it to him, and has since been a calm, steady source of support. To my editor, Naomi Gibbs, who has treated this book with such intellect and discerning care. My deepest thanks to her and everyone else at Houghton Mifflin Harcourt.

I'm very grateful for the continued support, both big and small, from my family — my mother Ragini, my sisters Uttara and Meeta, and my in-laws Andy and Yvonne.

To Ravi and Ishan, who will always be my boys.

And to Emilie, for everything.

A Conversation with Sameer Pandya

There are some shared details between your life and the pro-
tagonist Raj Bhatt's life—though mercifully for you, not all of
them. Could you tell us a bit about your personal connection
to this story?

First of all, let me just say that all the good parts in this
book are me and all the bad parts are Raj Bhatt! And
second, and most thankfully, I have never made the co-
lossal mistake Raj makes at the beginning of the novel.
With all that said, there is a lot of my life here. I didn't
set out to write a work of auto-fiction. But I felt so
emotionally tied to this book, an emotional honestly I
hope I have conveyed to readers. Raj's journey of figuring out his own racial identity, his engagement with
what it means to get older, to raise children, to be a son

and a husband and a father, is a journey I have taken. It's a journey I am square in the middle of taking. And so if I wanted to be honest about Raj, I needed to be honest with myself. But at the same time, I am a fiction writer, and this is a work of fiction. The book takes place over a week, and I've made up a lot of this crazy week. I do live next door to a blueberry farm, but I have not, knock on wood, had a heart attack. And also, because this is a work of fiction, with its demands for narrative tension, I have created a certain amount of necessary distance between what I would do in a situation and what Raj does.

Why did you write this book?

I wrote it, first and foremost, because I wanted to tell Raj Bhatt's story. One of my favorite lines from the book is early on, when Bill Brown, a key character, says that he knew a Raj in college. And Raj thinks to himself, "Everyone knew a Raj in college." In writing this book I wanted to flesh out that Raj everyone knew, or, for that matter, didn't know. I wanted to give him a past, a present, a deep inner life with wants and desires and failings. To make him human. To make his seeming difference recognizable. At the same time, I wanted to fill him with particularities—his memories of his early years in India, his growing up in the Bay Area in the 1980s, all the kinds of music he listened to, the books that have shaped him, the tennis he loves, and on and on.

Among other things, this novel is about race in our contemporary moment. What are you working through here?

Rightfully so, much of the conversation about race in America revolves around black and white. When I first arrived in the Bay Area in the early eighties, there were very few other Indian families. Thinking back to my own experiences, I wanted to write a novel about a character who exists in the brown space between black and white. It's a space of passing in particular instances, of not fully belonging in others. And here plenty of conflict and confusion and uncertainty arises. An ideal place, of course, to set a novel. At the same time, I also wanted to initiate a conversation about how we talk about race now. Raj is accused of being a racist by both a liberal and a conservative group of people. How did he get here? This is the question the novel tries to explore.

What did you have in mind with the genre of the novel?

I've had Raj in mind forever. The question was how to place him in some type of narrative. Once the inciting incident at the beginning of the novel was set, I had to figure out how to structure the book. I did it by combining three types of novels I am fond of reading: the immigrant, the midlife crisis, and the campus novel. By combining these three traditions, I wanted, on the one hand, to shake up the traditional immigrant novel:

while the experience of immigration certainly shapes Raj's life, I wanted to explore the life of a character for whom immigration is a distant memory. On the other hand, I also wanted to "brown up" the midlife crisis and campus novels, which have traditionally had white protagonists.

There's so much tension in this novel, but also moments of real warmth—conversations Raj has with his wife and sons and mother and with his officemate, Dan. There are so many great people surrounding Raj, even as he's facing some real challenges with others. Was that a hard balance to strike?

First, at the risk of sounding a little sentimental, I really like people. And Raj really likes people too. And out of that I tried to create warm interactions between Raj and the people around him. He is, after all, trying desperately hard to reach out to Bill Brown at the beginning of the book. He is reaching out to troubled young Robert, even as Robert makes Raj's life miserable. But the challenges that Raj is facing with others and the affection he has for the people closest to him are not mutually exclusive. Raj is ensconced in his community—his family, his kids, his friends. So often in books about men in crisis, they are devising ways to bail on their families and their kids, and that finding oneself requires a man to be on his own. I've read those books and liked them. But that was not the book I wanted to write here. A lot is in peril in Raj's life. His friends and family are not. And so in many ways it was a hard balance. But also a fairly easy one.

There is a lot of music in this book.

Like the father character. My own father used to listen to a Harry Belafonte record in our apartment in Bombay. And when we arrived in America, some older cousins of mine who had immigrated earlier introduced me to Cat Stevens, the Eagles, Pink Floyd, Tangerine Dream. But as I got older, I started to make my own musical choices as a way of forming a sense of myself. I went through plenty of phases: heavy metal, classic rock; Black Sabbath, *Physical Graffiti.* Dylan and Springsteen and Nusrat after college. But perhaps the clearest through-line, from high school up to now, is hip-hop: NWA in the late eighties, A Tribe Called Quest in the nineties; Biggie and Jay Z; the Kendrick Lamar that I listen to with my kids. All these years of music make their way into an iPod that makes a brief appearance in the novel.

Tennis is a central presence in this book. Why?

In India, I grew up playing cricket and watching it on a black-and-white TV. In America, I turned to tennis, though it is nothing like cricket. Maybe they have a sim-

ilar colonial/postcolonial sensibility about them. I have
always loved the feel of being on the court, of figuring out
when to use a racket as a tool of force or with the slightest touch. With singles, you are out there completely on
your own. At the same time, I have also watched a lot of
tennis over the years, particularly with my mother, who
is a huge tennis fan. There is a lot of intimacy in sports
talk. But in the context of this book, the tennis court—
like swimming pools and golf courses—is a fraught social
space, with said and unsaid rules that govern behavior
and social life.

*And finally, what would you like readers to take away when
they close the book?*

So many things I want readers to take away from their
reading. But let me mention three. First, I want them
to spend a week with Raj, in his head, seeing the world
through his eyes. Second, I want them to think about
what we talk about when we talk about race—more
broadly, but then also more specifically, to consider the
idea of brownness, an underdiscussed experience lived
between black and white. And finally, on the broadest
level, I want readers to think about the idea of belonging. What does it mean to want to belong? The heartbreak of when you don't. This is something we all feel.
It's at the heart of Raj's crisis; it's at the heart of Robert's
crisis. And perhaps as a country, it's a question we are

all asking ourselves right now. What is the group, the place, I want to belong to? When does that desire to belong become dangerous? These are questions worth considering.

Discussion Questions

1. Humor plays a big role in *Members Only*. How do particular characters wield jokes and playfulness? Do responses differ depending on the character's identity? How does the author use humor within the narrative, and how does that differ from the way his characters use humor?

2. While Raj is keenly aware of the microaggressions, biases, and uninformed assumptions of his white colleagues and community, he has also jumped to his own conclusions about people around him. What are some of Raj's blind spots, and how does he reckon with them?

3. Raj is quick to feel empathy for other people of color in predominantly white spaces, often envisioning mu-

tual points of connection with them. Do his expecta-
tions always match up to the reality of the relation-
ships?

4.   Raj is sometimes jealous of others in academia or at
      the club. What is he jealous of, and where does his
      jealousy come from? What other negative emotions
      does he feel, and how and when are they expressed?

5.   While the novel takes place over the course of a week,
      Raj has occasional flashbacks to his childhood, his
      graduate research in India, and the time he spent liv-
      ing in New York. Where and when did he feel most
      comfortable, or most uncomfortable? What parallels
      does the author draw by placing Raj's experiences in
      multiple cities next to each other?

6.   What does it mean to be between two cultures? Which
      other characters experience this? What do you think
      home means for characters, and people, who are be-
      tween cultures? "I've learned to make nowhere the
      somewhere I live," says Bill Brown. What do you think
      he means by this?

7.   In thinking about his formative years, and his place as
      someone who is neither black nor white, Raj says: "I'd
      come to see myself as the person in the middle, some-
      one who could talk to everyone, translate across the
      aisle, and bring people together." How does Raj con-

tinue to strive toward this idea of himself in his personal and professional life?

8.   We meet several generations of the Bhatt family. How does each generation experience exclusion and loneliness?

9.   In the middle of such a tumultuous week, why do you think Raj buys an expensive lamp to feel better? Talk about what the lamp represents, and Raj's relationship to money.

10. After hearing about a colleague's secret child, Raj wonders if he too is living a double life. Do you think he is? If so, how?

11. What are Raj's personal insecurities, and how does Raj picture security in his life? What does he think he needs to feel secure?

12. Something that many characters say is that a certain conversation calls for "further discussion." How frequently do deeper conversations actually happen? What gets in the way of further, and fruitful, discussions? What facilitates them?